CRUKAS

THIEF OF SHADOWS

AETHEAON CHRONICLES
BOOK FIVE

LEONARD D. HILLEY II

For my Family

CHAPTER 1

*T*hieves are scorned ...

THIEVES ARE DESPISED and few would ever yield trust to one. Even fewer would place their lives in a thief's hands, for fear of losing their possessions only to be abandoned or left to die. Trust's an attribute no thief can earn, nor afford to accept. Yet, no one—other than an aspiring or a professional thief—ever considers the invested years of training required to swipe a maiden's purse, an expensive ring, or a priceless broach without the victim realizing the loss until after the thief slipped away. A thief's greatest skill consists of the ability to blend into a crowd and slip past guards unseen with less than a shadow's trace and a whispered breath, while possessing the stealth of a begrudging cat.

Crukas—Aetheaon's master thief—moved like a finely dimmed wisp cloaked beneath a veil of shadow. His dues in training countless hours had been long-paid, but the reckoning for his misdeeds was closing in around him, much to his distaste. With all the stolen trea-

1

sures he'd accumulated throughout his life, penance beckoned. But his debt ranked higher than he could ever atone.

Luck seldom held longevity. The more he risked his chances, the heavier the odds weighed against continual success. Eventually, restitution would be required—either by blood, the theft of the goods he'd stolen, or his death by hanging; provided his execution occurred with such a sense of grace. Worse punishments could be issued, depending on which kingdom took him into custody. Some kingdoms required the amputation of a thief's best hand, and should such a verdict ever be issued for Crukas, he viewed death more favorably. Cutting out his tongue benefited none of the magistrates because Crukas seldom spoke to those outside his rare travels. He was known for being solitary. Whenever he died, his secrets died with him.

Besides, Crukas would never confess his crimes, so making him a mute for his travesties wasn't intimidating. Torture most likely wouldn't gain a confession, either. Mere accusations without proof meant nothing, even before a king or queen. In his mind's eye, his occupation wasn't a sin, so he'd never openly profess he deserved his accumulated wealth. He would, however, express that those he'd stolen from weren't worthy of the valuables he kept in his hidden caches.

For a thief, Crukas held his own set of rules. He never robbed the destitute, nor did he part with any coin to help the lessers, either.

What fool would?

Legends told of such renegades and how peasants worshiped them like heroes. The term "hero" left a bad taste in Crukas' mouth and he never desired to be considered one. He held enough fame throughout Aetheaon, not to be harassed by those who sought a redeemer of injustice and tossed coin to professional beggars, some of which he viewed worse than other thieves because of their guise. Though, some beggars should be commended for taking coin and pity from the higher class.

Yet, Crukas was living on borrowed time, and *time* was a luxury no amount of gold or silver could ever purchase or replace. He was no one's fool, except, of course, his own; a trait he seldom recognized whenever he gazed into a looking glass. His lofty pride prevented him from seeing past his handsome, dark reflection and the slyness of his perfect, affable smile.

Priests and priestesses, queens and kings, all disagreed with his lifestyle, even though they were equally thieves in a more *noble* sense of the word by using their pompous titles to justify padding their greedy coffers with gold, silver, silk, and gems. The money owned by the holy leaders and crowned royalties was tarnished by the dismal tales of the lowly men and women's sweat, tears, and blood. Not even the poor escaped taxation and tithes.

Without repentance, Fate's shadow crept behind Crukas, awaiting the proper moment to wrap around and crush him worse than the night blanketed the light of day. He felt the closeness of Fate and at times, its heated breath moistened the back of his neck. It was no secret Fate befriended Death and Death's footsteps often scraped slightly behind and awaited the moment to capture anyone's last fleeting breath due to Fate's folly.

Crukas understood the risks, but he would never offer any remorse for his thievery, nor part with a coin due to a burdened conscience. In order to thwart the demand for his blood, his life, and his luxuries, he planned to use his thieving skills to claim redemption, and for the betterment of Aetheaon.

Though no clergyman or royal official would honor a thief with a hero's cloak, he'd still become what he least desired: A Hero.

The Plague-bringer's powerful undead army continued growing in number, had toppled numerous small towns and villages, and amassed greater numbers. The larger kingdoms could not ignore the eventual threat but didn't have a clue how to defend themselves from attack.

Regardless of class or race, each who fought and stood against the Plague-bringer's advance were killed and resurrected as loyal undead soldiers. These undead warriors fought by the necromancer's side. Under his command, the Plague-bringer sought to further extinguish the living and acquire them into his horde. Mere weapons and magic weren't enough to stop the Plague-bringer's drive. No living army could defeat him.

A thief was not someone the kingdoms ever expected to defend them. While he plotted to find a way to defeat the Plague-bringer, bounty hunters plotted on how to capture Crukas and turn him in for the high bounty on his head.

Crukas needed to use his stealth to creep into the Shadowed Lands and steal an onyx pendant enchanted to protect the wearer from death. Obtaining this, however, might cost him his life, as the current wearer was a powerful cleric, but still he'd prefer the gamble than to become one of the Plague-bringer's minions. Instant death was preferable over becoming a slowly decaying corpse, mind-controlled by the necromancer.

The only way to physically get close enough to the Plague-bringer to defeat him was by being protected from death. The onyx pendant was but one item in his quest to save Aetheaon. The odds in success to obtain these magical relics were far greater than he anticipated.

Crukas had long held a huge bounty on his head, which could make a beggar richer than a lord. Since Crukas slinked with the ease of a shadow on a darkened night, he held little anxiety on being captured or killed by someone hoping to gain immediate wealth. What he didn't know, *yet*, was he was being tracked by one who held a grudge and one determined to bring Crukas to justice. This meant Crukas might have even less time to accomplish his unselfish goals. Eventually, their paths would cross and much sooner than either anticipated.

CHAPTER 2

*S*parrow Birme, a halfling, spent three days walking from Bridgebarrow to reach the small rundown, almost forsaken, township of Salem. Salem was nestled deep within the dark, haunted, Gloomy Forest. While pursuing Crukas, she tried to ignore the terrifying tales the forest bolstered. Had she her way, this wooded area would've been the last place she'd ever explored, but she found herself with little alternative.

Along her journey from Bridgebarrow, she'd stopped at every tavern and inn, searching for the master thief. Every time, she'd been only a few steps behind. So, she was close. Closer than ever. Eventually, she reasoned, she'd come face to face with Crukas. But, had she already, and not recognized him?

To better shroud her identity and to hide the thick scar along her left brow, she wore a hooded, forest green cowl. Her blond ponytail was hidden by the headpiece, but even in the darkest shadows, her radiant emerald eyes glowed like a cat's. Her leather armor was dark moss green, which helped conceal her while walking through thickets and forests.

Like now.

An old road, long taken hostage by saplings and bramble, was not inviting to outsiders and more attuned to usher less determined travelers away. Deep green ivy twisted and climbed trees like clinging serpents, often moving and mimicking the reptiles with slithering motions during wind gusts.

Brittle leaves crushed softly beneath Sparrow's feet, even though she was light in step and weight, but the faint sound of her footsteps seemed far louder than they actually were. Only one skilled with stealth could meander the overgrown trail without announcing one's presence.

A female halfling who'd lived most of her life in the grassy foothills beneath Willow Bend's rugged mountain ridge, Sparrow had been a thief—a quite successful one. That is, until her conscience befuddled her mind and partway convinced her a different path might redeem her wayward past.

Now a bounty hunter, the occupation's title still brought a strong, bitter taste in her mouth whenever she caught—*betrayed* was a better term—thieves and turned them in for posted rewards. The soured expression on those she'd captured said more than words ever described. She ignored their pleading, bribes, and threats. She promptly turned them in, collected the reward money, and traveled to the next city. Yet, she held no satisfaction in doing so. No matter what she told herself, she never quashed the haunting memories of their desperate actions while she transported them to local magistrates.

Her motto: 'What better way to hunt and catch a thief, than to have been one?', preceded her. Her reputation earned her more than bounties. She gained hostile enemies within every active thief guild in Aetheaon for her betrayal.

Most of her collected bounties had been for thieves she'd worked with in the past. Many vowed to separate her head from her tiny body whenever they escaped prison and found her. Fortunately for her, most of those threats were empty. Execution came quickly for known thieves in the major cities. Since she often sought thieves from the wanted posters on town or city work boards, she simply turned them over to the local officials. The higher the offered reward, the less likely the thief lived another day after the magistrate paid the bounty. Thieves seldom got the luxury of a trial. Their guilt preceded them and they were readily identified.

At times, remorse troubled her, especially since she had been a thief. She struggled with their pleas, often picturing herself in the place of the thief she held in custody. She could've been in a similar position not so long ago, pleading for her own release. The longer she worked as a bounty hunter, the more she risked having her heart become cold and hardened. Was her life as a bounty hunter actually a path toward redemption?

Unexpectedly, her bounty hunter reputation spread faster than her thieving skills for hire ever had. Her former guild placed a hefty reward for her to be captured *alive*—not harmed and especially *not* dead—and turned over to the thief guild master for a more fitting punishment. Her former guild master, and the majority of thieves as a whole, believed she'd turned on her own for quick profits, even though she'd earned far more as a thief than as a bounty hunter. They accused her of eliminating her competition. Rumors implied she secretly remained a thief and stole from those she arrested. She hadn't, of course, but since thieves trusted few people, the trumped accusations stuck within the thief guilds and garnered her as an enemy. Thus, the reason for the scar above her left eye. A thief she'd confronted—before taking into custody—slashed her with the mark by which other thieves could readily recognize her.

After Sparrow became a bounty hunter, she never stole another item. But abandoning her former occupation wasn't easy. The addictive rush of stealing a valuable object without being seen or getting caught remained a temptation she struggled to resist daily. But in one sense, the other thieves were right about her betrayal.

Sparrow knew thieves, where they gathered, and the underground areas where they hid. But rewards for amateur thieves weren't substantial. She understood why her new role worked against her. Eliminating other thieves broadened her field for stealing, if that was her intended goal. But she'd vowed *never* to steal again and worked solely for bounties. However, bounties were barely enough to cover traveling expenses and overnight stays at modest inns. She'd slept more nights inside a bale of loose hay and eating oats from horse troughs than at an inn.

Usually, after thieves stole a highly valued item in one city, they traveled to the next. Lingering too long tempted fate in getting caught. The same was true after she collected a bounty. Word spread fast through a thieving guild. Whenever one thief was captured or killed, the others were alerted and plotted to set a trap to capture her.

In hindsight, Sparrow might've considered another honest skill had she known collecting bounties wasn't a prosperous choice.

This was why she sought to capture Crukas. His lucrative reward was enough that she'd never need bounties or return to thieving ever again. Yet, he was impossible to trace, always out of reach, and most often, he seemed invisible. Ghosts were easier observed than he.

Sparrow spent six months researching Crukas' infamous burglaries, which he never kept secret and boasted to inflate his reputation. He flaunted his thievery, which broke every thieving law universally set by all thief guilds. Secrecy kept thieves less noticed.

Crukas held no alliance to any guild. No amount of coin could persuade him to work for another. But lately, Crukas' looting had lessened, which made following his trail more difficult. It also hinted that whatever he sought to steal next must be worth a fortune or highly guarded. Why else would his presence fade so drastically?

His trail wasn't completely cold, though. Moderately cool, she reasoned, and could only heat up again, if her luck for new clues increased. Bridgebarrow was the last place he was known to have visited but nothing had been reported stolen. For all she knew, he headed a different direction than she currently pursued. Her hunch was Crukas would pass through Salem. As with her most ambitious decisions, her hunches were seldom wrong.

Bigger towns and cities had squares, but Salem's center was circular with a fountain in the middle. Salem's old water fountain was stained with grime and a shallow pool of green, stagnant water. Bubbles rose to the surface. Small creatures wriggled along the bottom. If any coins had been tossed in the fountain for luck, they were camouflaged and tarnished and not worth risking possible disease, parasites, or a deadly curse by taking them. If any luck could be gained through such offerings, it certainly wouldn't be *good*.

The cracked statue inside the fountain was of four large serpents entwined. They spiraled upward with each head facing a different direction. Standing ten feet in height, the menacing serpents leveled an almost hypnotic gaze. Their jeweled eyes seductively stared, tempting the foolish who met them too long with a bewitching trance. Soon after, these folks disappeared into the Gloomy Forest, never to be seen again. These serpents were the town's watchers—*protectors*—and even the best thieves respected the power of these enchanted gazes. None ever attempted to steal these carved gems.

For Sparrow, the sculpted, towering serpents chilled her. Terror grated her spine. She refused to directly gaze into any of their eyes. She feared by doing so, the serpents would come to life and kill her.

The circular layout of the buildings outlined the cobblestoned walkway around the fountain. Each path from the fountain led to a unique shop. The town's design was in alignment with the constellations. The worn walkways between the old buildings were covered by brittle, dead weeds. As best she could tell, only two buildings were still in use: a tavern and a spell shop.

While she doubted Crukas would bother to stop at either, she didn't want to regret later that he had and she'd failed to check. After all, Crukas was a pompous thief who wanted the realm to know his reputation, but he was also wanted and needed to keep a low profile whenever he traveled.

Crukas was like other thieves, too, in his ability to disguise his appearance and blend into the crowds. He was a master with camouflage. This made her wonder if she'd ever stood right beside him and not known it. Crukas would taunt her in this manner, provided he knew she was tracking him. Belittling his foes fit his nature. Such a thought frustrated her and kept her wary of each stranger she encountered.

Sparrow assumed Crukas knew she was a bounty hunter. Did he worry she sought to find and arrest him? Most underestimated her abilities due to her small stature, so he probably never gave her a second thought. She hoped he didn't, as she'd have somewhat of an advantage and an element of surprise for when she eventually found him.

Sorceress Brew was the tavern's name. Its old wooden sign, pale and deteriorating, a haven for termites, swayed slightly in the breeze. The sign's rusted support chains squeaked. The only hints that the tavern was in use were the faint candlelight flickering through the filthy windows and a small, steady stream of smoke coming out the chimney.

Hunger made her stomach ache. The hickory smoke hinted of roasted ham and some type of stew. These scents reminded her of home. Her heart grew homesick for Willow's Bend, if only for a few moments. With her reputation, she'd never be welcome again.

Sparrow believed the deserted streets and rundown shops were a facade. All the wooden lantern posts were rotten except two: one at the front of the tavern and one at the Tomes & Scrolls shop across a narrow alleyway. The melted candles flickering in the breeze were the only obvious life remaining in the circle's power. This indicated, by her guess, those buildings were still in use.

She imagined eyes—other than the four sets of serpent eyes—were watching her from multiple vantage points in the abandoned buildings and from the thick forest surrounding the old hamlet. The warmth of their gazes produced chill bumps along her arms and down her back. Only after sunset would such observers make their presences known. They wouldn't chance being seen or recognized in the faintest light of day.

The look of death—in and around the hamlet—was a disguise. Even though she was incapable of performing magic, she felt the slightest prickle of the magical ley lines beneath her feet, which, for some reason, made her more uncomfortable than the gazes of the unseen.

With the Gloomy Forest slowly reclaiming the paths and the last remaining road leading to Salem, only those truly devoted to herbalism and alchemy risked entering the forest to find the quaint town.

Witches with their familiars, mages, and sorcerers hunted for the rarest herbs in this region; some of which didn't exist elsewhere. The scroll shop across the square from the Sorceress Brew was probably frequented more than the pub. Those who practiced magic needed to maintain keen senses. Fermented and distilled drinks blurred one's thoughts and understanding—except perhaps a dwarf's—so pubs were often shunned by the truly devoted.

A smaller shop near the tavern sold or once sold potions and incense. At least the broken sign hanging over the door indicated such. Yet, its light post was gone, and it was the only building no longer connected to the magical circle.

Even though Salem was known to supply herbs, scrolls, and potions, this didn't deter thieves from occasionally braving Gloomy Forest and visiting the hamlet. Robbing a herb gatherer, especially one with the good fortune of finding the rarest herbs, proved a prosperous looting. Good fortune turned to misfortune for such herb gatherers, but their misfortune became the thieves' monetary gain—a complicated way to define a thief's Circle of Life, but this summed it up rather nicely.

Thieves who robbed within Gloomy Forest tempted their own fates. A thief should never underestimate a gatherer being protected by some sort of magical amulet or protection spell. Some gatherers, which were obedient, loyal apprentices, never left the sight of their mage or wizard or witch. Some familiars were capable of inflicting almost as much damage as the witches they served, while a mage or sorcerer could shroud themselves in complete invisibility nearby.

Sparrow walked to the door of Sorceress Brew. She hesitated with her hand on the doorknob. She took a deep breath to muster enough courage to enter. Although she didn't expect to see many patrons or perhaps few at all once she entered, she kept a wariness in mind. After all, the forest was haunted. The town reeked of magic and death. The occupation of a bounty hunter was almost as dangerous as being a thief, possibly more dangerous, after she'd betrayed some of her former guild members. Depending on where she was, she found herself without a proper ground to defend—thief or bounty collector. She could never be in-between again, and at worst, she could become both.

Closing her eyes tightly and swallowing the heavy lump in her throat, Sparrow turned the doorknob and pushed her way inside.

CHAPTER 3

Standing inside the threshold of Sorceress Brew Tavern, Sparrow studied the immediate area ahead of her until she felt safe enough to shut the door behind her. Though an average door, it was constructed from heavy oak. Her head was almost even with the doorknob. Slowly, without looking away from the rundown bar and tables, she pushed the door closed. Her emerald eyes searched the deeper recesses of the room where the tables and patrons were almost hidden by shadow.

Despite no horses being tied outside the tavern, the bar overflowed with activity. Several seated patrons at the crude, round table closest to the door gave her quick, unimpressed glances before returning to their drinks and half drunken conversations. A few turned their noses up in disgust and slid their hands to the hilt of their daggers. She doubted any recognized her as a bounty hunter but her shady attire better suited an investigating thief who hoped to swipe a quick score when she passed by a table.

The air reeked of fermented mead, pungent sweat, and fresh horse dung. The heavy dung smell indicated a stable she'd failed to notice in the modest town ruins or perhaps at the forest's edge. The stench soured her stomach, and her building appetite from the smokey aroma of roasted boar outside slowly faded.

Perhaps these travelers—trappers, fishermen, and herb gatherers— had taken a different route from Crow's Point or Vylan and were headed farther inland to trade. The high cliffs around the point gave no immediate access to a commercial trading port or to the bay, for that matter. Vylan's port was small and occupied by fishermen and those who trapped lobsters in the bay. The seated men and women from Vylan permeated the fishy perfume one should always leave *at* the bay. She was surprised they weren't fighting off mewing felines begging for fish.

Sparrow counted four homely barmaids carrying trays of tankards from behind the bar to various tables. Their arms bulked with muscles most young peasants yearned to sport and no doubt, one day they'd achieve as well. The L-shaped bar matched the shape of the room. Behind the bar were shelves of various bottles, several large ale barrels with wooden spigots, and a locked door further secured with thick chains joined by a heavy lock.

Several WANTED posters were nailed to support beams and a small bulletin board. These posters displayed well-drawn images of thieves, murderers, and spies. Another sign presented a price menu of the drinks, the spitted boar, stews, and stale bread loafs. Burdened by the harsh smell of the place, she found herself without an appetite for drink or bread and refused to rest her gaze on the menu, despite the agonized growl of her stomach.

The small tavern didn't have a lounge or cloak or weapon check room, so she didn't need to surrender her weapons, but neither did anyone else. Her lingering gaze fixated too long on the locked door, so the frowning barkeep stepped in front of the door to block her view and placed a hand beneath the bar.

The gaunt, pale bartender appeared to be one of the walking undead, except his eyes were alert, and he spoke coherently to a patron seated at the bar. His sunken face and yellow, bulbous eyes were quite eerie. With his firm gaze directed at her and his hand reaching for something under the bar, she expected him to raise a hidden crossbow and aim at her. She turned her attention elsewhere. The longer she stood at the entrance and stared at the door behind the bar, the more suspicious she appeared.

Even though she'd turned her gaze from the barkeep, she wondered what or *who* was on the other side of the locked door. The locked rows of heavy chains wasn't necessarily a deterrent for thieves because it drew more attention to itself. The challenge lured curious, treasure-seeking minds to study it, but perhaps *not* as blatant as she. This bait awakened the thieving skills she'd chosen to abandon, but subconsciously, she entertained various ways to could gain entry to the mysteries behind the door.

No other doors led to accompanying rooms, like fancier taverns often had. No stairs led up to an attic or another floor. If the door behind the bar led to the cellar, there'd be no reason to overly secure it. Did the door open into an underground tunnel, a way for escape, or perhaps a network of tunnels that led to the former shops in Salem's odd circle? Did the door house a bloodthirsty monster seeking *to* escape? After all, the haunted forest was filled with legendary stories of beasts and ghosts. Perhaps, nothing more than a torturous trap lie on the other side. Regardless, she came looking to find Crukas, not to solve such a mystery or become the victim for whatever was locked away from visitors. Yet, the locked door teased her curiosity with a seduction no former vault ever beckoned. She itched to have a lockpick and five minutes alone with the heavy padlock.

Sparrow wanted to forget about what might be hidden behind the door. She stepped away from the entrance and looked for a corner table to sit and mull about how to find Crukas. But capturing Crukas entertained her less than discovering what was behind the bar.

"I'm no longer a thief!" she shouted inside her mind. "Bounty hunter. I'm a *bounty hunter.*"

The candle chandeliers cast faint light along the room's center near the bar. Along the walls, small tables with room for two rested in shadowy areas. Strangely, all the tables were occupied. Something she never expected.

Salem wasn't a secret place and drew travelers to its withering core. Each patron arrived on foot. Leaving their mounts at a stable or elsewhere, none had a quick getaway. But, thinking about the unseen eyes watching her from the forest, none of the patrons looked haggard or had suffered any attacks.

Suddenly her curious mind made her wonder what Crukas' means of travel was. On foot? She'd never heard about Crukas possessing a mount. While having a mount provided a quick escape, it also complicated things. Stable fees, keeping a mount fed, and proper tack must be maintained. Surely, he didn't invest in such. While a good mount was quick to flee a town or city, once he entered a forest or mountainous terrain, he was less likely to lose those pursuing him. Perhaps Crukas hitched rides from town to town. Was he here? Had he befriended the barkeep and persuaded the man to allow Crukas entrance through the forbidden door? No better place to hide ...

Sparrow shook her head slightly and attempted to pry her thoughts from the door. *Where are you, Crukas?*

Inside her robe, she kept the faded parchment of Crukas' wanted poster rolled tightly like a scroll. For some reason, with the high price on his head, she found it odd that none of the posters in the tavern displayed his image. While he was a notorious thief, wanted by rich aristocrats and the wealthy, a vast number of Aetheaon—especially the poor—viewed him as a hero. She never understood why, since he never offered charity to those in need.

With her hand gripping the rolled poster, she wondered if the underground thieving guilds had tacked wanted posters of her to their bulletin boards. More people hated turncoats than they did a prosperous thief or highwayman. She needed to make haste and leave, just in case others recognized her.

Even if Crukas wore a masterful disguise, he'd sit in a tavern where the least amount of light was available. Shadows were a thief's best friend when covertness was necessary. He'd want the best vantage point to watch the door and needed a quick exit should someone attempt to take him into custody. But this tavern only had one door, with the exception of the mysterious door, which might lead nowhere at all.

At the moment, she partially blocked the path to the door but not in an obtrusive way. Her size was hardly intimidating and the weakest, unarmed human child could toss her aside rather easily, unless she drew her weapons.

With the cowl and hood, no one could see her face. Since she was a halfling, few gave her a second glance, or as she often joked, "They always *overlook* me". Her entrance, not totally ignored, didn't spur anyone's sudden want to exit and any lingering interest in her arrival, either. Everyone was busy with their drinks and conversation.

"Ya ordering or what?" a husky barmaid asked with the shrewdest glare. The woman was missing most of her teeth and the remaining ones were black with rot. Her stare was cold, dark, and seemingly cast a soul-searching siphon that made Sparrow flinch. The barmaid came across as a crone who could readily put anyone in their rightful place if the need arose.

Sparrow's hand tightened on Crukas' poster hidden. She deepened her voice, but her attempt to sound tough failed. Instead, her voice rose higher. "I need somewhere to sit."

"Well, ya picked a busy evening. Nothing's available. I got an old crate you could use for a chair, provided anyone allows you to be seated with 'em."

Sparrow nodded reluctantly. "That'll do."

The barmaid walked behind the bar, set down her tray, and grabbed a rickety crate from beside the locked door. Sparrow pretended to follow the woman's steps but readily cast her gaze on the door, subconsciously working out how she'd unlock the chains. The barmaid returned with the half-rotted crate before Sparrow had enough time to evaluate the large lock.

Sparrow took the crate, careful not to get splinters in her hands, and inspected it. Anyone heavier than a halfling would crush the crate by sitting on it. She wondered how to sit on it without getting splinters in more delicate areas, should anyone share a table with her.

Though the barmaid had bothered to get the crate, Sparrow suspected the barmaid would rather Sparrow leave. Sparrow wanted nothing more at the moment, but not until she was satisfied Crukas wasn't here.

A bit apprehensive, Sparrow glanced around until she met the strange eyes of a young woman with elven features seated in the corner. Sparrow was certain another person had been seated across from her only moments earlier. No one had risen or left the tavern.

The young woman with an odd smile motioned Sparrow to the seat across from her. Eager to rid herself of the crate and tired of standing, Sparrow set the crate beside the door and hurried to empty chair.

CHAPTER 4

*S*parrow sat on the crude chair and wished she'd kept the crate to boost her closer to eye level with the stranger. To better maintain eye contact, Sparrow sat on her knees and rested her elbows atop the table.

"Thanks for sharing your table," Sparrow said, half embarrassed but with an appreciative tone. She kept her coif and hood barely above her brow. "From how vacant the streets are, I never expected so many folks inside this old tavern."

The young elfish lady grinned. Her dimples curled her lips mischievously. "No one ever does. So, if you thought no one was here, why'd you come inside? You're a long way from home. No?"

"Yes," Sparrow replied. "How'd you know?"

She rolled her odd colored eyes. "You're a halfling. Few halflings ever venture far from Willow's Bend. The determination set in your eyes and your attire indicate you're not on an adventure. Contrary to the brightness in your eyes, you pursue someone or something specific. Someone hired you to repossess a stolen item or—Hades forbid—you're a bounty hunter." She whispered *bounty hunter* as though it brought bitterness to her tongue. Disgust, perhaps. Whatever her tone, the elfish lady begrudged Sparrow's occupation. The lady's strange, reddish-yellow eyes brightened like smoldering coals kissed by a gentle breeze.

Sparrow swallowed hard and tried not to look away. "If I base my opinions about you, your eyes frighten me."

The young woman shrugged. "Am I correct?"

"Close enough," Sparrow sighed. "Are you a fortune teller?"

The young woman extended her hand and grinned. "I'm Fasha Clover, owner of Tomes & Scrolls, just across the way. I'm sure you saw the small shop across the alley. How could you not? It's the only other active shop in this wilting town."

Sparrow eyed Fasha's hand and hesitated. She feared a handshake with her required a fee of gold, blood, or something worth even more. The burly barmaid seemed less intimidating.

Fasha appeared insulted. "Unlike most patrons here, my hands *are* clean."

Sparrow winced and shook her hand. "Sorry. I didn't mean to be rude."

"What's your opinion of me?"

"What do you mean?" Sparrow asked.

"I've never met you. I told you what I *know* about you. What's your perception of me?"

"Except for your eyes, I'd say you're elven."

"Well, you're half right," Fasha said with a sly grin.

"I don't know about the other half?"

"Care to wager a guess?"

Sparrow shifted in her seat. Fasha's eyes underwent mesmerizing changes of flowing, fiery colors, and never held a stable color. Sparrow sighed and swallowed hard. "I'd ... rather not."

Fasha cocked a brow. "You disappoint me."

"Why?"

"You cut our guessing game short. Since you were a former thief and now you hunt thieves, you should read others better than this. How do you discern whether another thief's lying or not?"

"Have we met before?" Sparrow felt uncomfortable. With her coif and hood concealing her face, she felt confident no one recognized her, but she had given her first name. The air chilled between them.

Sparrow was a common name among halflings, sprites, gnomes, and other smaller Fae. Without revealing her last name, how'd Fasha know who she was. She glanced around the tavern with a great deal of suspicion. Had someone else occupied the seat Sparrow was seated in, like she'd thought? Often, fortune tellers worked in pairs. One spied and relayed information to the other, but this didn't seem to be the case. Sparrow feared something darker and more sinister was at play.

"No," Fasha replied. "We've never met."

"How do you know so much about me?"

Fasha smiled. "Back to the guessing game?"

Sparrow frowned. "Huh?"

"You said I looked elven other than my eyes. My eyes are indicative of my mother's side of the family. My father's an elf. So, I'm half elf. What's my other half?"

Sparrow looked down at the table. If she assumed incorrectly, she chanced insulting a stranger who knew more about her than Sparrow knew about Fasha.

"Go ahead. Guess. I won't be offended. After all, a thief and bounty hunter should be capable of deductive reasoning, right?"

Sparrow sighed. "Given you said, 'Hades forbid' and your eyes look nothing like any race I've seen, your mother must be a demon? Forgive me if I'm wrong."

Fasha winked and pointed her index finger at Sparrow while making a clicking sound with her tongue. "The most logical answer isn't always correct, but in this case, you're right."

"Is that why you read me so well?"

"No." Fasha shook her head slightly. "Not exactly. As I mentioned, I sell tomes and scrolls and various potions. I also write effective spell scrolls and practice divination so I can detect thoughts and intent."

"Of anyone in this tavern?"

"Only if they interested me, but few ever do," Fasha replied. "Most wanderers are quite … boring."

"*Why* do I interest you?" Sparrow asked.

"You're different from anyone in this pub, which drew my immediate attention."

"I'm a halfling."

Fasha nodded and whispered, "A female halfling who's a bounty hunter with her attention set on capturing Crukas."

Sparrow stiffened, glanced around, and pushed away from the table. She placed her hands inside her robe pockets and gripped the poster with her right hand. "You *have* read my thoughts?"

Fasha chuckled. "Every fiber of your being is focused on Aetheaon's master thief. Even now, your tight grip on his wanted poster inside your pocket is about to crumble it beyond readability. Your sweaty palm has probably smeared the ink."

Sparrow gasped and released her hold on the scroll.

Fasha's eyes narrowed. "This is why you caught my eye the second you entered the doorway. Fishermen and hunters come and go. The herb gatherers are too common a sight and all carry similar herb pouches. But you—a halfling with the grandest intent of going after Crukas—you loft and radiate an ambition far greater than your size. That says a lot. You've got heart and courage."

"I never expected anyone to notice. I'm trying to keep a low profile and stay hidden."

"To most, you probably go unnoticed. No one else paid you any mind, except the barkeep," Fasha said. "My guess is you stared at the locked door too long."

Sparrow nodded. "Yes. What's behind the door?"

Fasha's smile faded. Her eyes dimmed. "Some mysteries are best never known."

"He's overly protective of the door," Sparrow said.

"Chubs?"

Confused, Sparrow said, "Chubs?"

"Yes, that's the barkeep's name."

"You jest." Sparrow frowned. "He looks like a walking corpse. He has no meat on his bones, as my mother'd say."

"True, but he once was rotund. Thus, the name. And yes, his *real* name from when he was a young boy. Trust me, Chubs was actually a compliment with his immense size."

Sparrow glanced at the barkeep and shook her head in disbelief. "What happened?"

"Eh, he bought a spell scroll from me," Fasha said. "Unfortunately, he wasn't specific with how much weight he wanted to lose. The incantation was vague. He put too much emphasis on the wrong words, which messed it up. Magic can be fickle and unpredictable at times."

"Can't you undo it?"

Fasha shrugged. "Could, but he doesn't trust it'll reverse the effect. He fears he might waste away even more. But I think he fears returning to his enormous size. Either way, he's lost his faith in better expectations."

"He didn't get angry at you?"

"Sure, but he got over it. To be truthful, I'm surprised he allows me inside his tavern," Fasha said. "But since we're the only two shops remaining in Salem, we need one another's support."

"Why has the town diminished so much?" Sparrow asked.

"Hexes, curses, vengeance," Fasha said. "Bloodshed, sacrifices … hauntings, nature … the list of reasons are endless. Essentially, the town's being absorbed by the forest. Soon, Chubs and myself will find ourselves packing and moving elsewhere, if the forest doesn't consume us, too. Salem will cease to exist and the forest will erase what once was a pleasant town. Unless, I write the proper spell."

"Then why don't you?"

"Given time, everything dies. Any spell I cast prolongs the inevitable."

Sparrow studied Fasha for several seconds. There wasn't any coldness in her tone or her eyes. Her eyes blazed like dying embers, which masked coldness, and staring into them made Sparrow uneasy.

Fasha said, "You can't preserve everything. Have you ever planted a flower seed in a garden and watched it grow?"

Sparrow nodded and smiled. "Of course. As a halfling, gardening is a necessity. Well, second nature, I suppose."

"Over time, even with the best care, the seed sprouts, the stem and leaves emerge, and the flower comes to full bloom, reaching its glory. Once this peak is met, the flower withers. Pedals curl and one by one, they drop to the soil or the wind blows them away. Nothing stops this process. It's part of nature. The stem browns, becomes brittle, and crumbles to the earth to fertilize the soil. What remains afterwards?"

Sparrow thought for a moment. "New seeds?"

"Yes. The seeds. Salem's following this process. Sorceress Brew and Tomes & Scrolls are the last pedals of this town. Both are wilting even as we speak. Nature's reclaiming the forest paths to our town circle. No doubt you noticed that on your journey. Once these last two places close, and Chubs and I move on, each of us take our belongings and our knowledge to the next place we settle. Our knowledge and experience will join others. We'll transplant ourselves elsewhere."

"And you're fine with that?"

Fasha shrugged. "Nature *always* wins. Well, except in rare occasions."

Sparrow eyed the chain-locked door behind the bar while Chubs turned to fill a tankard from one of the ale barrel's tap.

A sly smile curled Fasha's lips. "Why does the door fascinate you? You've eyed it from when you entered. It mesmerizes you. Are you considering returning to your old ways?"

"What?"

"Once a thief, always a thief."

Sparrow shook her head. "Uh, no."

"You've considered several ways to get inside the door. I read your thoughts, remember?"

"An old habit."

"Ah. Temptations are difficult to ignore."

Sparrow grinned, but in the faint light, Fasha probably didn't notice, but with those eyes, perhaps she had catlike vision? "Do *you* know what's behind the door? Another room? Underground tunnel? A prison cell? Monster?"

"I answered you earlier."

"Not really."

"It's the best answer you'll get. But, if you're brave, feel free to ask Chubs directly. These patrons could use the entertainment."

Sparrow's chest tightened. "I'd rather not, thank you. Let's return to my rephrased question. Do *you* know what's behind the door?"

Fasha took a sharp breath, held it, and then motioned the closest barmaid.

"Yes, Fasha?"

Fasha peered directly into the barmaid's eyes. "Rose, two tankards of honey mead."

"Right away." Rose half-bowed and quickly backed away—careful, it seemed—to not turn her back to Fasha.

"Was she showing you respect or fear just then?" Sparrow asked.

"A little of both."

"Why?"

"As a spellcaster," Fasha said, "you gain a reputation quickly."

"The power of magic and words?"

"Yes. When both are properly matched, a spell can be advantageous. When mismatched, the outcome's devastating for almost everyone involved."

Frustrated, Sparrow placed her elbows on the table and leaned toward Fasha. "Why are you deliberately avoiding my questions about the door?"

"A lot of reasons," Fasha said. "One, you're a stranger in Salem. The door and the town are of no real concern to you. You'll be moving on your way soon enough. Mere curiosity doesn't merit an answer. Two, I gave a decent answer. Though *not* to your satisfaction, it's *still* an answer all the same. And three, it's *none* of your business."

Rose set two tankards on the round table. Sparrow reached for her coin purse.

Fasha slapped a silver coin on the table. "It's on me."

"Thanks," Sparrow said. "My apologies about the door. It's … I've never seen any door *locked* in such a manner."

"You'll probably never see another quite like it, either," Fasha said.

"And yet, you *know* what's on the other side of this one."

With a perturbed expression, Fasha said, "I can tell you what's *not* on the other side."

"What?"

"Crukas. After all, *he's* the reason you're here. *Not* the door. Unless, you're contemplating to use your thieving skills to break inside and see for yourself."

"No."

"Good to know. Chubs won't have to kill you." Fasha grinned.

Sparrow leaned on the table and pulled the heavy tankard to her. It was the size of her head. She took a sip off the top. "Since you read thoughts, can you read or predict the future?"

"*Your* future, you mean?"

"Well, yes."

"And whether or not, you'll find Crukas?"

"That'd be beneficial."

Fasha said, "For a fee, yes. But not in here."

"Your shop?"

Fasha nodded. "Of course. Where else?"

"The cost?"

"Depends on the reading and its outcome."

"Fair enough."

"Drink up. After you finish your drink, we'll head to my shop."

Sparrow shook her head. "I can never drink all this. A pint would've been difficult, but an entire tankard?"

"Drink what you can. Leave the rest."

CHAPTER 5

*C*rukas crept through the unlighted room with the stealth of a panther stalking its prey. Fortunately, for him, the object set in his focus was unanimated—a book—which could not flee, and he *hoped*, it wouldn't curse him.

Valuable books were often locked in safes or guarded by traps or spells, especially rare, magical books. Some mages and wizards set alarm spells. Others placed mimics inside false book binders to appear authentic. When a thief slid the book from the shelf, the mimic ate his hand or inflicted excruciating agony. A book mimic once attached itself to a thief's face and smothered the young man to death. Over the years, Crukas encountered various mimics disguised as books, doors, and chests, so finding the book on a shelf made him suspicious.

The book Crukas sought was not only informative about magic, the book was bound with a curse. Mimics aside, deciding which held a worse fate became his ordeal. To the bearer the curse attached itself. Because of this, Crukas would never have considered stealing it, except the book was a necessary tool to stop the Plague-bringer.

Before his arrival, Crukas never foresaw the book being out in the open. He certainly didn't expect it to be on a shelf between a basic herb book and an elementary potion-making book. A half hour later, he stared incredulously at the book's spine. Why was something so evil set in the open, unhidden, and unsecured? Taking the book seemed too easy, which was why he hesitated and mustered his courage to snatch it.

With a simple revelation spell, Crukas searched for snares or magical traps but none existed. A mimic could not be revealed by such a spell, so he couldn't rule out that type of trap. Not detecting common protective spells didn't offer him any ease. Perhaps it wasn't as odd as he believed. Only a fool would grab the *Cursed Spellbook of the Damned* and hope to keep it as a prize. *Cursed* prominently stood out in the title. The *first* word and one never to be dismissed lightly.

He imagined anyone who truly sought this book could've already found and taken it. The book gave away its presence and was easy enough for someone to find. The Gloomy Forest practically shouted the book's location, and thus far, there'd been no takers. The manifesting curse spread from the shelf, through the floor, and seeped bit by bit into the woods, possibly searching for living flesh to inhabit. With the magnitude of its destructive power, he was surprised that Tyrann didn't already possess the book. The curse seemed akin to whatever caused the Black Chasm to continue expanding. This book could be why Salem and the Gloomy Forest were dying.

Crukas was glad to find the book in Salem instead of the Black Chasm. While the Black Chasm slowly spread death and decay into its surrounding territories, its atmosphere was toxic.

Deadly.

Were the book in Tyrann's possession, Crukas could find no logical way to ever get his hands on it. But yet, the book on the shelf taunted him. If an ordinary heist, Crukas would've already nabbed the book and disappeared. This theft held higher stakes. He wagered his life by claiming the tome.

Stealing the cursed book wrought cautious thought on his part. He didn't want to *keep* the book, nor did he wish to touch it. He only wanted to *borrow* it. He'd readily return it after he skimmed the pages and discovered how to defeat the Plague-bringer. Regardless of Crukas' intent, a curse didn't make exceptions.

Faint voices outside the building grew louder as did their gentle, approaching footsteps on the cobblestone walkway.

Crukas closed his eyes and cursed. When he opened them, he took a deep breath and grabbed the book. Hurrying to the fireplace, he knocked dozens of rolled scrolls and several books off a table and onto the floor.

So much for a graceful exit.

Good fortune partially ruled in his favor. The scrolls fell first, rather quickly, and formed a cushioned layer on the floor, which kept the books from thudding loudly.

He'd come through the door—the lock an easy, quick pick—but the door was not an option for escape. Not with people approaching. Like other ruined shops in the town's circle, this building had no windows, which was an oddity in itself. The cold, dark fireplace was the only alternative route to flee. He'd exited worse places, but at least the fireplace didn't have a roaring fire or a metal spit. As much as he hated soot and grime, cleaning up later was better than the ultimate embarrassment of being caught in the act; something he rarely suffered.

"No time to leave a note." Crukas shook his head with a sly grin. He tucked the book behind his belt. "But, should I survive, you've my word, I'll return this."

Leaving a note was not something thieves did, but Crukas occasionally flaunted his greatest heists, not only to stoke his ego, but to mock his rivals. Even with his signature, the victims seldom believed Crukas was the actual thief. *Any* thief could leave a note and place Crukas' name for misdirection. So, over time, magistrates and other thieves readily discredited the personalized notes, unless a believable witness had seen Crukas steal the object. The less skilled thieves despised Crukas' growing reputation and wished to discredit him because no thief could be as slick as he. With so few believing his claims, Crukas seldom left notes at all.

For the time being, it was best no one knew he possessed this tome. His plan to covertly take the book and move to the next town without notice was gone. He'd triggered the book's curse. Knocking the scrolls and books off the table was the first clumsy moment during his life as a thief.

A metal key scraped the door's lock. Crukas crouched into the cold, darkened fireplace and squeezed inside the firebox. He climbed halfway up the flue before the door's lock clicked and the aged hinges whined, as the door swung inward.

Crukas froze and held his breath. Although he could scurry up the bricks quietly with his soft, enchanted boots without making a sound, he didn't chance it. Not yet. While the boots were blessed with feathered silence, this aided when he walked. Shimmying his back against the old chimney could break loose mortar and cause pieces of broken bricks to fall to the firebox below. The least noise could give his location away. All he could do was wait and hope the owner was distracted enough by his accidental mess for him to climb to the top and escape without further notice.

CHAPTER 6

Sparrow followed Fasha across the narrow alleyway to the Tomes & Scrolls shop. Fasha took a key from her pocket to unlock the door.

Sparrow belched, covered her mouth, and giggled uncontrollably. "S-sorry. I drank more than I intended."

"Partially my fault. I should've ordered you a pint instead."

"Told you!" Sparrow pointed and burst into a snorting giggle. "When I first saw this shop, I thought it was closed."

"It was," Fasha replied. "I always lock up when I go to the tavern."

Sparrow shook her head and regretted it. Doing so made her even more dizzy. "N-o-o-o. I mean per-ma-ma-ment-ly closed."

"Not yet." Fasha sighed and smiled, inserted the brass key into the large lock, and turned it. After a loud click, she turned the knob and pushed the heavy oak door inward.

"No fire or lantern?" Sparrow asked.

"No."

"How do you see?"

"Shh!"

Sparrow frowned. "Huh?"

"Quiet," Fasha said. "An intruder's about."

"Where?" Sparrow staggered forward and stumbled into Fasha. She caught her balance and shook her finger. "Is ... why you need ... proper lighting."

Fasha placed her hands on Sparrow's narrow shoulders and rested the halfling against the door post. "*Stay* here and be quiet."

Sparrow put her hand on the hilt of her dagger. "But I can protect you."

"Uh, no." Fasha shook her head. "In your condition ... you'll stab yourself or me, or both of us."

Sparrow snickered. "I'm good with a dagger."

"*No.* Stay put or we might both wind up dead. A dagger's of little use against magic. And us dying does no good at all. I need to find the intruder and see what he's after."

Fasha left Sparrow against the door post and entered the dark shop.

Everything spun in Sparrow's vision, though with nightfall, her vertigo wasn't nearly as bad. Other than Fasha grumbling and the rough scratching of a match being struck, Sparrow detected no other noises. Fasha hadn't screamed in pain or alarm, so the intruder must've already left.

A swaying light moved from inside Tomes & Scrolls and approached the doorway. Sparrow's fingers tightened around the hilt of her blade.

"All's clear," Fasha said in a gruff tone. She took Sparrow by the elbow and led the halfling inside the shop and secured the door. "Whoever was here is gone."

"Did they take anything?"

Fasha huffed. "That's yet to be determined. Here, take a seat. After I light a few more lanterns, I'll give you an elixir to sober you."

"You're sooo sweet." Sparrow slurred her words. "I seldom drink."

"That's rather obvious and probably best. Now, sit tight."

Sparrow closed her eyes and held the small tabletop with both hands. When she opened her eyes, three glowing lantern lit the room. Fasha also lit a small fire in the fireplace.

Fasha set a small flask in front of Sparrow. "Here, drink this."

"Oh, I couldn't possibly ... I'm tipsy enough."

Fasha's fiery, elven eyes narrowed. "It'll *sober* you."

"O-o-h, okay." Sparrow tipped the flask upward and downed the contents. "Yeesh. That's horrible."

"I know, but it works quickly."

Sparrow scrunched her nose. "Why didn't you tell me how nasty it tastes?"

"Because you wouldn't have drank it, would you?"

Sparrow shrugged.

Fasha leaned down and scooped an armful of scrolls off the floor. "What a mess. It'll take at least an hour to reorganize these."

Sparrow belched.

"How are you feeling? Has everything stopped spinning?"

Sparrow winced. "Yeah, but I have a terrible headache and breath harsh enough to slay a dragon. Thanks to the nasty stuff you gave me."

"The elixir sobers you quickly, but does nothing to alleviate the inevitable headache. Or, in your case, the bad breath."

Sparrow stood. The room no longer swayed and her vision cleared. "Tell me how I can help you."

Fasha showed Sparrow the faint differences in the parchment pigments. "Stack these according to the colors, so I can store them by spell type. Once these are sorted, I'll attempt to determine if and when your path crosses with Crukas."

"Thanks."

"Don't get your hopes up," Fasha said. "I may find nothing useful."

CHAPTER 7

*A*fter a half hour of sorting the scrolls, Sparrow's headache hadn't lessened, even though she'd tried to keep her focus on the task at hand. Because the spells were rolled and tied, she couldn't peek at at the written incantations. She marveled at the various types of spells, based on the color of the parchments. She never realized so many spells existed, which gave her more respect for the resources spellcasters used and added slight trepidation at the power the more experienced magic users possessed.

Sparrow shook her head. "You have so many types of spells. You could write books—"

"Volumes of books, I have. These scrolls are but a drop in a pail," Fasha replied.

"Really?"

"Of course." Fasha pointed at the bookcases behind Sparrow. "See? There are volumes of spell books and grimoires. Ancient ones. Some written in obscure languages. Others written in riddles, which can be quite dangerous to execute."

"Why?"

Fasha laughed. "The caster must be absolutely correct in the answer to properly cast the spell. Otherwise, he or she might jinx themselves with a curse or a temporary side effect. Some have even died."

"Ah. I never knew that."

"Most don't understand the dangers of using magic. Magic must always be respected. Any time someone casts a spell at another, the caster must pay a price."

Sparrow frowned. "What kind of a price?"

"Depends on the spell's level and its intent. Some use magic for good and reap good in return for blessing the less fortunate. Such means are rarer these days. Most view magic as a greedy attempt to gain more for themselves, but it's not meant for obtaining wealth, nor revenge. Eventually, these individuals learn their mistake, but often far too late. Those sorcerers who deal death or disease on others can only protect themselves by blood sacrifices or worse, sacrificing another regardless of race. These are the worst users of magic. Few of those who seek such a path seldom live a year or more. The price is too great to satisfy and the user's life withers and becomes the final token. Magic isn't free. It demands a cost and drains a user's vitality."

"Geesh."

"This is why one must use caution in the things they wish for."

Sparrow said, "With so many spellbooks, why do casters buy scrolls instead?"

Fasha shrugged. "To practice and test one's magical abilities. As a challenge. Or to learn something new to add to their mastery."

"Your door was locked when we arrived," Sparrow said. "How do you know an intruder had been here?"

Fasha gave a wry smile. "Wizards, witches, and mages don't *need* keys. Neither do thieves—well, good thieves. I sense the remnants of whomever came into my shop. The only way these scrolls ended up on the floor was for someone to bump this table hard. My shop has no drafts and opening the door couldn't have disturbed this table from so far away. Someone bumped the table."

"Did they take any of the scrolls?"

"No. I counted them before I left and I recounted moments ago. They're all here."

"But these scrolls would be worth quite a bit of gold, wouldn't they?"

"To a novice spellcaster, maybe. A more experienced spellcaster wouldn't waste time untying and reading them. And taking the whole lot of them … only a fool would do that."

"Why do you say that?"

Fasha smiled. "For those of us who write spells and sell the scrolls, we often place a tainted scroll in with the good ones. This scroll can inflict severe pain on the thief or, as mine do, cause the other scrolls to burst into flame. Which means the intruder came here for something specific."

"Something of more value," Sparrow said.

"Exactly." Fasha looked at the center bookcase behind Sparrow. She gasped. "Damn."

"What's wrong?"

"This isn't good." Fasha's eyes widened with concern and she hurried around the table to the bookcase. "Hades curse them!"

"What?"

"Someone took the Cursed Spellbook of the Damned."

"Well, *that's* a disturbing title for a book," Sparrow said.

"It is what it says it is. If the book gets into the wrong hands, the outcome could be disastrous."

Sparrow became uneasy. "For a book so dangerous, *why* would you leave it out in the open?"

Fasha's eyes narrowed as she stared at the bookcase. "I never thought anyone would be foolish enough to take it. Its reputation is well known, but no one knew I had it. Well, customers might've seen it, but we haven't gotten too many since I took possession of the book."

Sparrow said, "A customer could've mentioned the book to others."

"True. But again, the book's reputation sets fear in almost anyone's heart who has the slightest knowledge of magic. Not only is the book full of curses, the book is bound in cursed dragon leather. The bearer heaps curses on himself, which is one safeguard. Another is the spells are written in my mother's demonic language. A language no human, elf, dwarf, or any other race can read or translate. Only a *specific* sect of demons can read it."

"Can you?"

Fasha gave Sparrow a dead stare and then huffed slightly. "Of course I can. My mother taught me her language."

"Then perhaps a demon stole it," Sparrow said.

Fasha sneered. "Doubtful. Even demons are susceptible to the curse."

"It doesn't seem to have affected you."

"Not lately," Fasha said. "But, anytime I've ever had to carry it, in my travels, it has affected my health."

"How?"

"For me, it messes with my mind. For a human or a different race, who knows how the curse manifests?" Fasha pointed to a curtain on the far wall. "While I put the rest of these scrolls away, please take a seat at my table in the next room. I'll be there in a few minutes."

"For a reading?"

Fasha nodded. "Yes."

CHAPTER 8

Coincidence or the book's curse?
Crukas pondered with the heat of the growing flames in the fireplace slowly building into a hellish blaze. While his ice-silk armor protected him from blistering heat, it did nothing to lessen the smoke's effect.

Thick smoke burned his eyes. Involuntary tears flowed. Although he tried to hold his breath, the sage smoke burned his lungs and made his throat itch. He fought against the pressing urge to surrender to a coughing fit. Taking a black handkerchief from his pocket, he covered his mouth and nose and held the cloth tightly. He hoped to filter the smoke while taking short breaths to prevent passing out.

The fire crackled and popped. The increasing scent of sage and other fragrant herbs lofted within the black smoke. This was not an ordinary fire to light to warm a room. Powerful herbs and a generous sprinkling of powdered ingredients coated the burning twigs and branches to make the smoke more insufferable. Some herbs repelled ill omens or evil spirits, and others in this unique combination were meant to flush out an intruder, to make the invisible, visible.

A flurry of glowing embers flickered around Crukas' face. For several moments, he feared his weakening muscles would give out from pressing his back against the bricks in his awkward position. With his back pressed to one side of the chimney and his bent legs pushing his feet against the opposite side, painful cramps tightened in places he never imagined. The agony made him want to drop into the fire, roll out into the room, and take his chances fighting his way to the door.

While doing so might be an entertaining *grand* entrance, his watery eyes prevented him from seeing his way to the door while avoiding a powerful spellcaster. He'd probably bump and trip and find himself in a vulnerable situation, worse than smoke and fire.

Footsteps creaked on the old wooden floor and moved away from the fireplace. A light whispering hum, a chant perhaps, informed Crukas the owner was heading across the room. Taking the last opportunity he had before his fatigued muscles gave out or further inhalation caused him to cough, Crukas winced and shimmied upward with the use of his elbows while counter-forcing his feet against the other side for leverage. Once his back elevated above his feet, he raised each foot and secured them until he stretched into a near horizontal position. He continued this alternation until he reached the top of the flue.

Without the fire, time wouldn't have been an issue. But with the choking smoke and lessening oxygen, time was of the essence. The comfort of the cool, night air above the chimney lured him. He braced himself on his right side, and with a swift flip, he rolled over the chimney's edge and landed face-first on the roof's thatch.

He muffled his coughs into the thatch. Still wearing the handker-chief, he wheezed. Due to the smoke and the various mixtures of incense and sage, the soured, mildewy aroma of the old, rotting thatch was unnoticed. He'd escaped the fire without detection, and that mattered most.

Once Crukas ceased coughing and caught his breath, he rolled onto his back. The firelight glowed beneath the puffs of black smoke. He could've sworn the glowing embers rising with the smoke formed demonic eyes, and were searching the roof for his presence. They never looked directly at him and were nothing more than a hallucination from his inhalation of burnt mushroom spores or unknown herbs.

He was tempted to drop the cursed book down the fireplace, but the fire probably couldn't harm or destroy the book. After studying the cover in the faint light from the chimney, the fire wouldn't harm the book. Dragon-hide leather. He tucked the book inside a pouch and sighed.

Leaving the book behind, however, didn't release him from its inevitable curse. The curse marked him, and he couldn't deny its touch.

Shrouded by darkness, he listened to the slight howl of the night breeze. The warmth in the air indicated a storm brewed in the west where his destination was.

"Could this night get any worse?" Crukas whispered.

His wax-coated, leather thief pouch shifted at his side, as though a small animal was trying to escape.

Crukas held the pouch in both hands and examined it in the faint glow of the chimney light. He slipped his hand inside the bag, thinking perhaps a small rodent had somehow gotten trapped inside. Only the cursed book was inside. He removed the book. Immediately, an ominous discomfort overwhelmed him unlike anything he'd ever experienced. The power attached to the leather cover was undeniable. If the book's outside layer was shrouded with pure evil, he worried about worse things written inside.

He took a magic pebble from his inside pocket, spoke a simple word, and radiance beamed from the small stone. In its light, he opened the book and looked at the text. With a harsh frown, he stared at the strange lettering. The words and symbols made no sense. Flipping through the pages, he realized the book was useless without an interpreter. The book's curse had already taken a solid grip on him. Did he even have time to find someone to translate its contents? If he found someone, would the translator also be cursed? Would someone even chance the possibility, or would Crukas have to deceive someone into reading it?

Crukas feared little in his life as a thief. But magical curses were something he respected. He avoided stealing any cursed objects because the cost was too great. He could leave the book behind, but the curse would remain. Besides, for someone to counteract the curse, they'd need the physical book to successfully break it. Despite his fears, he needed to proceed forward with the duties. Regardless of the outcome, the worst was death. And if he died, there was nothing more to fear.

CHAPTER 9

Sparrow sat in the crude chair at a small round table covered with a black silk tablecloth. Two large candles glowed on a small shelf fastened to the wall, which provided adequate ambient lighting.

A small crystal ball resting atop a silver holder held her interest with a slight mesmerizing embrace. Several times, something swam inside the translucent ball, as though it sought to escape. Once, its eyes pressed against the crystal orb and stared at her with its darkened gaze.

If looks could kill…

Chills pimpled her arms, she shifted on the seat, and hoped Fasha would enter through the curtain soon. The crystal ball made her uncomfortable. This wasn't an ordinary magical bubble. Something inside the crystal sought to be released. *What* was imprisoned inside the glass?

Sparrow lowered her hood and removed her coif. She was hot and feverish. Whether this discomfort was the result of drinking too much or another side effect of the nasty elixir, she didn't know. She wouldn't have drank the elixir had she been sober because she didn't know Fasha well enough to trust. Nor did she now.

42

Were Fasha an elf or a half-elf that wasn't part demon, Sparrow wouldn't hold these doubts. Fasha being half demon troubled Sparrow. She viewed Fasha as more demon than elf and one who wrote spells. She possessed the Cursed Spellbook of the Damned without obvious suffering from the curse. Not only this, she controlled whatever was inside the crystal. Or worse, *it* controlled *her*. Since the book had been stolen and was only useful to a demon who could translate it, she doubted Crukas would've stolen it. Any good thief researched items worth stealing. Crukas couldn't be so foolish.

Yet, Sparrow tracked him to Bridgebarrow, which wasn't a far journey to Salem and close enough to make him suspect. Rumors about Crukas' ability to work magic and cast spells combed Aetheaon. These entertained rumors arose because of how he could get into such secure places without being seen or heard. Citizens speculated he must have used magic. Even so, since he was human, the cursed book offered him no help at all. Apparently by Fasha's explanation, no human or other race could interpret the language, so Crukas could easily be ruled out. Knowing Crukas' reputation, he wouldn't willingly risk his life for a book capable of cursing its bearer, nor would he sell his thieving services to steal it for someone else.

Would he?

According to Fasha, mages, wizards, and witches didn't need tools to get past locked doors, which further backed Crukas being capable of using magic. If so, what level of mastery did he possess? As a thief with enchanted powers, he was a double threat. He could enter places with his lock picks or by using magic whenever necessary.

Sparrow's thoughts toward Crukas bore additional scorn. She whispered, "This explains your success and ease to slip in and out of palaces, towers, and banks without ever being noticed." Feats she lacked the proper skill to do as a thief.

She was somewhat envious while hating him even more. After all, jealousy never bowed its green head to behold the slightest admiration.

She became more determined than ever to catch Crukas. Not only for the rich bounty, but she had questions—a *lot* of questions—that only he could answer. Provided he'd give honest answers. Fasha might allocate some information, but Sparrow doubted the half-demon would disclose everything or tell the truth. No doubt, Fasha already withheld more information than she'd readily share.

Sparrow looked at the curtain. *What's keeping you?*

She started to stand to look for Fasha when the curtain parted.

"Sorry to keep you waiting." Fasha walked past Sparrow and took the seat on the other side of the table. She lit a stick of incense, allowing the flame to rise and ignite the aromatic stem before she blew it out. The stream of smoke drifted with a sweet scent, and she inserted the end of the stick into a silver holder.

"Is something alive inside your crystal ball?" Sparrow asked. "Is it what tells you the future?"

A sly smile curled Fasha's lips. "Without divination, I must warn you to stay away from Crukas."

Sparrow gasped slightly, eased back in the chair, and rested her hands in her lap. The various fiery colors dancing in Fasha's eyes made Sparrow uncomfortable. Had Fasha played her all along? The sneer indicate she had. "Why? Are you in with cahoots him?"

"Cahoots?" Fasha scoffed and shook her head. "No. He's the one who stole my book."

"You know this how?"

Fasha's smile faded. "I cast a spell to see who invaded my shop. A ghostly image of every move he took played before me. He picked the lock on the door. Quite quickly, I must say. He's a master thief, no question about it. But for a thief, he tarried far longer than a master thief should. He stared at the book for a long while before finally taking it."

"So he knows about the curse?"

"Obviously."

"Then why steal it?"

Fasha shrugged. "Only he can answer that. But, I don't suggest you be the one to ask. Forget about Crukas. Let him go. Should you pursue him, nothing good comes your way. Confronting him might well be your death."

Sparrow shivered. The cold tone in Fasha's voice matched the coldness of her prophesy, which preceded the chill of an icy grave. Sparrow's gut led her to believe what Fasha said was true. She should cut her losses and travel a different direction, but a smidgeon of her pride forbade her from quitting the pursuit.

"But he can't read the book," Sparrow said.

"No. Perhaps he was hired to steal it for someone else?"

Sparrow shook her head. "No. Crukas never works for another."

"You don't know for certain. Perhaps he reconsidered? Or perhaps he's teamed with a guild."

Sparrow snorted and politely covered her mouth to hide the smile. "*Crukas*? He'd never lower his ego enough to join other thieves. He lives for the notoriety and his reputation."

"There's always a first time," Fasha said.

"Not with Crukas."

"You asked for my advice and I gave it, as I see it. Yet, you act as though you have the answers already."

"No." Sparrow frowned. "You never consulted whatever's inside your crystal ball."

Fasha's eyes blazed, brighter than the two candles' glow combined. The veins in her forehead swelled and mapped their way down her cheeks. Her voice deepened. "Dare you tempt your fate further? What more revelations do you need? Crukas stole the book. You seek him, and you seek your demise, as he has already done for himself. That's what you wished to know, correct? What happens when your path crosses his?"

Sparrow swallowed hard and trembled. She feared her breath had been taken from her. A chill crept throughout her tiny body. She'd never seen a true demon, though she'd heard about them, and although Fasha looked every bit of a half elf on the outside, there was no mistaking what she was inside—a demon.

Finally, Sparrow took a shallow breath and nodded, breaking eye contact with Fasha. "My apologies. You're correct. That's what I requested."

Fasha glared a moment longer. Slowly the glow and hardness in her eyes faded. "Just because the results aren't to your liking doesn't give you the right to insist deeper insight."

"Again, my apologies. I truly didn't mean to offend," Sparrow said, softly, while wondering if she'd get out of the shop alive. "What do I owe you?"

What had overshadowed and controlled Fasha subsided. Her eyes returned to their normal colors, provided one could consider them normal to begin with. A sly smile spread on her lips. "One gold and one silver coin."

"How much more to stay the night?" Sparrow asked, even though she wished for a better option. Based on the ruined nature of the small hamlet, residing with the half demon seemed safer than the alternative goal of finding a place in one of the abandoned buildings, a roof, or sleeping inside a hollow tree in the haunted forest.

Fasha met Sparrow's meek eyes. "No extra charge. You're welcome here. I've a small room in the loft. A little dusty, but not uncomfortable."

A chill shot through Sparrow. She felt as safe as a fly welcomed in a spider's web with the offer of a night's rest inside a tightly knit, silken cocoon. Her voice quivered. "You're too kind."

Fasha cocked a brow. "You and I both know you're lying."

"While I'm apprehensive about your brief transformation, I'm not lying," Sparrow said. "You could turn me out into the night and let me wander and fend for myself, but your offer for me to stay is kindness."

Fasha chuckled. "Let's not get all mushy. Come with me. I'll get you a blanket and a place to rest. But, don't let my hospitality get out, okay?"

"Sure. Okay."

CHAPTER 10

❧

The bright stars slowly faded behind a thin layer of clouds and the coolness of night settled. Crukas lie on the thatched roof and caught his breath. The harsh chimney smoke made his throat itch. The jovial laughter of three dwarves leaving Sorceress Brew caught his attention. The three spoke loudly and walked toward the town's circle.

Crukas had always had a difficult time discerning whether a dwarf was actually drunk or not. Dwarves could drink almost any human or elf under the table, depending on the choice of beverage. These three were boisterous and overly cheerful, but not one faltered in step.

A dwarf with yellow hair and beard pointed at his two companions. "And dat's when I said, 'Me ram could kiss better than your wife!'"

"What'd he say to dat, Adgus?" the dwarf with black hair and beard asked.

"At first, nothing, Bramnir," Adgus said. "After he kept his silence longer than a minute, I asked if he considered giving it a gander."

"O-o-h!" the dwarf with red hair and beard said. "Did he get mad then?"

"Mad's not the proper word for it, Ebden!" Adgus chuckled. "*Furious* was what he became."

"Did he kiss your ram?" Ebden asked.

"Nah, he changed the subject. But, his long pause indicated he might've been considering putting it to the test!"

His two companions howled with laughter.

Crukas wasn't certain how many more patrons tarried inside the tavern, but at this late hour, there probably weren't many. He worried how many were wandering the streets. He didn't wish to encounter others like Sparrow who might want to capture him for a quick reward. Had it not been for breathing in the herb-enhanced smoke in the chimney, Crukas would've long been gone. His lungs still ached. While the slight flickering embers flowed upward with the smoke, he truly contemplated returning the cursed book. He wondered if doing so removed the obvious curse latched to him and caused his sudden streak of bad luck. He doubted the curse would release him, regardless of discarding the book. Curses didn't recognize apologies or regret.

The magical items Crukas needed to steal for his mission were few, but now he wished he'd have collected these relics in the proper chronological order, as opposed to taking the shortest route to save time. He'd have endured a longer amount of traveling and circling back and forth to places otherwise. Time was crucial. However, had he gotten the other items first, he might've prevented the book's ability to curse him or at least lessened its effects.

After leaving Bridgebarrow, Salem was the next closest town, where the book was rumored to be stashed. After obtaining it, he could check it off his list. But now he realized his error in downplaying the dangers of the curse. Regret toiled with his mind.

Sparrow, the self-proclaimed bounty hunter, was in the shop beneath the roof where he rested. The thought of how close he was to her, and her being clueless about the irony, amused him.

Like her, he was on foot, but if he followed these three dwarves, he stood the chance of securing a ride to his next destination, provided he'd part with gold or offer them the promise of a barrel or two of strong stout when they arrived at Ravensdorf. Parting with coin in any amount violated his personal code, but the cost was worth paying to gain a day or more of travel to stay ahead of Sparrow.

At the edge of the hamlet, the dwarves stabled two ram mounts and two burros harnessed to a wagon filled with straw and a few empty barrels. He expected no argument to ride in the crowded wagon as long as he compensated them with stout. Few dwarves ever turned down a drink, and he doubted *any* dwarf would reject two barrels of stout. Should they decline his offer, he'd up the ante another barrel. The crowded wagon wasn't any worse than other places he'd stowed away in before. He'd hidden in tighter places for longer periods of time when he'd been on ships or the times he crammed himself into wooden crates to ride beneath the carriages of snotty aristocrats.

Crukas peered over the roof's ledge. The alleyway was empty. Gripping handsful of thatch and slowly turning and positioning his legs over until he fully lowered his body, he let loose of the thatch. With the quietness of a cat's cushioned paw pads, his enchanted soft-soled boots allowed him to land soft as a feather and without sound. In the darkness, he slinked and darted, following the faint echoes of the three dwarves' rolling laughter.

When light's absent, shadows are invisible and become a thief's best friend. Crukas moved without notice. Rather than approach the gleeful dwarves on their way, he moved past them. He decided to wait at the stables. No one liked being encountered on a dark street after midnight, as only thieves and murderers were expected to make such approaches with unsatisfactory outcomes for one or both parties. Crukas was the former, but had never been the latter, and he hoped to never be forced to kill another.

CRUKAS SAT on a bale of hay in the back of the three dwarves' wagon when they entered the stable. Several large flames danced in sconces on the corner posts to allow adequate lighting. Drab moths and other flying insects circled the flames.

"Evening," Crukas said softly with little emotion.

"Hey!" Adgus said when he locked eyes with Crukas. "What are ya doing up there? Dat's our wagon."

Crukas smiled apologetically. "I realize that. I was waiting for you."

"You've no business bothering our belongings!" Bramnir pulled his axe from over his shoulder.

"My apologies," Crukas said. "I didn't *bother* anything. I've got urgent matters to—"

"Do ya now?" Adgus pulled his mace, rather than the heavy broad axe off his back. "Cause if your aim's to rob us, ya'll find yourself minus a few appendages."

Crukas shook his head and spoke softly. "No. I don't wish to steal anything from you, but if you could oblige giving me a ride to Ravensdorf, I'd make it well worth your while."

"Meaning?" Adgus asked.

"Your barrels are empty." Crukas tapped the hollow barrel with his knuckles. "I'll buy enough stout to fill two of them once we reach the tavern in Ravensdorf."

"We're not *even* headed to Ravensdorf. It's completely the opposite direction." Bramnir ran a hand down his neatly braided black beard with a look of intense consideration of the offer in his gaze.

"You can pick the most expensive stout you desire," Crukas said, trying to coax the dwarves further into accepting his deal without being pushy. "I've no qualms about the price. Isn't that worth a half day's journey?"

"When you consider there and back, it'd be *more* than a day's journey out of our way," Bramnir said.

Crukas acquiesced a slight nod. "True, but Bridgebarrow's ale and stouts are no comparison to what you could get at The Mute Changeling."

Adgus' huge grin was evident through his beard. "Ah, I've heard of dat place. Never been, as it's always too far outta our travels."

Ebden, the dwarf with a wild bushy red beard, stepped closer. "Ya take us for fools? We know who ya are, master thief. We carry you halfway there and you'll steal our wagon and leave us stranded."

Crukas shook his head. "I've no need of your wagon."

All three dwarves gave him hardened stares with raised brows. They exchanged glances with one another and seemed only moments from bursting into another fit of laughter.

"Okay," Crukas said. "I see the irony. I've need of a *ride*, but I've no time or need to burden myself by stealing your wagon and then trying to hock it. I've urgent matters. Your hospitality's what I seek and I'm more than willing to compensate you for your troubles."

"How's dat?" Bramnir asked. "Ya don't seem to have anything on ya."

"Two barrels of the best stout when we reach The Mute Changeling."

"Dat's it? Bramnir asked.

"What more do you want?" Crukas asked. "The journey's short and there's enough room in your wagon to fit me. I've no need for food or drink."

"Whatcha got for a retainer?" Adgus asked. His yellow, bushy eyebrows leveled, and he placed his hand on the hilt of his axe.

Crukas smiled. "I travel lightly."

"Aye, I see. Then how do you plan to buy the ale?" Adgus asked.

"Bah!" Bramnir said. "Seems he's scheming to me. Let's load up and go."

Crukas sighed. "Devin Dusk is the barkeep at The Mute Changeling and is indebted to me. He'll give you the stout and then he and I will be even."

Adgus shook his head. "As me brother told ya. We know *who* ya are. We know you're a thief, and 'ave seen your wanted posters all over Aetheaon. So—"

"You have my word," Crukas said.

The three dwarves laughed heartily.

Adgus pointed a stern finger at Crukas. "Dat's me point. No thief can be trusted at his word."

Crukas sighed. "Fair enough."

Adgus cocked a brow. "We could turn you in for the reward and buy all the stout we crave and then some, eh?"

Crukas nodded. "You could *try*, but then you'll receive nothing."

Bramnir frowned. "Ya don't have to be breathing for us to collect the reward. Ya know dat, right?"

A sly grin crossed Crukas' lips. "You realize in thirty years, no one's ever succeeded in collecting my bounty. That's why the amount continues to escalate."

Ebden studied Crukas for a moment. "And how's dat? You don't seem capable of heavy weapons and you certainly appear unable to grapple with a muscled gnome."

Bramnir laughed. "Maybe so, but I'd *pay* two barrels of stout to see dat!"

Crukas cocked a brow. "I've never had a need for brawn. A good thief would rather be thin than musclebound in order to fit into places others cannot. You never see too many obese thieves, but it's not because they can't afford to eat. So, while I might not *appear* able to defend myself, the true art is in *not* being in a fight, but to disappear and escape."

"Is dat a challenge?" Ebden said.

Crukas stood and jumped off the wagon. He sighed. "No. Since we're unable to reach a satisfactory agreement, I'll wait for someone else to accept my offer. But, I was hoping to stay ahead of the storm. If you'd kindly reconsider, I'll bump the offer to three barrels, but I can't offer more."

Thunder boomed—almost on cue—in the distance with smaller quaking rumbles softly brushing over the forest and stable.

"Forgive me brothers," Adgus said looking outside the stables. "Your offer's more than generous, given the circumstances. None of us are interested in bloodshed, nor do we wish to take the time to bind you and wait for a magistrate to pay us. Most of 'em are grubbier thieves anyways."

"That's true," Crukas said.

"Since you stated how easily you can disappear," Adgus said, "you must put up some sort of retainer. Something of value or extreme importance. At least, *dat* would garner a wager of good faith between us. Do you 'ave anything of value dat we could hold until we reach Ravensdorf?"

Crukas winced, reached inside his cloak, and brought out the book. "Only a rare book, but I shouldn't let it out of my possession."

"Dat'll do," Adgus said. "Give it to Ebden."

"It's best I keep it. Safer, actually," Crukas said.

Adgus laughed. "It's *just* a book. Ebden can be trusted."

Reluctantly, Crukas handed the Cursed Spellbook of the Damned to Ebden. A slight prickle of static passed between the two during the exchange. Ebden's eyes widened slightly. He felt the energy and looked questionably at Crukas.

Crukas offered a slight shrug as though the charge came from the closeness of the storm, since lightning flickered outside above the trees. The burros shuffled their feet and brayed.

Ebden tucked the book into a leather pouch strapped over his shoulder. After a few moments of silence, Ebden seemed to have associated the static to the instability of the atmosphere, but Crukas knew differently. The weight of carrying the book lessened significantly for Crukas and because the book was light, Ebden received more than a tome for a retainer. By his demand and acceptance of the cursed book, he assumed *ownership*—albeit, only for a short time.

This didn't mean Crukas was immune from all risks. He was a traveling companion with the dwarf trio and as a member of their band, perhaps none of them were safe.

Yet, Crukas sighed with relief.

Bramnir walked to his ram and checked his bridle and saddle straps. "We'd planned to sleep in the wagon tonight. We don't travel at night, Crukas. But if we want to stay ahead of the storm, we've no other choice."

"Most severe storms bypass Ravensdorf and Salem," Crukas said. "*This* storm won't miss us, so we'd best leave now."

Adgus swung upon his mount and frowned. "How's dat? Rain's rain."

Crukas shook his head slightly. "No, not here. The quagmires are dry. Have been for months. They fill quickly with water and form sludge and pockets of quicksand. The ground becomes so viscous there's no pulling free."

"You've traveled through Salem often?" Ebden asked.

"Long ago. When the town was actually prosperous."

"What's the safest route to travel during the night?" Bramnir asked.

"From which direction did you travel to get here?" Crukas asked.

"From the northeast, a small port south of Vylan," Bramnir replied.

"How was the path?"

"Seldom traveled, after we took the southwest path to Salem," Adgus said. "No recent wagon tracks, dat is. A few places indicated riders on various mounts."

Crukas nodded. "Just curious. Since you have a wagon and the path was rough and overgrown, why head to Salem when you could've headed onward to Bridgebarrow on a well-traveled road?"

"Ask Ebden," Bramnir said.

Crukas looked at Ebden.

Ebden smiled. "I've long heard of the serpent statue in the town's center pool. Just, uh, wanted to lay me eyes on it."

Crukas returned the smile. "And you call me a thief?"

Ebden's smile faded and a harsh glare bore into Crukas. "Hey, I never touched it. I know better. Its precious jewels are heavy laden with curses. I'm not a fool."

"I meant no offense," Crukas said. "Believe me, many a thief and even those who've never stolen a single thing have stared at those gems far longer than necessary. The temptation is not trying to find a way to claim them as your own."

"Dat it is," Ebden said, nodding.

"Anyways," Crukas said. "Back to the trails. Follow the path back to the fork where you met this path. Take the left, which leads to Ravensdorf. Before you reach the fork, no clear paths remain in the forest. I'm sure you noticed that."

"Aye. So, let me ask ya this. With your knowledge as a thief, what's our best route to not run into a highwayman and get robbed?" Adgus said.

"No highwayman with any sense would ever hope to rob anyone in Gloomy Forest at night," Crukas replied. When he considered why no fool would hide along the wooded paths at night to rob others, he realized they'd be foolish to travel those paths at this hour. He had a difficult decision to make. Stay and be stuck in Salem for several days with the possibility of encountering Sparrow, or risk leaving what little protection Salem offered.

"Why's dat?" Bramnir asked. "Are these woods actually haunted?"

"So the legends tell," Crukas said with a slight nod. "But we're not in danger of ghosts and spirits tonight. With the storm settling in, and the moon hidden, we're more likely to be attacked by Wierwen than see any ghosts."

"Bah!" Ebden waved Crukas off. "Preposterous! Those wolfish men creatures are nuttin' but myths."

Bramnir and Adgus roared with laughter. Ebden joined in as well. Perhaps they were overly giddy from their stout at the tavern, or else, they actually dismissed the Wierwen altogether.

The heat from Crukas' slight embarrassment for the brothers to laugh at his expense reddened his face, but then it dawned on him. "Laugh if you will, but what's the reason for the three of you never traveling that direction, eh?"

Adgus' broad grin narrowed into a tight sneer. His brow tightened and he pointed a stern finger. "What you gettin' at? You think we're too frightened to travel through the wood? Bah!"

Crukas shook his head. "No, I wasn't implying that at all."

"Come on!" Adgus frowned at Ebden and Bramnir. "Saddle up! We'll show 'em we fear nothing."

"Seriously," Crukas said. "I—"

Adgus grumbled. "Not a word. We'll show ya those beasts are as mythical as the ambling ghosts. Besides dat, we want dat stout before you decide to welch on the deal."

Crukas sighed.

Adgus gave his brothers a quick wink and the three commenced to laughing again. Adgus howled and snarled like a wolf, and they laughed even harder. He widened his eyes and grinned at Crukas. "Dat's 'bout as close to a Wierwen ya'll see tonight."

Had the dwarves been fully sober, Crukas might've persuaded them the myths were truth. But them being dwarves with their unwavering love for stout, his offer of three full barrels in exchange for a short journey to Ravensdorf was the keenest focus they held. The trade overrode any fear they otherwise might've possessed.

Since no other travelers had arrived with a wagon, Crukas wasn't likely to barter for a different passage before the storm. His need to get farther ahead of Sparrow remained important. Crukas decided to let them laugh at his expense but hoped the journey failed to prove him right.

CHAPTER 11

*C*rukas would've loved joining their boisterous laughs but he couldn't allow a smile. He was too worried about the journey to be angry or embarrassed, but waiting until morning wasn't feasible. His obsession to borrow the book had nullified his worries about leaving the Gloomy Forest and traveling through Wierwen territory.

The Wierwen *were* real. Crukas encountered one long ago. If one existed, it was likely more of these bloodthirsty beasts lived in the thick forest. Now cursed by the book, the odds of crossing paths with them were far greater than none.

He'd love to boast that he'd killed the Wierwen that attacked him years ago, but the beast grabbed Crukas' only true friend and dragged her into the forest's depths. Jillann was dead before she left his sight. Of that, he was certain. No one could've survived such a vicious bite to the throat like she suffered. He did the only thing he could do to survive.

He ran.

Crukas was never proud for fleeing. But she was dead. What more could he have done? Had she been screaming or he'd heard her muffled cries, he'd have fought to rescue her. In truth, he'd have sacrificed himself to save her, which would've been almost as noble and selfless as his current quest to destroy the Plague-bringer. Plus, he'd never have done the same for anyone else.

The Wierwen resembled a cross between a human and a wolf. Unlike wolves, they were solitary, as attested by various bards' hymns. But since most bards sold lies disguised as truth, he couldn't hold strict confidence the songs were true. After all, what bard could've survived such an encounter to compose a truthful tale? From their tales, Wierwen never howled like wolves, either.

The one that killed Jillann had crept toward them like a shadow. Its uncanny stealth would've made any thief envious, especially himself. Because of its approach, Crukas didn't know how many more might've stalked them before this one attacked and killed her.

Bramnir looked at Crukas with genuine concern. "You okay? You seem suddenly uneasy."

Crukas was always good at hiding his emotions, but whenever he thought of Jillann, his countenance fell and the lingering pain from the depths of his soul prominently emerged, contorting his facial expressions. "Perhaps we should delay our departure until closer to dawn."

Adgus laughed. "No need to play it any further. I'll admit you had me almost believing ya."

"Aye," Ebden said. "Twas a hoot of a story! But, if Wierwens exist, we've got our axes and warhammers. We dwarves don't back away from a fight. If there be monsters, their heads become trophies on our walls."

"Besides," Bramnir said, "we can't risk getting mired in mud or sinking in quicksand, right? Dat's what you said."

Crukas offered a slight nod. He then acknowledged the beam in Ebden's eyes. The dwarf appeared eager to encounter a Wierwen. Since Ebden was now the temporary keeper of the cursed spellbook, Crukas pictured no good ending for the dwarf. Crukas recognized such determination. No amount of persuasion could make Ebden reconsider.

Crukas forced a slight smile and climbed on the wagon. He found a soft patch of hay between the barrels, not that it'd make the bumpy ride any more comfortable.

Crukas sighed. *So be it.*

CHAPTER 12

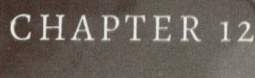

*S*parrow rubbed her tired eyes. She couldn't sleep in the modest loft room. The least wind rustled loose pieces of the thatch overhead. While she accurately discerned the reason for the strange sounds on the roof, she couldn't relax enough to doze off.

The small oil lantern Fasha left on the table, next to the tiny bed, burned but Sparrow refused to snuff the flame. She didn't want to be alone in the dark. Not in this shop. Even with the light, she couldn't close her eyes long enough for sleep to tempt her. She kept wondering if Fasha was on Crukas' side. And in a way she didn't understand, she felt almost certain Crukas remained nearby after his theft. Had they missed him by minutes?

Dumbfounded, Sparrow didn't understand Crukas' motive for stealing the Cursed Spellbook since he couldn't read it and taking possession of the book unleashed curses on him. Surely, he knew the consequences beforehand.

Although she didn't personally know Crukas, she was fairly certain of his actions. His continuous quest to obtain the rarest, most expensive jewelry, trinkets, and figurines would never have included jeopardizing his own life. Fasha hinted Crukas might've been hired to steal the book, but Crukas had long been known for *not* working with or for others. With the risks of reaping the curse or *curses* from the book, no amount of riches could persuade him to risk his own life. So why steal the book? A question suddenly occurred to her: *"Did he actually steal it?"*

Strange sounds creaked inside the shop—some *within* the room where she lie—but whenever she looked to find the source, she saw nothing. It didn't mean she wasn't being watched. She believed Fasha was using the odd creature living inside the crystal ball to keep tabs on Sparrow and was waiting for her to fall asleep. The unusual, strange eyes peering through the glass orb haunted her. Its piercing gaze was unlike anything she'd ever seen. A creature or being not from their realm.

Sparrow's pondering about Fasha remained torn. In Sorceress Brew, Fasha was the only one who'd shown her acceptance and kindness by allowing her to sit at her table and then buying her a drink.

People who are too friendly often have an ulterior motive.

Fasha was also the only one in the tavern who was half demon, so what was Fasha's game? Because Fasha was half demon, Sparrow was unable to fully trust her. She couldn't accept Fasha held Sparrow's best interests at heart. At this moment, Sparrow wanted someone she could trust as a true friend—someone to confide in. Sadly, Fasha appeared to be the only one willing to befriend her but Sparrow didn't have the faith to return the gesture.

Sparrow's eyes bore her shame. She had no reason to judge Fasha based solely on her heredity. As a halfling, Sparrow dealt with how other races viewed her race. While not degraded or treated with absolute scorn, her kind were often the butt of jokes and ridicule. She'd heard about every joke created, but she, like others in her culture, ignored the snide comments and worked harder to prove size held no bearings on one's accomplishments. And thus far, she'd proven that by being a fairly successful bounty hunter.

"Don't think I can *measure* up, eh?" Sparrow recalled telling the first thief she took into custody. Even though he was three times her size and weight, she brought him to the ground hard and bound his muscled arms behind his back. She grinned, remembering the stunned look in his eyes when she pulled him to his feet. The adrenaline rush of the pursuit and takedown had somehow increased her strength, which also surprised her.

If Fasha's advice and concern were genuine, Sparrow needed to heed the half demon's warnings about Crukas. Well, Crukas wasn't the *major* concern. He had the book. Whatever curses were bestowed on him might latch onto her should she take him into custody. The curses were bound to him, and if he became bound to her, would she become inadvertently linked to the curses? She had no way to know. Perhaps Fasha didn't know for certain, either. Yet, Fasha had warned her not to intercept and interact with Crukas—Was this *why*?

Could magic somehow transfer the book's curses to someone else? Was this Crukas' scheme? Crukas must have some means to remain unscathed. Otherwise, he'd never have stolen the book.

But what if Fasha was lying? What if Crukas *didn't* steal the book? What if Fasha staged the entire crime to stop Sparrow from apprehending Crukas? Should Sparrow catch Crukas and take him into custody, Sparrow would know for certain if Crukas had committed the crime. Then, she'd have absolute evidence.

Sparrow groaned. Her head ached, but not from the lingering hangover effects or her lack of sleep. The pain came from trying to sort through numerous scenarios. She'd totally alienated herself from everyone. The only advice she could rely on was her own.

Thunder rumbled overhead. The shop shook and her body quaked from fear and indecision. She planned to sneak out before sunrise and before Fasha awakened. But she was in the loft without a window or access to the roof. Despite her size and slight weight, the old stairs would creak with her every step. She couldn't reach the main floor without making noise. While the thunder could mask her movements, she couldn't time the thunder's arrival.

Should her luck prove successful and she slipped out the shop door unnoticed, the weather was against her. With the storm, however, she didn't need an additional obstacle. Traveling through the haunted forest in the dark would be bad enough. Adding rain and lightning created a more treacherous maze with a higher certainty of death.

Besides, leaving the shop without saying goodbye wouldn't be the worst offense because Fasha had never fully explained the fee for her advice. One silver and one gold coin was what Sparrow paid, but Sparrow didn't believe the amount was all Fasha required.

While Fasha's advice didn't emerge from divination, there was the possible matter of her night's stay. Without an actual inn in Salem, Fasha could legitimately request a fair boarding charge for allowing Sparrow to stay in a room overnight. Despite Fasha freely offering her a bed for the night, Sparrow learned long ago that *nothing* in life was free.

Again, Sparrow's mind raced. What was the true cost? If she snuck out without addressing these issues, her life might be cursed, too. She didn't need to steal the Cursed Spellbook for bad things to fall her way. She was quite confident Fasha had numerous spells at her disposal. Fasha could even seek to harm Sparrow's reputation by telling others she'd skipped out on paying room and board and had not abandoned her thieving ways. She could even accuse Sparrow of stealing the Cursed Spellbook.

Although either of these was a fabricated lie, it'd be Sparrow's word against Fasha's. People tended to believe a lie before accepting the truth, so Sparrow couldn't risk the possibility. The fact she was gone and unable to defend herself didn't matter. Her sudden absence implied her guilt. So, leaving before morning was out of the question.

Sparrow favored and wanted to sleep, as she could forget the expanding dilemmas for a while. But she feared what kind of situation she'd awaken to find. The forest was haunted. With the disturbing sounds rustling inside the walls, thumping on the roof, and the creaking footsteps of beings she couldn't see, she couldn't fall asleep. Instead of sleep, she stared at the ceiling and watched the flickering shadows from the oil lantern dance. Subconsciously, she counted the long minutes until dawn.

Although Time never actually stood still, this night seemed to argue against the notion. The next six hours might as well be an eternity.

CHAPTER 13

*C*rukas' conscience seldom troubled him because he chose not to align himself with anyone else. Nor did he want to be in need of someone else's services, except on rare occasions. Thus, he worked alone. He never thought twice about stealing from the wealthy, so what he took *never* weighed on his mind in the least. But, he had never stolen from a destitute individual, regardless of what treasure someone might have tucked away. Some fools held onto precious items and allowed their families to starve rather than barter for food. He never understood such people. Perhaps stealing their trophies might've changed these fools' mindset and forced them to take care of their families, but he doubted it.

Tonight, however, Crukas changed his pattern by hiring the Dwarven brothers for a ride to Ravensdorf. While the initial hiring wasn't immoral, the fact these three dwarves were risking their lives to travel out of their way to get him to his destination bothered him for two crucial reasons. One, the cursed book was in Ebden's possession, which impacted the dwarf's fate and possibly his two brothers'. Secondly, all of them might encounter a Wierwen and be attacked, possibly killed. All of this because Crukas wanted to put more distance between him, Sparrow, and the coming storm.

Sparrow was more an annoyance than any considerable threat. Compared to him, she was a novice. Her inexperience as a thief and bounty hunter rendered her pursuit in capturing him practically useless. He believed she craved the notoriety of being the one who finally brought Crukas to justice.

Good luck with that.

Crukas laughed to himself.

Some of the best bounty hunters had cornered him, only to discover Crukas' ability to seemingly disappear. His ability to blend in was enhanced by his unique armor. Before setting out on this thieving journey, Crukas had a tailor craft his armor and hooded cloak from ice-spider silk, which was far more expensive than he wished to consider. However, before he'd see Aetheaon destroyed, he'd become a pauper if necessary to save the world. After all, saving the world kept the people alive. Without people, there'd be nothing worth looting. Of course, practically everything of value he could claim if all the populations collapsed to the forthcoming plague, but he'd spend the rest of his days trying to stay alive and avoiding the armies of the living dead ruled by the Plague-bringer.

The undead owned nothing but the lingering rot and decay of their corpses. Even without flesh, the necromancer controlled them. This meant the Mors, the Plague-bringer, possessed everything. Crukas refused to allow such a victory.

The enchanted ice-silk armor clung to his body like a second skin and was fire resistant. Plus, it could block heatseeking eyes or spells from those who sought his presence. The thick layers of meshed silk threads were stronger than steel and readily protected him while allowing full flexibility. A thief couldn't ask for better lightweight armor. After Crukas paid the tailor, he tested the armor by slipping into an old dragon's lair. Though the dragon had long been rumored to be dead, fiery imps had claimed possession of the treasures hidden inside the old mountain crevice.

These imps generated a Hellfire globe that hovered over the center of the treasure like a miniature sun. This globe produced intense heat to thwart off invaders and the gold coins gleamed in a near-blinding fashion. Crukas thought their creation was close to genius because treasure hunters would assume the dragon was alive and was blasting flames to protect its lair.

Judging from the scorched piles of bones and pieces of armor scattered along the treasure, the imps killed those foolish enough to continue toward the fiery globe.

Crukas used his stealth-like movements to sneak past a few unsuspecting imp guards without notice. He stood close enough to touch them, but they weren't aware of his presence. Without the armor, he'd have been feverishly hot, sweating profusely, and easily detected by the imps. Instead, Crukas remained quite cool and comfortable. He made it to the center of their treasure pile and pocketed several rare gems. Later, he sold the gems for ten times the amount he'd paid the tailor for the armor.

Oddly, his satisfactory memories of robbing the imps with little fear were contrary to his mood tonight. He sat uneasily in the wagon. Bramnir's glowing lantern offered little more light than being a guide for Adgus to follow while he drove the wagon. The bobbing light indicated the roughness of the terrain ahead of the wagon.

Crukas could almost time to the second when he should brace for the abrupt jarring of the wagon wheels dipping into uneven pockets on the old trail. While this made the ride less harsh, he tried not to focus on the light. He needed to keenly watch for movement within the trees, in case the Wierwen attacked.

Behind the wagon, Ebden rode his mount and also carried a small lantern. Even with two lanterns, the lighting didn't make much difference. The lanterns were probably doing them more harm than good. They were the perfect beacons for stalking beasts to follow and to better decide when best to attack. Even without the faint light, the rickety, rattling wheels pinpointed their exact location. Most beasts, including the Wierwen, had night vision, so the glowing lanterns and campfires were greatly magnified. A lot of creatures feared blazing campfires and kept their distance, but a lantern carried in the night was almost a welcoming invitation.

Over the years, Crukas learned how to harness the slightest

sounds in order to distinguish what guarded a tomb or hidden cache, which took a great deal of concentration. Sometimes, a guardian was triggered after a thief or an innocent traveler stepped inside a certain radius of the treasure. It helped to remain keen to one's surroundings, but on a bumping, rocking wagon, he couldn't tell if they were being followed.

Without nocturnal animal sight, a spell he once used, he couldn't see them like night beasts could see the burros and the rams. To make matters worse, the night breeze—an indication of the swiftly moving storm—intensified. The wind bent the trees and caused the older trees to groan and creak. Dry leaves rubbed and rasped together. Even with Crukas' trained hearing and insight, a club-footed monster could thrash and stomp its way to them and he'd never hear it until after its attack.

Crukas stiffened when Adgus wailed in agony.

"Me arm!" Adgus dropped the reins and clutched his left arm. He fell over and the snarling beast went for his throat.

Bramnir raised his lantern and turned his ram. He pulled his axe and kicked the ram's flanks.

Before the Wierwen ripped into Adgus' throat, Bramnir's axe separated the beast's head from its shoulders. Warm blood sprayed Crukas' face. Acid churned in his stomach.

Crukas was on his feet with his dagger drawn and didn't remember moving from his seated position.

"Grab the reins, Crukas!" Bramnir snarled. "Stop the wagon!"

Crukas wiped blood from his face, sheathed his blade, and swung onto the narrow wagon seat. He grabbed the reins and pulled back. After the burros halted, he set the brake. He wanted to argue that they keep going but Ebden cried out in pain.

Another one?

Bramnir swung off his mount and moved to the side of the wagon to check on Adgus. Like a fool, Crukas drew his dagger and rushed across the back of the wagon to help Ebden. If Crukas were honest about his intentions, his first impulse was more to save the book from being stolen or destroyed, but since Ebden was the current possessor of the book, Ebden needed to be protected, too.

Crukas leapt off the rear of the wagon and brought his dagger back, ready to slash forward into the beast. But with Ebden's lantern on the ground and the beast's fur blacker than the night, Crukas attacked blindly. He hoped he didn't strike Ebden. Ebden was protected by armor, so Crukas could only accidentally harm him with a cut to the throat or head. He hoped neither of them were so unfortunate.

As Crukas swung the dagger for its connecting blow, strong clawed hands gripped his elbow and pulled him to the ground. Pain radiated through him. His ribs and back hurt. Breathing was difficult. Despite this, he gripped his dagger tightly, so he didn't lose the only good weapon he had to free himself.

Before he could stand, he was pulled from the path and dragged into the woods.

Not good.

Crukas underestimated the Weirwen's strength and realized the true danger he found himself in. The beast dragged him through small brambles and shrubs, but stubbornly, he held the dagger tightly, as though his life depended upon it, which was no exaggeration. It did.

He wasn't certain how far the beast had dragged him away from the wagon, but in the terror of the moment, it seemed miles. Other than his tight grip on the blade, he allowed his body to become limp. Perhaps his deception worked, or the beast became tired of dragging him, but it stopped pulling.

While he lie on his back, the Wierwen straddled his chest. Its wet, matted fur reeked of sweat, death, and decay. The beast pressed its slimy, moist nose against his. Its putrid, hot breath caused him to gag and thus, he lost the deception of being unconscious.

Its guttural growl indicated anticipated glee. Torture before killing must've been its goal. Licking its chops, a steady bead of saliva dripped and coated Crukas' lips. His churning stomach intensified. Acid crept up his throat. He'd rather die than be tortured by its stench.

Crukas tightened his grip on the dagger and was ready to thrust it multiple times into this thing's gut. He hoped Bramnir had followed and would help him escape, but such a notion was unlikely. Bramnir would tend to his brothers first. Since Crukas was a thief and had yet to make good on his payment, Crukas' importance to the trio diminished greatly.

Before Crukas stabbed the Wierwen, it suddenly whimpered and stiffened. "Crukas?"

Crukas' fingers loosened on the dagger. His want to kill the beast vanished. Stunned, he replied, "Jillann?"

She pushed off his chest and sprinted into the forest. Her footsteps crunched through leaves and twigs and faded deeper into the trees before silence indicated she was gone. Even if he chose to hurry after her, in the darkness, he could never catch her.

Crukas remained on his back for several long moments. He took a deep breath and swallowed the acidic lump at the back of his throat. He delved into a deeper remorse in knowing she was a Wierwen, than all the combined years of his guilt and remorse when he'd believed she was dead.

With his heartbeat ringing in his ears and overcome by dread and renewed loss, he closed his eyes and listened. Why didn't she kill him? Surely, she blamed him for leaving her years earlier. Wouldn't she have sought revenge?

Several minutes passed before he recovered enough to push himself to his feet. No footsteps approached from any direction, and he was confused in which direction to go. Had the dwarves travelled on without him? He couldn't blame them if they had. But Adgus' grumbles grew louder, in spite of Bramnir harshly trying to calm him.

Crukas sighed. At least he knew their location.

CHAPTER 14

Crukas followed the dwarves' voices until he left the woods and stood on the path near the wagon. Ebden lie on the ground, silent as a corpse. Crukas stooped and reached for the pouch that held the cursed spellbook.

Ebden clutched Crukas' wrist tighter than a vise and yanked Crukas to his face. "Whatcha doing, thief? Trying to steal back ya book?"

Crukas' eyes widened. "You're alive?"

Ebden released Crukas. "As much alive as you're still a thief. Surprised?"

"No. If you were dead, the book's no use remaining on your corpse. I'm relieved in knowing you're alive. Two Wierwen means there are more. I certainly don't want to be out here alone. We need all the help we can get."

Crukas offered his hand to help Ebden to his feet. Ebden readily accepted the offer.

"Thanks." Ebden stood and combed his beard with his hand.

"Don't mention it."

"Come on," Ebden said. "Let's help Bramnir with Adgus."

"What about you?" Crukas asked. "Weren't you injured?"

"Nah."

"But by your scream, I could've sworn—"

Ebden grunted a slight chuckle. "I must admit ... not my finest moment. I've never screamed out of fear. Of course, I've never been attacked by a Wierwen, either."

"Totally understandable," Crukas said.

Ebden picked up the lantern and pointed a stern finger at Crukas. "Tell *no* one."

Crukas clapped Ebden's shoulder. "The secret's safe with me."

"How 'bout you? You all right? The way the beast tore off into the trees with ya, I figured it'd kill you. Another reason why I acted dead. Ya know? So it wouldn't attack me again."

"Believe me, I understand. There's no shame in your charade." Crukas didn't feel any sharp burns often associated with deep cuts and abrasions. "No slashes or cuts. A lot of bruises, though."

"Did ya kill it?"

"No."

"Injure it?"

Crukas sighed. "Not likely."

"Hmm," Ebden said, seemingly confused. "Just let ya go, eh?"

"So it appears." Crukas cleared his throat and spit, still tasting Jillann's horrid breath. With his adrenaline waning, his shock remained steady. His core was chilled. His hands shook involuntarily.

Bramnir's voice rose. "Hold still, Adgus! I need to patch the wound to stop the bleeding."

"What's da use?" Adgus whined. "I'm going to become one of 'em. Won't I? Might as well lob me head off like dat one ya killed."

"Crukas?" Bramnir said. "Is what he said true?"

"Honestly, I don't know," Crukas said. But thinking about Jillann, he didn't want to outright lie. She'd somehow altered when he was certain she'd died. "Legends say so. In Ravensdorf, I know a trusted priest who can heal him, provided we hurry. We can seek her advice."

"We'll move overtime," Bramnir said. "Dat is, if you'll drive the wagon? Adgus is in no shape for the task."

"Sure," Crukas said.

They couldn't return to Salem. Flashes of lightning indicated the storm was picking up speed and heading their direction. With the rain and the Wierwen, it'd be foolish to stay in the forest any longer. The torrential rains would cause the wheels to mire down and trap them. Besides, he didn't know if Jillann would return or if she was gathering other Wierwens.

Bramnir held his lantern over the decapitated Wierwen, and looked at Crukas and Ebden. "Let's throw this thing's corpse onto the back of the wagon."

"What?" Adgus said. "I'm not riding with *dat* beast beside me."

"Bah!" Bramnir said. "It's *dead*. It can do ya no further harm. We might fetch a good amount for it in Ravensdorf."

Crukas looked over his shoulder, in the direction where Jillann had run. Was she watching them? A hunter's kill of an actual animal as a trophy was seldom frowned upon, but this Wierwen had once been a human or an elf.

Bramnir set his lantern and Ebden's on the wagon seat. He grabbed thick handsful of the creature's back fur while Crukas grabbed its ankles. They swung it up and it landed between two empty barrels on the wagon. With Bramnir's strength, he didn't need Crukas' help at all. The abrupt heavy drop of its dead weight caused one burro to bray.

In a gruff tone, Bramnir said, "We should've believed ya, Crukas."

Crukas shrugged. "I only wish it weren't true."

"Aye. We all do."

"Aye," Adgus said in a low groan.

The rustling wind swirled the highest tree branches. The burros became more uncomfortable. They stamped their feet but didn't attempt to pull forward. With the wagon's brake set, they'd never budge the wheels anyway. The rams, which seemed fearful of little, snorted and stepped side to side.

"I ain't riding back here with this thing," Adgus said.

Bramnir laughed and tossed the Wierwen's head on the wagon.

"Especially not *now*!" Adgus said.

A couple of growls came from each side of the overgrown path.

Crukas said, "I don't know how much these barrels mean to you, but perhaps we should toss them to lighten the load."

"Why?" Bramnir said. "You trying to squelch on the agreement already?"

"No," Crukas replied. "Of course not. But, we need to get out of this forest before they attack again. There are two Wierwen. One on each side of the road."

"No lie?"

"Honest. I tried to warn you to wait to leave closer to dawn."

"Aye, ya did," Adgus said with a harsh tone. "But you also said dat you wanted to stay ahead of the storm. Which is more important?"

"Neither matter now," Bramnir said. "Adgus, if it's true you might become a Wierwen due to your injuries, we need to not only stay ahead of the storm, we need to outrun these Wierwen."

Adgus grumbled. "I agree but now wish we'd not accepted the thief's offer."

"Nothing undoes dat," Ebden said. "I hear the growls, too. Let's get going."

"Look," Crukas said, "both of your rams can move swiftly when in war or in danger, right?"

"Aye."

"These burros can't. Even without the barrels, we'll be lucky to get to the fork in the path without losing one or both of them. Adgus is in no shape to fight. As you know, I'm a thief, not a warrior, and thus, I'm equally ineffective. We need to move fast. I'll provide you new barrels at Ravensdorf to be filled with stout."

Bramnir sighed. "Very well. We must hope the two burros can keep up with the rams."

"I have another proposal," Crukas said.

"What's dat?" Bramnir asked.

"Is it possible to hitch the two rams to the wagon and place the burros on the back?"

"Ya want to insult our rams by placing them in such degrading labor?" Bramnir asked.

"Not at all. But they're far more powerful and can get us to the forked path faster than those burros."

"Ya realize they've never pulled a wagon, right?"

"No, I never considered that," Crukas said. "But is it possible?"

Bramnir grunted. "With the proper potion or spell, we could get 'em wings and fly us to Ravensdorf, farting little rainbows along da way, but we ain't got dat, either, now do we?"

Despite his pain, Adgus howled with laughter and then groaned in pain.

"We're wasting time," Crukas said. "All I'm saying is that by hitching the rams to the wagon and putting the burros on the back, we can better defend ourselves."

"In what way?" Ebden asked.

"I take the reins. You and Bramnir can use your weapons to thwart off any aggressive Wierwen attacks that might come toward us. Adgus can lie safely between you and the burros."

"What?" Adgus said. "No! The burros will trample me to death."

Bramnir said, "Ya might be onto something there. But it requires some quick exchanges of halters and straps. Ebden, let's hurry."

"But we lose the Wierwen carcass," Adgus said.

"No," Bramnir said. "It rides with us."

Adgus grumbled and cursed under his breath.

"Ebden," Bramnir said. "Get our bundled rope from beneath the wagon. We 'ave to tie the burros securely. Otherwise, they'll fall off the wagon."

"Ya still forgetting about me!" Adgus said.

"If da ropes are tight enough," Bramnir said, "the burros won't shift their feet and trample you."

Two Wierwen howled. Others replied to their cries deeper in the woods.

"Hurry now!" Bramnir said.

CHAPTER 15

*C*rukas held the two lanterns while Bramnir and Ebden swapped out the lead lines and harnesses. They tossed the empty barrels off the wagon and forced the two stubborn burros onto the wagon bed. The burros brayed their disdain. Crukas was stunned and admired how strong dwarves truly were. They lofted both burros onto the wagon bed and secured them with rope, and were certain Adgus wouldn't get stepped on by their shoed hooves.

Adgus complained and angrily protested about the Wierwen's corpse and head being so close to him on the wagon, but neither Bramnir nor Ebden paid him any mind.

Once Bramnir nodded they were ready, Crukas cracked the whip above the rams' heads. He lightly smacked the leather lead lines along the rams' backs and hoped to prompt them to pull the wagon. The obstinate rams proved worse than the burros. The jest of the rams being hitched to the wagon as an insult was more factual than a joke. He could've sworn fire danced in their eyes when he commanded them. Fury rose in their gazes and they looked ready to break free of the harnesses and attack him.

Finally, Bramnir shouted a few Dwarven words Crukas didn't understand. The two rams snorted, grunted, and yanked the wagon forward into a dangerous sprint. Crukas was slammed Crukas back in the seat.

Perhaps the rams could see better in the darkness than he, but their sudden burst into a thunderous speed didn't make for a smooth ride. The extreme jostling of the wagon along the trail could rock the axles enough to pop off the wagon wheels, if they weren't careful. Perhaps their stubborn need to toss Crukas off the seat was their reason, but within seconds it was obvious their goal was self-preservation.

Growls came from both sides of the rocky path. The Wierwen moved almost as swiftly as the rams. Without the weighted wagon attached to the rams, the rams could've left the beasts far behind. However, the rams' temperament while pulling the wagon outweighed the vulnerability the burros would've shown under these circumstances. The rams pulled and ran with severe determination and grit. He better understood why dwarves preferred rams for mounts instead of horses. Did the oversized boar mounts possess this magnitude? Boars might not take to following the trail and choose to kill the Wierwen any way possible with their razored tusks.

Crukas counted six sets of glowing eyes closing in on the wagon's position from the forest. Two approached from the path ahead and charged headlong at the rams.

"So much for the Wierwen not roaming in packs," Crukas said.

"What?" Bramnir glanced over his shoulder and readied his axe to cut down any Wierwen that came within his reach.

"According to several bard's tales, Wierwen are solitary."

"Ha! No one told *them!*" Bramnir said. "A bard can no more be trusted for honesty in songs than a thief could be trusted with—"

Crukas caught the pause and turned toward Bramnir with a grin. "Go ahead. Say it."

"Erm," Bramnir said. "You be the exception. But I was going to say, trusted with one's treasure."

Crukas laughed. "Well, don't be *too* careful leaving valuables in my care. Such temptations are hard for a thief to resist."

Bramnir and Ebden howled with laughter, but silenced when several Wierwen howled their bloodthirsty cries.

The two Wierwen on the path ahead stopped and growled, apparently intending to set a roadblock. Their eyes glowed like large silver coins, possibly a reflection from the sudden streak of lightning blazing the sky. The other four Wierwen sprinted from the sides and from what Crukas could discern in the shadows, they were gaining enough speed to make a leaping attack to jump on the wagon.

Instead of the wagon slowing because of the two Wierwen in the road, the rams bowed their heads and charged. There was a brief moment where fear gleamed in the Wierwen's eyes. Each appeared uncertain and struggled to decide which side of the road to dodge out of the way. Before they could get out of the way, the rams' thick, metal-armored horns plowed into the Wierwen harsher than a battering ram struck a stone wall. Whimpers were muffled beneath the rams' hooves, and their brief wails echoed when the heavy wagon's wheels snapped and broke their spines.

"That'll teach ya," Bramnir said.

Adgus laughed heartily for a moment before crying in pain from his injury.

The beasts at the sides of the wagon gnashed their teeth, snarled, and leapt, trying to nip and bite Bramnir and Ebden. Bramnir's axe struck one Wierwen with enough force to disable it. The crippled Wierwen crumpled, whimpered, and rolled to the edge of a massive dark tree. Should it heal enough to survive, it'd never be the same.

Ebden swung with the same type of maneuver but missed. As he brought around his axe again, the Wierwen clamped its jaws around his right wrist. "Ah!"

Worse than an angry snapping turtle held to its victim after it bit, this beast clung to Ebden's wrist and refused to lessen its hold. The dwarf wore metal braces, so Crukas didn't think Ebden was actually injured, but the bite wasn't what concerned Crukas. The beast's weight bent Ebden over the edge of the wagon. One harsh bump on the path could cause Ebden's balance to tilt too far and he'd be taken off the wagon. The Wierwen would maul him to death before they could stop to rescue him. Not only would they lose Ebden, the cursed spellbook would be gone, too.

Crukas partially berated himself for even considering the value of the book at this moment, but Aetheaon's fate depended on the book.

"Bramnir!" Crukas said. "Help Ebden!"

"Can't at the moment," Bramnir replied, swinging his axe at a Wierwen. "These beasts be everywhere."

Another Wierwen charged the two rams. All Crukas saw was their glowing eyes. At first, he figured the beast's fate would be the same as the previous two, but this Wierwen surprised him and the rams. When the rams bowed their heads to pummel the beast, it leapt over their heads and aimed to land on the driver's seat with Crukas. Since it was coming directly at the wagon, and the rams charged in its direction with rapid strides, the Wierwen would hit Crukas with enough force to knock him into the wagon bed. Crukas' thin armor was not suitable to protect him from its sharp teeth and claws. He'd be dead within moments.

Crukas took a deep breath and braced himself. Fear prompted him to close his eyes, but if he were to die, he wanted to see his end. At no point could he readily defend the attack, but every muscle in his body tightened and prepared for the impact. He met the eyes of his deadly killer with an even, determined stare.

A second before the Wierwen seemed destined to end Crukas' existence, a shadowy figure struck the beast in its side.

"No!" Jillann said. She bit the attacking Wierwen's throat and her collision pivoted both her and the Wierwen onto the overgrown path. The male Wierwen yelped. She said, "Enough!"

She howled fiercely. The Wierwen latched to Ebden's arm released him. All the other Wierwens stopped their pursuit. The rams kept their pace and left the remaining pack on the path behind them.

Bramnir lowered his axe. "What da blazes?"

Ebden plopped beside Adgus and sighed. "No idea."

Adgus said, "Ya okay there, Ebden? Or are ya like me? Going to turn into one of those blasted beasts?"

"It had me bracer, nothing else."

79

"Lucky," Adgus replied with an agitated groan.

Crukas marveled at the comment. *Lucky?* If luck existed, he'd have thought all of them would've met their end before reaching the forked path. If not all, most certainly Ebden should've met his fate, since he had the book.

"What ya know about dat, Crukas?" Bramnir asked.

Crukas swallowed hard. "*What* exactly? Luck?"

"No," Bramnir chuckled. "Only a fool believes in good or bad luck. But the female Wierwen spared your life mere seconds ago. She ordered the others to fall back. Something ya not telling us?"

"Nah," Crukas said.

"Ah," Ebden said. "Perhaps something ya *don't* wish to tell us?"

"Perhaps a better answer," Crukas said. "For one, we don't have time. And for another, we're at the fork in the road. Let's get Adgus to the priest quickly."

Bramnir nodded. "No arguments 'ere."

CHAPTER 16

Sparrow watched the shadow creep from beneath the door and materialize. It stood at the edge of the small room. The shadow of *what* exactly, she didn't know, as it shifted into various shapes. But it stood between her and the door. She was cornered.

"Who are you?" She spoke with a friendly voice to lessen her chances of being attacked. "Why are you here?"

The shadowy figure didn't reply but snickered in a sinister, twisted way.

Sparrow pressed her back to the wall. How could she escape? The only option was the door, unless she could rip through the wall or ceiling. Of course, she had a better chance at demolition than suddenly learning to open a portal to transport her to a safer place.

The shadow moved like a curtain of smoke and drifted across the room to her. What harm it could do in such a form? She didn't know.

Petrified, Sparrow froze and the room's temperature plummeted. Chill bumps pricked her arms. She hugged the scratchy, woolen blanket to herself but couldn't find any warmth.

She was unable to determine whether this was a ghost or the product from one of Fasha's spells. Its presence was foreboding and somewhat threatening, since it refused to reply while moving closer. How did one fight an ethereal being?

Was this the sign of a bad omen? Had Fasha summoned it as a forewarning to reinforce Fasha's advice? To scare her into obedience?

Did Crukas have anything to do with its existence?

Was it a figment of her imagination or the result of her lack of sleep and fatigue? Or, had she fallen asleep and *this* was her nightmare?

Her mind raced but came to no beneficial conclusions. The longer she remained in Fasha's shop, the more she was convinced Fasha sought to protect Crukas and frighten Sparrow from trying to take Crukas into custody.

A gentle knock rapped the door. The smokey apparition vanished.

Sparrow took a sharp breath, leaned away from the wall, and placed her hand on her dagger beneath the thick blanket. "Yes?"

The door opened inward. Fasha stood at the threshold and peered into Sparrow's eyes. Sparrow shuddered and looked away.

"Is everything okay?" Fasha asked with interest. "What's troubling you?"

"Something was in my room. A shadowy figure."

Fasha glanced around the room and grinned. "I see nothing except you. Perhaps you dreamed it?"

"No. I've not slept. It vanished when you knocked."

"How unfortunate."

"In what way?" Sparrow frowned.

Fasha shrugged, but her eyes remained playful. "Perhaps I could've identified it, had I seen it."

You're toying with me.

Fasha's smile broadened. "No, I'm not. At least it didn't frighten you enough that you'd flee into the night."

Sparrow gave a nervous smile. "I wouldn't think of it."

"Ah, but you were considering it. You've contemplated leaving for hours now."

Sparrow cringed, suddenly remembering Fasha's ability to read minds. How she wished she could've kept her mind silent and absent in thought. But her thoughts meandered like a stream flowing down a rocky slope. Her thoughts swirled hopelessly without control and without her attempting to dam them.

"Are you certain I don't owe you more than one gold and one silver coin? I don't feel it's adequate payment and don't want to leave indebted to you."

"Still don't trust me?"

Sparrow's brow rose with sincere meekness, indicating how small she actually felt in the strange shop. "Please tell me. I'll gladly pay. As for my trust in you, you know my thoughts. So there's no need to ask, is there?"

Fasha offered a curt smile, but her strange glowing eyes became more unsettling. "Yes, I know how little you trust me, and I have to admit, it hurts my feelings. You question my intentions and are skeptical of my aid. Why? When I've been nothing but generous to you. And *no*, you don't owe me more than the modest fee I charged."

"I mean no offense. As difficult as it is for someone to trust a thief, and me having been one, I hope you understand how hard it is for me to trust anyone at face value. I lived my earlier life based on lies in order to escape charges and arrests, and I became quite good at telling lies. Because of this, I always question what anyone else tells me."

Fasha nodded. "I understand, and such a policy is beneficial to save you heartache and pain. But, it also leads to a life filled with loneliness and despair. Everyone needs a friend."

"I agree."

"Which is why I insist you keep your distance from Crukas."

"Because he's your friend?"

Fasha sighed. "No, because I hope *you're* my friend. I don't want to see you hurt or worse … *killed.*"

"Crukas has never been accused of assault or murder," Sparrow said. "His reputation as a thief is why he's wanted."

"And why you hope to be the one to capture him, am I correct? Your thieving skills can never match his. He's a competitor you wish to take out of the game?"

Sparrow bit her lower lip. "Honestly, I suppose I was jealous of him when I was a thief. But now—"

"Let it go," Fasha said. "Jealousy does more harm than good. If you pursue him, it'll end with your death."

"Is this a guess or did you use divination this time?"

Fasha nodded. "I did, at no extra charge, mind you, because I'm concerned about your wellbeing. You continue after Crukas and you'll be dead. The book's curse will become your demise."

"But *he* stole the book. I didn't."

"Ties bind."

"How?"

"You can't take Crukas into custody without the book's curse already on him," Fasha replied. "Should you shackle him, the curse attaches to you. It could attach to you after you release him."

"The curse can't be broken?"

"Only within the book can one learn and understand how to break its curse, but one must be able to read the language in order to understand. Good luck finding any demon willing to read the book's contents."

Sparrow frowned. "You've never read the book?"

"All the way through?" Fasha shook her head. "Hades no. The first few pages provide ample warnings about proceeding any further. No demon, regardless of its evil nature, would dare read past the warning. My skin crawls just thinking about it."

"Aren't you the least bit curious?"

"Curious? Oh, very much," Fasha replied. "Keeping the book has been a test of my resolve and willpower. The dangers of knowledge within those pages have been why no one before now has ever even attempted to steal it. Not even Tyrann."

"Then why was the spellbook even written?" Sparrow asked. "Why's there a curse?"

"Magic comes at a price. It always does."

"What price do you pay for using magic?" Sparrow asked.

"I *write* spells and only use modest incantations and not for selfish goals, so little's required in return."

"Okay, I understand that. What does one stand to gain if in return he's plagued by a curse or curses?"

"Immense power, albeit short lived," Fasha replied.

"That's not necessarily true," Sparrow said. "A lot of evil wizards and mages have lived far longer than the average life expectancy."

"Yes. But those made appropriate sacrifices to become a vessel for far worse beings than they were born to become. They're a shell of their former selves, lost to madness and lacking conscience. Some make offerings and sacrifices to sway the price from themselves and appease darker things."

Sparrow weighed the information and wondered what Crukas sought to gain, if it were he who wished to gain anything at all. He didn't need to seek wealth or reputation because he was richer than most kings and queens, if the legendary tales about him were true.

"I'm sorry," Sparrow said.

"For what?"

"My lack of trust," Sparrow replied.

"It's okay," Fasha replied. "For what it's worth, I understand. I have had few friends during my lifetime, and most likely, because I'm half demon. If not for my eyes, I could pass as an elf and fit in with folks in various towns and the major cities without second thoughts. As it is, more trust my abilities in writing spells and blessing charms than they can in seeing me as someone with a soul and feelings." She shrugged. "Because of my eyes, some mistakenly believe I'm an elf possessed by a demon. Ha! So, I've gotten used to being alone. Although I don't consider Salem a place I was ostracized to, I've stayed while the majority of the town moved on. So, I've allowed myself to be an outcast from neighboring villages and towns."

"That sounds … sad."

Fasha laughed softly, but genuine sadness showed in her eyes. "It's not your concern. When the day dawns, you'll move to the next town and forget about me, like so many others before you."

"That's not true." Sparrow edged to the side of the bed.

"I give you three days," Fasha said, "and you'll have forgotten me. You'll ignore my warnings about Crukas and pursue him anyway."

Chills ran down Sparrow's spine.

Although she wished to deny the part about pursuing Crukas, her heart agreed. She'd still go after him, but she couldn't do it alone. She'd need help. Swallowing her pride, she admitted Crukas was far more skilled than she, and his possession of the book was the greater problem.

"Look," Sparrow said. "Why not travel with me?"

"Me?"

Sparrow nodded. "*We* could capture Crukas and you'd get your book back."

Fasha shook her head. "Sorry, but no. I can't leave my spell shop unattended for long periods of time. I'd only left for an hour and Crukas stole my book? I can't carry all my belongings in a single carriage, either. But thanks for the offer."

"Won't you even consider it?"

"I just did. If you plan to travel in the morning, it'll be during stormy conditions. You need to sleep. The wooded areas around Salem are tricky after heavy rains, and you need to be at your sharpest."

"I doubt I can sleep."

"At least *try*." Fasha left the room, stood outside the threshold, and reached to close the door.

"What if the shadowy thing returns?"

Fasha gave a grim smile and spoke words in a foreign tongue, perhaps her demon language. "All evil is blocked from this room, so you can rest easy."

Sparrow glanced nervously around the room. "A protection spell?"

"Yes."

Sparrow wanted to sleep. By staying awake, her mind would continue weighing options and her doubts. Fasha would read her every thought. But, going to sleep? Sparrow would be most vulnerable, and she didn't know what had appeared in the room. What if it returned? Could the spell actually keep it out? She decided to remain awake and solely concentrate her thoughts on a knot on the ceiling beam or counting the tree rings on the bedpost. Anything to keep her mind focus outside of her deepest secrets and opinions.

CHAPTER 17

*A*fter reaching the forked path and heading west toward Ravensdorf, Crukas held the reins and thought about how their lives had been unexpectedly spared. Jillann had saved their lives, even though he hadn't fought to save her from the Wierwen years earlier.

In truth, he'd believed she'd been killed. But now, he chastised himself and grieved even greater for failing to protect her. She wasn't dead but was one of them, which he considered far worse. Of course, had he rescued her after the attack, she would've turned anyway. He hoped Irmine could help prevent Adgus from turning.

In all his life, Crukas had never given his heart to anyone, except her. She was the exception. For her, he'd have stopped his life as a thief, married her, and raised a family. The obsidian ring on the black gold chain around his neck was crafted by a master jeweler. He was only hours from proposing when the Wierwen attacked her. If she'd married him, they'd have had no need for anything. He was already wealthy enough to house and feed a family and the future generations to come. His heart ached.

The two rams pulled the wagon fast enough to stay ahead of the coming storm. Warm air flowed from behind them. Trees bent and leaves scraped harshly against one another. At times, the fierce winds whistled their fury, blowing debris from all directions. Streaks of lightning cut through the sky, followed by pounding thunder, which rumbled like orc war drums that foretold impending doom without escape.

They needed to find shelter in Ravensdorf quickly.

Crukas looked over his shoulder. Adgus lie on the wagon bed with Bramnir pressing a cloth against Adgus' wound. Adgus wasn't moving, but he groaned softly, indicating he wasn't dead, *yet*.

"How is he?" Crukas asked.

"Asleep, I think," Bramnir replied. "Eh, I hope."

Ebden sat with his back against the driver's seat with his broad axe across his legs. He seemed ready to rise and fight should any other attacks occur. Crukas was satisfied the Wierwens would not attack again; not on a clear road out in the open. But with the impending storm, he doubted anyone would lie in wait at this hour and under these circumstances. Then a chill shot through him. Perhaps Ebden was standing guard should Adgus suddenly transform into a Wierwen.

Crukas swallowed hard.

Would Ebden actually kill his own brother? After seeing Jillann as a Wierwen, Crukas couldn't find it within himself to do such a drastic act. He couldn't kill what she had become. Although the beast had overtaken her human form, inside a part of the woman he loved resided. Besides this, she'd recognized and protected him, which meant a small part of her mind was controlled by her remaining humanity. One day he hoped to return to talk to her, but deep inside, he knew he probably wouldn't. He could never face her. His guilt prevented it. Her beast side might be unpredictable. How long could she control its lust for blood or its primal nature?

Bramnir stood. Sadness weighted his words. "We need to pick up the pace. Adgus is boiling with sweat and shivering. He's going to become one of them."

Before Crukas could snap the whip to encourage the rams to

increase their gait, Bramnir spoke harsh Dwarven words. The rams automatically picked up the pace.

～

CRUKAS and the dwarves arrived at Ravensdorf with the storm still a distance from its arrival. The rams weren't fatigued or frothing at the mouth. The burros could never have achieved what the rams had in such a little amount of time and most likely, the Wierwen would've killed them before Jillann intervened.

Ravensdorf was a modest town set at the base of a steep mountain cliff. Atop the highest peak was a wizard's tower, known as Dark Ayr Tower. The town hosted sheep ranchers whose herds grazed the greener, grassy plains. Cloth weavers made garments to trade and sell at various markets near the docks on the eastern coast. The roads were more compacted soil than brick, but given the area and its inhabitants, the roads would never become any fancier. A few street lamps remained lit but at a low glow and ambient enough for Crukas and the dwarves to see one another. Perhaps the lamps were weakening as the last of their daily oil burned off the wick.

The old buildings were constructed from roughly hewn rocks carried from the mountainside. Heavy thatch topped the roofs.

"Now, for payment." Ebden held the spellbook in his hand and eagerly offered the book to Crukas. Ebden sensed something amiss about the tome.

Bramnir frowned at Ebden. "Payment? Are you daft? *First*, Crukas takes us to the priestess he mentioned and see dat Adgus is healed. Only *then* do we talk payment."

Ebden's hand shook with the tome held tightly between his thick fingers. The look in his eyes indicated he was wary of the book and uncomfortable keeping it. He wanted rid of the book and was embarrassed by Bramnir's harsh chiding.

Crukas was surprised Adgus had been the one attacked and was possibly near death or transformation. Since Ebden carried the cursed spellbook, shouldn't he have suffered the most? Or be dead?

Irony laughed in Crukas' face. Bad things immediately occurred to Crukas from the moment he snatched the book off Fasha's bookcase.

"Bramnir's right," Crukas said. "Adgus needs to be healed. She resides down this street."

"I see no temple," Bramnir said in a gruff, shrewd tone. His cocked brow indicated his confusion.

Crukas chuckled and slightly tapped the reins along the rams' backs to prompt them to pull forward. "And you never will."

Ebden reluctantly tucked the book back inside his satchel. "Why's dat?"

Crukas pointed at the towering mountainside. Due to the night and the heavy fog, the tower was mostly hidden and the narrow winding road leading to the tower was undetectable. "Scorpius won't allow it."

"Scorpius?" Bramnir squinted at the mountain.

"Mage," Crukas replied.

"Preposterous," Bramnir said. "How can a mage prohibit a temple? He's no ruler."

Crukas thought the remark odd, given that most dwarves worshipped some sort of a deity, the earth, and mountains but they never built temples, at least none Crukas was aware of. "Scorpius owns this mountainside."

"Ah," Bramnir said. "I see your point."

"Yeah," Crukas said. "He thinks he's a god."

Bramnir spat on the ground. "Those be the *worst* kind of mages."

Crukas sighed. "Any mortal who thinks himself a god is dangerous and best left alone."

"Dat be true," Bramnir replied. "Doesn't make 'em invincible though."

Crukas grinned and pulled the reins. The rams stopped outside a small house.

"Here?" Bramnir asked.

Crukas shook his head. "No. Down the narrow alleyway. The wagon won't fit, so we'll have to carry him."

"Dat's not an easy task." Bramnir's bushy eyebrows tightened. "Ebden, stay with the wagon."

Ebden nodded and pulled his axe.

Crukas would've rather stayed with the wagon, except Bramnir and Ebden didn't know Irmine, the priestess. She'd most likely turn them away or not answer her door. For all he knew, she might immediately turn him away or deny his request for her aid.

Helping Bramnir lift Adgus from the back of the wagon almost strained Crukas' back to the point he thought his spine would snap.

I'm not made for this type of labor.

"Lift wit' your legs!" Bramnir gave Crukas a stern glare.

"I don't think that'll help," Crukas groaned.

Bramnir chuckled. "Ya should consider mining a while. Strengthen your muscles!"

"No, thanks," Crukas said.

Dwarves were blocky, muscular, and short, but Crukas never imagined they weighed so much. Of course, Adgus' armor added significantly more weight, but they couldn't waste time removing his breastplate and leggings, which possibly equaled Crukas' weight.

What should've been a two minute walk took a quarter hour and seemed longer than a half hour to Crukas. He helped Bramnir prop Adgus against the wall. He took a deep breath while rapping softly against the small door. Adgus opened his eyes for a moment, groaned, and his head tilted to one side. Somehow, even as close to losing consciousness, Adgus' strong hands clung to Bramnir's forearms to prevent himself from collapsing in the alley.

"A priest? Here? In this little house?" Bramnir said.

Crukas nodded and arched his back in hope of relieving the pain.

Bramnir frowned. "He'll never fit through the door, much less the *three* of us."

Crukas smiled. "We'll manage."

A few minutes passed before the door opened slightly. A gnome peered out. Upon seeing Crukas, she opened the door wider. She gasped. "Crukas? What brings you to me at this hour? Nothing good, I must always assume."

"Irmine, I've a friend in need of your healing touch," Crukas replied.

She eyed him shrewdly and darted a glance at Bramnir, who propped Adgus against the wall. She knew Crukas well enough to know he never introduced anyone as his friend. He never allowed anyone to get emotionally close to him. Nonetheless, the compliment was more to lessen the shock of his arrival in the company of two dwarves. Crukas introduced them.

"I see," she said in her high-pitched, gnome voice with a tinge of disbelief. "Please, come inside."

Bramnir opened his mouth, possibly to explain they'd never fit, but then his eyes widened as the door suddenly expanded.

"Take him to the cot over there." Irmine pointed. She struck a match and lifted a glass globe on an oil lantern. After lighting the wick, she set the globe in place. She carried the lantern and held it while Bramnir and Crukas placed Adgus on the cot. The small bed sagged beneath his weight and threatened to snap the oak boards supporting the thin mattress. She peered closely at Adgus beneath the lantern's glow. "What ailment does he suffer?"

"He was attacked by a Wierwen," Crukas said.

Irmine retreated a few steps from Adgus. Surprise widened her eyes. "Wierwen? Are you sure?"

"Aye. There's no mistaking it," Bramnir said. "Will he become one?"

Irmine closed her eyes, whispered a prayer, and lowered the lantern. After a brief sigh, she asked, "How long ago was the attack?"

"Less than an hour," Crukas replied.

She nodded. "Then there's hope. Crukas, you come with me. Bramnir, stand ready by Adgus' bed. Should he suddenly change drastically, use your axe and strike him down before he attacks you."

Evident pain showed in Bramnir's eyes, but he offered no protest. Crukas held no doubt Bramnir would do whatever was necessary, regardless of the cost or loss.

CRUKAS FOLLOWED Irmine through a curtain and down a dark, narrow hallway, which opened into a cluttered storeroom of beakers, jars, dried flowers, and roots. From the outside, the house didn't seem large at all. No one would ever suspect the vast number of shelves in a room that appeared bigger than the house.

"I offer my thanks and gratitude," Crukas said.

"Do you now?" she said in a testy tone. "What else have you brought me?"

Crukas frowned. "Meaning what exactly?"

"No need to lie. You reek from an evil touch. Don't deny it. You no more brought Adgus for help than you did seeking a remedy for yourself. You've been tainted by something. Something dark and evil. Darkness looms around you. It's attacking your aura. So *what* have you done?" She sorted through several wooden supply boxes on a table.

"I've done nothing of the sort," Crukas replied. "I brought Adgus so you could heal him. As for me and my welfare, it never crossed my mind you could help me with my situation."

Irmine cocked a brow and looked into his eyes. She shrugged. "You tell the truth, but mind you, you've been cursed. A dark curse and its source is nearby. Tell me while there's still hope, so I can help you, too."

"Adgus first."

Her brow rose as she studied him. "Maybe this dark curse has distorted your mind. The Crukas I know never puts another above himself, nor has he *ever* introduced anyone as a friend."

"People change."

"Not you."

Crukas laughed softly and shook his head. "No redemption for me, eh?"

"Either take this seriously or you and your *friends* can leave."

"Very well. My apologies. I bartered with these dwarves to give me a ride to Ravensdorf. Along the way, we were attacked by Wierwens," Crukas said. "The dwarves weren't even traveling to this place, so

Adgus' injuries are *my* fault. They're brothers and certainly don't deserve to see Adgus become a Wierwen."

She laughed softly. "I'm certain Adgus will not turn."

"How do you know?"

"He was clawed but not bitten. I'll make a salve to prevent an infection. He's already feverish."

"Yes," Crukas said, "which is why he needs more than a salve."

"You practice alchemy now?"

Crukas shrugged. "At times, but that's not the point."

Irmine shook her head. "So tell me the actual issue. Your overwhelming concern isn't over this dwarf. You've only known him a few hours. Yet, your weighted guilt has *some* direct connection."

Crukas looked away. "True. I'd rather not chance Adgus turning into a Wierwen, even if he wasn't bitten. Treat him as though he might become one anyway."

"That'd be dangerous."

"Not as dangerous as him becoming one."

She nodded. "You'll pay the charges?"

"Yes, of course."

She smirked. "I'm not asking for gold or silver coin. I've no need for that. But I need a favor only a thief can perform."

"Ah, I suppose me stealing something for you eliminates you from being the transgressor?"

"Don't play self-righteous with me." Spittle formed at the sides of her mouth. "Will you or will you *not* do this for me?"

"Name it," he replied.

"After we're done. Why you think Adgus has a possibility of turning?"

"You remember Jillann?"

Irmine nodded. She poured white powder into a mortar, added a few drops of liquid from various bottles. "Yes. The one who had stolen your heart? Perfect match for a thief. I've wondered why you let her slip away so many years ago."

Crukas shook his head. Tears crested in his eyes. His words came slowly, suppressed by the strain of regret. "She didn't slip away. I thought a Wierwen killed her, but she's still alive. She turned into one of them. She remembered me. If not for her, the rest of the Wierwens would've killed us all."

Irmine's hand shook. She dropped the pestle before she began stirring. "I'm so sorry."

He shrugged. "Nothing we can do about it, but I fear Adgus will become one, too."

"Wierwen are rare," Irmine said. "You're worrying more than you should."

"Am I? Wierwen *were* rare and more a legend to scare folks from traveling into the Gloomy Forest. Tonight, I counted more than a dozen of them. That was from the sets of eyes I could see. There might be many more." Crukas resisted the slight rising giddy thought brought on by his lingering shock at seeing Jillann. Nothing about the situation was amusing but he didn't understand why he almost laughed. "Although, a few of them met their fate tonight. At least a half dozen are dead. One's carcass lies in the wagon on the street."

Irmine picked up another pestle and mashed the ingredients in the mortar. "Then we'll treat Adgus as though he's infected, but understand there are risks in doing so. Now, what did you do to become cursed."

His brow furrowed. He struggled on whether or not to reveal his theft. Could she really help him? He doubted it.

"Go on," she said, growing perturbed. "The night's a wasting."

"Very well. I stole the Cursed Spellbook of the Damned earlier tonight."

Irmine's eyes almost popped like a bugged-eyed toad's. "You fool! *Why?*"

"The reasons are my own."

"Of all the items for anyone to steal—"

"Save me the lecture," Crukas said. "I assure you, the theft was unselfish on my part. I plan to return the book should I survive the task. Technically, I *borrowed* the book."

Irmine huffed. "Return it or not, borrowed or not, the curse will remain."

"I assumed as much. So be it."

"Are you serious?" Irmine gazed narrowly into his eyes. Slowly, she shook her head. "You *are* serious. Oh, Crukas—"

"Yes. As I said earlier, I didn't come to seek help for myself, only for Adgus. If not for his situation, I'd not have bothered you at all. Because they agreed to bring me to Ravensdorf, he could die."

Irmine mashed the paste. "Seeing you is never a bother. More of a challenge since you'll never repent of your ways. I hate to admit it, but I lost hope of you ever doing that long ago. For what reason did you return to Ravensdorf?"

Crukas blushed.

"Ah," she said. "I should've known. Something else to steal, eh?"

"You know me all too well."

"You've never made it a mystery. Ya mind telling me what's in this small town worth stealing? Ravensdorf's dwellers have no valuables, which means you want something in Dark Ayr Tower. Only a fool sets his attention on entering the tower."

"Or, a master thief," Crukas replied.

"Don't be so foolhardy. Is that where you seek? As a priestess I'm bound to keep one's confessions secret or else, I receive great punishment from our goddess."

"Scorpius possesses an item I need."

Irmine set the mortar down. She stared at him in disbelief. "You're a greater fool than when you confessed about stealing the book. I might not get my favor after you cross paths with him."

"We might all perish if I don't succeed. The truth be told, I should've robbed him *before* I took the book. Doing so, though, would've taken too much time."

Irmine shuddered from sudden chills. "You have a death wish? You're not going to try to steal his mask, are you?"

Crukas grinned and shook his head. "No. I'm *going* to steal it."

She studied him for several long moments. Her stunned silence meant she had more questions than he had time to answer or would bother to answer. "What's really going on, Crukas? You're risking your life for items you've no need to steal and of no real importance to you. Why?"

"Again, I have my reasons. I don't want to say they're noble—"

Irmine waved him to silence and held up the mortar. "Very well. No more prattling. You have the corpse of a Wierwen in the wagon?"

"Yes."

"The entire body *and* the head?"

Crukas nodded.

Irmine handed him two glass vials. "For me to complete this concoction, I need you to collect its blood in one vial and as much saliva as you can in the other."

Crukas took the vials and frowned. "You're serious?"

She grinned. "Would a priestess lie to you?"

Crukas shook his head and headed down the narrow hallway. "Give me a few minutes."

Thunder rattled overhead. Bottles and beakers on the shelves and tables clanged a horrendous melody.

"I wouldn't tarry too long," Irmine said. "Run. Don't allow the rain to water down the blood or saliva. It's crucial for this is to work."

Crukas ignored his aching back and hurried to the door. While luck might not exist, he couldn't shunt the idea that the coming storm sought the Cursed Spellbook. So he obeyed Irmine's command to run, and run, he did.

CHAPTER 18

*B*efore Crukas returned to Irmine with one blood-filled vial and the other filled with viscous saliva, he studied the dead Wierwen with immense curiosity, wondering who the human had been before he'd gotten infected. Perhaps he'd never know.

Crukas had been fortunate the Wierwen's mouth was frothy with strands of drool hanging from its jaws. Otherwise, he'd have collected far less or been forced to touch its tongue and gums, which might infect him even with gloves on.

Ebden watched Crukas gather both liquids and seemed uncomfortable guarding the wagon with the flashing lightning growing more intense and steadily moving closer. Static hung in the air and the scent of rain was undeniable. Crukas gave him directions to the nearest stable, which was less than a block away. With the storm closing in, Ebden's safety was questionable, even more so since he kept the book on his person. But before Ebden departed, he did something unexpected.

"Crukas," Ebden said. "Take the book. I trust you'll keep your word. I can't carry this any longer. It makes me uneasy."

Crukas nodded. "I understand. Thanks. You best hurry. The storm's upon us."

~

"Here." Crukas handed the vials to Irmine. "It best be enough. The rain will begin soon."

Irmine took the corked vials and smiled. "This is more than enough."

With a narrow glass rod, she dipped the beaded tip into the vial of blood and allowed two blood droplets to fall in the mortar. She took another rod and did the same with the saliva. Then she vigorously mixed the contents with the pestle. While she stirred the mixture, she closed her eyes and mumbled words unfamiliar to him.

Crukas followed her to where Adgus lie. She rubbed the pasty mixture into Adgus' slash. He groaned. After setting the mortar on a side table, she placed her hands over the wound. Her hand glowed with enough radiance for the outline of her hand bones to become visible through her flesh. Crukas sensed and felt the heat of her touch. Bramnir's eyes widened. He steadied himself against the wall. A flow of power filled the room.

Adgus squirmed and his eyes opened slightly. He moaned but didn't attempt to sit up. His voice was weak and hoarse. "Where am I?"

"I'm here, brother," Bramnir said. "Rest easy."

Adgus looked around the dark room. "Where's *here*?"

"Ravensdorf," Bramnir replied.

"So we made it?"

"Aye," Bramnir said.

"I'm not a beast?"

Bramnir shook his head. "No more than what you were before."

"Hah!" Adgus' eyes brightened and he smiled broadly.

Bramnir met Irmine's gaze. "How does he fare? Is he cured?"

"By sunrise," Irmine said, "he'll be ready to leave."

Bramnir nodded. "Thank you, kind lady."

Irmine smiled. She grabbed Crukas' elbow. "Come with me."

Crukas frowned. *Again? Now what?*

Once they returned to her storeroom, she said, "How can I persuade you *not* to attempt to steal Scorpius' mask?"

Crukas gave an even smile and took her right hand in his. With a solemn expression, he said, "My dear Irmine, you've been far more than I've ever deserved as a friend."

Her eyes moistened with tears, as though he were saying his final goodbye, and quite possibly he was, he thought. Her emotions might've also stirred from him associating her as his friend since those words had never left his lips before. At least, not in her presence.

Crukas said, "Your kindness to a thief isn't something I ever expected. And your patience that one day I'd recant my ways is as close as you'll see. Understand, I've not stolen anything for myself in a long, long time. I've no need for wealth and thieving's no longer a satisfying challenge. There's no lock or pocket I can't pick. The thrill of those challenges waned some years ago. The book's not for me, and the mask, should I succeed in taking it, is to allow my safety until I finish what needs to be done."

Irmine squeezed his hand. "At least pray with me before you set off."

"I wouldn't know how to begin."

She smiled. "I can lead you."

"Fine." Warm tears shimmered in his eyes. "Afterwards, do you mind if I find a corner to sleep for a few hours?"

"For as long as you need." She released his hand, unlatched the gold chain around her neck, and pulled up the pendant hidden beneath her robe. "Take this."

"What's this?"

"A pendant to help protect you from Scorpius," she replied. "I blessed it, and it's protected me for most of my life. May it protect yours."

"I can never thank you enough." He fastened the chain around his neck.

"You can thank me by surviving and fulfilling your favor, eh?"

"I've made no plans for failure."

Irmine turned with a sly smile and took two small vials from a shelf. "You'll need these."

"What are these?"

"Antitoxin," she said. "Scorpius is a master alchemist who specializes in poisons."

"Thank you." Crukas slid them inside his pocket.

"Come, let's pray for your safety and success."

Crukas smiled.

For the first time, his subconscious didn't stubbornly protest the thought of prayer and redemption. Was this maturity on his part, or did he know his life would soon end? He held no allegiance to any deity, and with so many different gods and goddesses, he didn't have a clue to whom he should pray. Could someone praying on behalf of another actually benefit? It couldn't hurt, he reasoned. Perhaps Fate could be changed or delayed. In time, he'd discover the answer.

CHAPTER 19

Sparrow braved her way to the door of the little attic room and pressed her ear against its wooden panel. Although she didn't detect any sounds from the other side, her heart pounded so hard she became lightheaded. Chill bumps pricked her skin. Remembering how the mysterious shadow had crept under the door and into the room, she wished Fasha would return and escort her down the stairs.

"What kind of bounty hunter am I if I'm fearful of things I don't understand?" she mumbled.

A living one.

She held up the oil lantern and glanced nervously around the room, wondering from where the reply came.

Remaining in the room was no longer safe. Instinct and her gut feeling told her so. The scratching from inside the walls had ceased, but she didn't know what had made the sounds or where it might have gone. All she wanted was to get to the ground floor and out of the shop quickly.

Sparrow turned the latch, which clicked rather loudly. She pulled the door inward. The old hinges whined. Nothing stood outside the door's threshold—much to her relief—although she expected the specter to be waiting and ready to attack. In the faint glow of the lantern, the creaky stairs leading downward were daunting. She left the door ajar and moved to the top step.

Under normal circumstances, Sparrow never feared the darkness. She somewhat enjoyed the adventure in seeking out the unknown. But after seeing something inside the crystal ball and the sinister apparition approaching her in the room, her adventurous spirit took a sudden hiatus. Yet, to leave the spell shop, she needed to take the stairs, which were now far spookier than she remembered.

When Fasha guided her to the room, Sparrow never noticed the hanging cobwebs along the slanted ceiling and on each side of the stairway. The lantern's glow magnified the size of the crawling spiders' shadows, which were frightening to behold.

Her light weight allowed her to descend the stairs with hardly a sound, despite the earlier creakiness of the worn stairs. If the stairs made any sound, her thudding heartbeat in her ears muffled them. Should something have touched her, her shrilled scream would be heard far outside the Gloomy Forest, and perhaps frightened others like a banshee often preceded Death's timely touch.

At the bottom of the stairs, she listened. She halfway hoped Fasha was sorting through the spell scrolls on the table, but Fasha was nowhere to be seen. Since Fasha told her no addition costs were required, Sparrow made her way to the door.

Reaching for the doorknob, she looked over her shoulder. She thought it odd that she didn't want to leave without thanking Fasha again and telling her goodbye. It was rare for a halfling to disregard kind words to those who offered assistance. Plus, Sparrow needed the closure, needed to look into Fasha's odd eyes to have the certainty that nothing else was required of her.

With a reluctant sigh, Sparrow turned from the door and walked past the table piled with spell scrolls. She stepped into the neighboring room and slipped past the thin curtain to the table where the crystal ball rested.

Fasha wasn't in this room, either. Yet, the crystal ball illuminated at her presence. Sparrow stepped back, ready to retreat and bolt for the door.

She froze. An eye peered at her from inside the ball. Instead of leaving, her intrigue drew her closer.

What are you? she thought. As curious as she were, she didn't really want an answer.

"In need of another reading?" Fasha said from behind her.

Sparrow screamed and clasped her hand over her mouth to muffle the sound. She turned and Fasha's odd eyes narrowed. Fasha smiled but not in a friendly way.

"I'm s-s-orry," Sparrow said. "I—I thought maybe you were in here. I just wanted to say goodbye and thanks."

"A bit on edge, aren't you?" Fasha walked past her and seated herself on the other side of the crystal ball. "You didn't sleep, either."

Sparrow shook her head and couldn't stop the tears spilling from her eyes. "Not much, if I did at all. I can't sleep in your shop."

"Have you taken to heart the warnings I gave you?"

Sparrow wiped away her tears and nodded. "I have. I've had no choice but to think about everything all night."

"I'm glad you've taken time to consider the danger."

Sparrow stared past Fasha at the wall. "That's not what kept me awake."

"Oh?"

"Either you have some problem with vermin in the walls or else there's something worse."

Fasha grinned. "Just the weariness of an old building bracing the inevitability of impending decay. And as for my advice, you'll ignore me."

"What makes you so certain?"

"Lessons learned often come from hardship and experience, despite the most sound advice."

"That's true," Sparrow said.

"Death proves you failed to listen," Fasha said coldly. "Regrets are hard to dismiss, but in the afterlife, you'll relive your final foolish mistake over and over. Seek Crukas out and you'll learn firsthand. If you wish to live, I suggest you return to Willow's Bend."

"Is that a threat?"

Fasha shook her head. "No. It's what I've seen. Honest. Although my demon ancestry are known for their lies, the Elven side is not subjective to guile. As I've previously stressed, I wish to regard you as a friend. *My* friend."

"What of Crukas' fate?"

Fasha shrugged. "I've no idea. He's not asked and I've not seen his final outcome. All I know is he has the book and the curses associated with its possession will manifest over time. So, halfling, where does your heart lead you?"

Sparrow sighed and considered the question. "I truly don't know."

"Of that, you speak the truth. But only because you don't know which direction Crukas traveled, correct?"

Sparrow's face reddened.

"It's okay. My best advice is often ignored."

Sparrow's hand tightened on the wanted flyer for Crukas in her pocket. "I swore an oath in regard to his capture. I have an obligation—"

"Say no more." Fasha flicked her hand upward in dismissal. "You owe me no explanation. After last night's heavy rain, the swampy areas within Gloomy Forest are quite treacherous. You're welcome to stay another night or two. Free of charge, too."

"I appreciate the offer. Really."

"Then where will you go?"

Sparrow hunched her tiny shoulders. "I'll find my way. Perhaps the forest will give me the clues I need."

"This forest?" Fasha shook her head. "This forest will do its best to consume you, much like it has Salem. Dozens of travelers have been forever lost and their remains never found because they wandered astray."

A chill crawled up Sparrow's spine, and she visibly shivered.

"Since I know you'll still pursue your hunt for Crukas, perhaps I can give you a nudge in the right direction?" A slight, sinister curl of a smile came to Fasha's lips. Clearly, *this* was her demon side showing through.

"I—I don't know."

"All the same, if you know the actual route he's on, you'll be less likely to go off course and die prematurely."

Sparrow offered a nervous smile, knowing the future tempted Fate and the lust to obtain unknown knowledge was a craving few ever rejected. "Thanks, but no."

"Aww, I hear your words, but your heart and mind speak a different tune, don't they?" Fasha polished the crystal ball and gently pulled it toward her.

"Really, no," Sparrow said. "You've been more than helpful already."

"It's no trouble at all," Fasha said. "I'll find the direction Crukas went, and you decide what you wish to do with the information, okay?"

Sparrow knew she should decline the offer, but she didn't protest further. Knowing the details didn't increase her danger but allowed her to choose her next actions. At least she could evaluate better judgment and not waste precious time meandering false leads. The more distance Crukas gained, the less likely Sparrow would catch him.

Fasha peered into the crystal ball. The moving entity within the crystal swirled like a dark cloud and slowly it shaped into what appeared to be the iris of a mystical eyeball. It stared intently at her.

Sparrow swallowed hard and then bit her lower lip, awaiting an answer.

"Crukas is in Ravensdorf," Fasha said. "Seek him out if you must, but at your own peril."

After she spoke the words, she vanished and the crystal blackened, leaving Sparrow alone in the dark with only her thoughts and worries. Whatever had been inside the crystal ball must've left with Fasha.

"Now, that's an incredible exit," Sparrow whispered, slowly backing out the tiny curtained room.

CHAPTER 20

*C*rukas awakened after a long bout of nightmares about Jillann. In her Wierwen form, she was chasing and trying to kill him.

Although he often chided himself for not fighting to rescue her, in hindsight, had he done so, he'd have become infected and turned into a Wierwen, too. Or, they'd have both been killed.

He could've sworn the Wierwen had killed her immediately. At no time from her attack until she intervened to save him and the dwarves, did he ever consider she might've survived.

Covered in sweat, Crukas rose from the cot. He went to the room where Irmine had treated Adgus. The bed was empty. Neither dwarf was there.

"Your *friends* left several hours ago," Irmine said.

Crukas turned to see her standing in the doorway. Her emphasis on friends didn't make him uncomfortable. Perhaps a week earlier, having the term associated with him, he'd have cringed. Of course, he'd considered her a friend without ever openly admitting it. After last night, he found solace in the hope of friendship. Irmine had proven to be a friend, but the dwarves were only interested in the stout he'd bartered for the trip. He never anticipated more than that.

He introduced them as friends so Irmine would heal Adgus. Otherwise, should Adgus die, Crukas would suffer additional guilt.

"To where?" Crukas asked. His question tinged with panicked urgency he couldn't hide. After all, Ebden had returned the book to Crukas before Crukas settled his debt. Though a thief, he honored a promise. He never welched on an agreement. If matters grew worse, he didn't want to die with an unpaid debt attached to his legacy.

"They said they'd wait for you at the Mute Changeling."

Crukas gave a slight nod and sighed.

Irmine failed to hide her amusement. "Don't you worry. Those dwarves won't leave without their stout."

"How long did I sleep?"

"Through the entire storm. A bad one, too. The street flooded and I had to cast an invisible barrier to prevent the waters from seeping under my door. We've not had heavy rain like that in years. The hail and lightning were far worse. One would think Scorpius conjured the storm. Perhaps he knows of your arrival and your intentions?"

"Doubtful," Crukas said. "But you didn't answer my question."

"It's late afternoon, now."

Crukas cursed under his breath. "My apologies."

She smiled. "No need."

Crukas leaned down and hugged her. Her eyes widened at his sudden, unusual affection. He whispered in her ear, "Thank you … For everything."

"Keep the pendant on you at all times," she said. Her eyes were moist and near tears.

"I will."

"Be vigilant, Crukas. I sense I can't persuade you to not undergo the task you plan, so I've placed a protective spell around you. Should you—" She paused to choose her next words rather carefully. "Should you need healing afterwards, return to me. I trust you know your importance to me."

He caught her gaze and became uncomfortable. Few people had ever expressed even the slightest fondness for him, and less had shown what could only be platonic love. In a way, he'd always preferred that. With uneasiness and a jester's smile, he said, "Yes, I know I still owe you a favor."

Irmine playfully smacked his arm and shook her crooked, wrinkled finger at him. "The favor has nothing to do with your importance. In fact, I withdraw you owing me one."

Crukas displayed a warm smile. "No, Irmine, I've every intention of fulfilling my promise to you. Just tell me what you need."

She shook her head and took his hand in hers. "No, not yet. No sense adding another distraction to your already anxious mind. Do what you must first, and only afterwards, will I disclose what I need."

In the same manner as his hug surprised her, she caught him further off guard by wrapping her arms around his waist and embracing him. "Be safe. You have a friend in me. Never forget that."

CHAPTER 21

The Mute Changeling was a ruddy building near the center of Ravensdorf. Like all the houses and little shops, the tavern walls were composed of rock held together by aged, crumbling mortar. The thatched roof was a pale, sick yellow. Though not a fancy tavern, the place was far better than Sorceress Brew. A female bard stood in a corner and sang about the horrendous doom a long, lost party of explorers had suffered. None of them had a promising end.

The three dwarves had waited for several hours, watching the patrons come and go. Beside their round table set a modest barrel of stout and their tankards were filled a third time.

Bramnir shook his head. "Ya reckon he'll show? We've waited for hours."

"He's a thief," Adgus said with a shrewd stare. "I told ya he can't be trusted."

Bramnir smiled. "If he wants his book, he'll show."

"Bah!" Adgus said. "It's a book. What book be worth three barrels of stout?"

"Apparently, the one he handed Ebden." Bramnir pointed at Ebden's leather pouch.

Adgus sneered and grumbled. "Yet, he's not arrived and Ebden has his book. Plus, we're going to 'ave to pay this tab."

Ebden swallowed hard and looked away.

Adgus frowned at Ebden. "You still have the book, right? You didn't lose it when we were attacked by those blasted Wierwen?"

Ebden sighed. "No. I didn't lose it. I gave it to Crukas last night before the storm."

Adgus faced flushed cherry red. "Ya bloody fool! Ya did what?"

Bramnir glared at Ebden. "Why'd ya do dat?"

"The book's cursed," Ebden said.

"Nonsense!" Adgus said. "It's a book."

Ebden shook his head. His eyes held deep fear. "No. From the moment I touched it, darkness surrounded me. A dark force pulsed through me hand and up my arm when I took it from Crukas."

Bramnir's brow rose. "You're serious?"

"Yes. Nothing but bad things happened on our way 'ere. The Wierwen. Adgus nearly dying," Ebden said. "Twice, I was attacked, too."

"Dat be true," Adgus said glumly. "And even worse luck 'ave it, we're out of the stout. No way he'll honor his end since ya *gave* 'em back dat book!"

"He'll show," Ebden said.

"He's a thief," Adgus said. "Lest ya forget."

Bramnir clasped Adgus' shoulder. "Brother, he may be a thief, but he damned saved your life by leading us to Irmine. He didn't abandon us along the way, either. We left him with the priestess to sleep. Not once during our trip did I ever think he was deceiving us, nor do I now. He has business 'ere, whatever it may be."

Adgus wrapped his thick hand around the tankard, took a large gulp, and nodded. "Aye, you be right about dat. A time or two I thought I'd died. I owe 'em at least gratitude and should give 'em some benefit of the doubt."

"Life's worth more than three barrels of stout," Bramnir said.

"Aye," Adgus said and then winked. "But it be less merry."

A small bell above the entrance door chimed. In walked a kobold with a pack strapped to his back. His reptilian-like brown scales were covered with thick, red short hairs that resembled moss. His sharp, black claws were deadly weapons without the aid of his long dagger or the jagged pick sheathed on his belt. His long, scaly tail bent like a serpent ready to slither away. His emerald, green eyes gleamed brighter than the actual gems. With an intense glare, he glanced around the tavern. After a few seconds, he walked past their table and headed to a larger table near the back of the room. Another dwarf, wearing a patch over his left eye, greeted the kobold with a slight grunt and nod.

The three dwarves exchanged amused looks.

"They serve vermin 'ere?" Adgus asked with an outraged glare.

Bramnir shrugged. "Kobolds are miners, ya know? They find enough treasure to splurge."

Adgus shook his head. "No. I've never met one dat speaks well enough to be understood. Mostly, they're so primal and violent, we've had to kill them. Dwarves never rub shoulders with 'em."

"I know. But dat one seems different."

"Aye. Cause he is," Adgus said. "Still, I trust 'em even less than Crukas."

Bramnir chuckled. "One should hope."

The bard stopped singing and joined the kobold and the one-eyed dwarf at the table.

Devin Dusk, the barkeep, applauded. "Well sung, Miss Strella."

She stood, grinned, and did a prompt curtsy. Embarrassed that only Devin had applauded, she sat at the table and turned to her companions.

Devin stood a few inches taller than the average dwarf. He was dark skinned, thin, and appeared frail. He whispered to a young barmaid and less than a minute later, she carried several large tankards of brew on a tray to the table where Miss Strella was seated.

"An odd company," Ebden said, studying them with one brow cocked.

Adgus shrugged and chuckled. "At least she stopped her caterwauling. Maybe now, we can drink in peace and hope to forget the nightmare dat got us 'ere."

The door's bell rattled again. In walked another dwarf, whose reputation was almost as notorious as Crukas'. Unlike Bramnir and his brothers, this dwarf wore thick leather armor and boots. Strapped to his belt was an advanced snub-nose revolver known to have the ability to fire five subsequent musket balls. A marvel, really.

Revolvers were rare, mostly used by pirates and bounty hunters. Dwarves, in general, detested the use of them because they showed cowardice. A true warrior proved worthy in battle with blades and axes. For a dwarf to possess and carry a revolver meant he or she had probably killed a pirate in self-defense to collect the bounty and kept the weapon as a trophy. Either way, much respect and often fear were given to a dwarf brave enough to display the weapon as a preferred choice.

Bramnir and his brothers' faces tightened with resentment as the dwarf ignored them and marched past their table to join Miss Strella, the kobold, and the one-eyed dwarf at their table.

"What's going on 'ere?" Adgus stared at his tankard and shook his head. "This 'ere stout's too tame to cause me to be disillusioned. *Dat's* Triggor McLuft. He's a bounty hunter."

Bramnir's jaw tightened. "Aye. Tis a bit odd."

"Perhaps this is why Crukas hasn't shown?" Ebden asked.

"Could be," Bramnir replied.

"Ya still believe he's gonna show?" Adgus asked with a scowl.

"Not with these bounty hunters 'ere," Bramnir said.

Ebden glanced at the door. "Should I go warn Crukas? Or see dat he's okay?"

"Ya think he's still with the priestess?" Adgus asked.

Ebden shrugged. "It's possible. Only one way for us to know for certain."

"Not yet," Adgus said, focused on Triggor. "Let's watch 'em a bit."

CHAPTER 22

*A*fter opening Fasha's shop door, Sparrow backed her way outside. She kept her attention on the table piled with the sorted spell scrolls. Where had Fasha gone?

She closed the door. Rain had soaked the desolate streets. Small streams of water dripped from the thatched roofs. Wisps of drifting fog slinked like lost ghosts. Everything seemed more dreadful than when she had arrived. She considered accepting Fasha's offer to stay another night or two until the forest dried. But Sparrow had slept little more than occasional catnaps. Regardless of the kind offer, Sparrow could never sleep inside the spell shop. Besides, she didn't know where Fasha was.

Still uncertain of entering the forest to find a trail to lead her to Bridgebarrow, she entered Sorceress Brew. Unlike her previous visit, the tavern was deserted. Strangely, heavy layers of dust and cobwebs coated the tables and ceiling beams. It seemed no one had frequented the tavern in years. The night before, the place was modestly clean. What few tankards set on the table were dusty with spiders spinning new webs inside the handles. Were yesterday's events a dream or was she walking in a nightmare?

"Hello?" She worried she was alone but also fearful she wasn't.

Chills pimpled her skin. No one at all?

The odd door behind the bar stood ajar. All the locks rested atop the bar and the chains dangled loosely.

Sparrow eased closer to the bar, half wondering if the barkeep was on the other side of the door, perhaps getting supplies. In spite of her fear of him, she hoped to see what was on the other side of the threshold.

"Excuse me?" She rested her hands atop the dusty bar. "Sir? Chubs?"

No answer came.

The eerie silence troubled her. Her curiosity got the best of her. The door wasn't opened far enough to view anything. No one answered or stepped outside. And without knowing she'd moved, she stood outside the door on the other side of the bar.

Sparrow placed her hand against the door and pushed inward. A cold force embraced her wrist and pulled her into darkness where she saw nothing, but oddly felt herself suddenly falling.

Maniacal laughter echoed all around.

Fasha.

Sparrow recognized the distinctive laugh. Just when Sparrow expected to drop to her death, she was standing on a street outside a rustic building. Mystified, she studied the rough, wet streets. She was no longer in Salem. Looking up, she read the sign: The Mute Changeling.

Meet your Fate, little one.

The voice was Fasha's. A coldness rushed through Sparrow. She had a choice. Open the door and continue her pursuit for Crukas; or else, make the long journey to Willow's Bend and live a life of less adventure and chance. The latter choice seemed more difficult to pursue since she didn't know where her current location was on a map. The name of the tavern was familiar, though she'd never been to it. To figure out where she'd been transported, she'd need to ask someone local for possible directions.

Sparrow sighed. "What better place than a tavern?"

Sparrow took a deep breath, closed her eyes, and opened the door.

CHAPTER 23

*S*parrow had never visited the Mute Changeling, but she recognized its name and that the tavern was located in Ravensdorf. She only had a vague idea of how to find it. Thieves in her former guild had often spoke of it.

Hearing Fasha whisper for Sparrow to *meet her fate* left no doubt Fasha had somehow sent Sparrow to Ravensdorf through a portal on the other side of the mysterious door. But why?

While Fasha insisted Sparrow had choices, it seemed Fasha was forcing Sparrow to pursue Crukas.

Sparrow couldn't resist the temptation of knowing what was beyond the door should she get an opportunity to find out, and Fasha knew that. She explicitly warned Sparrow *not* to go after Crukas or else Sparrow would die. Sparrow's catlike curiosity lured her into a trap best set for a hungry mouse, and she had taken the bait without thinking her actions through.

Did Fasha *want* Sparrow killed? Only if Fasha was in cahoots with Crukas. If Fasha wasn't, as she'd sworn, then Fasha hoped to see Crukas captured or killed so she could get the Cursed Spellbook of the Damned back.

Even now, Sparrow couldn't determine what role Fasha played or why Sparrow had been thrust deeper into this maddening dilemma. Perhaps Fasha wanted to test Sparrow's bounty-hunting skills or she was challenging Sparrow's willpower to resist going after Crukas' reward because she feared dying. Or, perhaps Fasha wanted to see how much Sparrow really trusted her? For all Sparrow knew, Fasha had been lying all along.

"Why does everyone try to belittle me?" Sparrow smiled at her own pun.

Being a halfling whose heart had always been set on greater adventures while the cynical members of her family and community scoffed at her dreams, she fought harder to prove herself at every turn. Since Fasha had magically teleported Sparrow to Ravensdorf, her mindset became even more stubborn. She vowed to find and bring Crukas to justice without dying.

Sparrow's fingers tightened around the yellow parchment in her pocket with Crukas' image and the posted reward for his capture. She glanced at the table closest to the door. Three dwarves eyed her for a moment with slight grins on their faces but returned to drinking from their tankards without giving her much thought.

Her stomach tensed and for a serious moment, she considered leaving the tavern and abandoning her mission. Instead, she took a deep breath, tightened her jaw, and leveled an even stare at the dwarves before she headed toward their table.

CHAPTER 24

*B*ramnir's brow rose when the tavern door opened. A female halfling entered and promptly closed the door behind her. She stood in silence. Her cowl was pulled almost even with her brow. Her emerald eyes, glowing like a cat's, indicated she was unsure of why she was there.

Bramnir shook his head. "Quite an assortment of patrons 'ere."

"Indeed!" Adgus chuffed a laugh.

"I'd 'ave never thought this a popular place," Ebden said.

"Nor I," Bramnir said. "First a kobold, a gunslinging dwarf, and *now* a halfling. Most everywhere we travel, we be the most vertically challenged in the room."

Ebden laughed. "Don't forget the off-tune bard."

Bramnir groaned. "She be the exception, being as she's taller than all of us."

"Most elves are," Ebden said.

"What's next?" Adgus wiped froth from his braided beard with the back of his hand. His eyes lit up and he suppressed a roar of laughter. "Pixies?"

"Don't jinx us." Bramnir noticed the halfling's intense stare and whispered, "Careful, she's headed toward us."

"Me boots are quaking," Adgus said.

She stopped at the edge of their table, and even though they were seated, they were still taller than she was standing.

"You look out of place, little one. Can we help ya?" Bramnir asked.

Her brow furrowed. Her lips tightened with a moment of irritation. She yanked a crumpled piece of yellow parchment from her pocket and unrolled it. She fought to straighten it with her hands but failed. Her whispering voice shook slightly. "I'm Sparrow Birme, and I'm looking for *this* man. Have any of you seen him?"

Bramnir frowned, studying the picture, but kept a hardened expression. He met her eyes with an intimidating stare, which forced her to look away. "Nah. I've not seen 'em. What business you got with a thief anyway?"

"I wish to apprehend him and collect the bounty," Sparrow said.

Adgus scoffed and chuckled. "Do ya now? *You're* a bounty hunter?"

Sparrow's jaw tightened at his mocking tone. Apparently insulted, she said, "I am."

The high tone of her voice lessened the seriousness of the anger set in her eyes. Bramnir and his two brothers grinned, amused, and their beards helped hide their growing smiles. Although humored, they didn't wish to add any further insults by belittling her.

"Aye." Adgus nodded while staring at the wanted flyer. "Aww, now, don't be getting offended, lass. You're the first halfling bounty hunter we've ever seen. Took us off guard, is all. And besides dat, I've got to admire ya spunk. Highly ambitious to go after the most wanted thief in Aetheaon."

"You've not seen him?" she asked.

"Bah!" Adgus shook his head. "Ya think we'd hang around with a thief? We're miners. We *earn* our keep the honest way. The last thing we'd want is a thief to steal our ores."

Ebden pointed at the scar above her eye. "Ya get dat from catching a thief?"

"Yes," she replied, touching the scar. "I've other scars, too."

"Dangerous business for ya to be in," Adgus said. "You be at a disadvantage for most criminals."

"I know. But I've not failed yet," Sparrow said meekly.

"It'd be hard challenge for a thief to stab ya, eh?" Ebden asked.

"Because of my height?" she asked.

Ebden shook his head slightly. "I meant dat you look to be quick and agile. Dat's nothin' to do with ya size."

She frowned and cocked her head to the side. "Oh."

"Some might say dat it's hard for ya to measure up, eh?" Adgus said with a slight wink.

Anger flared in her eyes. Her mouth opened and her mixed expression teetered between crying or vehemently screaming.

"Easy, Sparrow. Forgive me brother," Bramnir said. "What makes you think Crukas is 'ere in the first place? This town doesn't seem prosperous. It's far from the ports and offers nothing but cliff walls overlooking the sea."

Sparrow sighed. "On sound advice, I was told he'd be in Ravensdorf."

"Maybe he is, but as you see, he's not with us, lass," Bramnir said. "But, should we 'appen to see him, is there a finder's fee?"

The question caused her brow to raise. She paused, uncertain how to answer. "I—I could pay a percentage, yes."

"Half?" Adgus said with a sudden glint of greed in his eyes.

She shrugged but failed to maintain eye contact with any of them. "Sure. The reward isn't as important to me as seeing him brought to justice."

Adgus chuckled. "Justice, eh? Is dat so?"

Sparrow leveled a glare at Adgus. "Yes."

Adgus didn't flinch or look away. "If justice is your true pursuit, ya best get busy."

Her brow rose. "Huh?"

Directing his nod toward the far table, Adgus said, "Seems some competition has already gathered. There be another bounty hunter 'ere."

She looked at the table. "Who?"

"Triggor McLuft. Since you're a bounty hunter, ya should know of his reputation, eh?"

"Oh," she said, uneasily. Any remaining self-confidence she held seemed to dwindle further. "Uh, yeah."

Bramnir gave her a shrewd stare. In a dismissive tone, he said, "We wish ya luck. Should we see 'em, we'll find you and let you know. How long do you intend to stay in Ravensdorf?"

"Provided my source was accurate," Sparrow said, "until I find him."

"Good to know," Bramnir said. "We'll keep our eyes open."

Sparrow offered a slight smile, rolled up the parchment, and tucked it inside her robe. "Thanks."

After she walked to the far table where the bard, kobold, and two dwarves sat, Bramnir looked at his brothers. "I find this entire situation unusual."

"Aye," Adgus said. "Quite troubling. Triggor's a known bounty hunter, as for her, I've never heard of her. But why are they 'ere for Crukas? Perhaps, we should consider handing him over to her? Dat's a lot of gold."

"You'd be a fool to think she'd part with half the reward," Bramnir said. "Besides, she was lying about sharing the pot. She made the promise without looking you in the eyes. No. We tell her nothing of Crukas. Ebden, return to the priestess' house and warn Crukas. Provided he's still there."

"What about the barrels of stout he promised us?" Adgus said.

"We won't ever see dat if they capture him, now will we?" Bramnir said. He looked at Ebden. "Hurry, but make sure no one follows ya, okay?"

Ebden stood, nodded, and went to the door.

"Perhaps we should talk to the barkeep and tell 'em Crukas sent us," Adgus said, peering into his empty tankard.

"No, not while the two bounty hunters are 'ere," Bramnir said. "For all we know, Devin might be the one who sent for the bounty hunters."

"Why would he do dat?"

Bramnir shrugged. "He's indebted to Crukas. Maybe he wishes to weasel his way out of paying him and get richer at the same time."

Adgus' bushy eyebrows tightened in anger. "Then he'd be a traitor to us, too. Why dat—"

Bramnir placed a firm hand on Adgus' shoulder. "Easy, Brother. I said, '*maybe*'. The barkeep could also be trying to send the hunters off course, too. Ya never know. Only Crukas would know. At the moment, I honestly don't believe Crukas will skimp on his word."

"I hope ya right."

CHAPTER 25

*E*bden rushed down the street toward the priestess' house. For a dwarf to hurry, without running, made one highly suspicious, but no one was walking along the roadway. All the windows of the shops and houses were boarded shut, but for all he knew, curious eyes could be peering through narrow slits.

The closer Ebden came to the alleyway where the priestess lived, the more he noticed shadows slinking at the edges of buildings and houses. Their large oval, yellow eyes fixated on him. Their sudden presence made him uneasy, as he'd never seen anything like them, and he certainly would never have expected to see such dark creatures during the day.

He patted for the spellbook in his pouch and remembered he'd given it to Crukas. Despite the absence of the book, a cold chill tingled and shocked his hand as though a remnant of the book's power lingered.

The tome was far from ordinary and unlike anything he'd ever handled. Though he could read, books were not his interest. He held no desire or want for them. Mining precious ores and gems was his passion, followed by his undying thirst for stout and strong brews. He didn't need a book to learn more about either passion. Crukas' book made Ebden uncomfortable. He wished he'd have given it to Crukas when Crukas thought Ebden was dead, and he caught Crukas trying to retrieve the book from the pouch.

In hindsight, Ebden wished he and his two brothers would've rejected the agreed terms of receiving the barrels of stout in exchange for giving Crukas a ride to Ravensdorf. Although the book was the only thing Crukas had of value on his person, Ebden didn't understand how it held any worth at all. He'd been uneasy ever since he agreed to keep the book until they settled their exchange. But returning the book to Crukas hadn't diminished the uneasiness haunting Ebden.

The eerie, creeping shadowy figures weren't the only noticeable oddities he'd witnessed. A sense of oppression and impending doom weighed on him. He was more anxious than he'd ever been in the deepest, darkest cavern. The reasons for this distress must be from the book, he reasoned.

At Irmine's door, he knocked. The few minutes he waited for someone to come to the door seemed an eternity. The shadows he'd seen on the street slowly moved their way down the alley.

The locks inside the door clicked, one after another, until finally, the gnome opened the door. "Yes?"

"I need to speak to Crukas immediately," Ebden said, looking over his shoulder. "Is he still here?"

"You bring with you much evil," Irmine said. "You carry the tome?"

Ebden shook his head. "No. I gave it to Crukas."

Irmine turned slightly and gave Crukas a sharp but partially confused stare. "Is this true?"

"Yes. I have the book." Crukas pulled the door wider. "Please allow Ebden inside."

Irmine mumbled a few words, and the doorway expanded. She ushered Ebden inside. "Quite odd."

"What?" Crukas asked.

Ebden looked uneasy with his gaze fixed on the alleyway.

Irmine frowned. "You have the book, Crukas? Of that you're certain?"

Crukas nodded.

She shook her head. "I never sensed it on you. Ebden reeks of its touch, more so than you. The pendant I gave you must've somehow concealed its evil, at least partially. I would never have allowed the vileness of that book to taint my home."

"Fine," Crukas said with a sigh. "He and I will speak outside."

Ebden shook his head. "No, Crukas, it's not safe for you. Bramnir sent me to warn you."

Irmine frowned at the dwarf. "What's wrong?"

"Bounty hunters." Ebden wanted to mention the odd shadowy figures, but if they were only a delusion on Ebden's part, Crukas would find more urgency in learning about the bounty hunters. "Several arrived at the Mute Changeling, only minutes ago. One, a halfling, carries a flyer with your picture and reward on it. She's demanding information to find you."

Crukas offered an amused smile. "That'd be Sparrow."

Ebden's eyes widened. "Yes. Dat be her name. I know not of her, but she's not our greatest problem. Another bounty hunter arrived minutes before her. Triggor McLuft."

Crukas's smile faded, and he couldn't hide his concern.

"Triggor?" Irmine grabbed Ebden by the wrist and tugged. She failed to have the strength to budge him. Ebden stepped across the threshold and the door shrank so small that from the outside it probably looked like a knot in the wood or perhaps, it was invisible.

Irmine glanced at Crukas and shook her head. "I suppose you've proven me wrong."

"About what?" Crukas said.

"You having friends." She laughed. "Only a true friend would warn you instead of turning you over for the reward."

Crukas acquiesced a nod. Ebden smiled.

"Look." Ebden took the small pouch off his shoulder. He opened it and where he'd set the book, a blackened outline of the book remained. "The book tarnished my satchel."

"May I?" Irmine reached for the pouch.

He nodded and handed it to her.

126

Irmine's brow creased with concern. "Whatever power possessed the book has attached itself to you."

"What do you make of that?" Crukas asked.

She met Crukas' gaze. "I've never seen anything like this. Do you mind if I keep your pouch to examine? I'll give it back."

"Keep it," Ebden said. "Burn it, if necessary. Since I've taken the book, I've seen and felt only darkness, which troubles me greatly."

Looking at the darkened place where the book had been, she said, "I understand."

While she inspected the pouch, Crukas slipped the book from his vest, and Irmine snatched it.

"Irmine," Crukas said, "I *need* the book."

"Only a fool seeks premature death," she replied.

"All our lives depend on what I must do, which also requires the book," Crukas said. "I have to steal the mask from Scorpius and head on for the next relic."

Ebden shook his head. "For now, ya best keep yourself hidden."

"He's right," Irmine said.

"I can't simply hide and wait for them to leave Ravensdorf. There isn't time," Crukas said.

"Confronting them would be the most foolish move to make," Irmine said.

Ebden gave a slight nod. "I 'ave to agree."

Crukas sighed. "I've no choice."

"As long as you have breath, you have choices," she said.

Crukas gave her an intent stare. "I'm open for suggestions."

CHAPTER 26

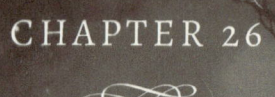

Sparrow walked to the table where Triggor McLuft and the others sat. She unrolled Crukas' wanted flyer and slapped it down on the table, interrupting their conversation. Their expressions offered no surprise. Instead, she was met by their sudden disdain, especially from Triggor and the kobold.

Her intended goal had been to look and sound tough so they didn't question her role as a bounty hunter. Without thinking her actions through, she forced herself to approach before she tarried too long and cowered from the opportunity. The three dwarves had not taken her seriously, so she hoped her charade settled better with a hardened attitude. Since she was dealing with other bounty hunters.

Like thieves, she reasoned, bounty hunters should hold and honor mutual respect for one another as comrades, but then she remembered thieves *never* trusted one another—not even within the same guild—and they often feuded in the same vein as bitter rivals. Bounty hunters, too, were highly competitive against other trackers and seldom teamed with anyone because they never wanted to split the pot.

Did bounty hunters hold the same distrust toward their competitors as thieves? She pondered whether the only true difference between a bounty hunter and a thief was on which side of the law and justice they stood. A gray line separated the two, which often made it difficult to see black or white, wrong or right. She realized she hadn't fully considered the aggressiveness of her approach but it was too late to back away.

"I'm looking for this thief." Sparrow spoke in a harsher, lower tone than she had with the dwarves and hoped she sounded tough. "Have any of you seen him?"

Triggor rose slightly in his chair. He grabbed the wrist of her hand that pressed the flyer to the table. In the same instance, he thrust the barrel of his revolver to her throat. His lips formed a snarl, and his breath reeked of stale cheese and sour mead when he spoke. "We're discussing business here, little one. Best you move on."

Sparrow held her breath, feeling the cold metal against her chin, which matched the fierce coldness in his eyes and voice. Triggor's gaze made her blood icy.

He was more than a bounty hunter, she now understood, and possibly worse than any criminal she'd ever captured for a reward. Her heart hammered against her sternum and the rhythm echoed in her ears. She fought not to show fear, but she was fairly certain her eyes already revealed her terror. Triggor's eyes gleamed with his suspected knowledge of her fear—he seemed to savor his dominance —but in the moment, she took advantage of his overconfidence.

The hardness of his gaze softened and a slight tinge of fear widened his eyes for less than a second. She pressed the tip of her dagger to his throat without him ever noticing her hand move.

"Be that as it may," she said, fighting tears and trying not to tremble or allow her voice to quiver. "We can either talk rationally, or else we both die right now."

Despite tears heating her eyes, and her voice unusually higher than normal, she waited.

Fasha had predicted her death should she pursue Crukas, but Sparrow didn't expect to die *before* she actually encountered and attempted to capture Crukas. If death was indeed her awaiting fate, she figured why not reach destiny ahead of schedule? She shrugged in

Fate's gaze, even though she didn't want to die. Fasha thrust her into this current situation without consent and possibly for folly. But this wasn't a dream or the result of her sleep deprivation.

It was real.

Far *too* real.

Triggor slowly released his fierce grip on her hand and waved his hand in a stopping motion. He gave a slight nod and lowered the revolver. He rebounded with a humored grin. "Aye. Quick reflexes. I like dat. You've earned ya-self a seat for a few minutes, as we decide the outcome of your intrusion."

Surprised, Sparrow slid her dagger into its sheath and took the last empty chair at the small round table. She sat quickly, before her shaking legs collapsed and garnered further humiliation. Only after seating herself did she notice the kobold's armed crossbow aimed at her. The one-eyed dwarf held his sharp, crude dagger. Neither took their attention off her, nor seemed ready to put their weapons away.

Triggor didn't wave his hand in surrender, as she'd assumed. He had motioned them to delay *killing* her. Her foolish confrontation with those around the table could've turned deadly. Being hardly able to stand her ground against Triggor, she'd disregarded the amount of actual danger she'd placed herself in.

Triggor's harsh eyes studied her. He seemed to be evaluating her strengths and weaknesses. She locked eyes with him, mustering all her willpower to not look away, especially with the kobold and dwarf training their weapons on her. She'd fallen into something as deadly as a serpent pit and wondered if she could ever become a cutthroat bounty hunter.

Halflings' nature was quite the opposite, notably affable, which was probably why those she encountered laughed at her assertion of being a bounty hunter. Few ever took her seriously. Even her scar didn't offer much clout.

Triggor turned up his tankard and emptied it with one big gulp. He set the tankard down hard and wiped froth from his beard with the back of his hand. He frowned and his eyes narrowed. "Bounty hunter, eh?"

Sparrow nodded.

The kobold emitted a sneaky chuckle.

"Never heard of ya," Triggor said. "And ya want to go after the most notorious thief in the lands? Name someone you've caught whose reputation *dat* I might know."

Sparrow thought for a few moments. Her captures had been less than a dozen, which she'd notched on her belt, but she never thought how those criminals were ranked throughout Aetheaon. One name came to mind who stood out above the rest. Apprehending him had nearly taken her life. "Locke Darby."

Triggor's eyebrows rose for a moment. Apparently, the news of her being the one to capture Locke caught Triggor off guard. "*You*? No jest?"

"It's true." She suppressed a smile. "Check with Crystal Ridge's magistrate. No doubt they recorded me turning him in and collecting the reward."

Triggor shook his head. "I find it hard to believe you captured dat fiend alone. He's three times your size, at least. Maybe five times. Who 'elped ya?"

"No one." She pointed at the scar above her left eye and smiled confidently. "I never implied the task was easy. He did *this*. Thus, the scar."

"Aye," Triggor said. "He was a known ruffian. Not a thief, like Crukas, mind you. Locke was a relentless thug. Crukas moves like a ghost, quieter than a slithering snake on glass and to my knowledge, he's never physically harmed a soul. Those of lesser fortunes consider Crukas a mythical hero, and I understand why. Locke, though, was a robber who enjoyed injuring or killing his victims before stealing their valuables. He was a dangerous menace. You're lucky he didn't stab through your eye into your brain and kill you. I went after him a couple times meself."

"Why didn't *you* capture him?" she asked, not realizing her tone was somewhat condescending.

The others at the table became more silent, and for a moment she wondered if she'd been too boastful. Their curious attention turned to Triggor. They seemed interested in his response.

"He was incredibly fast for his immense size," Triggor replied. "He swam better than a seal being chased by a shark. I can swim, but uh, leather armor weighs me down. I'd sink like a rock."

"You never answered my question," Sparrow said, a bit bolder but still wary of the kobold's crossbow trained on her. The one-eyed dwarf had sheathed his dagger and rested his folded hands on the table while listening intently.

"Dat being?" Triggor asked.

"Have you seen Crukas?"

The kobold snickered.

Sparrow cocked a brow and shot the kobold a fierce look, only to see it toying with the bow's trigger. "What's funny?"

Triggor laughed, as did the others. "The business we were discussing when you *foolishly* interrupted us, was how we could dismiss our competitive differences in order to capture Crukas and split the bounty."

Sparrow's shoulders slouched involuntarily. The stunning news deflated her optimism in capturing Crukas alone. She expected other bounty hunters to have contemplated going after Crukas from time to time and had given up. But now, the beginning of a joint effort was actually underway? She found the coincidence troubling.

Perhaps Fasha had not lied about Crukas being in Ravensdorf after all so she flung Sparrow into the mix, which didn't make any sense. Did this situation better Sparrow's chances to catch him, or did it increase the chances she'd die like Fasha predicted?

Except: *How badly did Fasha want her book returned?*

She looked at the kobold and then at Triggor. "Is the kobold your pet?"

"You idiotic girl. I'm no one's pet!" The kobold gave a fierce glare and bore his sharp teeth in an uneven sneer. Saliva dripped from the edges of his mouth. He stood at the edge of the table and seethed.

"Oh, you speak?" Sparrow gasped.

His cold, red eyes looked hungrily at her. "This kobold speaks and understands your words, yes."

Triggor roared with laughter. "Aye. His name's Gynx. He's a bounty hunter, too."

"My apologies," Sparrow said. "I never realized—"

Gynx halfway hissed. His serpent-like tongue flickered. "To use your brain? And folks say *my* kind are ignorant and unteachable."

The dwarves and the bard laughed.

"Again, I'm sorry." The heat of her embarrassment reddened her face. "I've never known a kobold to have learned the common language."

"Very few kobolds possess the ability," the elf bard said, holding her lyre. "Gynx is a rarity, though."

"Indeed," Gynx snickered.

Sparrow's brow furrowed. "Aren't you a bard?"

The elf was flattered. She smiled and gently nodded. "Why yes. Miss Strella's my name. Bard and part-time spy."

"Spy?" Sparrow asked.

"Yes. Taverns are filled with drunken patrons who are far more eager to reveal their secrets than they would elsewhere," Miss Strella said. "Afterwards, most don't remember what they said, or to whom they spoke, the following morning."

"But the lot of you aren't traveling companions, right?" Sparrow asked.

"Not until today," Triggor said.

"What brought you together?" Sparrow asked.

The one-eyed dwarf rolled his eye and shook his head. "Are ya seriously so daft, lass? Did ya not hear Triggor? The *gold*. The *reward*."

Triggor nodded. "Orgem's right. Dat's the lure, isn't it? Gold? Isn't it what brought ya to the table?"

"Partly," she replied.

"Partly?" Triggor gave her a shrewd stare. "If not for the gold, I'd wager ya 'ave a score of sorts to settle with him, eh?"

Sparrow sighed. "In a manner of speaking."

"Score?" Gynx said. "The biggest score isn't necessarily the reward for Crukas."

"What do you mean?" Sparrow asked.

"Legend tells that Crukas has stockpiled treasures beyond one's wildest imagination," Gynx said. "That's more wealth than we could spend in a hundred years without ever touching the reward."

Orgem and Triggor chuckled.

Sparrow never considered what would become of the stolen jewelry and other valuables Crukas stashed once he was captured and taken into custody. "He'd ever give up the location of his loot."

Gynx set his crossbow on the table and slid a wicked, double-edged dagger from its sheath. "Oh, there are ways to *make* anyone talk. His wanted flyer states *dead* or alive. It fails to state whether or not all his appendages still need to be attached." He licked the dried blood on the side of the blade and winked.

Chills reverberated down her spine. Even Triggor, Orgem, and Miss Strella appeared uneasy by the kobold's threat. She couldn't discern whether the kobold was part rat or full reptilian, or something in between. This one was coldblooded with a colder heart to boot, and it's mentality leaned toward a reptilian's frame of mind.

"True," Sparrow said, "but he can't be interrogated until he's captured."

Triggor nodded. "Yes. Which is why we joined together. To compare notes. But our gathering together today was secretive. How'd you 'appen to find us or know dat we were here?"

Sparrow wasn't certain how to respond. The truth behind her arrival was far from believable should she attempt to explain it. "Coincidence, I suppose. I guess you could say I was dropped at the door and ventured inside the tavern out of curiosity."

"You believe Crukas to be 'ere, eh?" Triggor said. "Otherwise, you'd not be in Ravensdorf. It's far off the beaten path."

"I've pursued Crukas for a long while," she replied. "Every time I get close to finding him, he slips away, still unseen."

Miss Strella nodded. "Yes, which is why *most* give up the hunt. Crukas toys with those trying to gain his reward."

"Not this time," Gynx said.

Sparrow met Gynx's cold gaze. "I vowed to find him, but inflicting unnecessary torture isn't part of my plan."

"Leave that to me, sweetie," Gynx said. "Perhaps Crukas would freely tell us where his hoard is without losing a finger, hand, or foot, huh? I might even forget the reward and allow him total freedom for the right price."

"You'd let him go for his treasure?" Her brow rose.

A sly grin curled on Gynx's lips. "Only to capture him later after he's had time to replace his losses."

"You're worse than a thief," Sparrow said.

"Ah, ya don't know the half of it," Gynx replied.

Triggor motioned the barmaid for another set of rounds and then eyed Sparrow. "Since you've been tracking Crukas and wound up 'ere, I suppose our hunch was correct? What clued you ta this location?"

"Chance? How about the rest of you?" Sparrow asked.

"Odd circumstances, if you want the truth," Triggor said.

"How so?"

Triggor ran a hand down his graying beard. "After washing ashore in Corvus Bay, south of Crow's Point, I planned to make me way to Bridgebarrow, but halfway there, me compass must've messed up from the salt water. It pointed me the wrong direction, and I wound up 'ere."

"Had you all prearranged to meet?" Sparrow asked.

Gynx snorted and shook his head. "I met Orgem near the swamps. Both of us were trying to find the mystical cavern where loads of aquamarines could be mined, if only someone discovered its actual whereabouts."

"We came up empty," Orgem said. "But at a tavern near the swamps, I heard Miss Strella's song about Crukas and his accumulated treasures. I tried to talk to her after her songs, to find out how much of the stories were true and what might be fabricated. But someone whisked her away, and I was too tipsy to go after her. She'd mentioned traveling to Ravensdorf, so I made me way here."

Sparrow frowned. "So none of you actually know if he's here or not?"

Triggor shrugged his broad shoulders. "Thus why we're making plans. Seems fate lead us together, so why waste the opportunity in sharing what we know?"

"No argument with that," she replied. "So who's taking the lead?"

Silence hung over the table. They all eyed one another about the question and suspiciously, no one seemed eager to take the command. Possibly because immediate arguments might ensue about why one deserved to be in charge rather than another. Such arguments could quickly escalate into bitter fighting, but she'd bet all wanted to give the orders to the rest. The gleam in Gynx's eyes indicated he was less trustworthy and might be scheming in how to steal all the loot for himself, even if it meant killing the other bounty hunters.

While they had inadvertently vowed to work together, her gut told her they would go to the extreme in holding back the most pertinent information for themselves in hopes of capturing Crukas alone. They could no more trust one another than a band of thieves not short-changing companions when divvying up their shares.

Triggor sighed. "We've chosen to make group decisions and keep one another informed. While Crukas might find ease in escaping one impetuous bounty hunter, he'll 'ave a harder time outsmarting four—uh, five, if ya join us—bounty hunters."

"So that's an invite?" she asked.

"Aye, it is," Triggor said. "Provided you share your knowledge of Crukas with us as well."

Sparrow smiled and nodded. "Happy to oblige."

CHAPTER 27

*E*bden returned to the Mute Changeling and rejoined Bramnir and Adgus. Keeping a wary eye on Triggor's table, he sat with his brothers.

"Anything happen while I was out?" Ebden asked.

Bramnir shook his head. "No."

"Was Crukas there?" Adgus asked.

Ebden nodded.

Bramnir smiled. "Did you relay the message?"

"Aye," Ebden said.

"And?" Adgus asked.

"He wants me to tell them where he is," Ebden whispered without suppressing a growing smile. "Well, where he's *going* to be."

Bramnir's brow rose. "What? He's a bloody fool!"

Adgus shook his head with disgust. "I knew we'd never get the stout."

Ebden grinned. "No. All's good, brothers. He's proposed a plan."

"Dat being?" Bramnir asked.

"His grand escape."

"Escape?" Adgus' expression soured. "*Preposterous* notion. There are five of 'em and he's one man, a scrawny one at dat."

"Perhaps we should aid him?" Bramnir said.

Ebden shook his head. "No. He doesn't want us to interfere and to act like we've never met him."

"I bet he does," Adgus grumbled. "Nice way to stiff us."

"On the contrary, brother." Ebden unfolded a piece of parchment he'd hidden in his strong hand.

Adgus eyed the paper suspiciously. "What's dat?"

"Our agreed trade for the stout with the barkeep." Ebden smiled and pointed at the bottom of the paper. "Crukas put his wax seal on it."

"And the book?" Bramnir asked.

"Irmine took it."

"Bah!" Adgus shook his head. "I should've been the one to tell Crukas. Ya were swindled."

Ebden sighed. "Have some faith, brothers."

"Ah," Adgus sighed. "I suppose the priestess persuaded you to see things *her* way?"

Bramnir clasped Adgus' shoulder. "I 'appen to believe Crukas is on the up and up."

"Nah!" Adgus said. "Not you, too."

Bramnir chuckled. "Beneath Crukas' seal, he's sworn to abide by the agreement. Ya see, Irmine has arranged particular runes in the order dat if Crukas breaks the oath, his immediate location will be known throughout Aetheaon at all times. He could never thieve nor could he ever hide where the bounty hunters won't know where he is. He'd never renege on this. So, Ebden, what's the plan?"

"He gave me no details," Ebden replied. "Only where they were to find him."

Bramnir groomed his beard with his fingers. "I still say we 'elp him, but if he insists otherwise, we best honor it. At least, for now."

Adgus held the sealed parchment between his fingers and stared at it. "This best be valid."

Ebden rose from his seat. "I'll inform them where Crukas plans to be. After they leave, we can approach the barkeep."

Adgus grumbled. "Aye. Get it over with."

~

EBDEN APPROACHED the table where Sparrow sat. She appeared somewhat uneasy when she noticed him walking to her. Ebden met the hardened gazes of Triggor and Gynx but offered a nod and a slight smile to let them know his approach was not hostile nor intrusive.

"Sparrow?" Ebden said.

"Yes?" She adjusted in her seat uncomfortably.

"Ya asked earlier if we'd seen dat man on the wanted poster," he said.

Sparrow nodded and eagerness widened her eyes. "Yes. That's right."

"When I stepped outside to check our burros, I'm quite certain I saw him."

Triggor straightened against the back of his chair. Gynx flicked his tongue and his facial features revealed sudden, keen interest.

"What was he doing?" Sparrow asked. "Is he coming inside the tavern?"

"No," Ebden shook his head. "I think not. He was walking down dat street."

"Alone?" Triggor asked.

"No. He had a companion."

"Who?" Sparrow asked.

Ebden frowned and shrugged. "How should I know? Until you showed the flyer, I wouldn't 'ave recognized the thief."

"Of course," Sparrow said softly.

Triggor eyed Ebden sternly. "Go on. What were they doing?"

Ebden said, "He and this man were talking. I overhead Crukas mention he was going to the Remholdt Supplies building at the edge of town."

Miss Strella frowned. "That place has been abandoned for years."

Gynx snickered and rubbed his hands together. "What better place to hide and store loot?"

"Dat be true," Triggor said.

Sparrow smiled. "Thank you for the information."

Ebden returned the smile. "Not a problem. Good luck with your endeavors."

Ebden nodded to those seated at the table and turned away. He returned to his brothers. He grinned wider once he was certain they couldn't see his face.

Seating himself, he winked at Bramnir and Adgus.

"They fell for it, aye?" Bramnir asked.

Ebden shrugged slightly. "Seems so."

"Once they leave," Adgus said, holding the parchment with Crukas' seal. "We take this and see if it's redeemable. If not—"

"Have faith, brother," Bramnir said.

"Perhaps," Ebden said, "we should load the barrels of stout and be on our way. We can open them elsewhere."

Bramnir frowned. "Ya think things are going to get nasty?"

"Not sure exactly what Crukas intends to do, but whatever it is, we'd best hope Triggor and that kobold don't somehow know we set 'em up," Ebden said.

"Aye." Adgus set a hardened gaze on Triggor. "Triggor's reputation lies more criminal than on the side of virtue."

Ebden waved the barmaid for another tankard. While he was glad Irmine had taken Crukas' book and his pouch, he couldn't shake the dark feeling that settled over him on his way to warn Crukas. Behind the bar, a strange shadow slinked along the wall. He shivered.

Bramnir said, "You okay, Ebden?"

Ebden flinched. "What? Yeah. I'm fine. Why?"

"You drifted into a trance," Adgus said.

"I did?"

"Aye," Bramnir said.

Ebden's uneasiness sent a chill down his spine. "I don't know. I've been uncomfortable since the Wierwens attacked us."

"Rightly so," Adgus said. "If not for Irmine, I'd be dead or worse, I'd have become one of 'em."

"Or even worse," Bramnir said. "I'd have had to lop off your head."

Shocked, Adgus looked at his brother. "What? You'd have done dat?"

"I'd have no other choice, brother. You'd have done the same if the situation was reversed?"

"Bloody right!" Adgus said with a sly smile. "And with pleasure!"

"Ya wouldn't miss this ol' face of mine?"

"Ah, it'd haunt me in me dreams. But thanks to Irmine, we didn't 'ave to make such choices."

"Don't forget," Bramnir whispered. "You'd have not found Irmine if not for Crukas."

"Bah!" Adgus said, waving his hand. "I wouldn't have been attacked, if not for him, either."

Ebden shook his head. Adgus always weighed the negative greater than the positive, but this time, he agreed. Crukas was the only reason they traveled to Ravensdorf. The book … something dark and sinister was associated with it. Crukas had warned Ebden not to take it and allow him to keep it on his person. What secret had Crukas kept to himself? Whatever it was, Ebden held an uneasy feeling he'd soon discover the answer and regret ever having touched the book. From the moment Ebden held the tome, a dark aura attached to his skin like sticky tar clung to flesh. This aura coated him. Nothing he could think of would detach it and that troubled him most of all.

CHAPTER 28

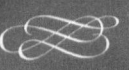

*S*parrow's eager eyes brightened. She grinned after Ebden left the table. "What's the plan since we know where Crukas is going?"

Triggor's brow leveled and his hardened gaze met Sparrow's. "And what's dat all about, eh?"

"What?"

"He *'appens* to give you information about Crukas?" Triggor asked. "How'd he know ya were looking for him?"

Sparrow's eyes narrowed. She nodded at the table where Ebden was seated. "Because I asked if they'd seen him after I came inside, just like I did you. Their table's the only one between this table and the door."

"Seems too coincidental," Gynx said. She'd have guessed his expression to be that of distrust, but his skeptical gaze appeared no different than earlier. But she could discern a difference when he grew angry. His fury couldn't be mistaken.

"I agree," Triggor said.

"Perhaps," Gynx said, "we should investigate the warehouse without her?"

Their mistrust cut deep and Sparrow almost wanted to cry. She fought the urge, swallowed hard, and reminded herself she must at least *appear* as cold and calculated as they actually were. "Look, I don't *know* those dwarves. I simply showed them the wanted poster and asked if they'd seen them. I offered a finder's fee should they provide any information, which helped me capture Crukas."

"Did ya now?" Triggor frowned. "Dat's on you."

"Of course," Sparrow said. "The reward isn't the importance of me pursuing and arresting Crukas."

"As you've said," Triggor said.

Gynx snarled. "Any fee to those dwarves comes from *your* share. However, if Crukas stashed loot in the old warehouse, you don't get a cut."

"Again," Sparrow sighed. "I've no desire for those things you've described. I never even considered his possible amassed hoard, provide he has one at all. Besides, at my size, how likely would I be to transport a large amount of treasure without being robbed and killed?"

Orgem nodded and seemed amused by the thought. He looked at Triggor. "She makes a valid point."

Triggor huffed. His eyes indicated deep thought, as he possibly weighed the situation. "Dat she does, I suppose. Do you agree to the terms Gynx established? You must pay the full amount of the finder's fee and take nothing of Crukas' cache should we find it?"

"Yes, of course," Sparrow said.

Miss Strella said, "The Remholdt Supply Warehouse has been in ruin well before I ever set foot in Ravensdorf more than a decade ago."

"Why's dat?" Triggor asked.

Miss Strella shrugged slightly. "Most of the village fled after Scorpius established his reign over the area."

"Pigs' mire!" Triggor said. "He's a mage, not a ruler."

Miss Strella shushed him.

Triggor leveled a glare that caused Miss Strella to visibly shudder. Sparrow feared to have him ever look at her in such a manner.

Miss Strella raised her hand delicately and with a gentle smile, she whispered, "Perhaps you should ask the remaining folks in Ravensdorf their views of Scorpius to give you a better perspective. Some are devoted to him or rather, *spellbound* by his power. Such spies could make us his target. I'm sure you'll discover a ruler doesn't need a crown or throne. His evil dominion and the threat of his power has placed everyone under his thumb."

"*Dat*, I won't argue," Triggor said.

Miss Strella placed her hands on her lyre, adjusting her fingers to play. "Perhaps, I could better explain in song?"

Orgem winced and shook his head. "No, lass, it's best ya don't."

Miss Strella's slight smile and the obvious enthusiasm she possessed only seconds before, withered. She set the lyre across her lap and sighed. "My apologies. I never thought my singing repulsed anyone."

"Oh, no. No." Orgem slightly shook his head. "You've a beautiful voice, sweeter than honey. But I've a roaring headache worse than the thundering rocks bashing me skull when a mine caves in."

Gynx snickered. "Don't you *hate* when that happens?"

"You've experienced it, too?"

With a sly smile, Gynx revealed a short stick of dynamite from his shoulder pouch. "No. Usually, *I'm* the cause."

"You weren't the reason Gomdurm Mine collapsed, were you?" Orgem said angrily, pointing a stern, stubby finger. "I lie under a pile of stone a day or more. Dat blast cost me this eye."

Gynx tucked the stick out of sight and chuckled. "No. Not my doing."

"Cause if ya did—"

"I'd've eagerly claimed the collapse if I had, Orgem. That being said, it could've been one of my *lesser* kin."

Orgem's thick nose crinkled from his obvious disdain for losing his eye.

Sparrow wondered how these bounty hunters could remain affable long enough to aid one another in capturing Crukas. They seemed too divided and headstrong to meet a mutual cause.

Triggor cleared his throat. "Enough nonsense. Let's set everything else aside for now. If the dwarf was honest in reporting his sighting of

Crukas to Sparrow, we're wasting precious time. Seldom is Crukas seen in the open, especially during the day. My guess is, he's in a hurry, a bit careless, so if we want to nab 'em, now's our best opportunity."

Orgem nodded. "Agreed."

Miss Strella set her lyre on the table. "Yes."

"How 'bout you, Sparrow?" Triggor asked. "You in?"

Sparrow smiled with relief to be included. "Of course. Let's go."

"Wait." Triggor glanced at Miss Strella. "This abandoned warehouse. Anything we should know? Possible dangers? Perhaps it's a hideout for a thief guild?"

"Crukas doesn't belong to a guild," Sparrow said.

"No?" Triggor's brow furrowed.

Sparrow shook her head.

Miss Strella said, "The last time I passed the building, the doors and windows are boarded. The entire structure is covered with vines and bramble. The building stands several stories high. I imagine getting inside might not be too difficult, but the soundness of the structure could be weakened by rot and termites. So, the floors and stairs could give way under our weight. We can determine better judgment once we get there."

"Aye," Triggor said. "Let's go make our assessment."

After Triggor and the others stood and walked away from the table, she followed. She didn't like the idea of having Gynx behind her since he'd seemed eager to shoot her with his crossbow and quite reluctant to remove his finger from the trigger. She liked even less the thought of his intimidating dagger plunging into her back while she walked.

Triggor opened the tavern door, and Sparrow made a causal glance at the three dwarves in passing. They offered slight nods with little emotion. She nodded in return with a smile of gratitude for Ebden's information. She'd hoped to see an eagerness in their eyes that she'd succeed and be able to pay them a great portion of her cut. But since she was in the company of a kobold, she assumed they held little faith she'd succeed.

She wondered the same.

The kobold seemed to detest the entire group and any race, including his own. If Crukas truly was at the Remholdt warehouse, her death most likely would be a bolt through the heart from Gynx, and she'd be wise to keep a wary eye on the kobold. Triggor was possibly thinking the same.

Sparrow walked through the door without hesitation. On the street, she thought again about her fate and how fragile life was. If Fasha truly believed her prediction, why'd she purposely transport Sparrow to Ravensdorf and put her into this oddly mixed band of bounty hunters? Sparrow understood her life was on the line, and should she back out now, Gynx and Triggor would most likely kill her, thinking she was setting them up. However, Sparrow knew she was the one being set up. Not by the dwarves, but by Fasha. Rather than run or back down, she decided to face destiny, even though she might not see the following sunrise.

CHAPTER 29

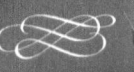

Bramnir sighed after the door closed behind Sparrow. "I still believe we should help Crukas with his scheme."

Ebden shook his head. "No. He explicitly warned us not to intervene. He doesn't want us hurt or killed."

"Hurt, eh?" Adgus said. "Damn near lost me life already."

"He holds genuine sorrow for dat, too," Ebden said.

"Ah, does he now?" Adgus frowned. "Since you're chums now, eh?"

Ebden shrugged. "He's a thief but his actions are sincere, brother. He showed true remorse."

"I 'ave to agree, Adgus," Bramnir said. "Crukas went to great lengths to ensure Irmine healed you. She didn't take your attack as seriously, but he persuaded her otherwise. Why hold such negative feelings toward him?"

Adgus held up the parchment with Crukas' seal. "If Devin the barkeep honors this, I'll consider a twist in me attitude toward Crukas."

Bramnir nodded. "Fair enough. Let's approach him and present it."

Bramnir placed a gold coin on the table to pay for their drinks with plenty left over for a hefty tip.

Devin looked perplexed and concerned when the three dwarves stepped to the bar.

"How might I help you?" Devin's brow furrowed, and he swallowed hard. "Was everything satisfactory?"

Adgus slapped the parchment on the bar. "We need this debt be paid."

Bramnir cocked a brow and looked at Adgus. "Straight to da point, eh, brother?"

"Business has no delay. At least *not* in this case," Adgus replied.

After Adgus removed his thick hand and left the paper with Crukas' seal up, Devin glanced nervously around the bar, slid the paper quickly to himself, and held it out of sight from the patrons and the barmaids. The paper crinkled as Devin unfolded it and read Crukas' note.

With a concerned expression, Devin leaned forward and whispered, "Crukas is in Ravensdorf?"

"Aye," Bramnir said softly.

Devin shook his head, suddenly pale, and more apprehensive than moments before.

"Can you honor dat?" Adgus said.

"Yes." Devin's voice shook. "Yes. But Crukas is in real danger. Those who left that table are bounty hunters."

"Aye," Bramnir said. "We know. We sent warning to him about them being here."

Devin sighed with obvious relief. "It's good you warned him, but unless he gets out of Ravensdorf quickly, I fear his demise falls today."

Adgus cleared his throat. "So you'll honor the note?"

Bramnir frowned at Adgus.

"Yes, of course. If you have a wagon, pull around to the back alley door, and we'll get these loaded for you."

"Just like dat?" Adgus said.

Devin nodded and cast a wary glance at the door. "Best hurry though. In case those bounty hunters return."

Bramnir motioned Ebden by nodding toward the door. Ebden

understood and left to get the wagon. In what might become a hostile situation, it was best to speak less and not give direct names.

ADGUS LEANED AGAINST THE BAR, met Devin's gaze, and whispered, "Why worry about a thief's welfare? And why obligate yourself to fulfill such a costly exchange without nothing in return?"

"It's a brother's duty to protect his own, is it not?" Devin asked. "By the similar runes on your weapons and the markings on your armor, you three must be brothers."

Adgus smiled. "Aye, we are. Good eye."

"So you're Crukas' brother?" Bramnir asked softly.

"Yes," Devin said. "Well, I'm his blood brother by pact, not birth. Almost the same age, we both grew up as homeless orphans in Hoff-nung. *I* was homeless, I should say, and starving. He stole food so I could eat. He had no reason to, since he was in a thief guild, which was better than the living conditions in an orphanage. His only oblig-ation at the time was to his guild master and no one else. He fed me anyway, and we became fast friends. You might say, out of my neces-sity. In return for his hospitality, I served as his watch-keeper to warn him when someone was coming. This helped him escape houses and stores whenever a guard or owner might otherwise have found him. Because he kept me fed and clothed, I kept him from being captured on the streets. We swore an oath in blood to always aid one another."

Adgus kept his silence and was surprised by the information. His chin suddenly quivered and his eyes moistened, shattering his former hardened resolve.

"Follow me to the back," Devin said.

Devin led them through a narrow hallway to the storeroom, and he unbolted the metal lock bar fastened to the door. "How is it you know Crukas, and why'd he pay his debt in stout? It's rare he'd ever place himself into a position where he'd compensate anyone. You realize the cost of these barrels?"

"Aye. We gave 'em a ride from Salem," Bramnir said.

Devin frowned with confusion. "That's all?"

Adgus cleared his throat. "All? It was a ride through Hell! A miracle we survived. Blasted Wierwens."

Devin nodded. "Those haunted forests have deadly consequences, I agree. Fewer travelers take the route through the Gloomy Forest. Most bypass it altogether. You're lucky to be alive."

Adgus grumbled. "Don't I know it."

"Did Crukas indicate his reason for coming to Ravensdorf?" Devin asked. "He's not visited me. At least, not yet."

Bramnir shook his head. "No. He never explained his reason. All he indicated was dat it's urgent."

"Hmm," Devin said, appearing quite troubled. He placed his hands on the top of a dark barrel of ale and tilted it slightly to the side on its rim. With careful maneuvering, he rolled it away from the wall. "This is Spider Haven's Stout. One of the rarest, finest stouts you'll ever drink."

Adgus frowned. "Never heard of it."

Devin smiled. "And you'll probably never hear or see another barrel."

"Why's dat?" Bramnir asked.

"The key ingredient is no longer attainable," Devin replied.

"How so?" Adgus asked.

"Goblins raided the underground distillery in Spider Haven, along with the rare crops that grew deep inside the caverns," Devin said.

Shocked, Adgus said, "Why then would you give us this?"

"Crukas insisted."

"On the parchment?" Adgus said.

"Yes," Devin said with a nod.

"I saw no mention—"

Devin smiled. "He only owns three barrels of stout. That one and two not so rare stouts, which is troubling, to say the least."

Bramnir frowned. "In what way?"

"Two reasons," Devin said. "One, since he hasn't visited me, he's about to do something he wants me to have no knowledge of, and two, it's a task that might cost him his life. Otherwise, he'd not part with the barrel. Something of great importance has brought Crukas to Ravensdorf, but it's a villa with little value to offer."

Adgus' heart sank. He should've been exuberant to have a stout he'd never tasted or known about, but the value of such was diminished by Devin's information. He'd sorely misjudged Crukas. For a thief, which was a despicable trade, Crukas was true to his word. "We can't accept the Spider Haven Stout."

Bramnir's brow rose and his mouth gaped. "What?"

Devin said, "He's freely given it to you."

Adgus shook his head. "No. We'll take the other two, but keep this for him."

Devin sighed. "Are you sure?"

"Quite."

"It's likely whatever Crukas is set out to do will cost him his life—"

"No," Adgus said. "He'll have need of it at a later date. I'm certain. And if not, you, as his brother, should keep it."

Devin offered a grim smile. "As you wish."

Devin opened the door to the alley. Ebden slowed the wagon and set the brake beside the loading dock along the rear doorway. Within a few minutes, the two barrels of stout were placed on the wagon bed.

"Thanks for your help," Bramnir said.

Devin nodded. "Should you see Crukas, give him my regards, and tell him to be careful."

"Aye," Adgus said. "We shall."

Devin turned and went inside the tavern. He shut and barred the door.

"A change of heart, brother?" Bramnir asked.

"Aye," Adgus said, softly.

Ebden frowned. "About what exactly?"

Bramnir grinned and groomed his thick beard. "Adgus turned down the most expensive, rare stout known in Aetheaon."

"*What?*" Ebden asked.

Adgus waved them off. "Bah! Considering Crukas' word is

honorary and he was more than willing to exceed his debt, taking dat barrel would've made *us* the thieves. No wagon ride, despite the obvious peril we encountered, should be so costly. Let's go."

CHAPTER 30

The Remholdt Supply Warehouse looked far worse than simply being abandoned from Sparrow's perspective. The building and surrounding landscape had fallen victim to a dark curse. Whether before the owner and workers left the property or after their departure, she didn't know. For all they knew, the workers' corpses might remain inside.

Mushrooms—with stems wider than massive oaks and towering above the height of the tallest tree—surrounded the building's perimeter like a towering forest. Their oversized, umbrella-like caps blocked the sun's rays. Thick vines and bramble covered the walls and tightly wrapped across the roof and meshed together like interlocked fingers.

Sparrow marveled. "I've never seen monstrous mushrooms before."

Miss Strella swallowed hard. She didn't attempt to hide her nervousness. "This place has been touched by the dark Fae's magic."

"Seems to be." Sparrow nodded. If true, it made entering the rundown building even more intimidating. But if Crukas had entered the warehouse, he must have a good reason. She wondered if Crukas stashed some of his treasures inside. He would choose an unbecoming, foreboding place.

Triggor frowned and shook his head. "Were it not for the clinging vines and thorny bramble knitted across the walls and roof, this building would've collapsed long ago."

"And yet, it stands," Miss Strella whispered.

Gynx made a couple of ticking sounds with his tongue. "I'd almost wager this place a lost cause, except—"

"Except for what?" Triggor asked.

A sly smile curled Gynx's lips. "I can't think of a better place for a thief to stash his loot. Clearly, no one's going to set foot inside."

Triggor laughed. "No one else but us! We'll have to cut through some vines to find the doors. Each of us needs to find a separate entrance to enter. Once inside, we work our way to meet one another at the center."

"You want us to separate?" Miss Strella's complexion paled several shades lighter. "Surely you jest?"

"No," Triggor said. "The best way to prevent Crukas from slipping past us is to corner him."

"Provided he's even in there," Orgem said. "I see no recent openings or even a footprint or path through the moss and bramble."

"He's a thief," Gynx said. "He's *not* going to leave a trail if he can prevent it. Besides, he probably has a secret entrance no one else can see."

Strella looked around with wide eyes. "Perhaps we should search for the secret door instead of wandering through these thorns and vines?"

"Where's the fun in that?" Gynx said.

Stella ran her hands down her blouse to straighten out the wrinkles. "I'm ... I'm not quite dressed for—"

The kobold laughed. "No one's asking you to stay. You can leave and our shares will increase. If you've not the stomach for pain and worry over your garments—"

Orgem placed a gentle hand on Strella's arm. "You can buy a dozen fine outfits or more after we catch Crukas."

"Provided he's even in here," Strella said. "Look at the mess we have to cut our way through."

Sparrow felt like a tiny insect compared to the height of the warehouse. "The building's at least four stories high."

"Aye," Triggor said. "Which is why we start at the cellar and work our way upward. But, dat means we can't leave any side of the place open for his escape."

When none of the others protested his proposal, Sparrow understood Triggor was in charge of their band. She said, "Have you considered traps? If Crukas has his cache here, he wouldn't leave it without some sort of protective means to prevent others from stealing it."

Gynx chuckled. "Thieves stealing from thieves. Where's the crime in that?"

"I suppose it depends on which side of the law one is on?" Sparrow said. "For a bounty hunter to savor the hope of stealing from a thief—"

Gynx hissed and pulled his grisly dagger. His hollow, almost soulless, eyes gleamed an odd, reddish glow. "I've gutted people for lesser insults, little one."

"It wasn't meant as an insult." She stepped back. "I stated a fact. If your interest is more in obtaining stolen goods than arresting the thief who stole them, you're no better than he."

"You've no stomach for this task." Gynx sneered. "Go back to where you came."

Frustrated, Sparrow slid her hand on the hilt of her dagger. "I came to arrest Crukas, and that's what I plan to do."

Gynx lunged for Sparrow, but Triggor punched Gynx in the side of the head, and sent the kobold to the ground. Gynx lost his grip on the dagger and it landed a couple of feet away. Gynx wiped blood from his creepy mouth and spat. "Strong strike, dwarf. But—"

Triggor pulled his revolver and shook his head. "No, Gynx. You reach for dat crossbow of yours and I'll end ya right 'ere. I'd rather not do dat, as you're an exception to your kind, but we came together as a group and dammit, I'll 'ave no squabbling amongst us. We do the job, split the loot, and go our separate ways. Is dat clear?"

Anger flared in Gynx's eyes. His jaw tightened. His primal urge to attack Triggor in spite of Triggor's aimed revolver was the instinctual rage known to the specific nature of kobolds. An ordinary kobold wouldn't have hesitated to calculate the risk, but after a few seconds of staring at the revolver, Gynx huffed and nodded. Perhaps his intellect kept his rage in check, at least for now. Sparrow feared, though, Gynx would seek revenge whenever Triggor lowered his guard.

"You can split the loot," Sparrow said. "As long as I get to arrest Crukas."

"See?' Gynx picked up his dagger and tucking it into its sheath. "She wants only the reward!"

"No," Sparrow said. "I want to ensure he's taken to the magistrate properly and without any *unnecessary* harm."

Triggor frowned. "No. As a group, we arrest Crukas, and together we turn him in. Dat way, no one runs off solely with the reward. Now, let's separate and find our way inside the warehouse. I'll take the south side."

Gynx's eyes narrowed. "She shouldn't be involved at all."

Feeling dejected, Sparrow said, "Fine. I'll remain outside, if that's your wish, but know this, should I capture Crukas while you're all inside, I leave with him, alone."

Gynx drew his dagger, bore his jagged teeth, and faced her. "On second thought, *you* stick with me. We go in together and you never leave my sight. Should you attempt to lose me, don't think I won't gut you."

Sparrow eyed the dagger. The nasty looking blade caused her to shiver, and the brief glance into his evil gaze struck her heart with renewed fear. She thought of Fasha and no longer seemed worried that she'd die at Crukas' hand. Most likely, her greatest chance for death resided in the hand of a demented, though intelligent, kobold.

Gynx pointed the dagger in the direction of the abandoned supply house. She nodded and reluctantly walked past him with the uneasiness of his drawn blade aimed at her spine. As much as she wished to capture Crukas, she'd be much happier should he not be inside the building. Because if he were inside, it was less likely Gynx would allow her to live. Either way, she didn't foresee a way she might survive. Gynx could kill her the moment they entered the door and discard her corpse without the others knowing and lay blame on some sort of accident.

Sparrow took a deep breath, grabbed the snaky vines and bramble, and pulled, hoping to find a window or door. While she tugged the vines, Gynx sliced through them with his dagger. The cuts were quick and wet-sounding, almost like a blade slicing through flesh. She continued pulling vines while he cut them, and her life never seemed bleaker.

CHAPTER 31

With a moment of luck—good or bad, Sparrow wasn't sure—she pulled aside a weaved curtain of vines to find an old wooden door. She sighed with a bit of relief. At least she could stop yanking more vines, most of which resembled snakes. Since the old warehouse appeared cursed, she feared the Dark Fae might've actually charmed venomous serpents into blending amongst the vines as deterrents and guardians. Each time a sharp bramble thorn stuck her, she feared she'd been bitten.

"We found a way inside," she said. She intentionally used *we* so not to boast but to persuade Gynx into believing she and he were part of a team.

Gynx chuckled. His sly grin curled his oddly shaped mouth and revealed his bloody teeth. His upper lip was swollen. Triggor had punched him hard. "Ah, yes! Go on, open the door."

"Perhaps you should have the honor?" she said.

"No, I insist." He frowned shrewdly. "Lasses, first."

Before she could argue, his dagger's sharp tip pressed against her back. Should this supply house be where Crukas hid his loot, all entrances should have armed traps or disfiguring spells to protect his accumulated wealth. Gynx seemed aware of the risk as much as she, but he wasn't about to chance his own injury or death. Instead, he chose to force her to open the door.

"Well?" Gynx said. "Time's slipping away. Go on."

Sparrow placed her hand on the rusted doorknob and attempted to turn it. "Either it's locked or too rusted to turn."

"Open it!" He pressed the dagger's tip harder. "If you don't, I'll use your tender body for a battering ram and break the door down myself."

The thought amused her more than frightened her. "Me? As a battering ram? I've not enough weight to put a dent—"

Gynx shrugged. "Perhaps not, but the results would be fun to see. Now, open the door."

Sparrow was no longer amused and raised her hands in surrender. "Give me a second, okay?"

She slid her left hand behind her belt and brought out a small pouch, which contained her best lock picks. Gynx lowered his blade. She took a pick and stuck it inside the door's lock.

"Interesting," Gynx said softly.

"What?" Sparrow asked without looking away from the lock.

"You accused us of being thieves. Yet, you've an interesting skill set, known mostly to thieves."

"Because I'm a *reformed* thief," she replied.

Gynx laughed. "No one's truly reformed. The lust and thrill are always in our minds and beg to be fulfilled."

Sparrow shrugged. "Perhaps, but I'm not willing to maim and torture someone for their loot, though."

"You only say that because you've never done it. But, once you discover the power of taking life or its vital source, the *blood*, you'll crave the next opportunity even more than the last."

Sparrow maneuvered the pick inside the lock, held it in place, and then placed a second pick inside with the first. "That's where you and I differ, Gynx. I'll never find myself in a situation where I'd agonize another for any reason."

Gynx leaned forward and whispered, "Never tempt fate, lass. In this business, you'll face all sorts of individuals who'll make you reconsider what you *won't* do."

Tempt fate? She'd been thrust directly in Fate's path.

"Individuals like you?" she asked. The lock clicked. She turned the knob.

"*Worse* than me," he replied. "But given the right circumstances, yes, I could change your outlook."

You already have.

He was the worst tyrant she'd met. If worse existed, she never wished to encounter them. The more she learned about him, the more she wondered why he didn't have a reward for his head. He probably had accumulated numerous enemies over the years.

"Go on," Gynx said. "Open the door."

Sparrow swallowed hard and held her breath. She pushed the door slightly inward, and Gynx stepped causally behind her. Should a bolt or arrow disengage from a wall trap on the other side of the door, she stood as his shield. It didn't mean he was totally safe from injury or death. A sharp arrow could pierce straight through her and strike him since she was small and wore modest armor.

Some traps released a rapid succession of bolts or arrows, which were meant to drop the first person and take out the next few should a party stand at the threshold. Since Gynx was approximately her height, he was less likely to take a shot to the head, which she halfway regretted. In their group, she trusted him the least.

As the gap of the door widened, old stagnant air wafted outside. Dust and specks of dry sawdust swirled and a slight breeze sucked the stale air outward. Even though the door had not been opened for years, the smell of old barley and dusty wool permeated the atmosphere. The place was dry, lifeless. No mice or rats scurried away from or out the doorway.

The hinges creaked. She paused for a moment before braving her first step across the threshold. No traps were sprung, much to her satisfaction.

"I think it's safe," Sparrow whispered.

Gynx shoved her through the door, into the darkened cellar, and almost caused her to lose footing. Were she not a halfling, she'd have struck her head on the low joints supporting the floor above. The cellar was not height friendly, but she and Gynx didn't need to worry about hitting their heads. Neither did Triggor or Orgem. Miss Strella, however, would have more difficulty.

"Hey!" She turned with a stern frown. "What's the purpose in doing that?"

Gynx placed a finger to his lips and glared. With a whisper, he said, "You said it was safe. Let's not give ourselves away, little one."

Angered, Sparrow's jaw tightened. Without realizing it, her fingers slid around the hilt of her dagger. Perhaps he didn't notice or simply didn't believe she was fast enough or capable of using the blade before he carved into her with his. The temptation for her to find out was stronger than an hour earlier.

The vast majority of halflings seldom turned to violence on behalf of themselves. For a friend or family member, they'd readily come to one's aid and fight if the situation required. But not for themselves. Either they'd flee or wait until they found a way to escape, rather than commit themselves to violence. Sparrow once held such a mindset, but after seeing how detestable others were outside of Willow Bend, and encountering near death situations herself, she chose *not* to be pushed around. She'd gained some respect in Triggor's eyes since he'd learned she had captured Locke by herself. And though he wouldn't admit it, she accomplished what he could not after several encounters of his own. She figured if she were able to handle Locke, Gynx couldn't be any worse. That is, if he didn't have a drawn dagger to her back.

"Let's get on with it," Gynx said. "We're not going to tarry here all day, eh? There's a thief to catch and treasures to find."

Sparrow sighed. "It's too dark to see where we walk."

"Ah, yes," Gynx said with a slight chuckle. "I can see quite well. Not much for the night vision, are you?"

"Well, no. I'm not a kobold."

"Obviously." Gynx pulled a yellow stone from his pack and tapped it against his dagger's blade. The stone glowed brightly, casting a light that spanned approximately ten feet in each direction. "That better?"

"Much," Sparrow said. "That's an Elven stone?"

"Yes."

"Those are hard to come by."

Gynx grunted. "Depends really. I got this one from a street lantern in Woodnog."

"You stole it?"

He shrugged. "Borrowed seems less appropriate, I suppose. Wanna turn me in?"

Sparrow shook her head. "I suppose you and I have different views in honoring the law."

Gynx snickered. "Honor? Law? Do those ideals actually exist?"

"Of course."

"Really? How can you believe that? The two don't coincide. Someone dictates rules of obedience, which are enforced as law. Correct?"

Sparrow nodded.

"There's no honor in law. If such is the case, *who* enforces those laws on the ones who write them? Most people of authority violate their laws altogether. They're exclusionary. The terms don't apply to them. No one holds them responsible. Two sets of rules and all."

"I suppose that's true in a lot of places," she said. "But we're bounty hunters and—"

Gynx shook his head. "No exceptions. We set out to capture criminals for the bounty set on them. Nothing more and nothing less. No rules are set for *how* we take them into custody or their condition upon arrival. Of course, the reward diminishes if the wanted criminal is dead, but a corpse doesn't put up a fight or try to escape. They're easier to transport."

"You've no regard for laws, if you're willing to steal Elven glow-stones and torture others in order to rob them," Sparrow said.

"You're right. I don't. Why should I? What does the law do for me? Say I'm an upstanding member of a city and never break the slightest rule, what am I given in return?"

Sparrow said, "A safer place to live?"

Gynx chuckled. "You're daft, lass. The law itself cannot protect me from a criminal. If someone wanted to rob or kill me, a law pamphlet isn't a shield. It's doubtful any aid would come to me from the guards or sentries before the murdering thief escaped."

"Thus, the reason why bounty hunters exist."

"Yeah, because they need *us* to do their jobs. Otherwise, they'd seek to find them instead of posting rewards."

Sparrow found no way to argue his points, even though she wished she could honestly disagree with him. The system seldom worked, which made her miss Willow's Bend even more.

The stone's light revealed crude stairs at the center of the left wall. He pointed. "There. We go up."

CHAPTER 32

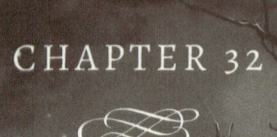

"*D*on't you think it odd?" Sparrow ascended the short set of stairs. "There aren't any vermin or spiders at all? Wouldn't that indicate the building's cursed?"

"Highly protected by something, I agree," Gynx whispered. "The only curse will be Crukas' cursing when we capture him."

She was surprised Gynx agreed with her. Well, *partly* agreed. He seemed more ready to offer conflicting responses than admit someone else was right. Based on the outside conditions of the warehouse and the absence of life inside the cellar where rats and mice and snakes often inhabit, what else except a curse overshadowed the place?

While Sparrow's first inclination was a curse, she held second thoughts. After spending the night in Fasha's shop, she'd seen better evidence of actual curses and sinister, ethereal beings. That type of sensation wasn't present here.

Something hung in the air. A strange scent, faint, but not dust or aged wood. She scrunched her nose.

The glowing Elven stone brightened the last upward step before they reached the first floor.

"You smell that?" Sparrow asked.

Gynx took a moment and a slow breath. "Yes. A pungent odor?"

She nodded. "What is it?"

"Spores." His eyes widened.

"Mushroom spores?"

"Yes. We're being poisoned." He turned and ran through the cellar toward the small door they'd entered. The light faded the farther he got from her.

"Wait!" She stood in the darkness.

Sparrow hurried down the short set of steps and chased after the dimming Elven stone as he ran toward the door they'd entered. She never thought Gynx would cower. Though, she suspected he'd abandon anyone else to save himself whenever danger arose. She wasn't wrong with her assumption.

Her balance tilted oddly, and she staggered while trying to run. If she lost sight of the light, she feared she'd die in the cellar. Dizziness overcame her and she dropped to her knees. The glow of the stone dimmed. Had the spores incapacitated Gynx or had he gotten out?

Running was the worst thing they could've done. They'd inhaled the spores deeper by overexerting themselves.

Sparrow shook her head, and slowly pushed herself to her feet. She struggled to keep steady steps but she reached the glowing stone. She couldn't tell if Gynx was dead, but in self-chiding shame, she sort of wished he was. His death wouldn't be a complete loss to their party. He couldn't be trusted, and his mental instability meant he could turn and kill them when they least expected it.

But, when she came within reach of the stone, Gynx sat on his knees and cackled a strange, crazed laugh.

"You okay, Gynx?" she asked.

"Get away," he hissed.

His laughter bellowed deeper. He howled and batted his hands at unseen things around him. The glowstone dropped on the floor near her feet, and she quickly snatched it. He snarled and lunged at her but she sidestepped from his reach.

"You see them?" he asked.

"What?"

"The ghosts."

"No."

"They've come for us!" He batted his hands and growled.

"There aren't any ghosts, Gynx. They're hallucinations. The spores are affecting your mind." She felt even more lightheaded and her vertigo spun. To prevent herself from falling she placed her hand against the wall.

"You don't see them?" he asked.

"No. But hold steady. I've got something that might help both of us." Sparrow reached into her leather pouch hidden beneath her cloak and retrieved two small vials. In the Elven stone's light, she handed him a vial. "Here. Drink this. It's antitoxin and usually works for most poisons."

His eyes narrowed and a slight hiss escaped his mouth. "You think me a fool?"

"Of course not." She meant it and refused to say what she truly thought about him.

"You're trying to poison me."

"Nonsense. Look." She tugged a cork from one vial with her teeth and then downed its contents. "See? I mean you no harm. It tastes nasty, but it's far better than suffering the delusions those spores cause. If you hope to capture Crukas and get his treasure, we'd best hurry."

Apprehensively, Gynx took the vial. He sniffed the cork Sparrow had dropped and stuck it to his tongue. After a few moments, he yanked the cork free from the other vial and poured the liquid down his throat. His gag reflex kicked in and he hacked like a cat coughing up a fur ball. She stepped back, fearing he'd spew all the stout he'd consumed at the tavern on her. Instead, he belched long and loudly. The stench wasn't quite as traumatic but unpleasant all the same.

Gynx remained on his knees and stared silently around the cellar. Even without the glowstone's light, he could see. Kobolds were blessed in that way. Due to this ability, his other senses were keener than hers. Why hadn't he detected the spores before her? Perhaps his excitement to capture Crukas preoccupied his mind?

"Thanks," Gynx said softly. "Whatever you gave me made those ghosts disappear."

"They were never here." Sparrow offered her hand. "Here, let me help you stand."

With disdained reluctance, he took her hand. She tugged him to his feet. "Never tell anyone."

"About?"

"My gratitude. I've a reputation to uphold, you see?"

Sparrow bit her tongue. He was worried about thanking someone more than his cowardice in running and leaving her behind? "I'm rather insulted."

He grunted. "What?"

"The way you left me behind in the dark earlier."

Gynx shrugged. "You had no problem catching me."

"That's not the point!" Sparrow glared. "We're grouped together for a joint purpose to capture Crukas. You left me to suffer and perhaps die from the spores."

"All turned out okay," he replied.

She slapped his face hard, and he recoiled in surprise. "It wouldn't have for you!"

Shocked, Gynx didn't resort to maddened anger. He rubbed his cheek, and she held his attention. "What do you mean?"

"The antitoxin," Sparrow said. "Had you succeeded in getting out of the cellar to fresh air, I could've still taken it and recovered. You, however, would've continued with hallucinations for no telling how long. What angers me is I freely gave you the potion without a second thought, when you didn't *deserve* it. You abandoned me, and you don't want others to know your appreciation?"

Still rubbing his cheek, he couldn't met her gaze. He stared at the floor and appeared meeker than a scolded child. "Forgive me, little one. You're far less selfish than me. I certainly didn't deserve your hospitality. For what it's worth, I'm sorry, and thanks."

"Was that so hard?" She turned to return to the stairs.

"But if you *ever* tell *anyone*—"

Sparrow shook her head. "Your secret's safe with me."

Gynx cackled with a loud, maddened squeal. She faced him. He pulled his dagger and glared at her. She slowly backed away and tried to figure out the best direction to run. Could she outrun him? The crazed look in his reddened eyes spiked fear in her heart almost equivalent to what his dagger could do.

He cocked his head to the side and his long tongue uncurled and stretched. A guttural growl rumbled in his throat. "Halflings. So simple minded. Always looking for the *good* in those who have nothing good to offer. Should you look into the depths of my heart and mind, you'll find no favorable virtue. Not a speck of kindness. The only difference between me and my kin is my intellect, and you have the foolish nerve to strike me?"

Sparrow swallowed hard, unsure how to respond, and a welling pool of regret flooded her mind. "I'm sor—ry."

Gynx laughed and his eyes narrowed. "You bet you're sorry."

"Truly," she said, "I thought—"

"Thought what, foolish one? Thought you'd frighten me, make me change for the better?"

"I hoped, yes."

He sneered. "There's no hope when it comes to me. I fooled you so quickly and so easily. I could be an actor in a palace play, but since I'm a kobold, I've no chance of that. No human or elf would want to look at my ugly features, but I'm a quick study. I had you believing I so readily was humbled and apologetic."

"Again, I'm sorry. I shouldn't have struck you."

"Damn right. And mind you, yours *is* coming. You'll understand the price for laying a hand on me."

Sparrow eyed the jagged blade in his hand. She closed her eyes and held her arms to her sides. If destiny predicted her death, like Fasha said, she'd as soon get it over. "Go ahead. Kill me. I deserve it."

"Death's too easy, halfling. I thrive on others' misery. You'll suffer before you learn from your error."

She opened her eyes. "What?"

"The fear of death is always worse than actually dying. Having to worry and wonder, looking over your shoulder and never knowing when the deathblow will strike," he said, with an odd smile. "I want that anticipation and fear to swallow you."

"What about Triggor?"

"I guess since he struck me, you figured you could do the same?"

"No."

"Ah, but you thought the earlier spat was over?" Gynx sheathed his dagger.

Sparrow nodded.

"You're too naive for this occupation and too stupid to quit. He knows it's not over, but even I know I'm not quicker than a steel ball fired from his revolver. His is coming, too."

"So you've no appreciation for me saving your life earlier?"

Gynx chuckled. "You didn't save my life. You spared me the delusions caused by the spores. They'd have passed on their own, given time. In an odd sort of way, such hallucinations aren't all bad. Despite the antitoxin you consumed, you're still delusional."

"How so?"

"You seem to think you and I will reach common ground. We won't. The five of us have a common goal, so don't fool yourself into thinking any of us are friends."

Sparrow stared at him in disbelief.

Gynx shrugged. "In time you'll understand I'm telling you the truth. Pirates and thieves aren't the only cutthroats. Bounty hunters are equally as vile."

"I refuse to believe—"

"It doesn't matter *what* you *believe*. Observe and learn. Before we accomplish what we've set out to do, each will show their true colors. Crukas' life isn't what any of us are concerned about. Not even you. Gaining the reward is the true prize. Regardless of how you spin it, that's the truth."

Frustrated, Sparrow considered his words. She was aggravated in knowing he was more right than wrong. Each of them, herself included, had kept pertinent information to themselves, unwilling to share knowledge that might give one of the others an advantage. His threat to make her suffer didn't add any additional fear, as she'd already expected he'd kill or try to kill her before the night ended.

Sparrow changed the subject. "I wonder how the others are faring since these spores are probably all through the cellar and perhaps every floor."

"I don't really care," he replied.

"They might be suffering from the spores," she said.

"Well, I'm not going to hunt for them. Crukas is my top priority, and if it's only you and I who capture him, I say we take him and split the reward and the loot."

"We'll do no such thing," Sparrow said.

"I've never seen a bounty hunter who wasn't in the game for the gold," Gynx said.

"It's not about the reward, as I've stated many times."

"Yeah, yeah. So you say. Which of Crukas' crimes made you so determined to turn him in for no money at all? I detect a great deal of resentment, more than anything else. Am I right?"

Sparrow walked to the short set of stairs. "That's a fair assessment. Are you coming?"

Gynx grumbled and stomped his way to where she stood.

Sparrow sighed.

She'd rather leave Ravensdorf and return to Willow's Bend and abandon the pursuit of finding Crukas. She would, except if he were in the rundown warehouse, she couldn't walk away. The threat of her death be damned. If she crossed his path, she needed to find out how Fate's hand played out. Fasha's prediction might be wrong, and if it wasn't, Sparrow would not flee. She needed to know, one way or the other.

CHAPTER 33

"*I* can't believe I agreed to this!" Miss Strella yanked thick ivy vines from the side of the warehouse wall. "Alone? Seriously? I'm a bard, for crying out loud! Alone? I'm used to a crowd. I'm not cut out for fighting. These sticky thorns are biting and ruining my dress. We should have stayed together. What a mess! I've no weapon. What to do if I'm attacked? It's a mystery. Should I sing my way to victory?"

"Whine your way out of it!" Orgem yelled from the other corner of the warehouse. "They'll die of boredom."

Miss Strella glared in his direction, which he missed since he couldn't see her. "You hush! I was rehearsing some lyrics for our current situation. Thinking out loud. Besides, you said you liked my voice."

"Aye! But that's when you're *singing*, and I've had a few rounds of stout. Okay. Make dat a *lot* of stout."

Miss Strella grumbled a few obscenities. Tears heated her eyes, from her frustration with the thorny vines and from Orgem's partial insult. She wanted to cry, but crying would turn to song, because singing was her only comfort when hardships fell her way. "Any luck finding a way inside?"

"No," Orgem replied gruffly. "You?"

"Nothing."

"Wait!" Orgem said. "I found something."

"A door?"

"Perhaps. Nah, it's a window. Come see."

"Gladly." She grabbed her lyre and hurried through the prickly bramble to the corner of the warehouse. With her dress ripped and torn by the thorns, she no longer needed to take her time. The damage was already done. She'd need to buy a new dress.

To her good fortune, her leather leggings beneath her dress prevented the thorns from cutting into her flesh. When she reached Orgem, he was on his knees chopping through thick ivy cords with his axe.

"Bah!" Orgem rose to his feet.

"What?" She frowned and looked at the window.

Orgem wiped sweat from his brow and adjusted the patch over his eye. "We can break the window easily enough, but there are bars on the inside."

"Oh," Miss Strella said. "Why not chop through the boards above and to both sides of the window? The boards appear partially rotted. Perhaps by doing so, you'll weaken the window frame enough that we can kick the bars inward."

"Aye! Dat's a good idea." Orgem brought back his axe and swung hard. The blade sliced through the wood with ease. The aged lumber was dry, rotted. He grinned. "Good assessment! I could kiss ya!"

"Let's not get *that* excited," she said glumly.

"All the same, we're almost inside now." He struck a sharp blow to the right side of the window. His axe and the side of the frame went through the other side.

"You really think my singing's so bad?"

"Oh, not at all," he replied, tugging his axe free from the wall.

"But you said—"

"I mentioned your *whining. Not* your singing," Orgem said. "I was already frustrated trying to yank away the ivy and all I kept hearing was your sordid complaints."

"I said nothing sordid at all. Like I told you, I was working on lyrics."

He shrugged. "Maybe after ya work more on it, it'll sound better. Me aggravation was getting the best of me and hearing you complain wasn't helping."

"I'm sorry."

"Don't be. Look! Your idea has 'elped us get inside, so there's dat."

Miss Strella forced a smile. "So can we enter together?"

"Sure, why not?"

"Triggor said—"

"Aw, who cares *what* Triggor says, eh? I've me doubts of Crukas even being in this warehouse since there's no obvious entrance."

"Really?" Miss Strella asked. "Then should we even bother going inside?"

Orgem combed his braided beard with one hand, thought for a moment, and then pointed a stern finger. "We should, yes. Just in case he is. Imagine if we didn't and Triggor watched Crukas escape and we were outside. Ah, he'd be sore for sure. Dat kobold would be even angrier."

"You hold some fear of Triggor?" she asked.

"Wouldn't you? He's the only dwarf I know with a revolver like dat. He's a shorter temper than any dynamite stick the kobold carries, and I swear if that stinking kobold was the one who caused the cave-in at the Gomdurm Mines, I'll remove his eyes with me thumbs."

Miss Strella took a sharp breath. "Perhaps entertain that thought *after* we inspect the warehouse?"

"Uh, right." Orgem nodded. He rubbed the patch over his eye socket and mumbled. "Let's get inside."

AFTER TRIGGOR CLEARED away vines and bramble from the wall, he kicked at a small door. The impact splintered the door with ease and much to Triggor's surprise. He chuckled.

He rammed his thick shoulder into the aged door and burst

through into the cellar. Taking a flint box from his pocket, he grabbed a handful of dead brittle leaves that had come through the doorway with him. He struck the flint and a few sparks ignited a leaf. Gently blowing the flame, the fire brightened and slowly rose, giving him time to find a pail of oil near the door with several unlit torches soaking inside.

Triggor took a torch from the pail, let the excess oil drip into the pail, and then carefully brought the torch to the small fire without an oil trail. The last thing he wanted was to send the building up in flames, at least not *before* finding Crukas.

He huffed. "Dat would draw you out, wouldn't it?"

The flames ignited the torch quickly, giving Triggor a good view of the cellar. He feared the torch would burn the cobwebs and once they burst into flames, he'd have to worry over whether the fire would grow and spread to the support beams. But, he didn't see any cobwebs, rats, or mice. Not even a bat.

"Odd."

A lot of old crates remained neatly stacked. None had been opened and all were marked with the signature of the company.

Triggor knocked on one crate with his knuckles. The thuds didn't echo, so the crates were filled with something. "Maybe Gynx was onto something. Is this where you've hidden your loot, Crukas?"

The room seemed to move in circles. Triggor leaned against the crate to keep from falling. "Bloody Hell. What's going on?"

A shadow moved on the other side of the cellar near some stairs. "Who's there?"

No answer.

Triggor fumbled to draw his revolver. "Reveal yourself or I'll shoot ya."

Triggor's vision blurred. "I know you're there. I hear ya."

He dropped to his knees and held the flickering torch away from himself, in case he lost consciousness. His head ached. A shadowy figure edged toward him.

"Crukas?"

"No," Sparrow said.

Triggor squinted. He recognized her voice but he couldn't see her image clearly even though she was only a few feet away. "How'd you get here?"

"We came looking for you and the others," she said.

Gynx grumbled. "Against my wishes."

"Ah, I see," Triggor said. Although he couldn't make out Sparrow's features, there was no mistaking Gynx's voice and attitude. "Then *why'd* you come?"

"Ask her," Gynx said in an agitated whisper.

"The air's saturated with mushroom spores," Sparrow said. "Here, drink this. It's an antitoxin."

Triggor took the vial and turned it up. The bitter liquid made him wince. "Any sign of Crukas?"

"Unfortunately, no, but we've yet to check the other floors," Gynx said. "What are in the crates?"

"No idea." Triggor sat and propped against the crate beside him. "This was as far as I got before my senses went wild and I got too dizzy to walk."

"Should I check?" Gynx asked.

"Sure. Go ahead." Triggor shook his head and tried to stop the ringing in his ears.

Gynx took his pick and pried the top panel off the crate. He reached toward Triggor. "You mind if I use your torch?"

"Help yourself. Just be careful not to send the building up in flames."

Gynx yanked the torch, grumbled, and said, "I'll keep that in mind, being as I'd burn to death, too."

Gynx held the light of the torch over the open crate and sighed.

"Well?" Triggor asked.

Sparrow moved closer to the crate and stood on tiptoe to look inside.

Gynx reached into the crate and rustled his hand through packing material, possibly old hay or straw. "Hmm. Nothing good or valuable. At least, not to me."

"What then?"

"Spools of yarn," Gynx said. "Cured sheepskins."

"So no treasure?" Triggor asked.

"Not in this crate, but there's at least fifty or more crates in the cellar."

Triggor's fuzziness of mind cleared, the ringing in his ears subsided enough to ignore, so he braced against the crate and pushed himself to his feet. "We've no time to check them yet. How much time 'ave we lost since we entered the warehouse?"

"A half hour?" Sparrow said.

"Seems right," Gynx said.

"Where's Miss Strella and Orgem?" Triggor asked.

"Don't know," Gynx replied. "We found you first."

Triggor took the torch from Gynx and looked at Sparrow. "You 'ave any more of that elixir?"

"Some, yes."

"How long does it work?"

"A few hours at the most," she said.

"Then we best get moving." Triggor pointed. "Over by the door are more unlit torches. Each of you grab one and light them off mine. Be careful though. We don't want to burn the warehouse down."

WITHIN THE NEXT HALF HOUR, Sparrow, Gynx, and Triggor found Miss Strella and Orgem huddled together against the wall near the window they'd come through. The size difference between the dwarf and elf was somewhat amusing, but not as much as what they were doing and how oblivious they were to their surroundings. Orgem's left arm wrapped around the small of her back while she strummed the lyre. The faint sound of her lyre and their muddled singing had led Sparrow to the pair. Apparently the effects of the spores worked differently for each individual.

"That's them." Sparrow held her torch to cast flickering light on their forms.

"What's going on with them?" Triggor asked. "They sound—"

"Drunk?" she asked.

"No." Triggor shook his head. "Of *dat* I'd be far more envious. But they appear to be having a better time from the spores than I."

Miss Strella and Orgem sang out of tune and their slurred words were difficult to understand. He followed her words in song, as if trying to learn the lyrics. Yet, both beamed smiles.

"They seem a bit chummy, I agree." Gynx chuckled.

"Sparrow," Triggor said. "Give them the elixir and snap 'em outta it. I can't bear to watch or *hear* any more of dat."

She nodded and hurried to administer the antitoxin. Another half hour passed before Miss Strella and Orgem were steady and stable enough for the five of them to separate and inspect the ground floor above the cellar, much to Miss Strella's chagrin.

"If anyone sees Crukas, call out before you attempt to capture him," Triggor said. "Is dat clear?"

Sparrow, Orgem, and Miss Strella nodded. Gynx sneered.

"Gynx?" Triggor gave the kobold a fierce stare. "I'm referring *especially* to you. Understand?"

"I make no promises," Gynx said.

"Then you can stick with me."

Gynx cocked a brow. "I trust you understand how undesirable that would be for us."

Triggor placed his hand on the revolver without breaking eye contact with the kobold. Gynx's level stare flicked to the revolver. He showed no fear and for several long seconds his defiant gaze seemed a challenge. Instead of opposition, he grumbled and headed for the stairs.

"Next time you're in trouble," Gynx said, "you're on your own. Sparrow's the only reason I came to aid you."

Triggor's jaw tightened and he didn't loosen his hold on the revolver until after Gynx walked up the stairs.

"I'll take the east side," Triggor said. "The rest of ya work it out amongst yourselves."

He walked to the stairs and went up.

Sparrow sighed. "I'll take the north side."

"South," Orgem said.

"South as well," Miss Strella said. "That is, if there's no objection. I don't like the idea of being alone. I've never had to fight and am at a great disadvantage."

"I've no objection," Orgem said with a slight smile. "Your company is rather pleasant."

Sparrow held back her smile. "Time to see if Crukas is really here."

CHAPTER 34

The game of cat and mouse often revolves around a cat stalking and killing the unfortunate rodent. But such a sport gets twisted when feral cats seek to attack and eliminate one another in order to become the sole champion claiming the mouse as its personal prize.

Sparrow headed toward the north side of the building after she reached the ground floor. She hoped Gynx had gone a different direction, as she disliked the kobold's constant threats. Since Triggor had sparked Gynx's dying resentment, the kobold's anger and attention were now focused on Triggor, so she felt a bit more at ease.

After a quarter hour, she returned to the center staircase where the others joined her. No signs indicated Crukas had been there. No new footprints cut a fresh path across the dusty floorboards.

"Should we move on to the next floor?" Sparrow asked.

Triggor nodded while exchanging an angered stare with Gynx. "We've come this far. No need to turn back now."

Gynx's eyes narrowed. "Agreed."

Miss Strella sighed with disdain.

"Bard," Gynx said, "You're free to leave the group if this is cutting into your long-needed rehearsal time."

Orgem's jaw tightened. He stepped around Miss Strella and pointed a stern finger. With the other hand, he pulled his axe."Don't insult her, ya rodent."

Gynx hissed, brought up his armed crossbow, and aimed at Orgem's good eye. At the close range, he wouldn't miss the dwarf's remaining eye. "Did I offend your love interest?"

Orgem frowned, but with hesitation. He studied the crossbow and seemed to withdraw his notion of charging the kobold. The boiling anger in the dwarf's facial expression indicated he wanted to tear the kobold apart. "You should apologize to her."

Gynx offered a crude stare. "No, I should praise her, don't you think?"

Orgem's anger subsided. His brow furrowed from confusion. "Eh?"

"I should praise her for *not* singing. The tremor of her voice could kill us all. These old boards and the rafters might collapse with her caterwauling. Or, perhaps she should apologize for having us endure her session in The Mute Changeling."

"Why you—" Orgem snarled and lowered his head, ready to charge.

Sparrow's jaw tightened.

Gynx delighted in being a ruthless instigator. He wasn't willing to work with the others to find and take Crukas into custody. His actions to draw Orgem into a fight were insane. Unless ... he hoped to eliminate the others in their party, so he alone kept the spoils for himself. Despite Gynx's uncanny ability to speak and communicate fluently with other races, were his primal, kobold urges trying to override his less aggressive nature? Could he ever succeed in abandoning the bloodlust to kill those around him?

Gynx grinned with an eager finger on the crossbow's trigger, and the wild glint in his eyes grew with anticipation. His expression was intended to kindle Orgem's anger enough to draw the dwarf into a fight, but the metal click of Triggor's gun erased the kobold's grin. Gynx's brow actually rose with sudden surprise.

Triggor cocked the revolver and trained it on Gynx. "Unarm dat bow before I shoot a hole through your hollow skull. We 'ave only two more floors to explore and if it proves Crukas isn't here, we go separate ways afterwards. We never really liked one another before meeting today and we certainly haven't kindled any new friendships, either."

Even though Sparrow was the smallest in the group, she lowered herself in the hope that she wouldn't become a casualty in the maddening disruption before her.

A heavy thud echoed on the floor above.

All five exchanged glances. Gynx lowered the crossbow and Triggor uncocked the revolver. Triggor placed his index finger to his lips. "Sounds like he's up there."

"Crukas?" Miss Strella asked in a low voice.

"Who else, you twat?" Gynx said.

Orgem snarled and tightened his grip on his axe handle.

Triggor frowned and shook his head. He kept his voice quiet. "Keep it down. If dat's him, he probably knows we're here. We've certainly made enough racket. Best I can tell, this set of stairs is the only way up or down from each floor. If dat's him, he's trapped."

A sudden rise of excitement caused Sparrow's heart to beat faster. Had her efforts finally paid off?

"Sparrow," Triggor said. "You go first."

A lump rose in her throat and she gasped. "Me? Why?"

"You're the smallest and make the least amount of noise," he replied. "Go quietly and move aside. Gynx, you go after her."

Still disgruntled, he gave a harsh glance and acquiesced a nod, saying nothing.

Triggor motioned toward the stairs. "Then Miss Strella. I pray your steps are as graceful as your voice."

Gynx snickered.

Orgem growled.

"Shh!" Triggor said. "Orgem follow her, and I'll take up the rear. Whatever ya do, don't leave the stairwell unattended. It's his only way down."

That we know of, Sparrow thought.

Sparrow met Triggor's gaze. He nodded for her to head upstairs. Lightheaded, she took the steps quietly, and like Triggor indicated, she moved without making the slightest creak on the steps. She reached the next floor and stepped aside to wait for Gynx.

His clawed feet surprisingly made little sound. After he reached the top of the stairs, he glanced at her with slight disgust and moved to the right while holding the crossbow with both hands, ready to fire if necessary.

While waiting for the other three, Sparrow glanced around. This floor was practically bare. No walls divided the floor and only a few crates were visible in the glow of their torches. She wished she possessed night vision like Gynx.

Perturbed, Gynx shook his head. "I see nothing or no one here."

Triggor reached the top of the stairs and huffed. "Nothing?"

"No," he said.

"We heard—"

"I'm aware," Gynx said coldly. "But the noise must've come from the next floor up. I detect no one else around us."

Another heavy thud dropped on the top floor.

"You're right," Triggor said. He clasped a hand on the kobold's shoulder as an appreciative gesture. "But there are no stairs leading up there."

"Ladders," Gynx said. "One straight ahead, and four others at the corners of the floor."

"Convenient. Almost as though it were meant to divide us up," Triggor said.

Miss Strella sighed. "Not necessarily. Since there aren't stairs leading upward, separate ladders at each corner of the floor and in the center make the best sense."

Sparrow nodded. "I agree."

Triggor shrugged and held up his torch to examine the ceiling. "Then we each take a ladder, but parts of the ceiling have collapsed in places."

Gynx huffed. "Worse than that."

"Eh?" Orgem said.

Gynx pointed. "The entire floor above appears rotten."

"Maybe no one's there after all." Miss Strella's soft voice rose with hope. The bard seemed ready to leave the warehouse and abandon hunting Crukas altogether. She certainly didn't want to separate from the rest of the group. "Could the roof be collapsing?"

"Not from what I can see," Gynx said. "If you're fearful, you should leave."

The bard took a sharp breath, stared at the stairs leading down, and after a brief moment, she shook her head. "All I'm saying is the loud thuds could be parts of the roof falling."

Triggor nodded in her defense. "But, we won't know unless we check it out, right?"

"That's true," she said.

Gynx craned his neck and placed a finger to his lips. "Listen."

A muffled cough broke the silence on the floor above. The floorboards creaked softly above them. Someone was moving toward the west side, away from the ladder where they stood.

Triggor grinned at Gynx. "Good ear. Dat answers the reason for the crashing."

"Either it's a person," Gynx said, "or the largest rat I've ever heard."

"Thieves *are* rats, don't ya know?" Orgem said.

"Sparrow," Triggor said. "You take this ladder. Gynx and I will take the two ladders on the west side, in case Crukas is trying to make his way to one of them."

Gynx's eyes almost gleamed in the glow of the torchlight.

Triggor looked at Orgem. "You and Miss Strella go to the east side and separate. You decide between yourselves which ladder you wish to take, but do *not* take the same ladder. We mustn't give him the slightest chance to escape. You two work your way to Sparrow, and Sparrow, stay within sight and quick reach of this ladder. Crukas is cunning, as you well know."

Sparrow nodded. She placed her hands on the ladder and prepared to climb to the top floor.

Triggor looked at Gynx and motioned for him to follow. The two of them walked toward the west side, and after a few seconds,

Miss Strella and Orgem headed to the east side, leaving Sparrow alone.

Sparrow disliked the isolation and peered up at the small square opening where the ladder ended. If Crukas was on the floor above, she wondered what Fate held for her. The possibility still existed that Crukas wasn't in the warehouse at all. No physical signs indicated anyone other than the five of them had even entered the building. Due to the massive growth of ivy and bramble covering the warehouse, it was possible Crukas could've climbed the ivy and entered through the roof; something she hadn't given much thought before they found their ways inside.

She placed her right foot on the bottom rung and pulled herself up the ladder. Within a few minutes, she'd find her way to the upper floor and discover what they'd soon encounter.

Midway up the ladder, the floorboards closer to the ladder creaked. She could've sworn someone looked down at her before the footsteps shuffled away from the opening.

Sparrow took a deep breath and hurried upward. She took comfort in knowing if it were Crukas, he'd never been known for violence or murder. Any confrontation might not prove fatal, but that was *if* it were him. Of course, falling off the ladder and landing on the lower floor could cause severe injury if not death. Regardless, she chose to take the risks and climbed the rungs faster without expecting an immediate confrontation.

CHAPTER 35

"*J*ealousy does not become you." Crukas set a lit oil lantern on a broken table. An amused smile curled his lips after Sparrow gasped softly.

"Jealousy?" Sparrow lowered her hood and frowned. "You're mistaken, if you think I'm jealous of you."

Crukas smirked. "Admit it, Sparrow. Your thieving skills could never compare to mine. Don't let it upset you. No thief comes near my expertise. None ever will. Even with me out of the way, you're hard pressed to ever place second best to me."

Sparrow's brow tightened. Her narrowed eyes revealed her festering rage and resentment for him. Other thieves over the years had given him similar looks, so her emotions were easily read.

She stepped between him and the ladder, which amused him. She wasn't a preventative measure to stop his escape, should he need to get to the ladder.

"Your arrogance does not suit you," she said.

Crukas shook his head and smiled. "No arrogance, little one. Simply, it's the straightforward truth. You were inadequate in your thieving abilities, so you flipped sides. But you'll never fill your purse with gold by trying to collect the bounty on my head."

"And yet," Sparrow said, sliding her fingers around the hilt of her dagger. "Here we are."

Crukas' dark eyes met hers. Her fingers tightening on the dagger's hilt didn't go unnoticed, even though he never broke his gaze with her. If she flung the dagger, she wouldn't be foolish enough to aim for a kill shot. His value was one hundred times greater alive than dead, depending on which city magistrate she handed him over to. Besides, her pride wouldn't be quenched knowing he was dead. She'd prefer he lived to suffer execution or a long imprisonment. And since she was a halfling, murder and torture were off the table.

From the corner of his eye, he realized she'd done something else to disappoint him. Ebden had told him the truth, but regardless, Crukas half expected Sparrow to pursue him alone. His capture was her vendetta and she probably championed the idea of boasting of her singlehanded success. She wouldn't want to share the glory should she succeed in capturing him.

Crukas' gaze narrowed. "To further prove you're nowhere near my equal, you brought others in your pursuit? Three others? No, wait, four?"

Sparrow's eyes widened. "How'd—"

"I know?" Crukas laughed. "It didn't help by bringing four thieves more amateur than yourself."

"I'm no longer a thief," Sparrow said.

"Says you," Crukas replied. "Otherwise, you'd have joined forces with actual bounty hunters and not posing thieves."

Sparrow's brow rose in confusion. "They *are* bounty hunters."

Crukas chuckled. "They've fooled you. Surely, you'd have done better research before partnering with strangers. Two of your wannabe thieves are dwarves. They haven't the proper build to earn a living as thieves, so they pose as bounty hunters. But dwarves are too cumbersome and heavy-footed."

"Hey!" one dwarf shouted.

"And even less covert when insulted, eh, Orgem?" Crukas looked past Sparrow into the shadows.

Orgem grumbled.

"You know Orgem?" Sparrow asked.

"Know *of* him. We've never met in person." Crukas laughed softly. "How's your one eye holding up, Orgem?"

Orgem snarled and stomped one foot. "Come 'ere and I'll show ya."

Sparrow half pulled her dagger from its sheath. Crukas recognized the blade. Her bandit dagger was the twin blade to the thief dagger on his belt. Both were made by Woodnog's master blacksmith, Beren Tiwele. Crukas couldn't insult her taste in weapons.

"Look familiar?" Crukas pulled his dagger from its sheath.

Her eyes widened.

"You even mimic me with your choice of weapons," Crukas said. "That could be construed as a tad bit jealous."

Her brow furrowed. "Beren Tiwele swore this blade was one of a kind."

"Almost. This blade is its twin and I've carried it for years."

Sparrow's nose twitched and her eyes narrowed. "I honestly had no idea. Otherwise, I'd have chosen a *different* blade."

"Really?" Crukas laughed.

"Yes," Sparrow said.

"You're better suited as a thief than the two dwarves with you." Crukas sighed.

"I'm sure their views differ from your compliment."

Crukas shrugged. "Sparrow, you might as well take your hand off the dagger. You understand, the same as your companions, how much my worth depreciates should you kill me. Even Miss Strella's best rendition in song won't soothe the pain of your monetary loss. Stick to singing your fables, Strella."

"*Sparrow*," Strella whispered harshly. "Whom did you tell?"

"No one. I swear."

"Someone surely did," Strella said. "He knows too much about our party unless someone forewarned."

The westside floor cracked and several slats broke loose and crashed to the floor below.

"That'd be Triggor," Crukas said. "Careful, the floor on that side of the building is more rotten than the rest. You might fall through."

Triggor chuckled. "As if you care."

Crukas grinned. "You're right. I don't. Just thought I'd warn you."

"Stay where you are," Triggor said. "You're surrounded. How dare ya call me a thief."

"The truth pains the conscience. The fact you possess the revolver is proof enough. Don't you think?" Crukas asked.

"You know nothing of how I obtained it."

"I know *everything* about the ordeal in Pirate's Cove. Such a dark secret's never safe with me. At least not that one. Another word of warning."

"What's dat?"

Crukas said, "If you fire your revolver, the impact's liable to cause the floor beneath you to collapse. Although it's not a long drop to the floor below, are you willing to wager *that* floor is sturdy enough not to crumble through as well?"

"Take him," Triggor said to Sparrow. Resentment rang in his order, which reinforced what Crukas had said about how Triggor had obtained the revolver was the truth. The only reason he didn't rush to take hold of Crukas or fire the weapon was because of the rotten floor.

Sparrow pulled her dagger and took a step toward Crukas.

"Remember," Crukas said. "The amount of my reward drops significantly should you kill me."

Sparrow's eyes widened slightly. In a near whisper, she said, "It's justice I seek. Not the gold or the offered reward. But, I've no interest in harming you. But, they do."

"At least one of us doesn't care about your bounty as a reward," a low voice said. "Or if you're taken in alive."

Sparrow cringed. "Sorry, I didn't realize his hearing was so keen."

"Ah," Crukas said. "Gynx? I thought I recognized the stench."

Gynx murmured. "Maybe you recognize *this*, too." He squeezed the crossbow's triggor.

By instinct, Sparrow ducked, even though she wasn't tall enough to be in the bolt's path or for it to strike her.

"Gynx!" Triggor said. "Bloody—"

The bolt passed through Crukas and struck the wall. Instead of Crukas falling or gripping himself in pain, his image rippled. In a few seconds, his image steadily returned to normal. He suffered no harm. Gynx loaded the crossbow a second time and prepared to aim.

"I've no time for this." With the gentle wave of his hand, Crukas and the oil lantern he'd set down, vanished.

"WHAT THE—?" Sparrow scoured the floor near where she stood. Bewildered, she shook her head. "How?"

"Blazes be!" Orgem hobbled to Sparrow.

"Ya let him get away?" Triggor eased one foot forward to test the soundness of the floor before he continued his treacherously slow, step-by-step, walk to the ladder.

Sparrow had listened to Bard tales that mentioned Crukas' magical abilities, but she figured the tales—like most Bards and even Strella's—were overly exaggerated.

Sparrow tapped the floor with her leather boots where Crukas had stood. The floor was solid. No trap door. Nothing that might've lofted him through the ceiling, which would've been obvious without checking. He didn't even use a smokescreen. He vanished into nothingness, much like … Fasha had.

"No! I never *let* him escape!" Although aggravated, Sparrow was partially amazed and regrettably relieved a fraction more. Crukas' escape would've angered her had Gynx not tried to kill Crukas on sight. And had the kobold only injured him, Gynx was prepared to torture Crukas until death, if necessary. All for Crukas' treasure caches. Since Crukas escaped injury and death, she could continue her pursuit later, hopefully without the others. "He never came past me. He vanished."

"Where is he?" Strella asked.

"Your guess is as good as mine." Sparrow spat on the dusty, cobwebbed floor and raised her hands in exasperation. "Unless anyone else can better describe what we witnessed, he's gone."

"Gone?" Orgem growled. "Blast it! How?"

"Not sure." Sparrow's curiosity swelled inside her. Crukas had stood only a couple of feet away from her. And yet, no brush of air touched her when he vanished. He'd have had to push her out of the way to get to the ladder.

Miss Strella stepped from the shadows. "Magic?"

Sparrow shrugged and pointed. "What else? He was right *here*. He didn't run. No trap door. Just gone."

Strella grinned.

Orgem glared at the bard. "Ya find this amusing, do ya?"

Her smile retreated, and she shook her head. "Not at all."

"Then why are you smiling?" Sparrow asked.

"It means the tales about Crukas are true, even those I believed were farfetched."

Stepping lightly across the floor, Triggor asked, "What tales?"

"About Crukas' magic," Strella said.

"Magic?" Gynx stormed past them and yanked the bolt from the wall. "He was never here."

"What?" Triggor said. "Are you daft?"

"You saw the bolt go right through him," Gynx said with a snarled lip. "No way my aim was off target in the slightest. His body rippled. Bodies don't ripple. He projected his image here from someplace else."

"Isn't that magic?" Miss Strella asked in an amused tone.

Gynx mumbled.

Sparrow nodded. "I've heard tales of Crukas' magical abilities, too. And like you, I didn't believe them, either."

"I never said I didn't *believe* the tales," Strella said. "We bards always embellish our stories. The better the story, the more coins the tipsy patrons toss our way."

Sparrow tightened her hands into fists until her entire body became rigid. Her eyes bulged and her face was redder than a ripened tomato. "Someone must've told Crukas about our alliance to capture him and collect his bounty. But who?"

"My guess is you told him," Gynx said with a fierce frown and pointing his finger.

Sparrow turned with flared contempt in her gaze. "Me?"

"*You* were the one the dwarf in the tavern came to. He told us Crukas was headed to this warehouse," Gynx said.

"I'd never met the dwarf before today," Sparrow said. "And only a few minutes before I approached *your* table."

Miss Strella said, "I've never seen the dwarf in the Mute Changeling before today, either. Even though he and his two companions seemed out of place, Sparrow's not to blame here."

Orgem nodded. "You might be right. Then who else could've aided Crukas?"

"The barkeep?" Triggor said with a firm brow. His eyes narrowed as he tried to think. "He recognized me, and he knows Miss Strella."

"Not on a personal level, he doesn't." She smiled, apparently flattered by a memory. "He saw my lyre and asked if I was a bard. After I sang one tale, he invited me to sing whenever I return to Ravensdorf, but he knows nothing of my spying to find criminals."

"He saw ya with me and Gynx," Triggor said. "Not hard to connect the three of us together. Besides, he seems the type who'd favor helping a thief escape."

"What reason could you have to believe he helped Crukas?" Sparrow asked.

"Smug jaw. Shifty eyes. Seemed to be eavesdropping to our conversation," Orgem said. "I kept my eye on 'em the entire time."

"You dolt!" Triggor said. "One eye's all ya got!"

"Aye," Orgem nodded fiercely, shrugged, and then crossed his thick arms. "Which is *why* I know I wasn't looking elsewhere!"

Sparrow gritted her teeth. "So us coming to the warehouse was all misdirection? He lured us here so he could steal something elsewhere. But what?"

"He was *never* here," Gynx said.

Sparrow examined the floor where Crukas set down the lantern, which disappeared the same time he had. "Gynx is right."

"Huh?" Triggor and Miss Strella said.

Gynx grinned. "You doubted me?"

Sparrow ignored Gynx and pointed at the floor. "Crukas left no footprints in the dust. Other than the five of us, no one's been up here in a long, long time."

Miss Strella came closer and looked. "Then how do you explain those crashing sounds we heard earlier?"

Sparrow shrugged. "Not sure. But as evidenced when Triggor was walking across the floor, a lot of the floorboards are loose. Some of the roof has collapsed recently, too."

"Since we can agree that Crukas wasn't actually here," Gynx said, "it means he's a head start on whatever he's really after."

Sparrow cringed. She took a deep breath and gave a regretful nod. "Gynx is right."

Gynx grinned and winked. "Two for two. This was a huge waste of our time."

Miss Strella held up the frayed ends of her tattered dress. Tears dampened her eyes.

Orgem grumbled. "No kidding."

"Right," Triggor said. "Best we cut our losses and return to the tavern and talk to the barkeep."

"Talk's cheap," Gynx said. "Torture's divine."

"No," Triggor said. "Friendly chat. Nothin' more."

"Aww," Gynx said.

"Look," Triggor said. "Our reputations are already at risk. We can't go about torturing people for answers, not if we hope to earn the trust of vendors and magistrates when it comes time to gather information."

"You can worry about your reputation all you want," Gynx said. "It's not my concern. Once I lay hands on Crukas, this is my last heist … erm, bounty."

Sparrow cocked a brow and eyed him shrewdly.

Gynx laughed at her expression. "What? You heard Crukas. He considers us all thieves."

"Because *you* are," Sparrow said.

"No need for flattery, in a time like this," Gynx said.

"I wasn't—" Sparrow formed fists and growled with frustration.

"Flattery?" Triggor said. "His remark I took as an insult, 'cause it is."

"I agree," Sparrow said. What had Crukas insinuated about Triggor's possession of the revolver? How'd Triggor claim the gun as his own? According to Crukas' accusation, Triggor had done something quite underhanded.

Triggor brushed past Sparrow and headed down the ladder. "We're only wasting more time, the longer we stay 'ere. Come on."

Miss Strella hurried after Triggor, but Sparrow decided to climb down behind the bard, rather than remain close to Gynx. Orgem didn't seem to have any bad blood between himself and Gynx. *Yet.* The quicker Sparrow distanced herself from the kobold, the better. But, she suspected the rest of the group would insist on her staying with them so they could keep tabs on her. Sneaking away was not her best option, as Gynx might begrudge her like he did Triggor.

She didn't know what the outcome would be once Gynx decided to seek his revenge on Triggor, but she didn't want to get caught in between or become Gynx's targets. She'd tried to warn Crukas about the danger he could expect from the kobold. Now, she needed to figure out a way to escape the trap she'd set for herself.

CHAPTER 36

Crukas blinked hard. When his vision returned properly, the familiar surroundings of Irmine's small library eased him. He shook his head, sighed, and attempted to shake away the sudden chills pulsating through his body. Though he boiled with sweat, his insides seemed bitten by an icy cold. Was it due to being projected into the warehouse while his body remained behind? Perhaps realizing how he might've died had his physical body been in the top floor of the warehouse had disrupted his core? Regardless of what was responsible, he placed his palm against the wall to steady himself and glanced at Irmine with a slight smile.

"Well," he said, "*that* was interesting, if not completely entertaining."

"In what way?" Irmine wrapped a knitted, wool blanket around him. Her creased brow revealed her concern for his wellbeing. As a priestess, maybe this was her attitude toward everyone, but somehow he doubted this was the case.

"I'd be dead if I had gone in person."

Irmine nodded. "I told you so."

"I know. How'd you project my image so clearly? They believed I was actually there. Enough so Gynx fired a bolt at me. Strangely, I felt it go through me without suffering any pain."

"He shot at you?"

Crukas nodded. "He *shot* me; my apparition or spirit or whatever you projected before them."

She shrugged, wiped sweat from her brow, and her eyes rolled back in her head. Her body shook slightly before she sank into a thick cushioned chair. Crukas knelt beside her and took her clammy hand. She'd exerted an immense amount of her energy in order to protect him, which sapped her strength and made her extremely weak.

Irmine took a slow breath and opened her eyes. Her tired gaze rested on him. She placed her other hand atop his. "I tapped into divine magic, as always, but I won't have enough energy to aid you against Scorpius."

Crukas squeezed her hand and shook his head. "Irmine, it's not your battle. It's mine. You've done far more than I ever deserve. Anything more is a debt I can never repay."

"You survive and it's payment enough," she said. "But Scorpius isn't the most of your problems."

"Meaning?"

"You fooled those bounty hunters into being lured to the old warehouse. After they discover your deception, they'll continue their hunt for you. Possibly more so, since your trickery got the best of them."

Crukas laughed softly. "The trickery was all you."

"Doesn't matter. Their anger will become an additional driving force to find a means to capture you. Or, in the kobold's case, *kill* you. A bard witnessed the ordeal. Such a story is treasure to her livelihood. The others won't like the likelihood of *how* you fooled them to be told throughout Aetheaon. And since you're not leaving Ravensdorf immediately, the chances they'll find you are even greater."

"I've been under Sparrow's nose for the past few weeks and even in the same room with her without her recognizing me. Her bounty hunter skills are far less than her ability to steal."

Irmine offered a weak smile. "Perhaps her conscience is keener than yours?"

"No question about it," Crukas replied. "She's a halfling, so she's not suited for either profession. Both are against her nature and culture."

"And yours?"

"I'm a product of my upbringing, Irmine. The streets were my home until I was mentored by a thieving guild."

"Not the best of examples."

Crukas shrugged. "They kept me fed and a place to stay, which is more than any temple or orphanage offered me. That instills a pattern of life I couldn't ignore when it came to where I placed my faith."

Irmine sighed. "Your childhood was far rougher than most and shaped you in ways that hardened you. And now, you're in a dire situation. Somehow, the most notorious bounty hunter and his company have found you. This wasn't designed by a higher power to make you atone for your transgressions. It's not by accident or coincidence, either. The book you stole plays a key, but I've yet to determine what the connection is. I see no positive end for you. My advice is for you to stay put, *here*, where I can at least shield you until they move on. Facing Scorpius now with these bounty hunters is the worst decision you can make. If you could postpone—"

Crukas squeezed her hand and stood. "I wish I could, but the luxury of time is *not* on my side. None of us, for that matter."

She cocked a brow and studied him for several long moments. With a frown, she said, "I sense your burden is far greater than the book's curse. What are you not telling me?"

"Should I succeed against Scorpius," Crukas said, "I'll tell you everything."

Irmine's eyes moistened with tears. "Oh, Crukas, I fear you won't get the chance."

"Nice to know you have faith in me."

"It's not that, Crukas. No thief is as sly and as fortunate as you. But, you've never been burdened and opposed by such oppressive forces. You've been marked by the book and something else. I'm too weak to aid you."

"Again, this isn't your fight."

Irmine formed a grim smile. "It's not *yours*, either."

"I've made it my fight and I refuse to turn back. Even though I can't explain it, I'm not alone in my endeavors."

"You've isolated yourself, Crukas. You don't want my help or plan to storm Scorpius' tower without anyone else's help."

"I've always worked alone. It's how I've gotten into the tightest places and inside highly guarded rooms. I move with the shadows in absolute silence. Others do not and would distract me. I work best alone because I don't have to worry about anyone else blundering the heist."

"Have you stolen from a powerful mage before?"

Crukas shook his head. "No, but there's always the first time."

"Death comes once, too."

Crukas nodded, even though he knew the statement wasn't exactly true. The Plague-bringer brought the dead back to life, and he was the sole reason Crukas needed Scorpius' mask. Clearly, the odds were astoundingly high against Crukas' success, but should he succeed, he knew his intuition was correct. Someone, be it a deity or something else, was directing his path and possibly could aid him where Irmine could not. Before the night ended, he'd know one way or another. If he failed and died, at least his death kept him from becoming one of the Plague-bringer's army. In that, he felt a slight bit of comfort.

CHAPTER 37

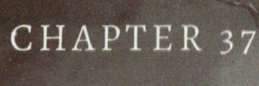

*N*ightfall was eerily darker than the short wagon trip through the Gloomy Forest. Crukas waited until Irmine had fallen asleep before he slipped through a small window and dropped quietly on the alley cobblestone street.

He crept along the edges of buildings and chose those that didn't have any lit torches or sconces, which was the majority. Oddly, he seemed to be the only thief moving through the silent town.

As he made his way toward the steep mountainside where Dark Ayr Tower rose into the sky, he wondered why Sparrow had chosen to join Triggor and Gynx. Miss Strella and Orgem weren't a threat and were more opportunists at trying to gain fortunes without additional labor. They'd probably abandon their hope for a quick rich bounty and return to other means to earn gold after Crukas' stunt.

Although Crukas had never encountered Triggor or the kobold, he knew their reputations. Any thief worth a bounty knew about them. Some thieves these two bounty hunters had captured never survived the journey to the magistrates. A carcass was easier to transport without worrying about the thief escaping. Had Crukas physically been in the warehouse, Gynx would've killed him.

Crukas was elated to have insulted both bounty hunters without either inflicting actual harm to him. His gloating was short lived. No doubt they'd seek revenge, not for the words alone, but Gynx was the one he worried about the most. Triggor might rough Crukas up for the ruse, but that was questionable since Triggor possessed a revolver, which testified to the dwarf's lack of morals.

He felt sorrow for the strain Irmine had suffered to project his image inside the old warehouse with such precision. The task drained her dangerously close to death. He could ask nothing more of her. Whatever favor he owed her after he confronted Scorpius he'd gladly honor, regardless of its risk on his personal wellbeing. However, before he could repay her, he must survive the encounter with the mage.

Crukas would've chosen a different way to confront Sparrow, Triggor, and the others, if he'd known Irmine would nearly sacrifice her life just to protect him. A tear trailed down his face. He wiped it away and shook his head. Something stirred deep within his soul he'd not felt since he lost Jillann. After losing her, he shut himself off from others, even though he never allowed anyone to be close to him, except Jillann and his blood brother, Devin. Now, Irmine—the most unlikely individual to accept him as a friend—made him realize he wasn't isolated in the realm. To survive mentally and physically required connecting to folks he could aid and those who could help him. Solitude held far fewer guarantees.

Crukas placed his back against the rock wall of a small shelter where a shepherd fed his sheep. Shrouded beneath the blanket of darkness and heavy fog, several sheep bleated somewhere nearby in the rocky field. Without the slightest ray of moonlight or any lanterns, Crukas was forced to rely on his memory of where Scorpius' tower stood. He wasn't certain if a moonlit night would've aided him, as then he'd be visible while advancing toward the tower while crossing the rocky ground.

Even though Crukas couldn't determine a crude path or see the tower, he shuddered at its presence. While he couldn't explain it, he felt the wicked magical power surrounding and fortifying the tower. Static hung in the air, prickled his skin, and made the hair on his neck stand on end. He held the suspicion that Scorpius *could* see him and knew about of Crukas' arrival. The blackness of night and the swirling fog wouldn't hide Crukas' approach. Scorpius might've used magic to obscure Crukas' sight to discourage the thief from proceeding with his plans. Was this a final warning or perhaps a dare to determine Crukas' fortitude or the lack thereof?

Staring at the dark curtain of fog, Crukas took a deep breath and held it. Once he walked away from the rock shelter, he feared his bearings would become lost until dawn. The small town was behind him. Stepping forward meant abandoning his only route of safety and means for a quick escape. He glanced toward the lightless streets. If any outside torches or lanterns burned, they were no longer visible. He stood in what seemed a black abyss.

While he insisted thieves worked best in total darkness, this was different than an ordinary nightfall. He'd be a fool to light a torch or lamp or cast a tiny luminescence orb spell to guide his path. An ignited spark would give his location away. He didn't dare risk it.

Crukas sighed and placed his fingers around the protective pendant Irmine had given him. He'd like to believe the enchanted piece of jewelry could save him from injury or death, but he felt nothing except the cold metal slowly warming between his fingers. Not even the slightest hint of magic or a goddess's blessing pricked his skin. The path he'd chosen to somehow thwart the Plague-bringer's coming reign was meant to be solitary. Crukas never intended otherwise, as he'd rather die alone than jeopardize the lives of others. He understood far too late the importance of having friends. Facing Scorpius was dangerous, but it was something he expected to do alone.

He took a step forward and a fierce hand grabbed his forearm and jerked him nearly off his feet. "Ya didn't think ya'd get away from us dat easily, did ya?"

CHAPTER 38

Sparrow sat in the Mute Changeling and drank honey wine. She thought of Willow Bend. Would they welcome her should she return home? She'd violated so many halfling standards by becoming a thief. Flipping sides to become a bounty hunter didn't redeem her former mistakes. Reality struck hard in learning she wasn't cut out for either profession.

She met Miss Strella's eyes and smiled. "No song for the evening?"

Miss Strella shook her head. "No. And after Triggor and Gynx finish interrogating Devin, it's doubtful I'll ever be allowed to sing at this pub again. I'm certain I won't be welcome."

Sparrow nodded. "I know the feeling. Where's Orgem?"

"With Triggor and Gynx," she replied. "But I've the feeling he'd rather be seated here with us."

"Ah. Why's that?"

Strella smiled weakly. "He doesn't seem to have the same vigor to threaten or harm others for gold as Gynx or Triggor. No more than you and I, if I understand you well enough."

"You've read me well. I'm ready to head home, but I fear leaving, too."

"Because of Triggor and Gynx?" Miss Strella asked.

"Yes. I'm afraid Gynx will shoot me in the back or in the heart if I bowed out and left your group."

"Why? You couldn't have caught Crukas since he wasn't actually in the warehouse."

Sparrow gave a feeble smile. "I know. But I warned Crukas that Gynx planned to torture and kill him."

Miss Strella frowned. "When?"

"Moments before Gynx fired his crossbow."

"*Why* would you warn Crukas?"

Sparrow shrugged. "I want Crukas to face justice. What Gynx plans to do isn't right. In fact, it's a worse crime than all of Crukas' combined."

Miss Strella cocked a brow. "All?"

"Okay, I greatly exaggerated," Sparrow said. "But Gynx shouldn't be rewarded with the precious items Crukas has stolen throughout the years. Especially *not* if he tortures Crukas in order to obtain them."

"While I understand your point, I see their side, too."

"Seriously?"

Strella nodded. "You were invited to help, *not* to allow him to escape."

Sparrow frowned. "You just said there was noth—"

"Yes, I know. But you warned him, and now he's gone with that knowledge, so you've made it harder for us to capture him."

"So you're fine if Gynx quartered Crukas to gain his stash?"

Strella's eyes widened. Her tone indicated the question insulted her integrity. "*No!* Of course not."

"And yet, you're fine with Gynx firing a bolt at him?"

Miss Strella sighed. "We don't know the shot would've been a kill shot."

Sparrow shook her head in disbelief. "I highly doubt Gynx would've missed, nor would he have allowed a slight injury instead of death from his vantage point."

"A dead thief cannot reveal where he's hidden his accumulated gains, so I don't think Gynx's aim was to kill."

"That's a good point," Sparrow said. "But he could've captured Crukas and—"

"The point is Gynx *didn't*, but you gave a thief pertinent information he didn't need to know. That violates most bounty hunter oaths. It's no worse than harboring a criminal. And you're right. You might want to watch your back until you redeem yourself. *If* you can."

Sparrow didn't bother to ask whether Miss Strella's inference was to watching her back or the slight chance she might gain redemption with Gynx. She doubted she'd be successful in either case. She disliked the irony of how she'd volunteered information to prevent Crukas' torture but instead, she'd only placed her life into greater danger.

The vagueness of Fasha's prophesy didn't help matters, either. She wondered if Fasha's intent would be to make Sparrow second guess every decision she made, which could very well cause Sparrow's death by keeping her off guard to less observant, surrounding dangers.

Fleeing the Mute Changeling while Triggor and Gynx were preoccupied only meant Sparrow would have to look over her shoulder for years. That'd keep her apprehensive and restless. So, she decided to stay with the group until better terms suited her. Besides, she expected the feat of watching her back was somewhat easier if she kept an eye on Gynx directly and not from afar. The distaste of being near him indefinitely was difficult to swallow but more tolerable than death.

CHAPTER 39

Devin had no sooner finished sweeping the thick layers of dust that outlined where Crukas' two stout barrels had stood before he was confronted by a dwarf and a kobold. A second dwarf with only one-eye stood at the doorway, and his blocky build filled the lower part of the frame. He recognized them from earlier and assumed they returned to get more information about Crukas.

Though outnumbered and boxed in, Devin leveled a glare at them. "Sorry, but no patrons are allowed back here."

"Dat so?" Triggor asked.

Devin met Triggor's gaze, never flinched, and never looked away. As a barkeep and the blood brother of Crukas, he'd learned to never show fear. Without glancing downward, he could see Triggor's hand was on the revolver and the kobold behind him held an armed crossbow with his finger on the trigger. Although he knew their reputations and their names, Devin thought it best to act ignorant. Orgem seemed no threat and appeared uncomfortable. He expected Orgem to retreat.

"If you need drinks, return to the bar, and I'll get what you need," Devin said.

"We need information," Triggor said.

"I'm sorry, but I've none to offer or sell," Devin said evenly. "I don't read Tarot cards or bones, either."

Gynx lowered his crossbow and unsheathed his intimidating dagger. "Look, you can freely tell us what we need to know, or … things'll get bloody soon enough."

Devin cocked a brow and showed no concern, but his hands tightened on the broom handle. "What type of information?"

"We came here to collect a bounty and another dwarf told us where this individual would be," Triggor said. "Instead of capturing the thief, someone tipped him off. Since we're visiting our first time in Ravensdorf, you seem the most likely to have revealed our plot."

"And you are?" Devin asked.

Anger flashed in Triggor's eyes. He was obviously insulted to not receive the proper recognition. "Triggor McLuft!"

"I'm Gynx." The kobold hissed and revealed his sharp teeth and long, slimy wet tongue. "No doubt you've heard of us both. What's your game?"

Devin shrugged. "No game. I'm not a traveler, and my patrons come and go from all over Aetheaon. It's difficult to keep track, so I don't bother."

Gynx frowned. "Ravensdorf's almost as dead as a cemetery. It's not likely you'd forget our faces from earlier."

"Oh, I *recognize* you, but I didn't wait your table, nor did I converse with either of you at all, did I? And as such, why should I even know your names?"

Triggor and Gynx exchanged puzzled looks and their anger subsided ever so slightly. Confusion settled in.

Orgem whispered, "Perhaps we should go order another round, eh? I'll buy."

Triggor shook his head. "Not until we get some answers."

"What information are you seeking?" Devin asked.

Triggor gritted his teeth. "We seek a thief by the name of Crukas."

Devin propped his broom against the wall and crossed his arms. He frowned and rubbed his chin in supposed thought. "Now, *that* name's familiar. I'm certain I've seen his wanted poster at some point, but I've not seen *him*."

"Word has it," Triggor said. "Crukas was traveling to Ravensdorf."

"*Rumored*, perhaps? Like you said, this town's almost as dead as a cemetery."

"We're quite certain he's already arrived."

"How so?"

"We saw him," Gynx said. "I shot at him, only it wasn't him. It was a reflection or an image of him, through magic, no doubt."

"I wish I could help you," Devin said. "But I know no magic so if you an *image* of him, as you indicate, it wasn't my doing."

"We didn't say *you* were the one who cast his image," Triggor said, combing his beard with his hand.

Rekindled anger flickered in Gynx's eyes. "He's lying."

Triggor frowned. "How can you tell?"

"Assumption," Gynx said. "But after a few minutes with my dagger, he'll—"

"Probably lie." Triggor glared at Gynx. "Especially if he's telling the truth now. He'd lie to avoid further pain and send us off on a differ-ent, pointless trail, which would waste too much *more* of our time. So put ya dagger away until we 'ave reason to use it."

Gynx looked disappointed. "Then what do you propose?"

"Look." Triggor met Devin's gaze. "Can you tell us anything at all? Did any of the barmaids happen to mention Crukas?"

Devin shook his head. "No."

"Would any 'ave given him warning?"

Devin sighed. "If none mentioned him, it seems they'd not have seen him, so how could they have given him warning?"

Gynx growled and pointed the dagger at Devin. "I'm telling you, Triggor, give me a minute or less—"

"Torture doesn't guarantee the truth," Triggor said.

"If I might offer any speculation," Devin said, "you mentioned Crukas appeared as an image?"

"Aye," Triggor said, nodding.

"Magic's a rarity in Ravensdorf," Devin said. "Unlike Salem, few sorcerers or witches venture here. However, at the western cliffside, there lives a mage, Scorpius, one who might well be deceiving your minds. He's a prankster."

"Why would he do dat?" Triggor asked. "He knows nothing of us or our intent."

"He reads and feeds off one's lustful intentions. You *desire* to find and capture a thief to collect his reward radiates his attention. After all, you're willing to torture me for an answer I can't possibly give," Devin said.

"Not I!" Triggor said with a firm brow.

"Your friend, though," Devin said.

"We're not friends!" Triggor and Gynx said in unison with such vigor that Devin almost smiled.

"Yet, you travel together."

Triggor cleared his throat. "Not by choice."

"No?" Devin asked with a furrowed brow.

"We share a common … ambition," Triggor said with a stern nod.

"Well," Devin said. "As I mentioned, I've no information to aid you in your pursuit."

Gynx slowly sheathed his dagger, obviously confused. "You think the mage might be responsible then?"

Devin shrugged. "I know of no one else, unless someone in your party is misleading you, it'd have to be the mage."

Triggor and Gynx looked at one another. "Sparrow?"

Triggor gave Devin a brief glance and firm nod. "Thanks."

Triggor and Gynx hurried to the door and Orgem stepped aside allowing them to pass through before following them out.

Devin chuckled softly and shook his head. "Brother, I know not what you're up against, but here's hoping they'll met their fates without harming you."

CHAPTER 40

*T*riggor rushed out of the Mute Changeling's storage room to the table where Sparrow sat with Miss Strella. The swiftness of his loud stomping steps, paired with the fierce anger in his eyes, caused her to hold her breath. His hand rested on the butt of his revolver. As though his movements weren't unsettling enough, Gynx was barely a step behind Triggor.

Sparrow tried to hide her inner fear at their explosive approach, but due to the suddenness, she couldn't hide her uneasiness. Her stomach churned and her heart beat like a hummingbird's frantic wings.

Orgem sat at the table and waved a barmaid to come over. She leaned close, and he whispered in her ear. The barmaid giggled and promptly walked to the bar.

"What's wrong?" Sparrow asked with a high-pitched tone.

"You're still 'ere?" Triggor asked, looking from her to meet Gynx's angry gaze.

She took a quick breath and nodded. "Where else would I be?"

Triggor studied her for several long moments. "I fully expected you to have fled into the night while we spoke to Devin."

Sparrow rested her cupped hands on her lap and offered a dainty, uneasy smile. Despite her obvious nervousness, she didn't rise to stand for fear they'd think she might run. "Nope. I've nowhere else to go. I don't like traveling at night. Nocturnal animals view me as a tasty morsel. Besides, we've yet to find Crukas. Did the barkeep offer any clues for us to follow?"

"She's hiding something," Gynx said with a low, guttural tone.

"Why do you say dat?" Triggor asked.

Miss Strella frowned at the kobold. "Yes, please explain your accusation. We were enjoying a delightful chat before you rudely interrupted us."

Sparrow didn't look at the bard and was surprised Miss Strella readily defended her after previously scolding Sparrow for warning Crukas.

"Her eyes are near tears," Gynx said. "She's fidgety."

Triggor chuckled. "Her uneasiness is no different than she showed when she first came to our table. Such timidness is part of most halflings' nature. They've no stomach for a brawl or confrontations. Gynx, according to you, everyone's hiding something."

"Because usually, everyone *is*." Gynx snarled and seated himself across from Sparrow. He seemed incapable of looking away from her.

Miss Strella adjusted in her chair. "So, Triggor, did your conversation with Devin pay off?"

"Bah! Dat was a bloody dead end," Triggor said.

"Not necessarily." Gynx grumbled with his eyes fixed on Sparrow.

"Leave it!" Triggor said to Gynx. "If she were completely guilty, she'd have fled while we were in the storage room."

"No information?" Miss Strella tried to redirect the conversation. "Nothing at all?"

"No." Triggor kept his angered gaze at Gynx for several seconds. He then looked at Sparrow. "Seems the information we seek sits with this one here."

Sparrow's brow rose. "What? Me?"

Gynx leered at her. "You."

"Why? What did the barkeep accuse me of doing?" she asked.

"Nothing. I heard you warn Crukas of our intent," Gynx said. "I'm certain the others did also."

"While I'm less inclined to fully lay the blame on ya, lass, you need to explain *your* reason for treating Crukas more as an ally than a thief," Triggor said.

"I did no such thing!" The nervousness in Sparrow's eyes was displaced by fiery rage. Her gut calmed and anger made her chest swell. Frothy spittle formed at the sides of her mouth. "Crukas is a thief. He's *not* my friend or ally. I'll never think otherwise. Besides, that's the first time I've ever seen him in person. Well, you know what I mean. So, no, I didn't warn him so he could escape. I wanted him to know Gynx intended to torture him. No one should be treated with such malice."

Orgem, Miss Strella, and Triggor all turned their attention to Gynx.

Triggor sighed. "Okay. I tend to agree with ya. However, my complete trust in ya can't be earned at the moment. Due to my suspicious nature, I'll be keeping an eye on ya, too."

"Me, too." Orgem grinned and tapped his eyepatch with a thick finger. He shrugged. "It's all I got."

"I'm serious," Triggor said with a tightened brow.

"And I'm not?" Orgem said. "I've only one eye, or are *ya* blind?"

Miss Strella laughed softly. Sparrow failed to suppress a grin.

Triggor shook his head and grinned. "Sparrow, from this point forward, you must swear to stay within our view at all times. Should you run, I'll assume you're in cahoots with Crukas and as guilty as he. Agreed?"

Sparrow sighed, hoping to dispel her boiling anger. It didn't, but she nodded. "Agreed."

Triggor looked at Gynx. "Is dat better?"

Gynx shook his head and shrugged. "Her oath makes no difference to me. She aided a thief, and only time can tell if she'll rescue him a second time."

"I *never* rescued him," Sparrow said. "He wasn't in the warehouse. Had he been, what I said wouldn't have benefited him. You fired without hesitation, without warning, or even asking him to surrender. He'd have either been severely wounded or dead. Either way, the information wouldn't have allowed his escape. He was surrounded."

Gynx grumbled and sneered.

"True," Triggor said. "Now, let's attend to a different matter. Devin gave us a slight hint in some direction."

Miss Strella's eyes brightened. "What'd he say?"

"He believes the mage in the tower overlooking this small villa might've lured us to the warehouse," Triggor said.

Miss Strella gasped and looked shaken. "Scorpius?"

"Aye," Triggor said. "I suppose dat's the name."

"Why would he assume that?" Sparrow asked. "Scorpius should have no interest in Crukas or *us*, for that matter."

Gynx studied her for a moment. "I suppose you've talked to the mage, too?"

Sparrow flicked an indignant gaze at Gynx but said nothing. He was needling her for a response to keep her riled up, so she held back the impulse to splash further fuel to satisfy his apparent need for chaos. "No. I simply made a point."

Triggor nodded. "Aye. It's a valid one, I suppose."

"Crukas somehow used a spell to pull off his act. Few individuals capable of magic venture to Ravensdorf," Gynx said. "Sort of makes sense Crukas might have a connection to the mage, perhaps they're associates in one way or another, but my suspicions continue to focus on the halfling."

Sparrow rolled her eyes. "Why? We've been through all of this. I've been honest."

"Well," Gynx said with a wink. "The dwarf who told you about seeing Crukas on the street earlier today. Why'd he give you the goose chase?"

"I told you, I don't know him or his brothers," she replied.

"Yet, they left rather quickly after we made our way to the warehouse. Any idea where we might find them?" Gynx asked. "I've a few questions I'd like to ask them."

Sparrow shook her head. "I *don't* know them. I've no idea where they might've gone. They could still be in Ravensdorf for all we know."

"Ignore 'em," Triggor said. "Maybe Gynx's mind will catch up with the conversation eventually. Devin insinuated Scorpius might've projected the image of Crukas to keep us off guard."

Sparrow frowned. "That makes no sense. What would his motive be for helping Crukas? Does Scorpius stand to gain anything?"

Silence hung over the table, and even Gynx failed to offer a slight possibility.

Finally, Miss Strella said, "To my knowledge, Scorpius associates with no one. He's a solitary mage, and a powerful one from the tales I've heard and gathered."

"What I think," Sparrow said, "is Crukas somehow conjured a spell to appear in the warehouse. He wants us out of the way so he can rob someone else."

"Like whom?" Gynx asked.

Sparrow shrugged. According to Fasha, Crukas stole the Cursed Book of the Damned and made his way to Ravensdorf. But why? Fasha somehow knew Crukas was here and had tricked Sparrow into falling through a portal to also arrive at Ravensdorf. Without a demon's aid, the book was useless to Crukas, so ... "He plans to steal something from Scorpius!"

"Preposterous!" Triggor said.

"I agree," Miss Strella said. "He's not *that* foolish!"

"Seems everyone knows more about Crukas than I." Gynx grinned. "Ah, but if that's Crukas' *plan*, we're going to miss his death."

"What would Scorpius 'ave dat Crukas would steal?" Triggor asked.

"I've no idea." Sparrow shook her head and frowned while thinking. She knew nothing about the mage and what he might possess that would tempt Crukas to steal from him.

"It doesn't matter," Gynx said. "An opportunity to watch an arrogant, foolish thief die at the hands of a mage is worth more than the reward."

"Let's not get rash," Triggor said. "The reward's most important."

"He bested us, Gynx," Sparrow said, "and you're elated he'd die a horrible death."

Gynx shrugged and innocently held up his scaly hands. "*Not* at my hands, sweetie."

"You're not listening," Miss Strella said. "Scorpius isn't a lesser type of mage. He's evil. Only a fool would dare attempt to find a way into his tower."

Gynx smiled. "Our intent isn't to confront Scorpius, but to watch Crukas' demise."

Miss Strella frowned. "Our *intent* isn't something Scorpius will take into consideration."

"Night's upon us," Triggor said with a tired sigh. "Dat'd be the best opportune time for a thief to steal. We should head there, just in case."

Miss Strella's eyes widened. She shook her head. "And should we be wrong? It's *our* lives in jeopardy."

An icy chill shot down Sparrow's spine. Again, she thought of Fasha's prophesy concerning Sparrow's untimely demise.

Triggor shrugged and pointed a stern finger at Sparrow. "We take our chances in dat. You, halfling, you stick close to us, or—"

Gynx raised the crossbow and his eyes gleamed with eagerness. "You'll find a bolt in your back and an excruciatingly, slow death."

"You'll hear no protest from me," Triggor said. "We'll leave ya body for the ravens."

Sparrow eyed the crossbow and nodded. "I'm with you to the end."

CHAPTER 41

*C*rukas tried to jerk his arm free of the tight grip around his wrist but couldn't. He couldn't tell if a hand held fast to him, or some type of toothless creature had clamped onto his arm. "Let go."

The grip lessened and Crukas pulled free.

"What are ya doing, thief?" Bramnir asked. "Whatever it is, we're 'ere to help."

"I can't ask that of you," Crukas said softly but sternly. Though he would never openly admit it, a sense of relief washed over him to know the three brothers were standing beside him. In the opaque darkness, they huddled together. They couldn't see one another, but their breathing allowed him to know the proximity of where each dwarf stood. Crukas didn't have to ask them to keep their voices at a whisper. They understood the danger of the mage locating them.

"We know. Ya didn't ask," Adgus said. "But we know if ya go it alone, you're dead, which is what you planned all along, correct?"

"No. To die is *not* my intention, but it's most likely the outcome," Crukas said. "What gave you such an idea?"

"Your gift of the rarest stout in all Aetheaon meant you knew you'd not survive," Adgus said. "Since we declined taking it, it means you *must* survive. Devin still holds it for you."

"Actually," Crukas said with a smile. "The gift was simply that. A gift. You deserve it more than I since you put your lives on the line for me. But, I didn't come here to die. I understand the possibility certainly exists. The odds are greater against me than in favor of my success."

"Nevertheless, dat's why we're here," Bramnir said. "To aid your success."

Crukas was almost moved to tears. "You don't even know *why* I'm here."

"Then enlighten us," Adgus said.

Crukas explained the Cursed Spellbook of the Damned and the correct order of the items he intended to steal in order to stop the Plague-bringer from destroying Aetheaon. His first stop should've been Dark Ayr Tower.

"Dat's a bold sacrifice for a thief," Adgus said.

"Nothing's sacrificed yet." Crukas took an Elven glowstone from his pocket. It was small but gave enough light for them to see one another without drawing attention to themselves.

"Except you and I," Ebden said.

Bramnir whispered in a hoarse voice, "What'cha mean?"

Ebden's voice shook. "E-ever since I touched dat book, I've felt an overshadowing evil hovering over me."

Crukas clasped a firm hand on Ebden's shoulder. "As have I."

"Shadowy creatures have been following me," Ebden said. "You've seen 'em, too?"

Crukas frowned and shook his head. "No. I've seen nothing like that."

"The book's cursed? And yet, you let our brother take the book?" Adgus asked.

"You insisted," Crukas replied. "I wanted to keep it in my possession. Remember? I tried to warn you."

Bramnir said, "Aye. Dat ya did."

"What can break the curse?" Adgus asked.

"Irmine's working on that," Crukas said. "The book's with her."

"Will she be cursed, too?" Ebden asked.

"Honestly," Crukas said. "I've no idea. She took the and refuses to give it back. Since she's a priestess, I hope she knows how to protect herself and perhaps find a way to release Ebden and myself from its tainted effect."

"Aye," Adgus said. "She saved me life, so perhaps she can remove the curse."

"What's your plan, thief?" Bramnir asked.

"To steal his mask without dying," Crukas replied.

"Dat's a bit vague," Adgus said.

Crukas shrugged. "I know, but since I've never been inside the tower—"

"Wait." Bramnir's voice deepened. "What?"

"Ya don't know the tower's layout?" Adgus' brow furrowed.

"No. How could I?" Crukas replied. "You can't approach during the day. We'd be seen well before we reach it."

"I've known brethren who've stormed a fortress during war," Bramnir said. "But most times, there's some knowledge of the layout. Even a crude map's helpful."

Crukas nodded. "This is why I chose to find my way inside, alone. I don't want anyone else injured or killed due to these dangers."

"Eh," Adgus said. "We've entered more dangerous mines for gemstones. What's the worst we can face 'ere?"

Crukas winced. He wished Adgus hadn't made such a statement, as those foolish enough to discount the dangers were often the ones who suffered the most severe consequences.

"You're sure I can't talk you out of accompanying me?" Crukas asked softly. He knew the answer before asking, but thought it best to confirm their oaths.

"Aye," Adgus said. "No sense letting a thief take all the glory in protecting Aetheaon. I'm in."

"As am I," Bramnir said.

Ebden stood quietly for several moments.

"Well?" Bramnir asked. "What say you, Ebden?"

"You've me axe as well. Cursed by dat book, what little more 'ave I to lose?" Ebden said.

Crukas said, "May the prayers of Irmine surround us with safety."

"Aye," the three brothers said.

CHAPTER 42

⁂

*C*rossing the near barren field in total darkness was almost equivocal to a blind man at the center of an empty banquet hall patting his way to find the exit. Without any proper bearings and light, a straight path proved difficult. Any slight deviation could keep Crukas and the dwarves walking in circles for hours without them ever reaching Dark Ayr Tower.

Crukas took the lead, crept with light steps, and barely made a sound. But behind him, the three dwarves' heavy boots crushed the thin shale stones into shattered fragments. Although the soft pulverization of stone wasn't loud, the sound seemed more amplified because a covert approach to the tower was imperative. Without a sliver of light, other than an occasional use of the Elven stone, Crukas decided to follow the howling breeze that carried a slight seawater flavor. He assumed these rushing winds swept inland from the bluffs, and after a half hour of blind wandering, his theory proved correct.

A slight gap in the night's heavy curtain of fog revealed the crude, broken steps that led upward to a small bridge ending at Dark Ayr Tower's fortified gate. Two sconces held dancing bluish flames at each side of the gate. The massive gate's iron bars proved impassable and no visible guards were posted. The absence of guards didn't mean the gate wasn't protected. Only a fool would believe such. As a thief, Crukas knew otherwise. No doubt, traps and other types of dangerous devices or protective spells lie in wait.

Poison darts, triggered spears, or a false floor camouflaged on the stone bridge before the gate were only a few apprehensive cautions Crukas kept in mind. He'd seen and escaped almost every type of trap during his lifetime. The most obvious path of choice tended to be the most deadly when dealing with a mage or wizard. Nothing was ever simple, and if it seemed so, one should be skeptical. Scorpius held a greater advantage over the folks in Ravensdorf, which was using their *fear* of him against them.

Perhaps Scorpius and his fortified tower were here long before the first settlements were established on the outskirts of Ravensdorf. Crukas doubted it, but Scorpius had probably made enough examples out of the townsfolk to keep others at bay, which destroyed any intention of them raiding the tower or attempting to assassinate the mage. Like magic, fear held a longer reach and the exaggerated rumors challenged only braver fools to risk their lives and limbs solely to prove they lacked any sense of dread. Or, they believed they were the exception and would become triumphant where everyone else had failed. Sadly, the dust of their bones and charred outlines on the stones testified a different story and outcome; though none of these attempted challenges seemed to have occurred recently.

This gave Crukas a slight bit of hope. If no intruders had raised an alarm set by Scorpius, perhaps the mage wouldn't anticipate trespassers.

Crukas stopped walking and Adgus bumped into his back.

"What is it?" Adgus asked.

The dark shadow of the narrow, short bridge leading to the tower gate caused Crukas to gasp slightly. He shook his head, almost in terror at the tower's height. "We've arrived."

Adgus and Bramnir stepped beside Crukas and peered at the cylindrical tower rising upward into the sky, seemingly endless. The outer stone walls were aged, but the fog prevented a clear view to determine whether gargoyles or dragonkin circled or perched on any of the shadowy balconies, waiting to devour new victims.

"Aye," Bramnir whispered. "Indeed. Where exactly ya suppose the mage is? From the looks of it, we could search a moon's cycle or longer without ever finding him."

"I've the feeling *he'll* find us," Crukas said.

Adgus nodded. "I agree. How do you propose we get inside? There are no guards, but I'm under the conviction he has no need for them."

"My thoughts exactly," Crukas said.

Static filled the air. Swirling dark clouds above the tower flashed with bluish cloud-to-cloud lightning. A set of red eyes peered downward from a subtle balcony. Several winged creatures hovered and circled the tower.

"Another storm?" Adgus asked.

Crukas shook his head. "No. He has watchers. We've triggered an alarm."

"Eh?" Ebden said.

"Scorpius knows we're here," Crukas said. "Run!"

Crukas turned and ran into the fleeting darkness. The hot yellow lightning bolt descended with an illuminating blast. He had barely crossed the small bridge and dove off the path when the lightning struck the stones. A wave of scorching heat washed over him. The intensity of the bolt caused a few stone slabs to glow bright orange and begin melting. Crukas rolled to his side and looked for the dwarves. Not seeing them, he feared the worst and pushed himself to his feet.

"Bramnir!" Crukas squinted. After being subjected to the pitch darkness in their trek across the field, the sudden bright flash of lightning wreaked havoc with his vision. "Adgus? Ebden? Where are you? You okay?"

Three shaken voices faintly replied, "Aye."

Crukas staggered to the side of the smoldering rocks and peered over the edge of the bridge. Two dwarves were crouched on the empty bed of what might've been a dried moat or a large stream at one time. The leftover, dry channel might've been where lava once flowed from the mountain's ledge.

"You all right?" Bramnir asked from near the gate. He sat on his knees and held his shield over his head. The metal glimmered with streams of smoke rolling off. The etched runes in his metal shield glowed fiery white. Those runes had apparently prevented Bramnir from being fried by the lightning blast.

"I'm fine," Crukas replied, stepping closer. "You?"

Beneath the faint glow of his heated shield, Bramnir's smile was visible through his frazzled beard. His wide eyes held prolonged, unexpected surprise and shock. "A bit toasty warm at the moment. Other than dat, okay, I suppose."

Crukas offered his hand and the dwarf readily accepted it. "Let's get down to your brothers."

Crukas looked for a small crevice or a possible set of footholds where they could safely move down into the rocky channel, but none could be found. "I suppose we've got to jump, too."

"Bah!" Bramnir said. "You first."

Crukas took a brief moment, spotted what looked to be a flat area of rock where he hoped not to twist or break his ankles, and then, he leapt. Due to his light weight and armor, he landed somewhat gracefully with a pitter soft scuff of his boots, no louder than a cat's paws.

Bramnir, however, wasn't as surefooted or graceful.

Bramnir's heavy boots struck the dry channel with a harsh thud. A few sparks ignited when the metal soles of his boots hit. He bent his knees slightly on landing, which helped slow Bramnir from pivoting straight forward and face-planting, but he was unable to maintain his balance. Crukas grabbed Bramnir's forearm, bent toward Bramnir, and braced his shoulder against the dwarf's breastplate. Otherwise, Bramnir might've skidded and toppled on top of his two brothers.

"Good thing the channel's empty," Crukas said.

"True." Adgus slowly rose to his feet. "Or we'd all be dead, one way or the other."

"The lightning came far too close, if ya ask me," Ebden said.

Overhead, a long thunderous rumble of doom shook from the sky to the ground. Loose stone fragments and pieces of mortar skidded and bounced down the side of the tower before pelleting all around them.

A mesh of sparkling light flickered in the small clouds, illuminating a couple of winged creatures circling. Stone scraped stone from above and a heavy flap of wings came closer.

"Gargoyle!" Ebden pointed.

Crukas and the dwarves hurried to get beneath the bridge for possible shelter, but the gargoyle swooped down and blocked their path. With a backward thrash of its wing, it sent Crukas into the air and he landed on his back. He winced and groaned.

Bramnir swung his heavy axe overhead and brought it down hard into the stone beast's chest. The metal chinked the stone and bits of small rocks exploded. Although damage was done, the strike was not a death blow. The gargoyle screeched and grabbed at the axe, but Adgus's axe blade lopped off its hand and shattered parts of its wing. Its red eyes widened and it gnashed its long fangs.

Unable to fly, it hobbled away from the dwarves and toward Crukas, perhaps its intended target. Crukas remained stunned and had difficulty breathing or moving.

Bramnir brought his axe overhead and drove the blade into the gargoyle's spine where its wings attached. The crushing blow broke through and exited through its chest cavity and heart, provided it had a heart. The gargoyle stiffened and broke into large stone chunks.

Bramnir and Adgus each grabbed one of Crukas' hands and hefted him to his feet. They carried him under the bridge, careful of the dripping molten stone where the lightning had struck. The long orange streams resembled magma. Crukas shook his head and wondered how much protection the bridge even offered.

"I figured." Adgus cleared his throat. "Dat's dar's no way Scorpius is the only occupant in this tower."

"I was under the same impression," Crukas said. "But more gargoyles are in flight."

"How many?" Adgus asked.

Crukas shrugged.

"Not dat numbers matter," Bramnir said. "Scorpius doesn't need an army. Not with stone sentinels guarding the place."

Crukas arched his back and stretched his neck from side to side. He was fortunate to not have suffered any broken bones or get crushed by the gargoyle. His lungs hurt less and the pain subsided. Another gargoyle could descend and attack at any time. Since they couldn't predict when, they kept occasionally checking the sky.

Static filled the air again. A crackling sound popped and moved from the bright flashes in the sky and danced down the sides of the tower and across the dry channel.

"Brace yourselves," Bramnir said.

Chain lightning swept across the empty channel toward them. The flowing, jagged lines of bluish-white lightning sizzled and reached outward like a jellyfish stretched its tendrils into a net to search for food.

"There's no way we can get outta the way or outrun it," Adgus said. "And if there's another gargoyle attack, lightning won't hurt it."

Bramnir gritted his teeth. "He's trying to flush us out into the open."

Without thinking, Crukas' forefinger and thumb grabbed the protective amulet Irmine had given him. The three dwarves placed their backs against Crukas, slammed their shields against the rocky channel, and formed a tight enclosure around them. Before the hissing chains of lightning reached them, the runes on their shields, weapons, and armor lit up. A curtain of static surrounded them and resisted the pulsating, chain lightning sweeping around them.

Crukas' hair stood on end, his skin prickled, and his hearing became fuzzy. He closed his eyes, and a light brighter than the chain lightning wrapped around them inside the small shield wall.

Something shrieked beyond them in the dried bed, but only for a moment. Crukas listened intently. What else lie in the lightning's path. Not a gargoyle, as Bramnir was correct. Lightning held no effect on them. At least, not like regular brick and mortar, as their lifeline of magical enchantments protected them from the elements.

The bright protective light diminished from inside their enclosure and after the lightning passed, Crukas opened his eyes.

The fading sparks of electricity buzzed and hissed, growing quieter and slowly fizzling out. Crukas studied the path ahead, where he thought something shrieked in short-lived agony. With the fuzzy static ringing in his ears, he couldn't be certain he'd heard anything at all. He'd rather inspect and know, than to regret not checking. They didn't need to be attacked by something from a blindside.

Where the elongated, jagged strands of lightning had reached the edges of the channel, numerous tiny objects remained lit, resembling glowworms or fireflies nestled against the stones. A closer examination revealed these to be a type of fungi glow-caps, not often seen when in small numbers. But with thousands meshed together like a sheet of moss, the caps offered a radiance in the pitch of night; enough light for Crukas and the dwarves to follow the channel's path with less hazards.

"We've got to find our way inside the tower," Bramnir said, lowering his shield. "Or, the next wave will most likely kill us."

"Agreed," Adgus said, "but how?"

"Follow me," Crukas said.

The three dwarves followed Crukas with their weapons drawn and their shields at the ready, perhaps in anticipation of another gargoyle or electrical attack. At this point, they had no idea *what* they might encounter.

Close to where Crukas believed a shriek shrilled, lie an enormous wormlike creature. It writhed and thrashed its large toothy mouth harshly on the stone channel. The chain lightning had killed the tunneling creature, but its nervous system didn't recognize it was dead. A good portion of its elongated body disappeared into a large burrowed hole beneath the tower. Its overall size was frightening. The tunnel's circumference was wide enough for a small wagon to enter with room to spare.

Ebden said, "Dat could've swallowed all of us and remained hungry."

"Might be more of 'em," Bramnir said.

"What do you make of dat?" Adgus poked its toothy mouth with the edge of his axe.

The giant worm had another mouth inside its outer mouth. Both bore sharp, serrated teeth. In between its outer teeth were several fangs the length of short swords that leaked venom.

Crukas shrugged. "Never seen anything quite like it before."

A small voice from near the bridge said, "It's a Fae-annelid."

The three dwarves turned with their weapons ready.

Crukas frowned and squinted, trying to see the figure. "Who are you?"

"Tamana," the pixie replied. She flittered lower and revealed herself with an illuminated magical aura. "What fools venture to the foot of Dark Ayr Tower?"

Crukas eyed her shrewdly. "You referring to us or yourself?"

She huffed, but allowed a slight smile. "Fair enough."

Bramnir's hand tightened on his axe. "Are you one of Scorpius' guards?"

She scoffed. "Far from it. Especially since his lightning killed Reaver."

"The worm?" Adgus asked with surprise. "Ya *named* it?"

Tamana nodded. "Yes. It's a dark Fae ... *Was.*"

"Why are *you* here?" Crukas asked her.

"These glowing shrooms," she said, as though he should've known. "They've magical properties."

"Ah," Adgus said. "We never noticed them until after the lightning."

"Thanks to the lot of you," she said, "You damned near got us all killed."

"We didn't cause the lightning," Ebden said.

"You triggered it!"

"Not intentionally," Crukas said softly. "And we'd prefer *not* attracting any further attacks."

Tamana glared. "So what's the purpose for your death wish?"

"Death is *not* our wish," Crukas said with a slight smile.

"No?"

"No."

She frowned and hovered closer to his face. The buzz of her wings reminded him of an annoying insect. "I suppose that's true, being as you crushed the gargoyle. Good job with that."

Bramnir smiled. "Thanks."

Tamana shrugged her tiny shoulders. "Then why are you here?"

Crukas sighed.

"It's doubtful we'll find what we've come for," Bramnir said. "As we can't find any entrance to get inside the tower."

"Few ever have successfully found a way inside that I know of," she said. "And those who have ... seldom ever find a way out. What's so important that you're too stubborn to flee after his attacks?"

"It's a life or death situation for all of Aetheaon," Adgus said.

Her eyes widened and actually beamed. She mockingly clasped her tiny hands together and grinned manically. "Oooh! Do tell!"

Crukas shook his head. "I'm afraid that's not necessarily the complete story. Only a part of it, but it fails to address the necessity. Not now, anyway, but since we're here ... I only require one object from the mage."

Her brow creased as she studied his face more carefully. "Wait ... You're Crukas!"

"We've no time for this," Crukas said. "Either we find a way inside quickly, or else, we must flee. Scorpius has attacked twice, but his next attack will be far more severe."

Tamana stared at the wormlike creature with a tinge of remorse. It stopped moving and expelled a loud blast of rank gas through its strange mouths. "There's a way inside, but it'll be messy."

"What'cha mean?" Adgus asked in a mean whisper.

"Reaver burrowed through the tower wall, turned, and cleared through his tunnel a second time," she replied.

"So?" Bramnir said.

Crukas shook his head and frowned with disgust. "So if we remove his corpse, we have a way inside?"

"Yes."

"If you used Reaver to make the tunnel, what's your intention?" Crukas asked. "The mage apparently has something you need, too."

She shrugged her tiny shoulders. "Leave that to us. You go after what you seek, and we'll tend to our needs. Deal?"

Adgus grumbled. "But dat means *we* 'ave to remove the worm?"

"All the pixies with me combined could never budge him."

"We can't tug this worm out. There's no way," Bramnir said.

"Like I said, 'it'll be messy'." Tamana cringed.

"You said that Reaver's dark Fae," Crukas said. "If we desecrate its corpse—"

"No. It's a worm, under our care and guidance," she replied. "Not intellectual, mind you, and even if it had been, he'd have had it no other way."

In the faint lighting of the fungi and Tamana's glow, Bramnir and Adgus grimaced.

Tamana smiled slightly. "It's either that or we wait to see what Scorpius hurls next."

Balls of lightning brightened the night sky.

"Let's get this over with," Adgus said.

"So we have a deal?" Tamana asked.

Crukas nodded.

"Aye," the dwarves said, each finding a place to slit open the worm's thick leathery skin with their axes.

CHAPTER 43

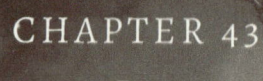

Sparrow stumbled slightly on the rocky field where the sheep grazed. With darkness surrounding her and the others, she considered running to escape. Surely, Gynx couldn't get an accurate shot with his crossbow. But, where could she run and be safe? Gynx would take pleasure in hunting her down from town to town. He'd make it his mission to kill her, and no reward was necessary. She didn't understand his reasoning, or lack thereof, in blaming her for Crukas' stunt.

Gynx was leading the party toward the tower without any light, as his eyes were best suited for the dark caverns, even more than the dwarves. In the darkness, the faintest light would become a foolish beacon. The black night disturbed her, perhaps not as badly as the ominous darkness inside Fasha's shop. Yet, with the growing tension between Triggor and Gynx, she believed she'd be safer in Fasha's shop. The more their angered fuses shortened, the more likely she might get caught in their crossfire.

"Gynx, are we even headed in the right direction?" She whispered with slight frustration. Although they hadn't walked more than five minutes, those few minutes seemed an hour in the void of uncertainty.

"Yes," Gynx said. "My sense of smell tells me Crukas and some dwarves headed this way recently."

"How can ya be sure?" Triggor asked. "Two dwarves are presently beside you."

"Your stench I already recognize," Gynx said. "The others have a different odor."

"I've not the nose of a kobold," Triggor said, "but there's no masking your horrid smell, either. So I suppose I'll 'ave to take your word dat you're tracking *their* scent. Keep sniffing, then."

"Hey! I'm not a mongrel you can command," Gynx said.

"My mounted boar follows directions better and has a better sense of smell. So, prove to me you've a good enough nose to lead us to Crukas," Triggor said. "Like a good pup."

Gynx growled and turned, bumping Sparrow in the process. She groaned slightly and fought to maintain her balance as she stepped aside. She didn't want to stand between them. In the darkness, Sparrow had no idea what was happening. The click of Triggor's revolver stopped Gynx's growls.

"Don't forget, kobold," Triggor said. "We dwarves have good eyesight in the dark, too."

"How could I forget?" Gynx said.

"Would the two of you stop arguing long enough to find Crukas?" Sparrow stepped farther to the side and hoped she didn't accidentally get shot by either of them. "Or just kill one other and leave the rest of us out of your squabble."

"I agree," Miss Strella said. "This isn't beneficial. You're wasting time."

Triggor uncocked the gun and the metal barrel scratched leather as he slid the gun into its holster. "Fine. For *now*. But this isn't over."

Gynx chuckled with sinister glee. "Not by a long shot. Let me do what I know I can, Triggor, without you butting your fat hairy nose into it, eh? I was already on their path, but *don't* order me to find them. Nor demand that I sit, fetch, or bark, either. I've a tail, but it's *not* the wagging type."

Orgem laughed heartily. "Good one."

229

"Please, Gynx, can we continue?" Sparrow asked. "Before Scorpius notices we're out in the open?"

"Since you said, *'Please.'*" The sarcastic emphasis on the polite term seemed sour coming from his mouth, almost like he had to scrape the word from his tongue.

"Dat's more than you'll get from me," Triggor said.

Gynx huffed. "Stick close. I've a feeling—"

A huge bolt of fiery lightning shot from the sky and lit up the night with such radiance, the light washed over them, and fully exposed their location to anyone watching the field from a greater vantage point.

Sparrow and the others dove facedown and peered up. The lightning struck the small bridge at the gate of the tower. Although the flash hurt her eyes, Sparrow was certain four figures were standing on the bridge moments before the bolt hit the bridge. Three dwarves and one human.

Gynx cried in agony. Since his eyes were keener in the darkness, the intensely bright, lightning bolt must've seared his eyes.

"They're there," she whispered.

"Who?" Gynx groaned.

"Crukas," she replied. "Apparently the three dwarves are with him."

"Where?" Triggor asked. "I can't see anything."

Sparrow whispered, "Near the tower."

"I see nothing," Miss Strella said.

"Nor do I," Orgem said.

"Half the time you don't," Gynx said.

"True, but my one good eye sees nothing but streaks."

Gynx groaned. "Understandable. My eyes ache. I see nothing."

Triggor grunted. "Dat's the same for me. Dat was one Helluva lightning strike."

"I'm afraid the weather wasn't responsible for it, either," Miss Strella said.

"Magic?" Sparrow asked.

"Nothing less," the bard said softly. "Scorpius must've raised his defenses."

Triggor grumbled. "We've nothing else to do except wait for our vision to return. Best we stay flat on the ground and hope Scorpius doesn't notice us."

"For once I agree with you," Gynx said. "My eyes might be bleeding from the sudden harsh light."

"We're quite vulnerable lying here," Miss Strella said.

"At least it's dark," Sparrow said softly. "It's less likely we'll be noticed. We're still a good distance from the tower."

"Sparrow?" Triggor said.

"Yes?"

"Are you sure you saw Crukas and the dwarves?"

"I can't say for certain it was them. But in the flash of lightning, I saw three dwarves and one thin human. The coincidence for another identical group is next to impossible."

"I 'ave to agree," Triggor said. "We wait until our vision returns. Then we head to the tower."

"Do you think it's wise?" Miss Strella asked. "We've no sorcerer with us or any way to protect ourselves from magic."

"Scorpius' attention will be on Crukas," Triggor said. "We can use dat distraction to our advantage."

Miss Strella didn't attempt to hide the fear in her voice. "I—I believe his tower's guarded."

"Don't worry about the situation until we get closer," Gynx said. "If we're fortunate enough for the mage to kill Crukas, we snatch the thief's corpse and turn it in for the reward."

"You're cold," Sparrow said quietly.

"Thanks," Gynx said. "I also have no soul, so no need to over embellish the flattery. Unless, this is your way of showing interest in me?"

Sparrow scoffed. She hated feeling weak and vulnerable, and at the moment she'd never felt so helpless. If the lightning had blinded Crukas and the three dwarves, they could possibly catch up to them. If not, they might never catch them. The most foolish decision they'd made when they left the Mute Changeling was not hiring a mage or wizard to accompany them. Miss Strella was right. They were no match for the mage, if he'd conjured the lightning. Only Triggor and Gynx were capable of defending their group but that was before the lightning. Against spells or curses, even they had no defense. She hoped Scorpius' attention was solely on Crukas and the dwarves aiding him. Since she and her group were somewhat outside the tower's territory, they might go unnoticed.

Her sight was next to nothing before the lightning made their surroundings blacker. How long before her sight returned? Since Triggor and Gynx had better night vision, her vision would probably recover faster. Once Triggor's sight improved, he'd make the decision to move forward. Until then, she'd fret.

CHAPTER 44

Crukas grimaced as he sliced through the worm's exoskeleton. The wet, gooey fluids gushed and splashed on the dry channel. He scraped worm guts off his dagger. The rotten stench of dung was far worse than he expected.

Aided by the glow caps' faint light, he and the dwarves hacked through the worm's flesh nearest the bored tunnel. Due to the worm's massive size, its entrails sloshed and rose like a rush of thick water after a dam broke. The four stood waist deep in the pungent, gunky sludge.

Crukas fought the urge to vomit. He took shallow breaths to lessen further nausea. "Tamana said it'd be messy."

Adgus gagged. "I've got worm poo and goo all over me. I'm wading in the blasted stuff."

"We all are," Ebden said.

"Where's dat pixie anyway?" Adgus asked.

"No idea," Crukas replied. He raked a handful of the worm excrement from his leggings and flung it against the tower's foundation. "Sticky stuff, almost worse than glue."

"Be thankful its digestive juices aren't strong enough to dissolve our armor," Bramnir said.

"Never considered that," Crukas replied. "How do we get this off of us."

"I'm hoping for a pool or an underground stream," Bramnir said. "But as dry as the field is, dat's highly unlikely."

"The pixie's gone." Crukas glanced upward at the looming tower. No flickering lightning or flying gargoyles was visible. "Why hasn't Scorpius issued another attack?"

"Shh! Don't jinx us," Adgus said sternly. "We should be grateful he hasn't and get through the tunnel fast."

"He hasn't attacked," Tamana said, flittering slightly above them. "Probably because Reaver's digested earth has masked your appearance. At least for now."

Ebden said, "How's dat?"

"Although a large worm, he was protected by my Fae magic and that lingering essence covers you."

"I'm coated with magical worm dung?" Adgus said with a hearty chuckle.

Tamana's eyes brightened. "I find no other reason for Scorpius to delay further assaults. He either thinks you're all dead or you fled."

Bramnir brought his axe overhead and plunged the blade through the tough worm's hide. He paused, glanced at the pixie, and swallowed hard. "Sorry."

She offered a weak smile. "It's fine. He's gone. In a way, he sacrificed himself as a means for us to enter the tower. If the opportunity arises for revenge, believe me, I'll take it, even though Reaver wasn't Scorpius' intended target."

Bramnir took a deep breath and pulled the blade toward him, slicing a long groove through the worm's hide. Tamana seemed amazed at how easily the axe cut through the tough skin.

Crukas' dagger kept its sharp edge even after slicing through a long strip of the worm's hide. The dwarves' axes and blades maintained their razored cutting edges. But their blades did nothing to rid themselves of the rising dung.

Standing in the sludge and fully disgusted, Crukas jerked back when something wriggled in the acrid mess. "Yah!"

"What's wrong?" Bramnir asked.

"Something's moving at my feet," Crukas replied.

"Back away!" Adgus stepped closer and readied his axe.

Crukas moved. "No argument from me."

Tamana waved her hand and illuminated the area where Crukas had stood. The cruddy mess jiggled, and a hand protruded upward.

"Careful," she said. "That's the arm of a ghoul or maybe a ghast. One scratch could paralyze you at the very least."

Adgus cocked a brow and was hesitant to chop the moving appendage. "How do ya know it's a ghoul's arm?"

"It's still moving," she replied. "If you hack it to pieces, each piece continues to move and search for prey."

Adgus lowered the axe.

"How'd it get inside Reaver?" Crukas asked.

"Reaver must have eaten the creature or ripped off its arm. Just know its whereabouts and it's possible the rest of its body might be in the waste."

Crukas winced. He'd been foolish to believe getting inside Dark Ayr Tower would be easy. Of course, dismembering Reaver's corpse wasn't easy, and an experience he'd long have nightmares about. He wished he had a crude map of the tower's layout, like Bramnir had pointed out, but the likelihood of finding such a map was impossible. From bard tales, no one ever ventured into the tower and escaped to boast of success.

The ghoulish fingers pulled the arm and crawled through the sludge and moved farther away, much to his relief.

Before learning about the ghoul being trapped inside Reaver's gut, he considered using the inside of the giant worm for a tunnel after emptying it. Should the ghoul's head be in the goo, it could bite and infect them. They couldn't chance that.

Flaps of worm skin draped loosely. The worm slowly collapsed upon itself like a wineskin after the wine was depleted. The more the gut contents oozed out, the lower the top half of the worm slumped.

"Back away," Crukas said. "I've an idea."

Since Crukas was the thinnest and perhaps the most agile, he climbed on the worm and crawled between the top of the tunnel and Reaver's deflating body.

"What are ya doing?" Adgus asked.

"I'm trying to squeeze out the rest of its waste to flatten its body," Crukas replied. "After it's flattened, we should fit through the tunnel without tugging out the rest of its body or stumbling on the rest of the ghoul."

Ebden and Adgus both grunted.

Crukas pushed against the top of the tunnel and pressed his back into the softened worm's body, but his weight and strength weren't effective enough to expel the remaining fluids. The thick exoskeleton was sturdier than he thought.

Bramnir grinned. "I see what ya are trying to do. Let me help."

Bramnir attempted to climb atop the worm, but the slimy ooze caused him to slip. Crukas extended his hand while Adgus and Ebden cupped their hands for Bramnir to step up on. Bramnir grabbed Crukas' hand and the two brothers hoisted Bramnir upward. He landed beside Crukas and together, they worked their way deeper into the tunnel, as the acrid waste shot outward. When the top part of the worm lowered, Adgus and Ebden walked onto the deflating carcass and joined Crukas and Bramnir.

From looking at Reaver's long body on the dry channel bed, he figured the rest of its body measured as long, if not longer than the part outside the tunnel. Their good fortune—if he could call it that after wallowing in worm dung—was the tunnel was a fourth the length of the outer end of the worm. And in less than a half hour, they stepped down *inside* the tower.

The stench inside the tower was harsher than the smell permeating from their bodies. Crukas realized he might've been better off not trying to steal Scorpius' mask at all. In a small watery chamber, several ghouls sloshed around. They grunted, groaned, and aimlessly tried to reach him and the dwarves. He wanted to retreat, but the dwarves readied their weapons. There was no turning back.

CHAPTER 45

A half dozen ghouls waded in the water pool. Reaching
upward, they sloshed and rippled the water. The smell of
death and decay permeated the air. Bluish-white fires burned in
several braziers around the pool's outer perimeter, approximately six
feet above the tallest ghoul's head. The glass-smooth rock walls encir-
cling the pool was impossible for them to climb. Otherwise, they'd
have scaled the wall and sprinted at Crukas and the three dwarves.

With the difficulty Crukas and the dwarves had to find a way
inside the tower, how had these ghouls gotten inside? Most likely,
they weren't ghouls when they entered, and after Scorpius captured
them, he cursed them to remain in this state. What had these foolish
intruders sought to steal? Several ghouls with pointed ears and this
faces favored elves before being stricken by Scorpius' magic. The
others were probably human before being cursed.

Crukas swallowed hard. His fate might equal theirs if he failed to
steal the mask. This end was worse than death, and oddly, quite
similar to what his fate and the rest of Aetheaon's would become
should the Plague-bringer succeed in his mission.

On the far wall, a dozen sconces with the same bluish-white
flames flickered. These flames seemed controlled by magic. Other

than the ghouls, nothing else lurked in the shadowy recesses. A shadowed door between a pair of the sconces indicated an attached hallway that lead to another large chamber room like the one they were in. Since the worm's tunnel led here, Crukas assumed this was the tower's base floor. Of course, he could be wrong. Dark Ayr Tower set at the edge of a high cliff. Outside balconies overlooking the sea could exist, with several more floors carved beneath this one.

A set of stairs circled a pillar and went upward. The wet walls shimmered in the glow of the flickering sconces. The lighting didn't fully dismiss the shadows, but glowed enough for them to see without the fear of being stalked or attacked unaware.

"We take the stairs," Crukas said, softly.

"Aye." Bramnir readied his axe.

Crukas took a torch that soaked in a small pail of pitch and touched it to a brazier to set the end ablaze. The dwarves followed suit.

"Dat's convenient." Ebden grinned.

"You realize this is a trap?" Tamana asked.

"Of course. The whole tower's filled with traps." Crukas glanced up the circular stairwell. "Scorpius won't come for me. I have to go to him."

"It's what he wants," she said.

"Since he has what I need, I'll entertain his hope."

"You're a fool," Tamana said. "And you're putting the lives of your companions in jeopardy."

"They're free to leave," Crukas said. "I never asked them to journey with me."

Adgus nodded. "He's right. We're 'ere to aid and protect him."

"Then," she said, "you're all fools."

The ghouls moaned hungrily. Their moans turned to slight growls when their aggravation increased from not being able to climb the smooth wall.

Adgus held his torch and glanced at the watery pool. The light washed over the ghouls' sunken pale faces. The ghouls shielded their eyes and hissed. "Ya think dat's all of 'em?"

Crukas shrugged. "Doubtful."

"How's dat?" Bramnir asked.

"Reaver had eaten at least one," Crukas replied. "Or *part* of it."

Tamana flitted closer, accompanied by eight more pixies. She pointed at the large, slimy swath at the lower part of the room. "That's where Reaver turned and reentered his tunnel."

In the long stretches of glistening slime, the ghoul that lost its arm was stuck facedown in the trail and not moving. Could the undead fake being dead?

Adgus studied it for a few moments. "Do we 'ave to worry about it coming after us?"

"No," she said. "That slime hardens quickly. The ghoul can't get up. The slime's why we had him cut our tunnels. Once the slime sets, cave-ins seldom occur and the tunnels last forever. It's far sturdier than mortar."

Bramnir shook his head. "Seems we dwarves should consider 'aving those giant worms burrow *our* tunnels."

Tamana smirked. "That wouldn't be wise."

"Eh? Why not?" he asked.

"Taming one requires a strong leashing spell to maintain control," she said. "But they're never fully *tame*. Any weakness in the spell allows them to break free."

"Ah." Bramnir nodded. "I see."

Tamana's eyes watered. "Reaver, though, was different. The magical harness we used didn't require much magic. He enjoyed our company."

The dwarves studied her with hardened gazes but offered no condolences. Perhaps they had a difficult time understanding why the Fae would feel loss over a worm?

"I'm sorry for your loss," Crukas said in a mellow tone.

Tamana gave a slight smile and then pointed at two pixies near her. "Azzy and Pom, fly before us and see what's on the higher floor. Any sign of danger, report to me immediately."

Crukas frowned. "You've no need to scout ahead for us."

"You?" she said with a haughty laugh. "What we seek isn't on this floor. We, like you, need to reach an upper floor."

Crukas grinned.

The two pixies darted up the stairs and disappeared around the bend. Crukas drew his dagger and stepped on the first step, which was cracked and dripped moisture.

"No." Adgus clasped a firm hand on Crukas' arm. Using his shoulder, Adgus pushed Crukas aside and ascended several steps. Instead of pulling his axe, he drew his mace, which seemed a better weapon for a narrow squeeze. "I'll lead since you've already confessed your lack of fighting abilities."

"My gratitude," Crukas said.

Although he didn't want others injured or killed during his confrontation with Scorpius, he was relieved others were willing to fight with and for him. He was beginning to understand the value of what true friendship meant, and because of this, he also found himself worrying more for their welfare than for his own life.

CHAPTER 46

*S*lender trails of meandering water trickled down the catacomb walls. The fiery sconces hissed when occasional water droplets dripped into the magical flames. The stagnant air was colder than what the night air had been outside. Crukas shook slightly, more from his growing fear than the cool temperature. Although he'd yet seen Scorpius, he *felt* the mage's presence.

Adgus showed no fear and took the stairs bolder than Crukas ever could have on his own.

Bramnir followed Crukas. Crukas met his eyes only momentarily, but long enough to recognize Bramnir's eagerness for a possible melee engagement. The dwarves' nature to entangle with an occasional foe in battle wasn't something Crukas understood, but it was commonplace. Dwarves viewed combat as a high-stake sport or an excuse to escape the mines and underground cities, which was the opposite of a thief's agenda. Crukas always sought a way *not* to get caught in a skirmish.

But when Crukas stared past Bramnir, he noticed Ebden did not possess his brothers' zeal. The whites of his widened eyes revealed his fear, despite his intense frown. Had the book's curse weakened his resolve? His vigor had diminished after he took the book from Crukas.

Dwarves seldom feared anything, except magical curses and attacks or an ale shortage. From the shared tales surrounding the Battle of Hoffnung, the dwarves fought valiantly against the Vykings, an undead army, and an undead dragon. Though outsized and outnumbered, they never retreated. Crukas had heard the tales about dwarves' bravery long before the Battle of Hoffnung but dwarves often resisted battles against the undead. Dwarves longed to see fear in their enemies' eyes during confrontations. The undead showed no fear or any emotion. For a warrior, fighting an undead soldier under a necromancer's control was an unsettling dilemma.

A sharp shrill pierced the air. Crukas ducked, but Adgus turned and smashed the strange, red-eyed bat with a prompt tap of his mace before it could fly up the circled stairs. He grinned. "Pesky critters."

"Indeed," Bramnir whispered. "When one flies past ya, a hundred more might follow. So ... stay alert."

Crukas didn't like the idea of a bat swarm fluttering past them. Their shrieks, sharp claws, and teeth could become maddening. He hoped this bat was a stray or the others had not yet awakened. With the ghouls on the floor below, did this indicate Scorpius was a necromancer or had he simply cursed the intruders and trapped them to use whenever other uninvited visitors found a way inside the tower? The ghouls might've accidentally trapped themselves by being unable to claw their way out. Others could be wandering anywhere inside the tower and the idea disturbed him.

The majority of evil wizards and mages held infamous reputations while the favorable sorcerers who used their magic to aid and heal the less fortunate were seldom acknowledged and remained unknown to the general populations. Fear motivated and magnified recognition and the tales of immoral sorcerers' sinister nature spread hotter and wider than a volcano spewed molten rock.

Adgus paused at the second turn in the circular stairs. "Watch ya step."

This section of the stairs was comprised of missing or broken stones. The area where the worm's tunnel had entered indicated the tower's foundation was solid, but the stairway was slowly deteriorating and collapsing upon itself. Bits of green ooze pulsed in the cracks with small slithering slugs moving up from the crevices.

"Hurry upward," Crukas whispered.

"Why?" Adgus asked.

"Ooze slugs are hidden in the stairs."

"What?" Bramnir looked at his feet. "Bah! Go, Adgus!"

Adgus gripped his mace and hurried up the broken stairs until they reached the threshold of the next floor. Crukas was more agile and kept up with the dwarf. After Adgus stepped out of the stairwell, Crukas tossed his torch to the side and tackled Adgus.

"Bloody—" Adgus rolled and turned with his torch. On the floor, he glared at Crukas. The zip and harsh thud of an arrow struck the far wall and echoed. Adgus' eyes widened. "How'd you know?"

Crukas shrugged, stood, and offered his hand. "The trigger pin kept tightening the closer we came to this floor."

"You 'eard dat?" Adgus said.

Crukas nodded and tugged Adgus to his feet. Even Crukas wondered how he'd heard the trigger over the sound of their boots rushing up the stairs. Instinct?

The path the arrow had flown would've struck Adgus. Even though Adgus wore decent armor, the thrust of the arrow could've injured him. Of course, if the trajectory path was set for a human or an elf, the arrow might've struck a deathblow to a dwarf's head.

Bramnir and Ebden exited the stairwell and stood beside Crukas and Adgus on a wide circular floor. The stairwell continued upward.

"We're not going to use the stairs?" Bramnir asked.

"You saw the slugs," Crukas said.

"Aye."

"A large gelatinous monster recently shed them," Crukas said. "It's probably higher up the stairwell."

"Then what?" Adgus said. "We're stuck 'ere?"

"No," Crukas said. "Scorpius isn't foolish enough to only have one way up."

"Where'd the pixies go?" Ebden asked.

"Who knows?" Adgus said. "A lot of good they did warning us about anything."

"They've their own reasons for being here," Crukas said. "Because they are so small, they're less likely to trigger a trap, so they probably weren't aware of it. Obviously, we're not their concern."

"What about those slugs?" Bramnir asked. "Won't they come after us?"

"When they're that size, they're opportunists," Crukas replied. "They'll probably feast on the bat Adgus killed. The scent of its blood should draw them downward."

Adgus sighed. "This floor's empty."

Crukas grabbed his torch, lifted it higher to view more of the open floor and nodded. Like the floor below, bluish-white flames flickered inside wall sconces. He estimated the distance to the farthest torch on his right a bit more than twenty feet away. To his left, another sconce seemed to be about the same distance. The center of the floor remained swallowed by darkness, even with the aid of their torches.

"Appearances can be deceptive," Tamana said, swiftly descending the upper stairwell.

Bramnir nodded. "More than true."

Crukas gave her a questionable stare. "What'd you find up those stairs? More slugs?"

"No slugs, but it's good you didn't head farther upwards."

"Why's dat?" Adgus asked.

"Several traps," she said. "Some obvious ones, but some even Crukas might've missed."

Adgus' lips snarled. "Well, ya did us no favors by not warning us of the arrow."

"I warned you by magnifying the sound of the trigger for Crukas. But the stairs leading upwards has a camouflaged hole in the center of the stairs. The drop to the floor below might not kill you, but there's a greater chance of you dropping into another water pit with ghouls or something worse."

Ebden wiped sweat from his brow. "A fate worse than death."

Adgus nodded. "Aye."

"Is there another set of stairs?" Crukas asked.

"Not on this floor," she said.

Adgus frowned. "There must be another way up."

"Yes," she said with a slight grin. "But you're not going to like it."

"Why?" Crukas asked.

"Crukas won't mind," Tamana said. "But the dwarves—"

"What about us dwarves?" Bramnir asked with a firm brow.

"A tall ladder's at the center of this floor."

Adgus' hand tightened on his mace. "A ladder? You sure there aren't another set of stairs?"

"Not on this floor," she replied. "My scouts are searching each floor discreetly."

Crukas met Adgus' hardened gaze. "What's the issue with climbing a ladder?"

"You're joking, right?" Adgus said.

"No."

"I'd rather keep me feet on solid ground or broken stairs. With our stature and weighted with heavy armor, shields, and weapons, it's difficult to maintain balance. It's not about strength or fear of heights though."

"How about the fear of falling?" Tamana teased.

Adgus cocked a brow and narrowed his gaze. After a few seconds, he grinned. "Now dat ya mention it, there's *dat* possibility to consider."

"How long's the ladder?" Crukas asked.

"Seems like it bypasses several floors. Other than falling, there's little to fear as far as being attacked while you climb," she said. "However, the higher you go, the more vulnerable you are to arrows, magic, or falling."

Crukas turned and walked to the center of the room. "The longer we stand around, the more likely something might come from the stairs to attack."

"True," Adgus said, following him.

When they reached the tall ladder, they looked up. The top end of the ladder vanished into the darkness out of the torches' glow. From Crukas' best guess, the ladder was forty feet high.

"You first," Adgus said.

"Why?" Crukas asked.

"I can easily defend you on the stairs, but not on a ladder. Besides, you're more agile and quicker. Once you reach the top, you'll have to wait for us to catch up."

Crukas nodded and while precariously holding his torch in his right hand, he began his climb.

CHAPTER 47

*S*parrow rubbed her eyes, causing little sparks of light to appear behind her closed eyelids. She opened them and waited for the bursting lights to subside. Afterwards, she studied the swirling clouds overhead but no further threats of impending lightning flickered.

Sparrow stood. "I think the storm's past."

Triggor said, "I wonder if the lightning killed them?"

"Hard to say without getting a closer examination." Gynx was somewhat less enthusiastic than before. "I see no sign of them on the bridge, but my vision's still partly blurred. Perhaps they're already dead."

"Then we go see for ourselves," Triggor said. "If the lightning killed Crukas, it saves us a lot of time."

SPARROW DIDN'T LIKE the idea of getting any closer to Dark Ayr Tower, especially *not* after seeing the mage's powerful control over the storm and the massive strike of lightning.

At the bridge, no crispy, fried dwarf or human remains were on or beneath the bridge. Several glowing rocks continued to melt. The glittering array of the glow caps illuminated the sides of the channel. Cautiously, they climbed into the channel and walked until they came to Reaver's severed body and the spilled contents of its gut.

Sparrow's stomach churned. Miss Strella turned away and vomited on the channel floor.

Gynx stood at the edge of the worm feces. "The lightning didn't kill them. There are four sets of boot prints through the sludge and going into the bored tunnel. We're going in after them."

Strella turned and vomited again. She wiped her mouth with the back of her hand and shook her head. "Surely, you jest."

"I never jest," Gynx said with a stern voice. "We go through the tunnel, same as them. That means you, too."

"I'm sorry. I *can't*."

Gynx growled. "Suit yourself, but it won't be any safer for you out here."

"Why's that?" Strella spat on the ground.

"Gargoyles are circling their way downward." Gynx pointed. "Unless you can sing a high enough note to shatter magical stone, I'd say your odds of surviving are next to none. And should you decide to make a run for it, you've no idea where you'd be running in this darkness."

Miss Strella dry heaved.

Sparrow placed a gentle hand on Strella's shoulder. "He's right."

"I know, but I'd rather gargoyles crush me than to wade through the nasty sludge." She sighed. "The thorns and bramble tattered my dress at the warehouse. This was my finest dress, too."

"You can sing a dirge about it later," Gynx said sourly. "But right now, let's get on with our pursuit."

Sparrow wasn't sure how to offer a brighter side of the situation to Strella, so she said, "Imagine the new tales you can sing about after this is all over. How many bards could paint these images into song? You'd make enough coin to buy a dozen or more fancy gowns."

Strella snorted and wiped tears from her eyes. "That's true, I suppose."

"Ah, lass," Orgem said, "if it'll make ya feel better, I offer to hold your hand until we get through to the other side."

"Ug," Gynx said. "How un-endearing. It makes *me* want to puke."

"Hey!" Orgem said.

"Be kind," Strella said, giving Gynx a stern look.

Gynx shook his head. "I know not how. Not a part of my beloved nature."

"Your offer's sweet, Orgem," Strella took his thick hand into her long, slender fingers. "I accept."

Orgem swooned with a bashful smile that seemed more radiant in the light of the glow caps.

"We 'aven't time for this," Triggor said with a gruff voice. "We've no idea what type of mazes or tunnels dat are inside the tower. Crukas and those other dwarves 'ave the advantage of a head start. We're so close to catching 'em. But, once inside, we've no idea which direction they went."

"I agree," Gynx said. "Let's go."

"Wait! Careful," Triggor said, pointing. "Dat arm's moving toward you, Sparrow. Must be from a ghoul."

Sparrow backed away, and Strella gasped. Orgem put himself between Strella and the arm. He pulled his ax.

Seeing the moving arm with its strange lively movements further made Sparrow want to withdraw from their pursuit and quit tracking Crukas altogether. Willow Bend harbored nothing so grotesque. Perhaps she and Strella could successfully find their way across the darkened field together?

Gynx wouldn't allow it even if she begged. He'd kill her without a second thought.

She stared at the large spreading pile of worm guts and muddy feces and cringed. No amount of reward or satisfaction in capturing Crukas was worth swimming through that. Swimming was exactly what she'd have to do, because of her height. She couldn't wade through it and keep her head above the flow. Death was a better option.

She shook her head and whispered, "I'm too short to do this."

As if sensing Sparrow's turmoil, Miss Strella extended her free hand to Sparrow. "Sparrow, climb on my back and hold on. You can't possibly swim through that mess without—" Strella strained not to dry heave again. "Getting it in your mouth and ... nose. Straddle my shoulders but watch your head inside the tunnel."

With a sigh of relief, Sparrow said, "Thanks."

Miss Strella whispered, "If I had my way I'd return to the Mute Changeling and forget I ever volunteered for this."

"Me, too," Sparrow said softly.

Orgem chuckled. "I'd rather drank another keg of their weak stout than find out what awaits us on the other side."

Sparrow nodded, but rather than say anything more, she worried about the putrid muck swallowing her. It never crossed her mind this might be her demise. Perhaps, since she'd soiled her life by her decisions, it was a fitting end.

CHAPTER 48

Crukas climbed the ladder rungs nimbly, leaving Adgus and the others over a floor below. He hated leaving them behind. But after careful reflection, he didn't want them near him should Scorpius exert a magical attack while they climbed the ladder. He wanted Scorpius focused on him, and not the dwarves. At their height on the ladder, should they fall, they'd be critically injured or dead. The fall and the weight of their armor would crush them.

Adgus had not lied about the difficulty the dwarves had with climbing ladders—perhaps long ladders like this one were a bigger handicap. Although they were muscled and physically stronger than most humans, their short arms and legs slowed their ascent, especially carrying their heavy shields and weapons while climbing.

To Crukas' surprise, the iron ladder was sturdy, especially considering its extreme length, and seemed resistant to any physical damage they could cause. The ladder seemed enchanted. No rust had eaten through the rungs and the side rails offered no shakiness. Even with the combined weight of the dwarves nearing the middle, the ladder didn't bend in the slightest.

Tamana flitted to Crukas and hovered several inches above his face. Her fanning wings irritated him like a pesky insect. He couldn't be certain it wasn't intentional, since his party was the target for the chain lightning that killed Reaver.

Crukas met her eyes. "Have you not found what you seek?"

She shook her head. "Not yet, but this tower's immense."

"That's true. How much farther before I reach the top of this ladder?"

"Another thirty feet or so. Not far."

"Not far?" Crukas shook his head. "That's easy for you to say since you've no need to climb."

She giggled and shrugged her tiny shoulders. "While flying looks graceful, it makes us weary and we require sustenance to maintain our strength. Since we're patrolling the areas and reporting back to you, we're expending valuable energy."

"I appreciate that, but in all fairness, I never asked you to search ahead for us," Crukas said.

"I know. But if your group fails, we're all dead, so consider us extra sets of eyes for you."

"And in return?" Crukas understood no deed, great or small, ever came without a price.

"Help us find food."

"Fair enough."

CRUKAS REACHED the final rung and hesitated at the square opening in the floor above. His arms ached, not so much that he couldn't react quickly, but he didn't like the idea of confronting anything alone. Adgus and the others were not even visible on the ladder below, which meant they were quite a distance below. Otherwise, the flicker of Adgus' torch would be visible. Crukas couldn't suspend himself on the ladder until the dwarves reached him.

He took a deep breath and hoisted himself onto the floor above. While he lie on his back, his heartbeat pounded in his ears. He relaxed and took slow, methodical breaths. After his pulse lessened, he closed his eyes and listened to his surroundings. Nothing stirred, but he felt the uneasiness often associated with being watched. Rather than be alarmed by the feeling, he chose to wait for its approach, as apparently, it knew he was there.

CHAPTER 49

*R*iding atop Miss Strella's shoulders prevented Sparrow from swimming through the worm dung to get to the other side of the tunnel, but her boots and pants were not spared from being coated by the gunk. Sparrow cringed her dainty nose and coughed. She hoped for fresher air inside the tower, but instead, she inhaled the decayed stench of corpses.

Miss Strella bent slightly so Sparrow could climb off. After Sparrow stood on the damp tower floor, she gagged and wondered how she'd get the worm goo off her clothing, Miss Strella leaned against the wall and dry-heaved. Tears formed in her eyes and she softly sobbed.

Orgem and Triggor waded out of the tunnel with worm feces up to their necks. Their thick braided beards were matted and slick. They clawed handsful of the earthy dung from their beards and flung it to the tower floor. They stared at their mucky hands with disgust.

Gynx, also being vertically challenged, wiped away the thick goo from his face and mouth. He mumbled without opening his mouth to prevent the dung from leaking into his mouth.

Crukas and his three dwarf companions had gone through the

tunnel without getting completely covered by the worm entrails since they walked along the outer skin of Reaver. But, once inside the tower, the back flow of the entrails slowly reentered the tunnel and almost filled it to the top.

Sparrow placed her hand against Strella's shoulder. "You okay?"

Strella reached to wipe away tears but seeing the crud on her hands, she refrained. She simply nodded. "I'll be okay, once I wash off this excrement."

Sparrow nodded. Had Strella not carried her, the dung would've covered Sparrow worse.

Water sloshed nearby.

Strella offered a half smile and turned. The faint light off the sconce revealed the rippling water pool. She hurried toward the water. "Finally, some good fortune! A small pool to wash this mess off."

Sparrow turned to follow Strella, but Triggor's grumbling anger caught her attention and stopped her in her tracks.

Triggor growled while trying to strip the mess from his beard. "Bloody Hell! I'm beginning to wonder if Crukas is worth the reward!"

Spitting and wiping the remaining feces from his lips, Gynx snarled. "Oh, it's worth it! But, before I get the reward, I'll take several pounds of Crukas' flesh for payment."

"*You* get the reward?" Triggor cocked one brow and gave an even stare.

"You know what I mean. *We*, okay? *We* get the reward!" Gynx said. "But that thief's going to pay for this."

"How is *this* his fault?" Sparrow asked.

"For someone bent on catching him," Gynx said, "you spend more time defending than hunting him."

"I'm here with you, aren't I?" she said.

"I'm guessing not by choice," he said.

Sparrow scowled and crossed her arms. She huffed. "You've given me no other choice."

Strella bent over the edge of the water pool and stretched to reach the water. She stood a head and a half taller than the dwarves but still couldn't reach the water. She groaned.

Gynx winked at Sparrow and chuckled. "That's true."

Strella shrieked.

Orgem ran to aid Strella without a second's hesitation or without knowing *why* she'd screamed. "Strella needs our help!"

Triggor and Sparrow hurried to the pool.

Orgem wrapped his thick arms around Stella's slender waist and pulled her up. He fell backwards. She landed atop him with him hugging her waist tightly. "What 'appened? Did ya nearly fall in?"

She vigorously shook her head. "No. The pool's filled with ghouls!"

Instinctively, Triggor pulled his revolver, not that the weapon could kill one.

Orgem looked Strella over. "You didn't get bitten, did you?"

"No." She sighed. "They were on the opposite side until they saw me or they'd have pulled me into the water before you could've gotten me."

Triggor found a crude rock to step on. He looked down into the watery pit. His eyes widened slightly and he shook his head. "You're lucky Orgem got ya in time, dear bard. They be rather hungry. Doesn't appear they can get out, so dat's a good thing."

Strella's body shook.

"Dar, dar." Orgem patted her back. "You're safe now."

"I'd like to believe that," she replied softly. "I'd wager I'm safer wandering through the dark to find Ravensdorf than being in here. But if these ghouls are trapped, what worse things await us?"

Gynx held a sour expression and looked around the room. "Nothing else like them is wandering around."

"That's my point," Strella said. "Unless we want to go back through the dung tunnel, and I most certainly do *not*, we have to find another way out."

"I only see the stairwell," Gynx said.

Triggor aimed his revolver at one of the ghoul's heads but didn't take the shot. It seemed apparent he considered shooting one of them.

Sparrow considered what Strella said about how few options they had escape from the tower. But Crukas was in here. Somewhere. He couldn't be too far ahead of them.

She glanced at the tunnel. More of the worm sludge oozed from the opening. Although the height of the gunk had lessened a great deal, her stomach soured at the thought of having to slosh her way through to get outside.

Seeing the ghouls in the watery pit brought a lot of uneasiness, too. She didn't want to encounter one outside the watery pit, and she wished she and Strella could abandon their pursuit of Crukas, at least for now.

Escaping with a comrade was much harder than by oneself. And while Orgem, Triggor, and Gynx busied themselves to help alleviate Strella's shock before they weighed their options for their next move, Sparrow took the opportunity to sprint up the spiral stairs. Though she ran fast, her rush to the stairs didn't go unnoticed.

"Hey!" Gynx snarled. "Get back here!"

Sparrow dared a glance over her shoulder a moment before he raised the crossbow and blindly fired. She rounded the corner of the stairwell and the metal bolt scraped across a rock a little more than a hair above her. Her heart thudded like a frightened rabbit's but she kept running.

"Get up!" Triggor said. "We've got to catch her."

Sparrow guessed he was addressing Strella. She hated the idea of leaving the bard behind with the present band of bounty hunters, but she didn't have any other choice. She felt ashamed because Strella had helped Sparrow through the tunnel to spare the halfling the agony of crawling or swimming through it.

Heavy footsteps thudded below her at the bend of the stairs. She held no doubt Gynx was pursuing her. The only advantage she held was the sharp turn of the stairwell prevented him from getting a clear, easy shot. But what happened once she reached a landing or if the stairs suddenly ended? At a closer range, the crossbow was useless. He'd have no use for it, but his dagger he'd take far more pleasure in using.

"Gynx!" Triggor's voice bellowed up the stairs. "Don't ya harm her!"

Gynx panted and snarled, as he got closer to Sparrow.

The moisture dripping off the cobblestone walls made the stairs slick. She slipped and stumbled but caught herself against the wall. Instead of slowing, she pushed off the wall and propelled herself up the next step.

"You think you can get away?" Gynx spat.

That's the plan.

Sparrow caught a glimpse of him from the corner of her eye and shrieked.

The animal side of Gynx emerged. His wild eyes indicated his need to spill blood, and while he had teased of doing so several times inside The Mute Changeling, there was no question of his animalistic rage. Something flipped a switch inside him. She feared nothing could cage the monster that had broken free.

"I knew you'd betray us," Gynx hissed.

He lunged for her. She leapt two steps up instead of one, which was an incredible leap for her, given her height. Even though she moved nimbly, he was faster and grabbed her ankle tightly.

Sparrow screamed, but rather than allow her fear to consume her, she mule-kicked with her free foot and caught his huge nose full-force. She fell forward and braced against the fall by landing on her elbows.

Gynx winced, released her ankle, and rolled down the stairs. He covered his nose in both hands. Mumbling curses, he pushed off the side wall and staggered to his feet. His eyes watered and apparently blurred his vision. Blood leaked through his hands and colored his teeth.

"Run," he whispered. "You best run because when I catch you, you're dead."

Sparrow took a deep breath, shoved herself to her feet, and without an argument, she ran. But, she couldn't exactly call it a head start, because Gynx tore into a sprint a second after his last muffled word. There was no way to rationalize with the crazed kobold. Especially *not* at this point. With disturbing glee, he'd threatened to kill her several times since they'd met, and the pursuit before carrying out his murderous desire was the thrill of the hunt. The only way she could take that away from him was to give up. *That* she couldn't do. Not if she wanted to live.

"Gynx!" Triggor yelled at a lower turn of the stairs. His thunderous voice echoed.

Sparrow came to a landing that opened into a dark floor. For a second, she contemplated dashing into the room, but Gynx was too close. She continued up the stairwell, hoping the sharp turns of the spiral stairs gave her an edge. The open room gave him ample time to fire a bolt into her leg or shoulder and once she fell, he could torture her with his dagger until she died.

She bounded up another step with Gynx's snarls growing closer, louder. Triggor shouted her name. He seemed to have almost caught up to them. She wondered why he suddenly took a stern interest in preventing Gynx from killing her. Did he possess a better conscience than she'd thought him to have? Did he abide by some moral code? Crukas had implied Triggor had gotten the revolver through some underhanded means.

The ongoing rivalry between Triggor and Gynx was never going to allow them to find common ground. They didn't want any, as there was no chance of losing friendship between them. They butted heads harder than stubborn rams and it had little to do with collecting Crukas' reward.

Sparrow stubbed her toe on a step that was a couple of inches higher than the previous one. She winced and fell. As much as she wanted to massage away the pain, she wanted to keep running, but Gynx rounded the corner. The kobold's eyes widened with great excitement.

"Oh!" he grinned. "You've made this *too* easy."

Sparrow raised her hands in surrender and tried to scoot up to the next step.

Gynx lowered the crossbow and reached for his knife. "Any last words?"

"Pl—" she said, closing her eyes, but was interrupted before she could plead for her life.

"I got a few for ya," Triggor said.

Sparrow chanced opening her eyes in time to see Triggor round the stairs and lower his shoulder. He hit Gynx with incredible force and lifted him off the ground. Gynx dropped the crossbow and his knife clanged on the stony wall. But Triggor's momentum didn't slow, and while he carried Gynx, the two of them rammed into Sparrow, too. All three moved up several steps before triggering the trap Tamana had warned Crukas about. All three dropped through the fake steps and plummeted downward.

MERE SECONDS after the three vanished from the stairwell, Orgem and Strella exchanged uneasy glances.

"Did ya see dat?" Orgem asked. He closed his eye and rubbed it, before looking again.

"I did," she replied.

"Good," he said. "I didn't want to think my mind was playing tricks on me. I'm far too sober for dat to be happening."

"Oh, no," she said. "They vanished."

"Dat much is obvious. But how?"

Strella shook her head. "It could only be—"

"Magic? Yeah, dat seems to be your answer for everything."

"And I suppose *you* have a more definitive answer, Orgem?"

The dwarf scratched his bearded chin. "Not right offhand. But magic can't be the answer for everything we can't explain."

"You're right," she said with a gentle smile. "But, in this case, there's no other reasonable explanation."

"Aye. I suppose you're right. What should we do now? How can we find them?"

She shrugged. "Perhaps we continue upward? Nothing good below."

"That's true."

He offered his elbow. She smiled and looped her arm in with his. They took two steps and fell through the stairs to join the rest of the bounty hunters.

CHAPTER 50

Chains rattled and clanked beyond the darkness near the almost unnoticed door. Still lying on his back, Crukas turned his head slightly and squinted, hoping to see what sought to emerge. The clinking metal links indicated an imprisoned beast of some sort. Without knowing the chain's length, he couldn't determine if the captive creature was capable of entering the room or was placed conveniently to guard the floor's only other exit.

He couldn't determine how far the chained beast could walk, but it never seemed to strain the chain to its full tension. The loose rattling indicated it respected its granted limit of movement and was apparently unable to break free, which, for Crukas, was an advantage.

Crukas was almost certain the guarded door led to a different set of stairs, which would delight the dwarves. They could exit the tower without descending the ladder.

After fifteen minutes, Crukas regained some strength and rose into a seated position. The dwarves had not reached the top of the ladder, which he thought odd. Although Adgus had inferred the difficulty dwarves were able to climb ladders swiftly, Crukas became concerned. By now, Adgus' flickering torch should be visible. It wasn't.

Rather than waiting, he considered moving closer to where the chained creature was. Knowing he'd been watched since stepping off the ladder, he shouldn't have been caught off guard when the atmosphere in the large circular room sizzled and crackled with dark magical energy behind him.

Jagged bluish-white, electrical flames fingered outward. The hairs on the back of his' neck stiffened. He slid his hand over his dagger's hilt and whispered, "Scorpius?"

"Crukas," Scorpius replied.

Crukas glanced over his shoulder. Lines of electricity stretched from Scorpius' fingertips. The dark shadows in the room skirted away.

The chained beast whimpered, scurried to the door, and dragged the clanking links with a harsh clattering sound.

Crukas met Scorpius' gaze. Confusion shimmered in the mage's eyes, despite wearing the affixed death-mask Crukas so desperately coveted. Hindsight reminded him of his regretful mistake in not obtaining the mask *before* he stole the Cursed Spellbook of the Damned, perhaps preventing the curse from ever clinging to him or Ebden.

Standing in the same room as Scorpius, Crukas expected his own courage to wane and for fear to overwhelm him. But oddly, boldness crept inside his mind and heart. Having the curse's weight on him lessened his fear of death and torture. He was already doomed. The curse was inevitable, it seemed, and with that in mind, dying released him from the curse's clutches.

Scorpius lowered his hands to his sides. Threads of electricity formed sparkling nets between his fingers. "You're the last person I'd expect to be so foolish to enter my tower. Surely you realize how near your death is."

"Much closer than yesterday," Crukas replied. "As is yours, I fear."

Scorpius laughed manically. "I've heard you were entertaining, no less than a jester is to a king."

"By whom?"

"No one in particular," Scorpius said.

"I imagine you have few guests." Crukas cocked a brow. "My life's one of solitude, as is yours. I only grace the presence of others when the need presents itself. The fewer acquaintances, the less chance of betrayal."

"You and I hold that in common, thief."

"I gathered that by your hostile welcoming committee."

A sly grin creased the mouth of Scorpius' mask, which sent an uneasy shiver down Crukas' spine. Like the spellbook's curse had gripped Crukas, he wondered if the mask controlled the mage. The mask seemed to be an entity, too. These were the seldom expected dangers of magical items. The item's magic seemed more willing to possess the possessor.

"It's amazing you survived," Scorpius said with an amused smile.

"I almost didn't."

The mask's smile deepened. "Your companions, however, will find their fate much sooner than yourself, I fear."

Crukas held a stoic appearance, but his gut tightened with fear for his three dwarf companions. Was this why they had yet to reach the top of the ladder?

With a calm voice, Crukas said, "What are you talking about?"

He searched to see Scorpius' eyes but the mask made a clicking sound and shielded the mage's eyes with an obsidian sheen, making it impossible to read the mage's intent. The mask had buried the mage's thoughts where few could ever delve to find and unravel. Crukas had seen the eyes of the undead, and strangely, the eyes of the mask were far more frightening.

Scorpius shrugged and changed the subject. "What do I possess that a thief would risk his life and hope to steal?"

"It's not a question you need even to ask, is it?"

"Amuse me, entertainer," Scorpius said.

"I'm not a jester, nor do I dress the part," Crukas replied. "Unlike yourself."

The mask creased dramatically. Scorpius' jaw tightened and his nostrils flared at the insult.

Crukas smiled. Only one weighted by deep insecurities would take immediate insult from mere words. Crukas questioned how powerful the mage was by how easily offended he suddenly became.

"Are you implying *I'm* the fool?" Scorpius' voice amplified and echoed through the room. From near the hidden door, the creature's chains rattled.

"No implication's necessary." Crukas sneered. He seemed to have found a weakness in Scorpius' fortitude and so, he sought to prod deeper into the fresh bruise. "You dress as though you're headed into battle while you've securely locked yourself in a tower protected by minions you control with magic. Why the need for such pompous armor in the absence of company?"

Scorpius' jaw tightened. "You realize this armor was made from the deadliest giant scorpion in the Desert of Torrenth? Besides, you and your party managed to somehow gain entry into my tower, despite my guardians."

"No lock or gate is foolproof," Crukas said with a mischievous smile.

"Not to a notorious thief, as I'm aware. Yet, you mock me for my attire, knowing full well how rare this scorpion leather is to attain? No poison or venom can harm me while I wear it."

Crukas shrugged. "It makes you look bloated, like a dead animal in the heat of a midsummer's day."

Scorpius examined how the abdominal section of his chestpiece protruded farther than his upper chest muscles and since he was looking downward, it seemed a larger extension than normal. For someone concerned with their outward appearance, Crukas' comment struck fiercer than an arrow to the heart. "Bloated? How dare you!"

"Yes. Almost as much as your inflated ego. So if the suit fits, wear it. Seems appropriate enough."

Crukas walked away from the square opening where the ladder attached. Riling the mage might've been enough to make him attack Crukas. Since Scorpius seemed to favor using magical electricity as his weapon of choice, Crukas didn't want to chance falling several floors downward should such an attack render him unconscious.

While Crukas might survive the electrical shock, he'd never survive the fall to the floor below.

Scorpius studied Crukas for several long seconds. "Why waste your time with this useless banter? You've come for my death-mask, no doubt. At least tell me *why* before I end your pilfering life."

Crukas ignored the statement. "You mentioned my companions' fates earlier. What have you done with my friends?"

"Friends?" Scorpius snorted a short laugh. "I've tucked them away in a small cage for now. Why you thought two dwarves, a halfling, and a kobold could aid you in any way is beyond me. The elf bard will prove quite useful on dark days, provided she's capable of singing a pleasurable tune."

Crukas frowned. "You're mistaken if you think I'd travel with such a squad."

"I figured you'd deny having any association to them. That's fine. No need to worry over their fates since they're of no importance to you."

"I'm not worried. I've no interest in them."

Crukas worked his way farther from the ladder and edged toward the outer circular wall until Scorpius stood between him and his only route for escape. As best Crukas could tell, this section of the large circular room was the mage's library. The curved walls were lined with bookshelves. Each bookshelf was packed with weathered books about spells, astrology, and potion making. While none of these books could remove the curse on him, he wondered what other tomes might benefit the battle against the Plague-bringer. Should he survive his encounter with Scorpius, Crukas would scan the bookshelves in hope of finding a codex useful to his mission.

"Why am I not surprised?" A slight teasing smile creased the mask. "Like most thieves, you con others into helping you until they're no longer beneficial to you."

"Those you've trapped? I do *not* know them," Crukas said evenly.

"So you say."

"I'm more concerned about whatever you've shackled near the door on the other side of the room."

"Ah. No need to fear something you'll not survive to encounter."

"Perhaps not, but I'm curious. Whatever it is, it's not loyal to you. It fears you."

Scorpius smiled. "As should you."

"I've no time for fear to delay me any longer. I'd soon get this over with, take the mask, and be on my way."

"That's a bold assumption. You actually *think* you'll win?"

Crukas said, "Unless your plan is to bore me to death with this deadening conversation."

The mask frowned with obvious contempt. "Boring? I thought I was being hospitable."

"You don't host enough gatherings, do you?"

"With whom? No one in the miserable town draws my interest."

"Have you forgotten that you almost killed me and my party? Nothing hospitable about that."

Scorpius nodded. "But you survived. Don't you see why you intrigue me? Thus, perhaps a bit of conversation before one of us dies?"

"Nah." Crukas shook his head. "The less we know about one another, the better the fight."

Scorpius scoffed. "If that's truly how you feel, at least answer one question."

"You've never answered mine."

"About your friends?"

Crukas nodded.

"They're in a prison cell several floors below. I've not killed them ... *yet*, if that's what you wish to know."

Crukas studied the cold death-mask, which didn't necessarily control Scorpius but seemed to reveal the mage's emotions. The group of individuals he'd stated to be Crukas' party weren't, but Scorpius seemed convinced they were. So where were Adgus and his two brothers?

"So now answer my question. Why do you want my mask?" Scorpius asked.

"The same reason as you," he replied.

"Ah. Immortality? Then I suppose you'd like my armor, too?"

Crukas shook his head. "The armor would be a handicap for the tasks I perform. And the bloated look … not an image I'd like to see on my future wanted posters."

The mask contorted with an expression of pure rage. The obsidian eyes grew even darker. "That's assuming you survive. Neither the mask nor the armor are yours for the taking, thief. So let's end this. Now."

Crukas shrugged and smiled. "I won't leave without the mask."

"Without your life, there's no need to possess the mask."

"That's true. I knew the risks before I entered your tower and I'll be satisfied either way. So, let's see the mighty power you claim to possess."

"As you wish." Sparks flickered and sizzled on Scorpius' fingertips. He poised himself ready to strike but the set rage on the mask's countenance softened and its eyes widened. Scorpius hesitated. "Wait. You *want* me to attack you. Why?"

"Often reputations are overly inflated, with the exception of my own, of course," Crukas said. "You frightened a small town of shepherds, weavers, and cheesemakers into boasting about how powerful you are to those who visit, but that doesn't impress me."

"You wish to challenge me?"

Crukas shrugged. "If the outside performance is a fraction of what you can do, you don't seem as dangerous as I was led to believe."

Scorpius looked skeptical. "No. You already mentioned how you barely survived getting to the tower wall. And we stand inside closed quarters where my power is far greater. So, that's *not* the true reason." The mask's brow rose in surprise. "You've been touched by a dark force. Thus, why you want the mask."

"Actually, I should've taken the mask days ago, before I became cursed. But I decided to take a shortcut. I thought I'd save time, which now I regret. Perhaps, there's another way that benefits both you and I. If you'd lend me the mask for several days, your death won't be necessary today."

Scorpius chuffed an odd laugh. The mouth of the mask formed a mocking sneer. "You're a fool. The mask *prevents* me from dying."

"Yes. *If* you're wearing it," Crukas said.

"See? I'd be a fool to offer it to you, even for a few days. You'd take advantage of my vulnerability and kill me."

"You have my word that I won't."

Scorpius laughed deeper. "I'd be an even bigger fool to take the word of a thief."

"Thieving reputation aside, I'm a man of my word. While I may steal valuables, I've never gone back on my word. Any promise I've made, I've kept. My word's more precious than gold, silver, or gems to me. I value it above all else. Even my own life. For the most part, I don't steal from those who have little or nothing to spare. In this case, I've greater need of your mask for a short while than you do for the remainder of your life."

Scorpius said, "That still sounds like a veiled threat."

"It's not meant to be," Crukas said.

"The only way you'll get this mask is by taking it. That'd prove you worthy to wear it. And since this is my tower, my strength is the strongest here. It's highly unlikely you could pry it off my face, even in the event that you happened to get the upper hand and kill me."

Crukas shook his head. "So you'd rather die?"

"I don't foresee my death tonight."

Crukas offered an even smile. "Then the mask has blinded you. You can't say I didn't at least offer a reprieve."

"True, so in all fairness," Scorpius said. "I'll forgive your trespass and allow you to leave my tower without further harm. Once you're past the bridge, I'll release your party to you, also unharmed. What say you?"

No more than Scorpius seemed capable of believing Crukas, could Crukas trust the mage. Neither held faith in the other, so a final confrontation was imminent. One or both would die. Crukas couldn't walk away, not without the mask and not without his three friends.

"If that's the best you can offer," Crukas said, "I suppose we play this out."

269

"So be it."

CHAPTER 51

Sparrow found herself facedown in a gooey puddle of mud. She pushed herself to her knees, wiped mud from her face, and tried to gather her bearings. The stagnant air and acrid, muddy water triggered her gag reflex but she resisted vomiting. The potion Fasha had given her had been much worse.

Confused, she wondered why the spiral stairs she'd bounded up were gone and how she'd fallen through them. Had she fallen alone?

No.

Beside Sparrow lie Strella. The distraught bard sat in a deeper muddy pool with her back against a crude, rock wall. Orgem lie unconscious beside her. His head rested on a flat stone mere inches above a puddle.

Triggor and Gynx were nowhere to be seen.

"Where are we?" Sparrow whispered, more to herself than Strella.

Strella didn't respond. She was trapped inside her own inner turmoil. Momentarily, shock stiffened the bard like a statue set in a stagnant fountain. All the glamour and beauty Strella had presented while singing at The Mute Changeling was soggy and stained by mud and worm feces.

Sparrow's heart hurt with compassion for Strella. Like her, Strella didn't want to continue pursuing Crukas and had Gynx not forced them to stick together, she and Strella could've sought to travel to a neighboring city. Sparrow had deceived herself into believing Scorpius had bested Crukas, but Crukas had survived. His survival didn't mean he'd escaped the tower though.

For now, Sparrow couldn't worry about Crukas' welfare or his whereabouts. Her greatest concern was where Gynx was. With his desire to kill her before they'd fallen through the stairs, she didn't expect his bloodlust to have lessened. Somewhere, he might be hiding and preparing a surprise attack.

Miss Strella broke into tears and sobbed loudly.

"Are you okay?" Sparrow moved closer to the bard.

Strella held up the tattered, soiled fringes of her shredded gown and shook her head. Frustrated, she thrashed the long strands of cloth in the mud. "Do I *look* okay?"

Sparrow placed a gentle hand on Strella's shoulder. "It's going to be fine. Like I said earlier, you can get a new dress. I'll even help pay for it."

"I'm not upset about the dress." She closed her eyes and sighed. "Okay, I am, but that's not the reason I'm crying."

"Oh?"

"The longer we pursue Crukas, the worse my luck becomes. And now Orgem's injured, possibly severely. Truly, Triggor and Gynx are the two who wish to capture Crukas the most. Well, you do, too."

Sparrow agreed with Strella's luck correlation, but she feared and expected worse to befall her. "No. I'm like you. I wouldn't be here if Gynx hadn't threatened my life. Have you seen Gynx? He was trying to kill me before we somehow wound up here."

Strella put her hand on Orgem's forehead. "No. I've no idea where he or Triggor is. My concern's for Orgem. He won't wake up."

Next to the flat rock where Orgem rested his head, Sparrow knelt. She reached inside her herbal pouch and retrieved a small corked bottle filled with bluish-gray liquid. She handed the bottle to Strella. "See if you can get him to swallow this. It should help his recovery."

"Thanks." Strella's eyes flickered a slight bit of optimism.

Sparrow's nervous eyes searched the layered stones behind Strella that resembled an old wall. The wet mossy stones dripped rust-colored water. "Are you sure you haven't seen Gynx?"

"He shouldn't be far," she replied, uncorking the bottle. She pressed her thumb against Orgem's lower lip and applied enough pressure to open his mouth. Tilting the bottle, she let the potion slowly leak into the dwarf's mouth.

"What makes you certain?"

"See the iron bars over there?" Strella pointed. "We landed inside a prison cell."

Sparrow's eyes widened. "We're trapped?"

Strella nodded. "Well, I've not walked the perimeter, but my guess is we are prisoners. Unless you see a way out."

Sparrow hadn't noticed the bars until Strella drew her attention to them. Glancing up, she searched to see if she could find an opening to the floor above. Only the rock ceiling was visible. Even if she could've found the place where they'd fallen through, the slick stone wall was impossible to climb.

She stood and walked to the bars. The bars stretched from the floor all the way into the high ceiling without any gaps. Outside the cell was Gynx's unloaded crossbow. During their fall, he must've lost his grip on it. Where the fired bolt ended up was questionable. She was partially relieved to see the crossbow on the other side, but if Gynx was also on the outside of the cell, she was trapped and an easy target whenever he obtained it.

Sparrow followed the barred wall but found no door. The odd prison was narrow, approximately seven feet from the stone wall to the bars, but it steeply descended and curved, similar to the circular stairwell.

Outside the cell wall was a narrow path with a crude rock wall. Several flickering sconces offered dim light. No guards were present and there seemed to be no signs of anyone having walked the path recently. She noticed several skeletal remnants near the wall, partially hidden beneath the shallow muddy puddle. A few gnawed bones with teethmarks too large to be a rodent's were scattered on the floor, which meant former prisoners must've fed on one another. The back of her throat tightened and her stomach turned. She pictured Gynx doing that to all of them.

Muffled growls and sputtering caught her attention. She pulled her dagger from its sheath and followed the iron-barred wall. Rounding a slight curve, only fifteen feet or so from where Strella and Orgem were, she came upon Triggor and Gynx. Triggor had Gynx pinned to the wet rock floor. He shoved his full weight on the kobold and since Triggor's armor weighed more than Gynx, the kobold couldn't wrestle free. With fierce grips, both clutched one another's throats with their strong hands. Each fought to choke the other one to death.

Gynx's eyes bulged. He snarled and bared his sharp teeth. His long, strange tongue thrashed like a dying snake. Triggor's stern grip around the kobold's throat prevented Gynx from biting Triggor. However, Gynx's hold didn't seem any weaker. Triggor grunted and fought to breath.

Triggor mouthed words but she didn't understand what he said. His face was beet red and sweat dripped from his brow. A look of desperation reflected in his eyes. Despite obvious death grips, neither relinquished their stubbornness to give up. Neither held an actual advantage over the other, either. The first to lose consciousness would be the one killed.

The battle was fought by physical strength. Triggor's revolver remained in its holster, and Gynx had not pulled his wicked blade. Although Gynx had tried to kill her, he was in no position to make an attempt on her life at the moment. She'd expected these two to eventually go at one another's throats, but she didn't think it would be this literal. If one of them died, and she felt ashamed to consider it, she hoped Triggor was the victor.

When Gynx had become crazed with his bloodlust, Triggor ran to stop Gynx and protect her, which she never expected. Surely, their current scuffle wasn't because of his attack?

The more their group learned about Gynx, the less they wanted the kobold around. None could trust he wouldn't eventually turn on them. Triggor realized it and had challenged and put the kobold in his place several times. Now, Triggor was trying to end Gynx's life.

Since they were all trapped inside the small prison, they likely needed Gynx to help break them out. She hated to admit it, but it was the truth. To request Triggor to spare Gynx meant she'd have keep watch over her shoulder while inside the cell and then after they escaped.

Gynx gagged as Triggor squeezed his thick hands around the kobold's throat. The veins in Triggor's hands resembled flesh-covered ropes. She guessed a mere human's or a halfling's neck would've already snapped from such force.

Knowing she might regret it later, Sparrow said, "You're both wasting valuable time! Would you *stop* trying to kill each other?"

Neither lessened his hold on the other.

"Triggor!" Sparrow said. "Gynx! Continue this fight later, if you wish. Right now, we need to figure out how to escape this prison cell."

Triggor and Gynx slightly turned their heads toward her without loosening their grips on each other's throat. Informing them they were prisoners seemed to have caught their attention.

"Yes." Sparrow pointed at the iron bars. "We somehow fell through the stairs above and landed inside this cell. Orgem took a nasty fall, and Strella's too distraught to think rationally. Call a truce for now! Okay?"

Triggor and Gynx looked one another in the eyes. Their anger subsided slightly, they nodded, and slowly but cautiously, they stopped choking each other.

Triggor pushed himself to his feet and rubbed his throat. Rather than offer a helping hand to Gynx and help him stand, Triggor stepped on the kobold's long, scaly tail and walked closer to Sparrow. Gynx coiled in pain, snarled, and rubbed the tip of his tail.

Triggor took a deep breath and exhaled while massaging his throat. "He tried to kill you, Sparrow."

"I'm aware." Sparrow kept a wary eye on Gynx.

"Given time and more air to breathe, he'll try again. And ya just want to let him go?" Triggor said.

"Go? Unless he has a way to get through the iron bars, *where's* he going to go?" She asked.

With one hand on his throat, Gynx leaned against the stone wall. He wheezed and craned his head to give her a side-glance. "Down at the pool, you tried to escape and leave us behind."

"Escape?" Triggor asked. "She knows as much about this tower as any of us. By running, she placed herself into more jeopardy than securing safety. Dat's why I wanted her to stop."

Gynx coughed and frowned. His jagged teeth made his grin even more wicked. "Perhaps. But she looked like she was fleeing."

"Yeah," Triggor said. "Ya were trying to kill her."

"The beastly side of my kobold took over," he said. "I lost control."

No remorse tinged his voice and his eyes remained sinister. He at least acknowledged he held no permanent control over his primal urges. She didn't expect an apology, and by all means, she could never lower her guard as long as he breathed, and they were banded together.

"Call a truce for now," Sparrow said. "Besides, if one of you kills the other, we'll have to deal with the stench."

Triggor's nose scrunched. "Dat's a nasty thought since he smells bad enough *alive*."

Gynx hissed.

Triggor said, "Look, I had your best interests in mind, Sparrow."

"More like you had hopes of killing me to get a larger share of the bounty," Gynx said.

"The bounty be damned! Her life's worth more than dat. We allowed her into our party, and as such she must be protected."

Sparrow offered a kind smile to Triggor. "I appreciate that, Triggor, but why would you kill him?"

Triggor combed his beard with his hand. "The two of you are opposites. Gynx is vile, greedy, and murderous—"

Gynx snickered. "You can stop with the flattery."

Triggor cocked a brow and gave the kobold a stern glare. "And you, Sparrow, are far too kind and innocent to have chosen the life of a thief *or* a bounty hunter. It'd be a shame to see you die at this fiend's hands."

Sparrow worried Triggor's insults would cause Gynx to hurl into another rage and attack Triggor.

Gynx, though, seemed to have read her thoughts and shrugged. "No love lost, lass."

Sparrow sighed. "We need to set aside our differences and find a way to escape. I've not found a door to the cell."

Gynx laughed. "I'm surprised you never took the opportunity to leave, rather than search for us."

Sparrow frowned. "How could I leave without a door?"

"Lass," Triggor said. "As small and thin as you are, you can easily squeeze through those bars."

Sparrow blushed from embarrassment. She never considered that. Turning to her side, she slid her slender body between two bars and fit without having to squeeze through. She felt like a fool. She could've fled without searching for Gynx or Triggor, but even so, she couldn't have left Strella and Orgem behind. Not with him injured and Strella's mental outlook in shambles. Neither was in any condition to pursue Crukas; provided they ever got free. Also, realizing the harsh differences between Triggor and Gynx had gotten worse didn't reassure her that the bard and Orgem would be safe until she returned to help them escape. Gynx might decide to kill them first, due to their weakened states.

Pushing through the bars to the narrow path outside the prison, Sparrow walked the incline until she reached the place where Orgem and Strella were. Gynx and Triggor followed her along the inside.

Orgem's eyes were open, and he leaned slightly against Strella. The potion had awakened him. She hoped it helped him regain his strength.

Strella's eyes widened. "Sparrow? You found a way out?"

Sparrow nodded.

Triggor gripped the bars with his hands. "Ya sure there's no door?"

"I didn't see one," she replied. "Of course, I didn't walk the entire length of the cell around the bend."

Gynx slipped closer and extended his hand through the bars. "Be a dear, lass, and hand me my crossbow."

Sparrow reached down and picked up the crossbow. Cradled in her hands, it was heavy. She shook her head. "Not until later."

"It's mine!" He hissed through gritted teeth.

"Yes," she said, "but I need to borrow it."

"Foolish girl," Gynx said. "You can't even pull back the string to load it. And even if you could, it's useless without a bolt."

"Give her a bolt," Triggor said, "and I'll help her load it."

Gynx glared at Triggor. "What?"

"Hey," Triggor said in a reasonable tone. "She's our only hope to get out of this place, and if she gets herself killed trying to find a door, we're *never* getting out of here. Besides, what good is it to you in this cell?"

"It's a weapon I've carried for years." Gynx pulled a bolt from his pack and handed it to Triggor. "It has sentimental value."

Sparrow's brow rose.

Gynx grinned. "Ironic, you think? The sentiments are for those eliminated by its accuracy. Which is why I don't want anyone else taking it."

"Well, ya still got your dagger and I've me revolver," Triggor said. "I say dat makes us on equal ground, if we butt heads again."

Triggor took the bolt, reached through the bars, and pulled back the string, and placed the bolt into place. "There. Be careful not to pull the trigger until you need to shoot. Ya only got one shot."

Sparrow nodded. "Thanks."

"One shot against ... how many ghouls were in that pool?" Gynx grinned.

Sparrow swallowed hard. Her nervous eyes widened.

"Pay 'em no mind," Triggor said. "Those we saw 'ave no way out of the water."

She nodded, but his reassurance didn't ease her mind. Those might not be the only undead in the tower, and who knew what else she might encounter. With the weight of the bow, she doubted she could hold it steady enough to peer through the site. One misfired bolt from a weapon she'd never used before could be wasted by poor aim or by accidentally pulling the trigger.

"Is there a problem?" Triggor asked.

Sparrow said, "I've no idea where to go."

Triggor said, "I'd follow the path upward and see where it leads."

"Yes. True. But how'd we wind up here?" she asked.

"Magic," Gynx said. "I'm guessing we fell through a disguised trap. What we thought were stairs, weren't."

Obviously.

"I won't desert you," Sparrow said. "That's a promise."

"From a former thief," Gynx said.

"*Reformed* thief," she said. "My conscience would never let me rest if I left you to die and rot. So should I not return, something will have killed me."

Triggor nodded. "I believe ya. Halflings hold more compassion than the rest of us locked in here."

Gynx's face soured but he offered no words.

Sparrow smiled with regret and turned away, slowly making her way up the ascending path.

CHAPTER 52

Crukas moved closer to the bookshelf on the opposing wall while Scorpius' magical energy surged. From his fingertips, impressive bluish-white, electrical sparks lengthened into a jagged mesh. Static buzzed within the light, and Crukas had stirred something worse than a hornet's nest.

"Quite a show," Crukas said. "I've seen similar stunts by street corner magicians."

Scorpius stiffened. His lips curled into a snarl. "Have you?"

Anger built in Scorpius' eyes, but from the corner of Crukas' eye, Adgus gently slid his broadaxe onto the floor near the square opening. Adgus eased off the ladder and helped each his brothers onto the floor.

Scorpius' attentive wrath focused on Crukas, and he didn't notice the dwarves. Apparently, the mask held no omniscient sight and could only view whatever the wearer could see, much to Crukas' relief.

"Have you seen these magicians do this?" Scorpius asked. He hurled the ball of lightning at Crukas.

Crukas dove between a large table and the bookcase. The floating energy moved slower than he expected and fizzled out before it reached the bookcase. Was he toying with Crukas to prolong their banter?

Crukas wondered if Scorpius had intentionally snuffed the lightning ball or if some magical, protective barrier prevented the lightning from destroying the books? Or perhaps, Scorpius didn't wish to chance setting the tomes on fire so he limited its reach?

Scorpius was a master at mixing deadly poisons for traps and to coat blade and arrow tips, so why did he use lightning so much?

"Coward," Scorpius said in a harsh whisper.

Maybe the static energy was distorting Crukas' hearing but he could've sworn two overlapping voices had spoken the insult: Scorpius and the mask.

"Coward?" Crukas stood and brushed dust from his leggings. "Survival's instinctual, not cowardice. Even you would duck an attack to prevent an injury or your own death, wouldn't you?"

Adgus, Bramnir, and Ebden separated from one another and formed a semicircle behind Scorpius, out of his immediate sight. The mask seemed to partially block the mage's peripheral vision.

"I'm guessing not since you wear the mask, eh?" Crukas said with a sly smile. "What cost must you pay for the mask to prevent your untimely death and allow you to live. Magic's never *free*. It also has its limits. What's your sacrifice?"

Scorpius stared at Crukas in long silence. The unnerving mask enhanced the quiet of the room, as if it had a mind of its own, which would explain Crukas hearing two distinct voices whispering only minutes before. Other than the mask protecting the wearer from death, he knew nothing more about its abilities.

Crukas wondered what he might suffer once he placed the mask on his own face. He held no knowledge of what Scorpius' personality was like before he took possession of the mask. How might the mask have altered the mage's behavior? And what more did Crukas stand to lose after he claimed it as his own?

"Something must be sacrificed in your place so you don't die," Crukas said. "What?"

The chains confining the beast from the other side of the room rattled and slid across the floor until fully extended. The monster didn't growl or act aggressive, but whimpered in hope of being freed.

Crukas' brow rose. "Ah. Now, I see."

"Do you?"

"Whatever you've restrained dies in order to spare you. But after that, then what?"

"Does it matter?" Scorpius asked. "Should you be successful enough to kill me once, you'll be dead before you get another chance."

"Don't be so certain."

Scorpius laughed. "Thief, your amusement has no end."

Crukas opened his mouth to reply, but a faint voice whispered in his ears. "You mustn't kill him."

Irmine?

The priestess said, "If you kill him, the mask dissolves. It benefits you none at all. Instead, Scorpius will kill you. I warned you, your hope to attain the mask was a foolish endeavor."

What should I do, then?

She whispered inside his mind. "That I do *not* yet know."

"Step away from the bookshelf," Scorpius said.

Crukas frowned. "Why?"

"Do you fear facing me out in the open, alone?"

"I'm not as well trained in magic as you." Crukas pressed his back against the bookcase. Power pulsed behind him from the books, or perhaps only one of them. Whatever oozed the magical force must be what made Scorpius wary of hurling chain lightning too close to the tomes.

As exhausted as Irmine was when he left her home, how had she recovered so quickly? Was she aware he and Scorpius deadly conflict was near?

"You use sorcery, too?"

"Some."

Scorpius scoffed. "Dabbling with spells doesn't make you equal to a mage."

"I never insinuated such."

"You boasted about stealing my mask. How'd you plan to succeed since it's obvious you can't match my abilities?"

Crukas smiled. "Trickery?"

"Oh? Who's the street corner magician now?"

Crukas shrugged. "You must go with what works, but it pays to have the help of friends."

"Those locked away in the dungeon?" Scorpius asked.

"Nah!" Adgus roared He raised his broadaxe and ran at Scorpius' back. "He be needing *our* help. Not those imposters!"

Scorpius gasped. He turned his neck in such a harsh, quick manner Crukas was surprised the mage's neck hadn't snapped.

Bramnir and Ebden charged from opposing sides with their weapons drawn. Not far away from where Crukas stood, a shimmering light brightened. More surprising than the sudden light was the dark image of Irmine slowly materializing.

Several books on the shelf behind him thudded on the floor.

Irmine whispered, "Take those. You'll have need of them."

Crukas knelt and read the books' spines. One was a Codex of Infra-light and the other was a Witch's Libram. The books were small, so he tucked them inside a pouch and hurried to find a safer place to stand. The fight was underway.

CHAPTER 53

*S*parrow's skin prickled. Static filled the air the farther up the winding, sloped path she walked. With the massive lightning display she'd seen hurled down on Crukas and his party outside the tower, the source of this energy meant Scorpius was close.

The narrow path she followed seemed a hidden passageway between the walls, as a way to escape unnoticed, which was odd since it led to the doorless prison. Had she gone deeper into the dungeon, where would she find herself?

The path took a sharp left turn upon itself. She walked along a crude set of stairs. Shouts echoed above. For several moments, she considered returning to the prison, but that would prove a fruitless endeavor. The farther she got away from Gynx, the safer she'd feel. She'd promised to return to find a way to release them, and her promise was something she'd never rescind, even though she'd have to deal with Gynx again. Strella and Orgem were the only reason she'd attempt to help them escape. With the tension between Triggor and Gynx, though, she might return to find them all dead.

The shouting voices sounded like Triggor and other angered dwarves she'd heard in different taverns across Aetheaon whenever a skirmish arose. But, Orgem and Triggor were trapped below. For them to have escaped and be on the floor above so quickly was impossible. Besides, they'd have had to have walked past her. She was confident the shouts were from those dwarves accompanying Crukas.

Chills combed through her and prickled her skin. The flowing, electrical energy pulsed around her. A conduit of magic was being drawn through the floor below her and from the surrounding walls. She hurried up the stairs, careful not to trip or wedge her foot between broken steps. After the third abrupt turn in the squared stairwell, she came to a locked door.

The tendrils of the building static sparked ribbons of light. Though the light wasn't bright enough to shun all the shadows, it was enough to reveal the plated keyhole on the door. For someone without lock picking knowledge, the lock presented a problem, but for a former thief with a set of lockpicks, this lock offered little challenge.

Sparrow took her leather pouch with various lockpicks from behind her belt and slid out two of the sturdiest picks. Although the lock was iron, the lock wasn't the most difficult to manipulate and disengage, but doing so required a heavier metal pick to prevent breaking her valuable tools. Where this door was hidden, a better lock was not required because what fool would enter this mage's tower in the hope of robbing him?

She laughed.

Crukas.

Sparrow fumbled a few minutes and smiled when the lock clicked. She pulled down the handle and eased the door outward. Blazing blue strands of lightning stretched throughout the round room in a blinding manner. The display left no question as to where Scorpius was. She winced from the glare and raised a hand to shield her eyes. Afterwards, a large creature bounded right at her.

Fear overtook her, and she opened her mouth to scream. Instead, her vocal cords suffered paralysis. The creature was over four times her size and the way it rushed at her seemed threatening. Its massive jaws and jagged teeth could crush and rip her tiny body to shreds with little effort. However, it whimpered, full of anxiety, and plopped its large misshaped head on the floor in front of her. Its long, sloppy tongue coated her boots with slime.

Sparrow couldn't rightly discern what it was, but its actions reminded her of an oversized, mistreated mutt. She placed her hands on the flat ridge above its eyebrows and between its ears and gently scratched. Its odd coat was a mixture of soft fur and ruffled feathers.

Its long, wet tongue unrolled from its mouth and it panted like a dog. It seemed to appreciate her comforting petting. It shook its head and the heavy chain looped around its thick neck shook and rattled.

"Aww," she whispered. "You poor thing."

It stuck its wet nose against her hand and nuzzled her fingers while wagging its tail. The end of the tail was like a hard, rounded piece of bone that resembled a mace head. Its tail could deal an incredible amount of damage should one get too close.

"Easy." Sparrow knelt. "Let me get you loose of that heavy chain."

Seeming to halfway understand what she said, it sat back on its haunches. Its mouth widened as though it smiled. In the fiery blue glow of the dancing lightning and electricity, she realized how huge its mouth was. If it had wanted, it could gulp her down in one quick swallow. Not only did it have enormous teeth, on its bottom jaw were two thick tusks. What was this creature?

Rubbing its wide chest with one hand, she patted along the chain with the other to find the heavy lock that fastened the chain.

"Hold still." She fumbled and worked the pick until the pin inside the lock clicked. She turned the open lock and struggled a few seconds to pull the shackle free of the chain's links. After she succeeded, the chain slid off its neck and clattered on the floor. She dropped the lock.

Excited, the mutt-like creature wagged its tail so hard, its entire body shook. To prevent being battered and suffering any broken bones, she stayed outside its tail's wide, swinging arc.

Sparrow smiled. "You're welcome."

She turned her attention toward the harsh chains of lightning near the center of the room. The strands of lightning stretched outward from Scorpius' fingers and up to the high ceiling. Three dwarves—who were spaced a fair distance apart—growled and raised their axes to charge Scorpius. The runes on their shields and axes glowed. Beyond Scorpius stood Crukas. He was between a long table and a bookcase. He appeared helpless, but he showed no fear.

The sizzling, bluish cloud of lightning swelled and drew into itself more energy. Soon, she expected large bolts of fiery lightning to descend and kill those attacking Scorpius. At close proximity, she wouldn't be spared, either. Nothing should survive such a strike of electrical fire.

Scorpius meant fierce destruction to Crukas and his party, but why wasn't he concerned with his own life? Surely, Scorpius would die along with the others. What did Crukas seek to steal that was worthy enough for the mage to end it all and snuff out the lives of everyone else?

The large, unusual mutt guttered a low growl and snarled at Scorpius.

Sparrow placed a gentle hand on the side of its face. "No. He doesn't concern you."

It chuffed and its eager eyes implied the ongoing battle greatly concerned the mutt. She didn't quite know why she could read its thoughts or how it somehow projected its thoughts to her, but she felt its determination and need to stop Scorpius' madness.

Through the charging clouds of pulsating lightning, a dozen or more sprites glowed and flew in sharp descents toward Scorpius. Sparrow's eyes widened.

What's going on?

Scorpius stretched his arms up and his fingers stiffened. Her body involuntarily tightened. He looked almost ready to bring his wrath down on everyone. It was then, Scorpius turned his head slightly. The hideous mask on his face glowered a severe look of pure hatred and disdain but to no one in particular. The mutt growled.

"Enough, Scorpius!" a female shouted.

Slowly, a gnome dressed in a priestess gown materialized to the left of Crukas. Crukas looked stunned. Clearly, he hadn't expected this gnome to show up.

Her appearance and the sharp demand in her voice caused Scorpius to jerk. Whether fear or the sudden surprise of her presence shook him from his focus, Sparrow didn't know. But it was obvious, Scorpius was suddenly uneasy. His stiff fingers curled slightly and the intensity of his spell dimmed several shades lighter.

From the rafters, even more pixies glided downward and drifted almost silently and as lazily as autumn leaves or snowflakes falling to the ground in the absence of any breeze.

Sparrow was dumbfounded, lost in wondering about what was unfolding. The prison cell seemed to have been safer.

The dwarves rushed Scorpius with their weapons drawn and the sudden appearance of the priestess forced the mage to regain his footing to concentrate on his chain lightning spell. But, he didn't seem capable of taking his eyes off the priestess.

"Irmine," he said. "Why are you here? I banished you from Ravensdorf years ago."

"I never left, even after you destroyed my temple," she replied.

The brows of the mask rose. "No?"

"No."

"That's strange, as I've never detected your presence ever since your temple became a heap of rubble."

Anger flickered in Irmine's eyes. Her jaw tightened. Even a priestess was capable of seeking revenge.

Scorpius met her gaze. "Why intervene to save a thief's life? Wouldn't that be a contradiction of what a priestess should convey?"

"Not when I seek to destroy an *evil* mage," she replied.

The mask contorted and formed a smug smile. Scorpius shrugged. "You may join in sharing your demise with these assembled here, Irmine."

Scorpius turned his attention to rebuilding the strength of his lightning mesh.

"End this now!" Irmine said. Between her hands a powerful white glow of energy formed into a ball.

"I can't," Scorpius said. "These trespassers must die. Their trespassing alone is enough reason to eradicate them, but they've come to steal my death-mask. And since I failed to get rid of you, years ago, I won't make the same mistake again."

Chain lightning encircled Scorpius. The growing static pushed Adgus and his two brothers backwards. Above, the jagged webs of energy knitted together and in less than a minute, Sparrow expected a larger bolt than the one that nearly blinded her outside to blast the floor. With the right amount of force, the entire tower might collapse upon itself.

"So you wish to die?" Irmine asked.

Scorpius laughed. "Die? I'm the only one in this tower who'll survive this."

The white orb in Irmine's hands expanded. "Don't be so sure. The mask won't protect you from injuries. The mask only saves you from death *once*. After it shatters, this holy fire will cut you down before you have a chance to recuperate from your self-inflicted injuries."

"That's not true," Scorpius said. "I've a sacrifice ready to accept my injuries and my death. The mask will stay intact."

"Then you've been misinformed," Irmine said. Her eyes blazed the same white glow as the holy fire orb in her hands.

The dwarves shoved against the circle of sizzling energy. The runes on their shields and weapons glowed, but even so, they couldn't push their way through Scorpius' protective circle.

The mutt beside Sparrow roared and charged past her.

"No!" She reached for the cumbersome beast, but it paid her no mind. Even if she secured a handful of its feathery hide, she didn't have enough weight or strength to slow it.

Irmine said, "Adgus, don't hit Scorpius with a deathblow. Otherwise, the mask turns to dust."

"Eh?" Adgus frowned. "Bloody blazes. How do we stop 'em?"

"Patience."

Desperate to help the galloping monstrous mutt, her hand rested on her dagger, but the weapon was useless unless she were capable of getting close enough to stab Scorpius. That was impossible.

The crossbow!

Sparrow had placed the loaded crossbow against the stairwell wall while she'd picked the lock. The charging mutt caused her to forget the weapon. With the mutt running headlong into a dangerous confrontation, she hoped to use the crossbow to save the mutt. She only had one bolt, so the shot needed to be accurate.

CHAPTER 54

Crukas turned toward Irmine. While he'd always known she was a priestess, he never realized how much power she could summon from her deity until now. She'd been frail and near death when he left her, or so he believed. A renewed fierceness glowed in her eyes, and he'd never seen her like this. The heat from the holy fire she wielded forced him to step farther away. The waves of heat rippled worse than the midday sun in the middle of a desert. How she wasn't consumed by the fire surprised him.

Sweat dripped from her forehead. With the magnitude of power flowing out her body into the orb of holy fire, one might think her a giant instead of a gnome. The undulating force sent pulsating flares outward like she'd harnessed a small sun.

"Irmine," Crukas said. "You didn't need to come to my rescue."

"Yes, I did." Her lips never moved. She whispered inside his mind. "What you said was truth."

"About *what* exactly?"

"Everything. The mask. The Plague-bringer. Aetheaon's fate. I'd have never thought the fate of Aetheaon rested on the shoulders of a thief."

Crukas swallowed hard. He frowned. "Nor I. I still don't."

291

"Oh, it does. *More* than you know."

"What can I do to help ... right now?"

"Stay where you are. Don't get caught between me and Scorpius. But as I warned Adgus and the others, Scorpius can't suffer a death blow. Otherwise, the mask crumbles to dust."

The expanding heat made him want to move away, but then the protective amulet Irmine had given him glowed. Coolness washed around him and shielded him from the holy fire.

Crukas frowned. "That leaves few options."

"I'm aware, but we have something Scorpius doesn't."

"What's that?"

"My faith."

CHAPTER 55

Sparrow grabbed the bow and returned to the round room. The mutt charged in a clumsy gallop across the room determined to reach Scorpius. Its massive paws thudded as it ran. The room shook. The mutt's hook-like claws dug grooves through the floor tiles, sending wood chips into the air. The beast's flapping jowls revealed its large teeth.

A dwarf noticed the mutt. His eyes widened. "Bloody hell!"

Sparrow closed her eyes. She worried the dwarves mistook the mutt's attack was directed at them and they'd kill it.

Please don't hurt him.

Heated tears formed at the edges of her eyes. When she opened her eyes, she was relieved to see the dwarves had stepped aside to let the beast continue toward Scorpius.

The bluish electrical tendrils of the building chain lightning intensified, and since the dwarves were unable to interfere, Scorpius was close to completing the spell and incinerating everyone within range. Someone needed to intervene. The priestess' holy orb was too bright to look at directly. While Irmine's spell might strike Scorpius with enough power to immobilize him, if not kill him, Sparrow worried about the catastrophic devastation should both magical forces collide.

Sparrow raised the crossbow and took a deep breath. She aimed at the Scorpius' shadowy form and pulled the trigger. After the bolt fired, the giant mutt leapt. Sparrow bit her lower lip and hoped the bolt missed the beast and somehow struck Scorpius.

CHAPTER 56

*C*rukas stood in front of the bookcase. The swelling, enhanced power building between the mage and the priestess overwhelmed him. As with any magical spell, the energy source came from various planes: Air, water, fire, earth, and holy. The Fae and Elves drew from others as well. The more casters attuned themselves to these various planes aided in how much magic one could draw and control.

Not certain how this eruptive battle was about to end, Crukas understood Irmine's previous warnings to not enter the tower were valid. Experienced mages used dangerous magic, far greater than anything Crukas could ever hope to attain. In all fairness, Crukas ranked himself below the meekest wizard apprentice. An evil mage, like Scorpius, was far worse. Regardless of any trickery Crukas might've attempted, he wasn't a worthy challenge to Scorpius at all.

Since Scorpius wore the mask, this burglary wasn't a simple sneak-and-grab an object before being discovered. Scorpius not only owned the mask, he obviously never took it off. To steal it meant to meet the mage on a personal level, face-to-face. He could never have gotten close enough to the mage without additional help. Crukas doubted if he'd said, *"Please"*, during their banter that the polite request would have changed the outcome. Then, Crukas wondered if Scorpius never took off the mask because he *couldn't*. Was it affixed to his face?

Crukas regretted not arguing harder for the dwarves to stay in Ravensdorf. But the dwarves were stubborn. They wouldn't have heeded the request or changed their minds, no matter how much Crukas tried to persuade them. They were with him regardless. They'd have all died without Irmine miraculously recuperating enough to appear and fight in their stead. Of course, they all might die anyway after the last thread of magical energy exploded and then evaporated.

Crukas felt the warmth and comfort of what having true friendship meant, but now, terror and possible heartache consumed him in understanding what it meant to *lose* those friends. He would've rather remained solitary and sacrifice his own life, instead of others including themselves in his mission. Should he be the sole survivor of this impending battle against the Plague-bringer, Crukas would become the most miserable soul in all of Aetheaon.

"Crukas," she said without taking her eyes off Scorpius. "Should I not survive this, I placed a parchment on my alchemy table. Follow the instructions I wrote."

The heat of her glowing, white orb intensified. An invisible force pushed him. His ears rang. "What?"

"Do what's on the parchment. That's the favor I need from you."

Crukas wanted to tell her that she'd survive. All would be fine. But at the moment, even he questioned if any of them would survive. The tower floor quaked. Bits of mortar and dust fell from the cracking ceiling. This didn't seem to be her doing. Scorpius was trying to make his tower collapse.

"Brace yourself," Irmine whispered.

Crukas gripped the heavy oak table in front of him. Remembering how the lightning had melted the stone slabs on the bridge outside, whatever happened within the next minute could be far more catastrophic.

"Wait!" a female yelled from across the room.

Crukas squinted to see who was hidden in the darkness. The sprites flew at Scorpius with small flames firing from their wands. Scorpius' armor was resistant to venom, but what about fire? Or Irmine's holy magic? Since Scorpius controlled lightning and it seemed his choice of weapon, anything electrically charged probably wouldn't have any effect. The fiery flames struck the scorpion leather armor, smoldered, and didn't penetrate it.

Scorpius yelled in pain and his left shoulder jerked slightly. He maintained enough balance and strength to focus on his spell. Then, an angered, deafening growl that sounded like a mix between a mongrel and a predatory bird's shriek echoed. The floor vibrated as its heavy, thundering feet bounded at Scorpius.

"You'll all die!" Scorpius seethed. His mask creased with a furious frown and its mouth bent to reveal incredible agony. His hands trembled. The burst of lightning flickered with a slight rumble of thunder, but not like what shook the floor.

Crukas braced himself. The brightness prevented him from seeing the dwarves. Would the runes on their shields, armor, and weapons be enough to protect them? No. Not if the floor fell through.

"No-o-o!" Scorpius stammered. He turned to face the charging creature.

The giant, feathery mutt leapt and its huge mouth clamped around Scorpius' right arm. The chain lightning blazed brighter and sizzled. The swarming pixies fled lower. Over half of them darted down the ladder opening at the center of the room.

Scorpius screamed in agony, dropped to the floor, and cradled the stub of his right arm. The mutt's momentum kept the beast moving. It slid to slow its pace. Its claws dug into the wooden floor with a nerve-grating annoyance. Shaking its head, it dropped Scorpius' arm and sniffed the partial limb.

Scorpius wailed and lie on his side. He whimpered with his back fully exposed. Even the most evil mage or wizard succumbed to pain and could lose control of their spells. Agony sometimes held greater power than the strongest spell. Irmine thrust her hands outward and released the glowing holy orb, which shot forward and struck Scorpius dead center in the back. His body tightened with sudden paralysis and his moaning cries ceased.

The huge cloud of chain lightning dissipated upward through the ceiling and most likely exploded in a spectacular array of colors for all to see in Ravensdorf. As the chains of vibrant blue lightning stretched and crept through the ceiling and cracking walls, every sconce suddenly lit with the same white fire Irmine had released. The room brightened, akin to a midday sun on a cloudless day, almost as though her power sought to purge Scorpius' control and evil over the tower.

Profusely sweating, Irmine dropped to her knees. She panted, resting on her elbows, and clinging to her last threads of consciousness. Exhausted and near fainting or succumbing to death, her weak stare focused on Scorpius.

Crukas rushed to Irmine, knelt beside her, and placed a gentle hand between her shoulder blades. "Are you okay?"

"Claim your prize, thief," she whispered. Boiling sweat streamed from her brow and her fatigue slowly consumed her. "Before his paralysis fades."

Crukas looked into her tired eyes. She was too depleted to meet his gaze and her breathing became frighteningly shallow. He didn't want to leave her side. The mask seemed less important when the price for the triumphant victory might've cost her life.

"Hurry," she said. "There's not much time. Should his paralysis fade, I've no strength left to fight."

"I don't think he has any, either."

"All the same," she replied. "He could kill himself to prevent you from getting the mask. Hurry."

Crukas leaned and kissed her sweaty, furrowed forehead.

"Don't forget. The parchment I left for you. It's … essential." She attempted a weak smile, closed her eyes, and collapsed.

He rose but hesitated leaving her side. Had she died? He closed his eyes tightly. Tears leaked from the edges of his eyes. *The parchment.*

Her voice whispered inside his mind. *Go!*

Torn by the uneasiness in leaving her and fearing she'd died,

Crukas walked to Scorpius. The mage was down, severely injured, but for some reason, this wasn't the victory he'd hoped.

The giant mutt returned to Scorpius and peered down at the mage. The mongrel seemed ready to finish Scorpius' life. This beast must've been the chained sacrifice at the other side of the room. It was supposed to die so Scorpius would live. How had it gotten free?

It leered over Scorpius. A guttural growl rumbled inside its thick throat. It seemed hesitant to injure the mage any further.

"Easy." Crukas raised a cautious hand like he might coax a stray dog. "Don't kill him until after I've gotten the mask, okay?"

Crukas looked in Scorpius' eyes. While the rest of the mage's body remained paralyzed, his eyes were not. A plethora of emotions reflected in his gaze. The most noticeable was his fear. If Scorpius could speak, Crukas expected the mage might express his unexpected disbelief in losing everything due to his haughty nature and underestimating his mortality.

The beast seemed to understand what Crukas said. It eased back and allowed the thief to stand over Scorpius. The fear in Scorpius' eyes filled with sudden defiance, as though he thought he might still escape his defeat.

A crossbow bolt protruded from the mage's left shoulder, which confused Crukas. Who fired it? Somehow the bolt had found its way through a segment in the scorpion chitin and was driven into Scorpius' flesh. Quite possibly, this was the only weakened place in the armor.

Scorpius' blood loss seemed minimum, but the thick, tight armor probably prevented the bleeding from leaking to the surface. The armor was only slightly dented but not torn or ripped where the mutt had bitten. It had jerked the mage's arm apart, but the armor remained intact. Considering the strength and size of the beast's jaws, the scorpion leather proved quite difficult to penetrate.

Blood leaked and pooled from Scorpius' jagged arm stub. With the amount of blood loss, Crukas needn't worry about the mage taking his own life to prevent Crukas from getting the mask. Unless the mage somehow stopped the bleeding, he'd die soon enough. Scorpius seemed aware of how close death was, which was the reason for the fear dominating his dark eyes. Such a painless death was too easy and not a rightful reward for all the evil this mage had shed on Ravensdorf. While the mask had shown various emotions in addition to Scorpius', it was now smooth and calm, perhaps contemplating its own fate.

Crukas gave a somber gaze to Scorpius. "You probably wish you'd let me borrow this now?"

Crukas carefully gripped both sides of the mask. Scorpius couldn't stop him. Crukas expected the mask to resist being taken. The way Scorpius had boasted earlier, Crukas thought he'd have to pry the mask off. Instead, the mask dislodged without any force. Skeptical, Crukas wondered if the mask wanted him for its next victim. Taking the mask was no challenge, unless ... *whatever* possessed the mask disliked the idea of crumbling to dust. Crukas didn't want to yield himself to its control after placing it on his face. Was the mask a type of predatory parasite that latches to and feeds upon its victim? In the near future, he'd find out.

CHAPTER 57

With the mask in hand, Crukas backed away from Scorpius. The three dwarves met and joined him.

Crukas stared at the eye, nose, and mouth holes in the mask. He sighed. "I never expected the mask to release itself."

"Aye. Dat be easier than I thought it'd be," Adgus said.

"*Easy?*" Bramnir said. "None of *this* was an easy task."

Adgus roared a hearty belly laugh. "Okay. Ya have to admit climbing the ladder was far more challenging."

Bramnir huffed. "No argument there."

Ebden nodded. "Especially with our shields strapped on our backs."

"You forget," Bramnir said. "Irmine's the reason we're alive. Now, she needs our help."

Crukas nodded and looked at Irmine lying on the floor. She seemed even smaller than a gnome should be. "We owe her our lives. She's so weak now. We need to get her home."

Adgus grinned broadly. "Happy to oblige."

Crukas pointed at the bolt in Scorpius' shoulder. "Did one of you fire a crossbow at him?"

Bramnir shook his head and frowned, partially offended. "Are ya kidding? Don't insult us. We'd never stoop so low. Axes, hammers, and blades are the glory in our fights."

The feathery-haired mutt whined and its jaw dropped with slight sadness. It pawed the floor and its actions indicated it was pointing to Scorpius.

Crukas grinned at the mutt. "He's all yours."

The mutt yapped an eager sound, wrapped its jaws around Scorpius' midsection and shook the mage like it might a straw scarecrow. Due to the mage's paralysis, he offered no cries, but the loud snaps and pops of his bones made them cringe. When the mutt stopped thrashing Scorpius, the mage's body hung limp and lifeless in the its mouth. Every bone in Scorpius' body must've been splintered and broken.

Blood leaked from the mage's eyes, nose, mouth, and ears. Scorpius was dead.

Crukas winced and gently tucked the mask under his arm.

"No stomach for dat?" Adgus asked.

"Nah. I hate to see such a waste of good armor though," Crukas said. "It's priceless."

"Oh?" Bramnir asked. "How's dat?"

"Scorpion leather is rare, particularly *this* leather. It's resistant to venom and poisons."

"We could pry it off him," Adgus said, "if ya want it. The beast has no interest in eating the mage."

"Doing so would probably leave a worse taste in its mouth," Ebden said.

The mutt dropped Scorpius on the floor and studied the corpse; perhaps waiting for any further signs of life.

"That armor's too heavy for a thief," Crukas said. "If none of you fired the crossbow, who did?"

"Me." Sparrow cautiously walked out of the shadows.

"Sparrow?" Crukas gave her a shrewd stare. In spite of the fiery white sconces, she approached unnoticed until she spoke. She possessed the stealthiness of a thief. "You? Why?"

"I thought Scorpius might hurt this pitiful beast," Sparrow said.

Adgus's brow rose. "Doubtful much could hurt it."

The mutt panted and stared at them with large, playful eyes. Other than its intimidating size, it didn't seem an immediate threat unless provoked or attacked. It acted proud of killing Scorpius.

Bramnir stared at the crossbow propped atop Sparrow's shoulder. "You 'ave much experience using dat crossbow?"

She shook her head. "First time I ever used one. I only had one bolt."

Adgus' eyes widened. "Oh? Quite a good shot then."

Sparrow blushed. "It was luck, really."

"No," Crukas said. "The bolt struck the only weak spot in his chest piece."

Sparrow shrugged. "Honest. I've never used one before."

Crukas changed the subject. "So, you released this cumbersome beast?"

Sparrow grinned. "Yes. I picked the lock that kept the tight chain fastened around its neck."

"Ya timing couldn't 'ave been better," Adgus said. "Scorpius kept us from reaching him with all dat lightning."

"Still pursuing me, eh?" Crukas asked her.

She shook her head. "No. Not anymore."

"Where are your new friends? Triggor and Gynx?" Crukas gazed past her. "Should we prepare to defend ourselves?"

Sparrow shook her head. "No. They're not my friends."

Ebden said, "You seemed awful chummy with them."

"No. Honest," Sparrow said. "After they talked to me about the wanted flyer I showed them, they forced me to join their group."

Crukas chuckled. "Forced? Adgus told me you walked to their table and sat down."

"True. They offered for me to join them," Sparrow said. "I wanted to decline but with the evil glint in Gynx's eyes, he wasn't about to let me go freely. He intended to kill me whenever I turned my back to leave. At the warehouse, he insisted I stick with him. Then, after I warned you of his intentions, he's looked for any opportunity to fire a bolt through my heart."

Crukas kept his attention on her eyes as she spoke. Not once did she look away. Her voice never quivered. Her bold words indicated she wasn't lying. A seasoned thief could lie through his teeth without flinching and never hint that his words were lies. Sparrow, though, being a halfling with much innocence and a conscience that guilt and remorse could easily bruise, couldn't blatantly lie without having a tell. She spoke the truth.

"So what's become of them?" Crukas asked.

Sparrow sighed and looked at the floor. "They're locked inside a prison cell a floor or two below."

"Your doing?" Bramnir asked with a questioning frown.

"No. We fell through a trapdoor in the stairwell," she replied.

Crukas nodded and glanced at Adgus. "The one Tamara warned us about."

"Aye," Ebden said.

Always skeptical, Adgus tightened both hands on his broadax and with a grim expression chiseled on his face, he looked at Sparrow. "Ya still interested in obtaining the reward set on Crukas' head?"

Her fearful eyes studied the axe and his not so subtle threat. She swallowed hard. "No. All I want is to return to Willow's Bend, my home. I stopped being a thief not so long ago, and now, I won't be bounty hunting any longer, either. Neither suit me. Besides, I don't measure up to the standards required."

The three dwarves eyed one another and roared with laughter. Adgus wiped away a fresh tear. "Measure up! Now, dat's a good one."

Sparrow blushed. A smile tugged at her lips. "You know what I meant."

Adgus grinned. "Aye. We get it all the time from these human folk and elves 'bout our stature, but we find no offense. I'd hate to be a miner with height. I'd always be bashing me head in."

Bramnir frowned "So, you're going to leave Triggor and Gynx in the cell to die?"

"I promised to return and help them escape," she said.

"Don't think we'll 'be helping ya with dat," Adgus said.

"I don't want to, either." Sparrow's hands trembled and the

nervousness in her eyes increased. "Gynx chased me up the stairwell and was going to kill me before we dropped through the stairs. He's threatened my life many times. Freeing him won't change his view of me. No matter how flattering or persuasive he might be when I free them, he'll kill me once he's released."

"Dat may be, lass," Adgus said, "but some people deserve an earlier death than others."

Her brow rose and her mouth gaped.

Adgus waved his hand. "Not you. The kobold."

"Yes. Perhaps, Gynx." Her eyes became remorseful. "But not Orgem and Strella …. I can't justify leaving them to starve to death."

Bramnir shook his head. "Not dat I want them to die, but you won't find any of us wishing to help Triggor and Gynx escape. They'd consider us in cahoots with Crukas."

"We haven't time to free them, anyway." Crukas walked away from Sparrow to Irmine. She lie still, barely breathing. "We need to get Irmine home quickly or else she may die."

Without addressing another fear aloud, he worried she'd die before they reached her home.

Adgus motioned Ebden and Bramnir over to Irmine. "The three of us can take turns carrying her, provided we can find another way down, other than the ladder."

Sparrow pointed to where the beast had been chained. "There's a set of stairs beyond the door, but they lead to the prison below."

"Bah!" Bramnir shook his head. "We can't take her past them."

Crukas nodded. "I agree. No sense drawing their unwanted attention to us since we won't help them escape. That'll only infuriate them more."

"Another path forked into the downward one I took," Sparrow said. "I've no idea where it leads, but the prison cell is out of view. They'll never know we came close to them."

Tamana flittered between Sparrow, the dwarves, and Crukas. She said, "That path leads to the outer wall to a balcony overlooking the sea. Another set of stairs on the outside of the tower will take you to an entrance several floors below the prison cell where you can bypass the ladder. You'll find a stairwell to the main entrance."

Adgus narrowed his eyes. "And ya know this, how?"

"We've combed these floors," the pixie replied. "Scorpius didn't invest much in his lines of defense."

"He believed he was invincible," Crukas said.

"Indeed," Tamana said. "Such false security makes one blind to real threats."

Sparrow sighed. "I can't let Strella and Orgem die in the cell, so I'll go see if I can find a way to get them out."

"No," Tamana said. "I and those with me will help free them."

Sparrow looked relieved.

"We appreciate that," Crukas said. "I know we're in no position to ask, but could you wait until we get some distance between them and us?"

Tamana smiled. "One day or two?"

Crukas frowned. "I didn't expect that wide a gap."

Tamana scrunched her dainty nose and shrugged. "For you, dear thief, we'll ensure you have an adequate head start."

"You haven't found what you were looking for yet, have you?" Crukas grinned.

The pixie blushed. "Not yet, no. But since you killed Scorpius, we've more time to search. Besides, Scorpius killed Reaver. We can't allow that to go uncompensated."

"How do ya put a price on dat?" Adgus asked.

She sighed. "You can't really, so we'll keep the most important necessities we find."

"I didn't kill Scorpius," Crukas said.

"No one will care about the truth, thief. He was collateral damage and the folks in Ravensdorf will view you as their rescuer. You've freed them of his reign."

"But I didn't," Crukas said. "It was a group effort, but truth be told I cowered behind the table over there. I was no match for Scorpius' power, I admit it, and I didn't want to get caught in the crossfire.

Irmine immobilized him, and that large mutt-like beast ended Scorpius."

"Aye," Bramnir said. "We couldn't even get near the mage."

"Pish posh," Tamana said. "Those details don't matter. No matter how you try to tell the tale, it'll end up exaggerated a hundred different ways. Each listener will choose her favorite version and tell it to others. And just wait until bards get ahold of the story."

Crukas rolled his eyes. "I can't wait. If you can wait two days to release Triggor and the others, we greatly appreciate it. For now, we have to get Irmine to her cottage and hope she heals. Unless you could heal her?"

Tamana glided closer to Irmine, glanced the priestess over, and sadly, shook her head. "No. Sorry. Her life force is far beyond what we could do, even with all of us focusing our magic together."

Crukas winced and hung his head.

"My clan will scour this tower for several days, but we'll keep check on the prisoners. They won't starve or die of thirst," Tamana said. "That much mercy we'll allow."

Sparrow said, "The kobold. You can't trust him. He might attack you once you free him."

"Gynx?" Tamana giggled. "Yes. We watched him pursue you. None of us will come within his reach."

"His crossbow's over by the door."

"We'll let him find it later," the pixie replied. She flitted off.

Crukas watched Ebden heft Irmine over his broad shoulder and then turned his attention to Sparrow. "What of you, halfling?"

"Mind if I tag along with you?" she asked. "At least until we get to Ravensdorf?"

"Can I trust you won't drive a dagger in my back?" he asked.

Sparrow met his gaze. "I left the hunt, remember? Besides, carrying a dead body would slow us down."

Crukas eyed her and attempted to read her intentions.

A slight smile curled her lips. "I jest. You may carry my dagger if you don't trust me."

Crukas studied her a few seconds longer and then shook his head.

"No. Keep it. We've no idea what else we might face before we get out of the tower."

"Thanks." She looked at the mask he held.

"You might not've had any more bolts, but you should consider taking the crossbow. We might find more bolts on our way out."

"I don't know," she said softly.

"You did remarkably well for your only shot, provided it was your actual *first* shot."

"I swear it was."

"You may have a natural talent for using it."

Sparrow smiled. "Be right back."

She sprinted to the spot where she dropped the crossbow, grabbed it, and hurried back. She glanced at the mask. "That's what you came for?"

He nodded. "Even wearing the mask, Scorpius didn't escape death."

"I doubt much would've survived the jaws of this beast," Sparrow said, ruffling the feathery-hair on its chest.

"True," Crukas said.

"What's the mask for?"

"It's a long story," Crukas replied. "I'll tell you on the way to Irmine's cottage."

Sparrow smiled. "Sure."

"Are you taking this beast with you?"

"I can't leave him here, can I?"

"Perhaps not. Come on."

CHAPTER 58

While Adgus carried Irmine up the narrow stairs and through the passageways inside Dark Ayr Tower, the intended sacrificial beast followed and squeezed his way behind them. Once they got outside, the large mutt stepped in front of the dwarves and lowered its huge head.

"What's it doing?" Crukas asked.

Sparrow smiled. "I think he wants to help."

Adgus frowned. "How?"

She shrugged. "Perhaps he wants to carry Irmine across the rocky field."

The creature looked even more massive and taller in the ambience of daylight. Its undercoat shimmered like tiny, sparkling gems and more feathery than hairy. The dwarves stood almost eye level with the beast.

"What is this beast?" Crukas asked.

"Never seen anything like it." Adgus cradled Irmine in his arms while cautiously observing the mutt.

"Perhaps it's a product of magic?" Sparrow asked.

Bramnir nodded. "Maybe. I've never seen one, either."

Adgus studied the creature and it chuffed. "What's it want?"

It moaned and whimpered.

Crukas said, "I think Sparrow's right. It wants to carry Irmine."

Adgus' brow rose. "What? Ya think dat's safe?"

Sparrow stepped to the large creature and rubbed the bluish-gray, feathery-hair on the side of its jaw. "He wouldn't hurt a thing."

Bramnir cocked a brow. "Uh, ya saw what it did to Scorpius, didn't ya?"

"Okay. Self-preservation isn't the same. Scorpius was going to sacrifice him. I'm certain he wouldn't hurt Irmine. He's worried about her and wants to protect her," Sparrow said.

Adgus adjusted Irmine in his arms. "I'm not so sure."

"Let's give him a name," Sparrow said. "Bolt? How about Bolt?"

"Why Bolt?" Adgus asked.

She shrugged. "Scorpius was going to sacrifice him to spare his own life with chain lightning. Bolt seems strong, fierce."

Crukas nodded slightly. "You also fired a bolt to distract Scorpius, which gave this mutt an opening to attack."

"Let's forget naming it for now." Adgus frowned. "So ya want me to place Irmine on his strong, fierce neck? You sure dat's safe?"

"He can be trusted."

Adgus flicked his gaze to Crukas. "How 'bout it, thief?"

"Bolt holds genuine concern for Irmine," Crukas replied. "Letting him carry her would save us time, and you wouldn't have to strain yourselves by carrying her."

"Strain ourselves?" Bramnir said. "She weighs hardly nothing."

"All the same. Let's see," Crukas said. "We need all the allies we can get."

Ebden sighed. "Dat's true."

Adgus huffed. "All right. I'll be keeping a wary eye on it though."

"*Bolt*," Sparrow said.

Adgus eased Irmine between Bolt's massive shoulders. Bolt stood slowly and carefully walked toward Ravensdorf. Despite his diligent stride, his heavy weight pressed, cracked, and crushed large paw prints into the brittle shale stones. The sea breeze flowing from the bluffs caressed Bolt's feathery-hair and sent ruffling, wavelike movements across his puffy coat. A near metallic sheen from his undercoat reflected when the faint morning sunlight touched it.

Keeping his attention on Irmine, Adgus hurried alongside Bolt while Bramnir and Ebden stayed on the opposite side. Each of the brothers seemed fearful Bolt might drop her. He didn't. The sway of Bolt's shoulders gently rocked Irmine as he walked.

While following behind the dwarves and Bolt, Crukas explained the mask to Sparrow with sparse details since the mask might prove useless unless he managed to obtain the other artifacts he needed. But time for collecting them was escaping him.

Once Crukas, Sparrow, and the dwarves reached the outer perimeter of Ravensdorf's cottages and stone buildings, they were met by a large crowd of townsfolk who'd been drawn to the magnificent chain-lightning display firing out through the top of the tower into the sky. Due to dawn approaching, the lightning grew fainter and was fading. If not for the misty sunrise, the magical display might've lasted longer.

Crukas covertly glanced at the mesmerized faces. He was relieved few even noticed him and more satisfied no one recognized him. Most kept their attention on the tower and others watched in astounded dismay as Irmine's limp body lie in between Bolt's massive shoulders. Upon seeing Bolt, the crowd parted in fear.

Adgus placed a thick hand against Bolt's side. The dwarf's eyes moistened with tears. "Give us room! Back away!"

Crukas was touched, seeing how much Adgus cared about Irmine. He was the most outspoken and skeptical of the three brothers. But she had saved his life and might've even sacrificed her own to save all of them and Ravensdorf from Scorpius.

Although Scorpius had destroyed her temple long ago, the people knew her. She, no doubt, had never stopped being a priestess and many secretly sought her for healing. She was a treasure they only whispered about to keep her whereabouts unknown to Scorpius.

Crukas admired Irmine greatly for not fleeing Ravensdorf and chuckled that Scorpius was foolish enough to think he'd frightened her away. Such audacity had led to his downfall.

Murmuring passed through the crowd. Several whispered their fear of Bolt, but Adgus and Bramnir each patted Bolt while walking alongside him. The dwarves offered calming words to the townsfolk that Bolt meant them no harm.

Concern rose in their voices, as they wondered aloud if Irmine was going to live or if was dead. She clung to life loosely and might have an hour or less to live.

"This was Scorpius' doing," one whispered.

Crukas stared at the ground, saddened and filled with grief, questioning why Irmine had placed her life on the line to save his again. He'd admit his fault—had he asked her to intervene—but he hadn't asked or even hinted for her to offer assistance. Her energy had waned before he left her. Yet, guilt pressed his heart and mind. He ached to understand her devotion for a thief. He thought about the parchment she demanded him to read. Had she aided him to ensure he'd fulfill his favor to her? He grinned. Quite possibly.

Someone stepped in front of him, causing him to glance up into familiar eyes. Crukas stopped, perplexed. "Devin?"

Devin smiled and clasped Crukas' shoulder with a firm grip. He whispered, "Brother, you're alive."

Crukas forced a smile and flicked his gaze side-to-side to see if anyone noticed who he was. "Barely. Irmine didn't fare as well."

"And Scorpius?"

"Dead."

The quiet whispering crowd suddenly cheered and praised Irmine for his demise. Elderly folks began offering prayers for her healing. They encircled Bolt and blocked the crude street. Crukas took a moment of relief and hoped they'd revere her as the hero and not himself.

Adgus waved them back and snarled. "Irmine's injured. Back away!"

Devin motioned with his hands and attempted to calm their unnecessary blockade. "Make way, please. We must get Irmine home immediately."

The crowd parted, allowing Bolt and the three dwarves to pass through.

Sparrow weaved her way through the townsfolk and hurried to catch up to Bolt.

Devin walked in stride alongside Crukas. "So the dwarves found you."

Crukas nodded. "Much to my surprise, and they ignored my vehement protests to allow me to face Scorpius alone."

"Good for you, eh?" Devin frowned. "Did you actually believe you'd have survived without them?"

"Highly doubtful," Crukas said with little emotion. "But Irmine arrived unannounced and carried the battle for all of us. Scorpius was attempting to collapse the entire tower on top of us. She stopped him."

Devin shook his head. "For what purpose did you find it necessary to trespass into his tower? Nothing's *that* important."

"For this." Crukas opened a small pack and showed him the mask.

"A death-mask?"

Crukas nodded. "Yes."

"I see. They're rare, but ... What's its significance to you?"

"I'll explain later." Crukas hurried his pace to catch the dwarves.

Devin matched his pace. "When the dwarves told me you'd given them the last barrel of your finest ale, I doubted I'd ever see you again. Well, *alive*, that is."

Crukas half grinned. "I had my doubts as well."

"Now what?"

"Before anything else, we need to find Irmine's healing potions and hope we're not too late for her to drink one. She's drained to the point of death."

"I agree. I'm sure she has them."

"I know she does," Crukas said. "But I'm not sure if I'd know one from the other."

"We'll figure it out. Then what do you intend to do?"

"I make my way to Moonharvest Tavern."

Devin frowned with curiosity. "At Pirate's Cove? Why? It's dangerous to steal from pirates."

Crukas shrugged. "Even more dangerous to rob the dead."

"What?" Devin's brow rose. "The dead? You mean to steal from the graves?"

Crukas grinned. "But is that really stealing? The dead have no need for items or riches."

"I always thought grave-robbing was beneath you."

"Generally, graves *are* beneath me, but mausoleums and sepulchers are above ground. None of these are what I plan to rob. A ghost has a magical item I desire."

Devin clasped a hand on Crukas' shoulder and shook his head. "I think it best you offer no further information."

"As you wish," Crukas replied.

CHAPTER 59

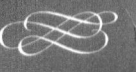

*C*rukas pointed to the cot. Adgus placed Irmine on the same cot where he'd lie only a day or so earlier. Consumed by his inner turmoil, Adgus's reddened eyes studied the room. He seemed to be remembering Irmine's grace when she'd healed him.

"Thanks for getting Irmine home," Crukas said.

Each dwarf offered a solemn nod.

"Ya think she'll recover?" Adgus asked.

Crukas inhaled deeply and released a slow sigh. Though Irmine's situation appeared bleak, he didn't dare speak his worries aloud. "I hope so. Time will tell."

Sparrow came into the room with a vial filled with a lavender-colored liquid. "I found this on a shelf in her alchemy room."

"*Dat* will help her?" Bramnir's brow narrowed and enforced his skepticism. "You sure?"

Sparrow nodded. "This was with other healing potions. There are more of these. One was recently used."

Crukas assumed Irmine had drank the emptied one to revitalize her strength to battle Scorpius. Projecting Crukas' image to the bounty hunters in the warehouse had weakened her. Without some type of healing potion, it was unlikely she'd have recovered fast enough to fight the mage. If she had consumed it, would a second dose present further risks? Since they couldn't ask her, they could only speculate.

Adgus looked wary. He snatched the vial from the halfling's hand and inspected it in the light. "Dat means nothing."

"We must try *something*," she said. "Irmine's near death."

"How do we know you didn't already 'ave this potion when you got here?" Adgus asked.

"I've been out of potions for a while," Sparrow said. "I used all of mine at the warehouse when we succumbed to the poisonous spores. This vial I found in her alchemy lab. I'm only trying to help."

"You wish to wager her life?" Adgus' firm eyebrows intensified the flare of his anger. His nose flared. "I can't allow dat."

Crukas cleared his throat. "Ordinarily I'd agree wholeheartedly. But, Irmine has a greater risk of dying if we do nothing. She's always been efficient and organized. When you were here near death, Adgus, I spoke with her in her alchemy workshop. A recently emptied vial indicates one of two things. Either it's the vial she gave to heal you, which I doubt because I watched her mix the ingredients for your cure. Or, she drank the potion so she could fight Scorpius. So if this vial was on a shelf marked as healing potions, most likely it is."

Bramnir's brow rose. "*If?*"

Adgus kept his frown on Sparrow and cocked his head to the side, studying her. "Lest you forget, Sparrow approached us with your wanted flyer. She was seeking to collect the bounty on your head. You seem so quick to forget."

"I've not forgotten," Crukas said.

"Well, don't think for a minute dat this might not be a trick."

Sparrow's eyes widened. "A trick? In what way?"

Adgus spoke in a gruffer tone. "Dis might be something to make Irmine worse, so you can blackmail Crukas into surrendering to you."

"I'd never do that." Tears crested in Sparrow's eyes.

"Perhaps you would or perhaps not," Adgus said. "Due to the circumstances over the past couple of days, I'm not as trusting."

"I thought Gynx's accusations were bad enough, but what you're insinuating—" Sparrow's eyes softened with a pleading gaze to Crukas.

Crukas sighed. "Adgus, Sparrow warned me about Gynx's intention to capture and torture me should he ever get ahold of me. Gynx resents her for that and marked her for death. Halflings have always exhibited a purity no other race has. She wouldn't deliberately kill a priestess or use her life to blackmail me."

Bramnir said, "Ya sure?"

"I'd wager my own life on it," Crukas said.

"You might just be doing dat," Bramnir said.

Crukas shrugged. "It's a chance I'm willing to take for all Irmine's done to protect us, and me."

Adgus eyed the vial and then glanced at Crukas. After several seconds, he shook his head and handed the potion to Sparrow. "Ya best be right, thief, cause if you're wrong, the halfling suffers an early death."

Sparrow held the vial and gave Crukas a questioning look for permission to administer the potion. Crukas nodded. She uncorked the vial and with shaky hands, she poured the contents into Irmine's slightly open mouth.

Irmine made a shallow gulping sound, but other than that, she didn't move or have any sudden reaction.

Crukas placed the back of his hand to Irmine's forehead. Her skin was cold, blue.

Adgus grunted. "Well?"

"Sometimes these potions take time," Sparrow said.

Adgus flicked his gaze to Crukas.

Crukas nodded. "She's right."

Devin eased closer and nodded. "It's true."

"I'm not dat patient," Adgus said.

Crukas said, "We witnessed the amount of power Irmine drew and exerted from the ethereal planes. It's a miracle she didn't die in the tower or before we got her home."

Adgus swallowed hard. As gruff and stolid as he chose to portray, he couldn't diminish the tears heating his eyes. "I suppose. But what do we do in the meantime?"

"Crukas needs escorted to Moonharvest Tavern," Devin said with a sly grin. "I'll stay and keep watch over Irmine."

"I never said I needed any assistance," Crukas said. "I plan to go alone."

Ebden offered a disappointed expression and crossed his thick arms. "Alone? You and I are both cursed, because of dat book, and you'd abandon me?"

"No," Crukas said. "That's not my intent. I'll find a way to lift the curse."

Bramnir grumbled. "Not if ya get yourself killed along the way."

"He's right," Adgus said. "We stick together until the curse is removed."

Crukas sighed. "Fine. As you've already proven, it's fruitless to argue with you."

Sparrow appeared stunned. She confronted Crukas. "So it *was* you who stole Fasha's book?"

Crukas winked. "I stole the book right beneath you and Fasha's noses with only seconds to spare before the two of you entered her shop. Come with me."

CHAPTER 60

Crukas walked down the narrow hallway with Sparrow to Irmine's alchemy workshop. He stood at a table with various beakers and vials. He turned to face her.

Dumbfounded, Sparrow balled her hands into fists.

Crukas said, "What's bothering you?"

"How'd you escape Fasha's shop without us seeing you?"

"Thieves don't reveal their secrets," he replied.

"Did you go through the chimney? But Fasha lit a fire."

"I'll answer your question provided you answer some of mine."

She gazed into his eyes for several long moments before she acquiesced a slight nod. "Okay."

"Are you still jealous of me?"

"Preposterous! I'm *not* envious of you," she said, but quickly broke eye contact.

"For a former thief and for a halfling, you're a horrible liar."

Her mouth dropped but she offered no argument. She wrung her delicate hands together at her waist and glanced at the floor with shame in her eyes.

"No one has ever pursued me like you," Crukas said. "Especially not another thief. Such determination only evolves from absolute obsession or resentment. If you can't best me, you've been bent on ensuring my demise. No?"

Sparrow swallowed hard. "Maybe I was a smidgen jealous."

Crukas grinned. "Why?"

"Your reputation. You're the most wanted thief *ever*, with skills no other thief can match. It's not so much about the amount of riches you've accumulated. It's more about the game in not getting caught. You disappear like a vapor."

"Those skills don't happen in a few days or weeks or even years. It took decades to develop and fashion them," Crukas said. "How long were you a thief?"

"A few years, but I was never good. A bit above average, maybe."

"In such a short time, no one could hope to be more than medi-ocre. It takes years to hone one's skills and perfect the craft. Orphaned, I didn't have any choice except to become a thief," Crukas said. "I lived on the streets. Few cared. Mongrels got better scraps from strangers than I. To eat, I learned to steal food without being seen or caught. A master thief, not as masterful as myself, mind you, took me into their guild and trained me. But, he and his guild betrayed me. They stole an item I treasured the most. After stealing it back, I set out on my own. The drive to feed hunger pains makes stealing food necessary when no one cares about your welfare."

Sparrow's eyes teared. "Your reasons make better sense to me now."

Crukas said, "I didn't choose the profession. Destiny, perhaps, chose my path. The wealthy who never offered to feed my hunger were the ones I stole from the most. I stole from temple coffers because priests sit on piles of wealth while others live destitute lives. That's beyond hypocritical. It's a greater crime than my thefts."

"I always thought you freely chose to become a thief."

He shook his head. "No. That's the difference between you and I. You chose to steal for whatever reason, which is contrary to a halfling's nature. But, your conscience is your enemy. You question each act because you fear how others view you. You need to steal without fear. Fear causes hesitation, and hesitation gets you caught. Never allow anyone to read your emotions through your eyes."

"That's all true."

"One thing you've never considered, though."

"What?" Sparrow asked.

"While your fortitude as a halfling may twist your conscience, being a halfling thief could've worked far greater in your favor."

She frowned. "How?"

"Few expect a halfling to steal right beneath their noses," Crukas replied.

"Like I mentioned, I was never great at swiping items. But I can pick locks quite exceptionally. Locks are like puzzles, and I *love* puzzles."

Crukas said, "Puzzles keep your mind sharp."

Sparrow's eyes softened. "I believed you to be arrogant, but your actions indicate you're the opposite."

Crukas placed his index finger to his lips. "Don't let others know."

She gave a solemn nod.

"Most believe rumors to be truth. Few ever seek the actual truth," Crukas said. "Over the years, some copycat thieves left notes to flaunt what they've stolen to frame me. I've left notes on occasion, but rarely. It'd be foolish to draw attention to every theft I committed. A fool could connect the dots and follow my path to find me. I was selective in what notes I left. Under suspicion, some magistrates forged or patterned notes to sound like I was the criminal but the stolen items weren't things I considered valuable enough to steal. I'd never commit petty thefts."

"Why would they frame you?"

Crukas gave a modest shrug while examining small crates on a corner table. "I suppose it made the loss less painful. After all, would you rather an unknown thug steal from you when you thought your possessions were safe or have the most notorious thief break through your security and take them? The latter might lessen the sting and give a story to boast to others."

"I suppose," she said.

"Besides, the more thefts to my name, the higher the reward for my capture becomes. Thus, more bounty hunters are interested in hunting me down. Like you, Triggor, and Gynx."

"In hindsight, I should never have set out to try to capture you."

Crukas smiled. "You'd be surprised how many times you were standing only a few feet away from me."

Sparrow's eyes widened and she gasped. "No-o-o."

Crukas' grin stretched longer. "It's true."

Embarrassed, Sparrow didn't seem to want to linger on that likelihood. She changed the topic. "Okay. So, how *did* you escape Fasha's shop?"

Crukas explained the chimney and how the smoke had almost done him in. Had it not been for his ice-silk armor, the flames might have become detrimental. Soon after he left Fasha's shop, he met the three dwarves and bartered for a ride to Ravensdorf.

"How'd *you* know I was going to Ravensdorf?" he asked.

"I didn't." Sparrow explained the sealed, off-limits door in Sorceress Brew. When she returned, she found the door unlocked and opened. After she stepped across the threshold, she was transported outside the Mute Changeling. And although she believed Fasha was responsible for teleporting her, Sparrow lacked any proof or any reason for why. "For a while I thought she was in cahoots with you."

"Me?" Crukas shook his head. "No. With time fleeting for what I must do, I didn't think my actions through. While I needed the book, this mask should've been my first priority."

"You think it would've protected you?"

"Quite possibly."

"So the book's really cursed?" Sparrow asked.

He nodded. "I assure you the book's curse is real. I sensed it before taking it off the shelf. I only rushed to grab it because you and Fasha were about to open the door. When Ebden took the book as a retainer, and he later said he immediately felt the curse's binding grip. As for Fasha, I've never met her in person, to my knowledge. Why she sent you after me is a mystery."

"She foretold my death should I pursue you for the bounty."

"And she deliberately directed our paths to cross?"

Sparrow nodded. "Yes."

"Does she want you dead?"

"I hope not."

"What other reason would she have?"

"No idea," Sparrow said.

"So is that why you decided to quit being a bounty hunter?"

"No. I'm not cut out to be a thief or bounty hunter," she replied. "But the thought of death does change one's mind."

Crukas searched the shelves along the wall across from Irmine's powdered herbs, dried roots and leaves, and other odd potion ingredients, which included dried animal organs, feathers, hair, and vials filled with blood. He frowned and sighed heavily. Kneeling, he looked beneath the tables.

"What are you looking for?" Sparrow asked.

Crukas stood, put his hands on his hips, and scanned the tables and open cabinets. "Before Irmine cast the holy orb at Scorpius, she told me she'd left a parchment with a message for me. I don't see it."

Sparrow reached inside her cloak's hidden pocket and pulled out a rolled parchment. "Perhaps this is it?"

Crukas frowned and his eyes flared with anger. "You took it? For *what* reason?"

"To give to you," she said with a sheepish smile.

His jaw tightened and his gaze hardened. "Did you read it?"

Sparrow blushed and looked at the floor. "I'm sorry."

Crukas snatched the rolled message from her. "Maybe the dwarves' warning about you is right."

"When I first picked it up, I thought it might be a spell scroll and we could use it to heal Irmine. But then I noticed it was a message written to you. I didn't read it any further and put it in my cloak to give to you. Honest."

"No," Crukas said. "You withheld it and didn't offer it to me in the other room. You waited until now to give it to me? And only *after* I couldn't find it."

"Not intentionally." Her hands shook almost as badly as her voice.

"I swear it. After Adgus accused me of trying to poison Irmine, I got flustered. Those were harsh allegations. The message being in my pocket slipped my mind. I'd never do anything to hurt Irmine, and I'm sorry I forgot to hand you the message."

The meekness in her trembling voice and the guilt in her eyes assured him she was telling the truth, but he found it difficult to quash his anger and distrust. For all the time she'd spent seeking to capture him for the reward, he felt betrayed. He partially wondered if she still sought to turn him in.

Sparrow's eyes and facial expressions held genuine regret, like any halfling might express. How had she ever stolen an item or captured a thief to collect the bounty? He could picture her apologizing and trying to pay someone for what she stole.

Crukas shook his head and unrolled the parchment.

> Crukas,
> Through prayer I've discovered you seek to obtain the Ghost-flame lantern from Kane Greaves' ghost. This relic is essential in finding other useful tools for your cause. The lantern was the favor I needed, even though I had no prior knowledge it was one of your goals. Obtain the lantern and return to me. Never underestimate the smallest factor. Together, we can aid one another. Holy light shine and protect you.

Crukas' frown deepened.

"What's wrong?" Sparrow asked.

Crukas rolled the parchment and sighed. "Not sure, yet."

"I know you probably don't believe you can trust me—"

"You're correct, but I trust few people," Crukas said. "I've little time to evaluate everything. But fate or misfortune thrust you into the mix. Neither you nor I understand the reasons why. However, how we stumbled into one another wasn't a mistake."

"Really? So Fasha was trying to frighten me?"

Crukas studied her for several moments. He had told the truth about Fasha. He didn't know her. To his knowledge, they never interacted with one another. For the moment, provided Fasha had sent Sparrow to Ravensdorf, he wasn't ready to discard the possibility that Sparrow was essential to obtaining the artifacts Crukas deemed essential. And with Irmine's letter, he wondered what Irmine meant by the *smallest factor*. Had Sparrow not stood before him, he'd have thought the reference was about Irmine, which it could infer. Yet, Sparrow could be the factor he'd never expected. What did Fasha know that he didn't conceive?

Crukas walked to the door. "I'm sure we'll find out soon enough. Come on, let's rejoin the others and head to Pirate's Cove. You may join us if you wish."

Sparrow appeared surprised. "Why would you want me to come? Especially after I had taken the note and forgotten to give it to you?"

"You gave it to me."

"But still?"

Crukas gave her an even smile. "A thief never knows when he might need another thief's assistance."

Confusion set in her gaze. "But, I'm nowhere near as good as you."

"You said you're good at picking locks."

Sparrow's eyes beamed, and she smiled. "Yes. I am. But, it's well known you work alone."

Crukas chuckled. "Not lately. Who knows? You might learn some new skills through direct observation."

"I retired."

"No thief truly retires. The itch for the thrill of possibly getting caught never gets satisfied. Are you game?"

Sparrow blushed and gave a sheepish smile. "Sure, but what about Bolt?"

"Leave him in Devin's care," Crukas said with a grin.

"Do you think he'll mind?"

"No more than I minded him telling the dwarves of my journey to Pirate's Cove. Besides, Bolt would be too difficult to hide during a covert task. He has a fondness for Irmine. She and he are safer in Ravensdorf. Let's go, but before we do, how about we borrow some of Irmine's potions for the trip. Never know when we'll need them."

Sparrow grinned and nodded. "Sure."

CHAPTER 61

*C*rukas cushioned and separated a dozen potion vials between thick layers of wool inside a burlap sack. Because Irmine's favor was an object he already sought, he didn't need to fulfill the obligation later. Why did she need the Ghost-flame lantern and for what purpose? Could the power of this lantern remove the curse on he and Ebden?

With the cushioned potions inside the sack, he and Sparrow returned to Devin and the dwarves.

"How's Irmine?" Crukas met Devin's gaze.

"Extremely weak," Devin replied. "But, she opened her eyes for a few seconds and mumbled something."

"What did she say?" Crukas asked.

Devin shrugged and shook his head. "I didn't understand anything she said except … I think she whispered your name."

"Ah," Crukas said.

"Still, *dat's* a good sign, eh?" Adgus' eyes beamed with hope.

"Yes," Crukas said. "She'll be safe with Devin and Bolt while we make our way to Pirate's Cove."

Adgus gave a shrewd stare. "Ya mentioned dat earlier. As I recall, Pirate's Cove is filled with Ravenfolk."

"Aye," Bramnir said. "Unless absolutely necessary, dat's not a place to venture."

"Ravenfolk are far more hospitable than the pirates," Crukas said.

Ebden frowned. "Not by much."

"True," Devin said. "But they've learned how to tolerate the pirates and other races."

"Long enough to kill one another," Bramnir said.

"The reputation they've earned was not attained by unscrupulous means," Devin said.

Adgus shrugged. "It's there all de same."

Devin gave a narrow smile and nodded.

Sparrow became uneasy. "What caused the skirmish between the Ravenfolk and the pirates?"

Crukas said, "Pirates encroached the Ravenfolk's nesting ridges and built Moonharvest Tavern during the Ravenfolk's migratory season. When the Ravenfolk returned, they butchered and filleted dozens of pirates. What flesh and bones remained of the pirate corpses were buried in Bone Hollow Cemetery."

Bramnir combed his beard with his hand. "And yet, the tavern remains?"

Crukas nodded. "Skretch Krall, the barkeep, claimed ownership of the tavern."

Adgus chuckled. "Let me guess. Skretch is a Ravenfolk?"

"Yes, he's the Overlord of the Ravenfolk," Crukas said. "The Ravenfolk reclaimed the cliffside bluffs and small caves. Any ship that ports in the cove must pay a hefty tariff or risk losing the ship."

"Either sounds hefty to me," Ebden said.

"Indeed," Sparrow said.

"Just a heads up," Crukas said. "The cutthroat pirates are dangerous, but getting on the bad side of the Ravenfolk has greater repercussions."

"Why would pirates continue returning to the cove after the Ravenfolk reclaimed control?" Sparrow asked. "Couldn't they find another suitable port?"

"They could," Crukas said. "But rebuilding a post with such a nasty reputation in a new place wouldn't be easy. Pirate's Cove is a landmark trading post for pirates. Pirates are lawless, but the Ravenfolk tend to oversee and keep them in line. If total chaos ruled, only the most ruthless would set foot on the shore and hope to survive. Pirates require the same supply needs as merchant vessels and captains need new recruits time and again. The seas are treacherous even without the fierce plundering against merchant and naval ships."

"Dat makes sense," Bramnir said.

"Still," Sparrow said, "wouldn't the pirates fare better trading elsewhere, outside of the Ravenfolk's order and without tariffs?"

"Contrary to how we view pirates," Crukas said, "they're not completely lawless. They have their own rules, codes, and laws, by which they abide. They won't kneel before any kingdom's crown. Perhaps, those pirates who built Moonharvest Tavern had done so innocently and never knew the cliffside caves were the nesting place of the Ravenfolk. After all the bloodshed and the loss of pirates' lives ended, maybe they yielded to the Ravenfolk? No one rightly knows. Except, of course, any pirates who survived the bloodbath."

The three dwarves' faces became grim. Each slightly nodded while taking in the information.

"So," Adgus said. "The Ravenfolk are more trustworthy?"

"To a degree," Crukas said. "Unless you're a bounty hunter."

Sparrow gasped. Her eyes widened. "Wait. Is this why you want me to accompany you? To hand me over to them?"

"No," Crukas said. "Of course not. We've no reason to travel into Pirate's Cove. Besides, you've not the reputation they'd view as a threat. Not like Triggor or Gynx."

She sighed with slight relief, but the fear in her eyes didn't lessen. "Does that mean you, the most recognized thief in all Aetheaon, could wander into the tavern and not be accosted?"

Crukas grinned. "With the bounty on my head? There's no guarantee, but I've been inside Moonharvest Tavern several times. Always in disguise though. Why take unnecessary chances? Someone's always foolish enough to violate the rules to collect a hefty bounty. If ever you get a chance, ask Triggor how he obtained his revolver. You'll find he failed miserably trying to take a pirate named Barnacle into custody. The dumbest part was attempting this *inside* the tavern."

Sparrow shook her head. "I hope to never cross paths with Triggor again. Or Gynx. Especially not Gynx."

"Oh!" Adgus' eyes beamed with sudden interest. "Tell us how Triggor got dat revolver."

"Sparrow," Crukas said, "Pirate's Cove is probably the last place you'd ever encounter Triggor."

"Why?" she asked.

"Triggor traded for the revolver from a backstabbing pirate, Dawg Rad, some days before. From what I understand. Had Triggor been less observant, he'd have been buried in Bone Hollow Cemetery. Triggor cornered Barnacle Reed at a table inside the tavern. When Triggor reached to place shackles on the battle-scarred pirate, Barnacle grabbed the revolver. Triggor clasped his left hand around the revolver and caught the trigger between his thumb and index finger before Barnacle could shoot.

"He and Barnacle wrestled over the gun. Triggor's right hand gripped Barnacle's throat. He pinned Barnacle against the wall, which wasn't an easy task. Barnacle's odd armor was covered with razor-sharp barnacles. After Triggor pried Barnacle's thick hand off the gun and clumsily fought to get a better grip, the revolver fired and killed a Ravenfolk inside the tavern."

Bramnir's brow leveled. "O-o-h."

Crukas paused and noticed the eagerness in their eyes as they listened. He understood why bards loved telling stories to an audience. Listeners fed off the words and were anxious to know what happened next.

Crukas nodded. "Barnacle made his run to escape while Triggor stood shocked by what had occurred. He stared at the revolver in disbelief and swore he'd never fired a shot. His finger was nowhere near the trigger. Other pirates, seeing the dead Ravenfolk, scurried out the door. Triggor fled with them and somehow escaped Pirate's Cove without the Ravenfolk catching and killing him."

Sparrow said, "Is this occurrence a bard's tale?"

Crukas shook his head. "No. I witnessed it firsthand."

The dwarves and Sparrow slightly gasped.

"The only wanted flyer you'll ever see inside Moonharvest Tavern and Pirate's Cove is the one for Triggor McLuft," Crukas said.

Adgus bit his lower lip. "So, Triggor killed one of the Ravenfolk?"

Crukas nodded. "The worst part is the shot killed a Ravenfolk Elder brood mothers. If ever they capture Triggor, the end of his life will be sheer agony."

"Did you actually see him fire the revolver?" Sparrow asked.

"No," Crukas said. "I watched them scuffle. It was the first time I'd seen a weapon like that. From my understanding, Triggor had taken the revolver from another patron. When the gun fired, the unexpected explosive sound caused a few of the meanest pirates to shriek like young lasses. They fled, especially after seeing who'd been killed. Seeing how fast it killed the Elder, I went out a door with the rest of the pirates."

Sparrow asked, "Then do you think someone else shot her?"

"Doubtful," Crukas said. "Such weapons are rare."

"So, it's possible he didn't?"

Adgus frowned at her. He scolded her with a harsh tone. "Are ya missing Triggor, lass? 'Cause if ya are, you know where to find him."

"No."

"Ya seem to be defending him," Adgus said.

Bramnir and Ebden nodded. "Aye."

"No," Sparrow said. "Triggor doesn't seem to be the type to flee. He'd own up to any wrongdoing."

Bramnir cocked a brow. "What makes you think dat?"

"Gynx kept threatening to kill me the entire time I was with them," she said. "Several times Triggor pulled the revolver on Gynx and warned him to back off. Inside the prison cell, he was trying to strangle Gynx to death."

"He's a bounty hunter," Adgus said. "Not much better than a thief, if ya ask me."

"All the same—"

Crukas interrupted her. "All the circumstances point to him, Sparrow. He still carries the revolver, as a trophy and a warning to those he encounters. He apparently uses it, so he wants others to know he has it."

"And that makes him guilty?" Sparrow frowned.

"Look, lass," Adgus said. "Ya can go back to Dark Ayr Tower and ask him if ya want."

"No thanks!" Sparrow scowled and crossed her arms. She glared at him. "But sometimes things don't look as they seem."

"Perhaps," Crukas said. "As you now know, I witnessed the fight. The only revolver I saw was the one Triggor now carries. In a tavern filled with cutthroats, it might be possible more than one of those weapons were in the room."

"I'm probably wrong," Sparrow said. "But with the animosity between the pirates and Ravenfolk, killing an Elder could be viewed as revenge or a plot to revolt against them. It could've been planned."

Crukas nodded. "True, but all the same, it's not our concern."

"Ya are more than welcome to investigate if ya'd like," Adgus said.

"I agree with Crukas," Sparrow said. "It's not our concern."

CHAPTER 62

Moonharvest Tavern was nestled on a flat ledge between two jagged high cliffs, which overlooked the calmer waters of Pirate's Cove. The sea inlet was the only calm attribute along this section of the coast. A rocky path cut through the cliffs and past the old tavern. At the highest peak was the crude cove's lighthouse.

Beyond the tavern was a shadowy border of dead conifer trees that separated a cursed swampland from the rocky ledges. In between the tavern and the swamp was Bone Hollow Cemetery. Its buried occupants were mostly pirates and unfortunate sailors who had accidentally docked in the wrong harbor.

Docks and short piers lined the inlet beaches of gritty, grayish-black sand, dotted with broken shells, smooth stones, and lobster hulls. Several vendor huts stood weathered and bent. The vendors sold smoked, dried fish, various wares, repaired nets, and some offered carpentry services to repair the hulls of ships riddled with cannonball holes or slightly punctured by reefs. Some sold and repaired weapons while others repaired torn, ratty sails.

Along the various grooves in the steep cliffs, Ravenfolk stood watch with sheer scrutiny at the various races and cultures of pirates.

In the fading light surrounding the shadowed crevices, the actual number of Ravenfolk was impossible to determine.

Only pirate ships were allowed to drop anchor in this port and at their own risks. Merchant ship captains were ordered by their kingdom's crown to never sail within a telescope's sight of Pirate's Cove. Any trading captain's ship foolishly anchored in the cove was ransacked. An all-out brawl ensued amongst the hostile pirate captains to lay claim to the ship as its new captain. These brawls often succeeded in adding more numbers to the clifftop cemetery. Once the ruckus ended, the Ravenfolk ultimately decided and assigned a new captain to the ship.

The Ravenfolk seldom interfered with such physical squabbles but gleaned the benefit of the aftermath by taking the freshly splayed corpses off the sand. Much like their raven descendants, the Ravenfolk were scavengers. These brief pirate scuffles were nothing more than entertainment before their upcoming feast. Both amusement and banquet were reaped without having to toil for flesh and blood. The unruly pirates seemed the perfect alignment to supply the Ravenfolk with both without being coaxed or coerced.

Even amongst the seasoned pirate captains, no one was free from mutiny or an opposing pirate killing a captain to claim a new ship. Those coups occurred later on the high seas, far from the Ravenfolk's observation.

Although recognized as a gathering place for marauders, Pirate's Cove wasn't a safe haven for any pirate. It was quite the opposite. Everyone was subject to the loss of treasure, limbs, and life; if not from one another, the Ravenfolk often dictated subtle outcomes. Sometimes to overcome their boredom, the Ravenfolk covertly instigated fights between opposing shipmates.

Above all else, no honest being was spared and only the nastiest in Aetheaon chose to venture to Pirate's Cove.

Crukas thought about what Sparrow's theory that Triggor might not have fired the shot to kill the Ravenfolk Elder mother. Could she be right? Was it possible someone else with a revolver took the opportunity to deliberately kill the Ravenfolk Elder to regain control of the tavern? Triggor could actually be innocent, but Crukas had never met Triggor, so he couldn't speculate. Dawg might have had an accomplice who tried to shoot Triggor, missed, and the projectile struck the Elder instead.

Everything had happened so quickly that day, so Crukas couldn't deny he might've missed other clues.

Crukas needn't worry about encountering the ruthless pirates on the docks or along the shoreline since he was traveling with the dwarves. Adgus sat on the wagon seat. Bramnir and Ebden rode their rams to each side of the wagon. Sparrow had tucked herself behind the wagon's seat and was hardly noticeable even though the wagon bed was empty.

At the edge of a clear bluff where the forest left the crude road no covering, they stopped and observed the cove, the lighthouse, and Moonharvest Tavern.

Crukas' goal wasn't the tavern. Instead, he needed to visit the cemetery. He hoped the moonlight was the proper tint to find and see the ghost of a pirate long dead. All the same, they needed to hide the wagon a good distance away from the tavern so no one was tempted to steal it.

The dwarves stashed the two barrels of ale inside Irmine's home, and Devin promised to keep them safe. No need to attract a thief's or pirate's attention by traveling with ale in the wagon. After all, pirates could *almost* drink dwarves under the table. The pirate's life was not a glamorous one. Without successful plundering, the long stretching days were depressing, especially when the ship's rum went dry after weeks of searching the high waters. Desperation often set in. Once they reached the shore, they drank themselves into stupors. So, even though ale was not the pirates' drink of choice, after the senses were overtaken by alcohol, taste no longer mattered as long as the fuel flowed to keep the buzz active.

AFTER LEAVING Irmine's home and taking the road northeast from Ravensdorf, Adgus stopped the wagon along the edge of a grassy field where Bramnir and Ebden tied their mounts.

"Perhaps, after defeating Scorpius," Bramnir said, "we should get some sleep before taking the treacherous road to Pirate's Cove."

"Aye," Adgus said. "Devin packed us several baskets of cheese and hard bread, and a few flasks of wine and a short barrel of mead. I'm exhausted and famished."

Crukas yawned and stretched. "We should rest, but briefly."

Sparrow nodded.

SEVERAL HOURS PASSED while they slumbered. One of the ram mounts angrily bellowed and awakened Crukas. He rose from the wagon bed and stepped onto the grass.

"What's upset your mount?" Crukas asked.

Bramnir rubbed his eyes and shook his head. He aroused against a massive oak where he'd fallen asleep. "He's angry we've slept this long."

Crukas looked at the angle of the sun. "We've overslept. At least half the day."

"We were exhausted," Sparrow said.

"Maybe so," Crukas said. "But we need to put as much distance between us and Triggor as possible."

"You think he'd risk his life to go to Pirate's Cove?" Sparrow asked.

"Depends on how badly he wants the reward," Crukas replied.

"I thought you told the pixies not to release them for two days," Adgus said.

"Yes. But there's the off chance they won't wait that long," Crukas said. "Especially if they find what they're looking for."

"You can't trust anyone, can ya?" Adgus directed a harsh stare at Sparrow.

"What are you implying?" she asked.

"Mere speculation," he replied. "Wasn't aimed at ya, little one."

"Your eyes were." She frowned and crossed her dainty arms.

Crukas sighed. "Look. It'll be dark within an hour or so. Pirate's Cove is a day or more away. It's too dangerous to ride after nightfall."

"Then we ride as far as possible and set up another camp," Adgus said.

"I've already slept too long."

"Then we'll be well rested by sunrise."

Crukas studied the rough hillside forests and shook his head. "Doubtful. We know little of what hides in these dense trees."

Sparrow's eyes widened.

"Wierwen?" Bramnir asked.

"None to my knowledge," Crukas said. "But their population has increased since I last went through Gloomy Forest. Just be on guard at all times."

CHAPTER 63

*A*fter sunrise, they traveled a half day up a rugged mountain road. They stopped at a clearing with a perfect scenic view of the cove and the seas beyond. Crukas pointed. "The sharp bend on the ledge on the other side of the cove is where the cemetery lies."

"Dat's still a good distance," Adgus said. He tapped the reins against the burros' backs. The burros pulled the wagon forward. "It'll be dark before we reach it."

Echoes of music and shouts from the beaches rose with the stern winds. Small bonfires blazed and grew brighter as the sunlight slowly faded. Drunk pirates sang and staggered in what could be mistaken for awful dancing. Others lie unconscious on the sand with empty rum bottles gripped in their hands.

Crukas nodded and stared at the setting sun. The pastel colors of pink, reddish-yellow, purple, and indigo swirled into a peaceful array. The deceptive beauty masked the treacherous dangers nightfall brought to the cove and the rough roads leading to the tavern and cemetery. Nature had a way of ignoring the pathetic lives of villainous bandits.

The roadway steadily climbed upward and meandered along the steep ledges overlooking the bay. Once darkness blanketed them, the shrouded night invited more sinister foes into play, as nighttime often did in forests, haunted or otherwise.

"I hate to see the sun fade, but we'll be better concealed," Crukas said.

Adgus nodded. "From the looks of it, those pirates won't likely climb their ways up here."

Crukas chuckled.

"Despite the dangers and hostilities we might face with those pirates and Ravenfolk below, this sunset's glorious," Sparrow whispered.

"Aye," Bramnir said. "There be no greater beauty in the sky."

"Except a mine cart full of diamonds, rubies, and emeralds captured in the sun's light," Adgus said.

Bramnir laughed. *"Dat's* a better array of colors."

"Are ya sure this trip be necessary?" Adgus asked.

Crukas nodded. "I hope it's not a complete waste of our time."

"Eh?" Ebden asked. "How so?"

"Yeah," Adgus grunted. "What exactly are you looking for?"

"A ghost." Crukas whispered.

Sparrow sat upright, pressed her back against the seat, and hugged her knees to her chest. Her nervous eyes widened.

The dwarves kept their silence and exchanged glances with one another. The wagon creaked and bounced on the rough rocky path.

After a long pause, Adgus frowned. "Did I hear ya right? A ghost?"

Crukas nodded. "Yes."

"Are ya daft?" Bramnir asked.

"It'd make things better if I were," Crukas said. "But no. He has something I need."

Ebden frowned. "What could a ghost possibly have that you'd need?"

"A lantern," Crukas said.

"Ghosts can't carry objects," Adgus said. "They project images of things they once had. But having the ability to tote one—"

"For the most part," Crukas said, "that's true."

"What's the name of this ghost?" Bramnir asked.

"Kane Greaves."

Sparrow's brow furrowed. She seemed to be contemplating whether she recognized the name or not, but she said nothing.

Adgus' frown deepened. "Name means nothing to me."

"Nor to me," Bramnir said.

Crukas shrugged. "His name's not important, but the item he possesses is vital. He has the Ghost-flame lantern."

"Why's dat so important?" Adgus asked.

"I've a hunch—" Crukas said.

"A hunch?" Ebden frowned. His eyes burned with sudden anger. "You bring us here on a *hunch*? You and I are cursed—"

"Let him finish," Sparrow said with a slight smile while unable to hide her nervousness. "When it comes to ghosts, I'd like to know more. Besides, Irmine requested Crukas get the lantern."

Bramnir narrowed his eyes. "Is dat so?"

Crukas acquiesced a slight nod. "Thanks. The lantern's blue flame prevents a necromancer from forming undead from the buried dead."

"Bah!" Ebden said. "It's as I told ya before. A ghost *projects* items. Ya won't be able to take the lantern because he's a ghost and can't carry it."

"Oh, he has the lantern," Crukas said.

Bramnir cocked a brow. "How do ya know dat?"

"From a reliable source. One who knew Kane."

"Oh?" Adgus said. "Who would dat be?"

"Skretch Krall," Crukas replied.

The dwarves shrugged.

Ebden shook his head. "The barkeep?"

"Yes. The barkeep at Moonharvest Tavern," Crukas said.

"So? How does he know Kane has the lantern?" Sparrow asked.

"Ebden's right about ghosts not being able to carry things, but Kane keeps the lantern hidden between planes," Crukas said.

"If dat be the case," Bramnir said, "how do you expect *us* to retrieve it? There aren't fancy little gateways dat lead from one plane to the next. Ya'd need a mage to open such a portal and last I checked, we just killed one."

"I've not figured out how to get between the planes yet."

Adgus mumbled. "Don't tell us ya brought us all dis way for nothin'. We could be seated at a warm fire drinking those two barrels of ale."

"Dat I'd prefer," Bramnir said.

"I can't say it's for nothing," Crukas said. "I'm quite certain the journey's well worth our time and effort."

Adgus groaned. "Most of the time when I follow a *gut* feeling, it turns out to be from eating spoiled meat. You best 'ave more than dat gut pointing ya out here."

Crukas smiled and took the rolled parchment from his satchel. "If it makes you feel better, Irmine requested a favor from me before we went to Dark Ayr Tower. She wanted me to obtain this lantern. I owe her that much. See? She left this for me."

Adgus read the message and sighed. His eyes softened. "Aye. If she needs it, I owe her dat much as well."

Bramnir nodded. "We all do."

CHAPTER 64

The shroud of darkness cloaked the swamp. Frogs and insects presented a pleasant chorus, which might be nothing more than a facade to hide the intent of lurking creatures with strange glowing eyes.

At the sharp bend on a rising hillside, a beam of light cut through the sky over Pirate's Cove. The lighthouse beamed its light toward the rough seas for several minutes and then cut off as abruptly as it'd turned on.

"We should probably find a place to hide the wagon and your mounts," Crukas said.

"Here?" Adgus said, pulling the reins.

Crukas pointed. "That grassy stretch between the trees might be more suitable. The burros and rams could graze."

Sparrow said, "Aren't you worried someone might try to steal the rams?"

Bramnir laughed. "The rams can take care of themselves. Besides, each mount responds only to a single worded command. They won't walk off with anyone. And if ya think mules and burros are stubborn, they're nothin' compared to these rams. A word of caution, though."

"What's that?" she asked.

"Never look a ram directly in the eyes or you'll find yourself waking up next week not remembering who ya are," Bramnir said with a slight grin. "These rams view eye contact as a challenge and it won't go unmet."

"What about the burros?" she asked.

Ebden smiled. "The rams won't allow anyone to come near them. Bears aren't a match against 'em."

Adgus gently tapped the burros with the reins and directed them to pull the wagon onto the grassy knoll. "How far on foot do ya expect us to travel?"

Crukas said, "I can go alone."

"Dat won't be happening," Bramnir said. "We've sworn to protect you with our lives."

Adgus sneered. "Don't know 'bout going *dat* far."

Crukas looked perplexed. Adgus laughed heartily.

"I've never asked that of you," Crukas said.

"Maybe not," Adgus said. "But, you need protection since you're not skilled with weapons and can't rightly defend yourself."

"While that's only partly true," Crukas said, "I know a thing or two about getting away from those who wish me ill will. And, I have a dagger if someone tries to grab me. On rare occasions I've used it but never killed anyone. But I doubt any of us have effective weapons against spirits."

The dwarves and Sparrow exchanged uneasy glances.

Adgus said, "Dat's true, but it's the undead we could fight, should such a situation arise."

Crukas took a deep breath and then sighed. A slight shiver went down his spine. "Let's hope it doesn't come to that."

"We all be hoping dat," Ebden said.

CHAPTER 65

*B*one Hollow Cemetery, after twilight faded, was probably no different than most cemeteries. Except, a thick, haunting atmosphere hung over the half hidden gravestones with such a choking quality, breathing was difficult. Within the eeriness of the graveyard, the lurking presence of protective unseen spirits hovered. Their unsettling presence was due to the inhumane body desecration the Ravenfolk had performed. The painful torture inflicted on those buried in the graves lived on, well after the souls left their bodies, and created a place for the living to dread.

The freshest graves were shallow—obviously dug in a rush—with the body remnants dumped and covered with barely enough soil to hide the bones. Not even the weakest necromancer would waste the magical energy necessary to call forth an undead minion. He'd reap animated body parts. Few bodies had been buried with enough anatomy to function with mobility, but those were few and far between. Ravenfolk prized skulls for trophies, so not many rotting heads could be found in the cemetery.

Kane Greaves had also suffered a grueling death but his corpse had somehow gone unnoticed by the Ravenfolk, along with Chimz's body. Chimz was Kane's pet chimp. The primate had tried to spare his owner's life. He rushed between another pirate's cutlass and Kane. The cutlass pierced the chimp's gut, but not before Chimz bit and nearly ripped off the attacker's face. Heartbroken, while holding Chimz during the chimp's final breaths, Kane allowed the next attacker to deliver his final death blow, rather than to continue living without his pet.

Their deaths left the pirating thieves empty handed. They attacked and hoped to attain the Ghost-flame lantern Kane owned, but Kane tucked the lantern in between planes before the thieves confronted him. Kane and Chimz were buried in the cemetery with their bodies mostly intact. Perhaps their murderers planned to return later with a necromancer or a spell scroll to revive Kane long enough to learn where he'd stashed the lantern. But these thieves met their fates before having a chance to return to the cemetery alive.

On certain nights, the moon rose over the mountain peak with a strange crimson glow, which lasted only a couple of hours. During this time, Kane and Chimz appeared in a bluish spectral glow and moved about together as though their lives had never been lost. Companions in life, they also remained friends in the afterlife.

DRIED conifer needles deceptively camouflaged the thick layers of sphagnum moss. Some sphagnum pools were deep enough to suck a body down to be seen no more. Crukas, Sparrow, and the dwarves walked cautiously. Their crispy steps pressed their boots several inches deeper than the mossy surface. Acrid water rose and covered their boots. Adhesive mire clung to the bottom of their boots. Sucking noises smacked each time they took another step. Despite searching for a more solid place to plant their feet, none were found, especially not for the dwarves. The dwarves' heavily weighted armor and substantial body mass caused them to sink deeper.

Crukas stopped at a bent, rusty fence wall. "Adgus, perhaps you and your brothers should wait here. Sparrow and I are lighter. Who knows how deep these sphagnum pools are? They could be deep enough to pull you under."

Standing beside Crukas, Adgus studied the water rising over his feet. The wet moss bubbled around his sinking feet. "Aye. How far do you plan to walk? We can't protect you from a distance."

"Not far," Crukas replied. "Actually, we need only to wait."

"Wait for what, exactly?" Bramnir asked.

"For Kane to appear."

"But ya don't know he will, right?" Adgus asked.

"That's right," Crukas replied.

Adgus humphed. "How long do we wait?"

Crukas sighed. "Hopefully not too long."

CHAPTER 66

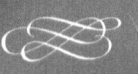

Faint echoes of boisterous, drunken laughter drifted from the cove.

Crukas wondered if Kane's ghostly image would emerge tonight. The moon gleamed a soft, reddish glow, but was it the proper shade of red to beckon the dead pirate from his grave?

Sparrow shivered, pulled her cloak tighter, and hugged her arms beneath it. Her chills were due to her fear of encountering a ghost than from the actual cold. The night was balmy and the salty breeze lofting off the seas foretold another set of thunderstorms heading inland. He hoped not. The cove was known to have more rain than sunshine. Regardless of the weather, they couldn't afford to be delayed any further.

"You're uneasy." Crukas turned slightly to face Sparrow.

Her nervous eyes met his. She offered a slight shrug. "It's not like I spend a lot of time in cemeteries well after dark."

"Nor I," he said with a slight grin. "Until recently, however, I never had reason to fear the dead."

"I understand."

More eruptions of faint laughs and wails from the cove made the pirates seem better company than standing in an empty cemetery looking for ghosts. The mood on the beach was definitely contrary to standing ankle-deep in a soggy sphagnum cemetery.

"At least *someone's* 'aving fun." Adgus propped against the back of a crude gravestone. Bramnir and Ebden chose different stones to prevent sinking deeper into the mossy pools.

"You can return to the wagon," Crukas said. "There's no guarantee Kane will show. I might have to count the loss and move to my next destination."

"Nah!" Adgus grumbled. "Irmine needs the lantern as much as you. If dat be the case, we'll wait all night."

"Yes, she does, but—"

Bramnir cleared his throat and pointed at the moon. "The moon's red. Where's Kane?"

Crukas shook his head and started to repeat his disappointment and apologize for wasting their time.

Sparrow nodded at the row of tombstones ahead of them. "Look! What's that? Is that him walking in our direction?"

Adgus, Ebden, and Bramnir straightened and drew their weapons. Each dwarf set the heads of their axes against the crude tombstone foundations and clasped the ends of the axe handles in their thick hands.

Near the spot Sparrow had indicated, a slender tendril of fog looped from around a gravestone and slithered along the mossy cemetery like a smoky serpent. Resembling an expanding mist tainted by watery blood, a human form materialized with a medium-sized primate figure hobbling behind it.

"Dat him?" Adgus asked.

Crukas nodded without knowing for certain it was Kane, but who else could it have been? "Yes."

Sparrow stepped behind Crukas, which amused him. He'd have done the same if he were closer to the dwarves, but he didn't perceive Kane as a threat.

"He's a spirit, Sparrow," he said, trying to reassure her.

"I realize that, but there were spectral beings at Fasha's shop."

Crukas frowned. "Did they harm you?"

"Not physically. I believe they could have, but Fasha entered the room. They seemed to fear her, or else, she could manipulate their coming and going. But I can't shake their frightening appearance from my mind. That could count as harm, right?"

Crukas agreed but offered no further words to settle her mind.

The two ghostly figures seemed nothing more than misty images and had yet to fully materialize. Kane lifted the dark image of a lantern upward in his right hand and caught a beam of the red moonlight. A bluish flame inside the lantern burst into sudden brightness. Kane and his chimp stood in full form, as though they were still amongst the living.

Sparrow gasped while the three dwarves mumbled their uncertainty between themselves.

"I'm more worried about the chimp than I am Kane," Crukas said.

"Why?" Sparrow asked.

"He might be too unpredictable."

The chimp hobbled and carried a banana that had not suffered rot since their death. Upon closer inspection, neither the chimp nor Kane could be mistaken as fully fleshed and living. Both were in solid form and vivid in color without transparency but obvious decomposition had taken effect.

Kane's grizzled beard and sunken eyes with red pupils were enough to reveal he was undead. His hollow eyes set on Crukas. "What brings you here, thief? Have you come to take my lantern?"

Crukas tried to swallow the growing lump in his throat, but he couldn't. The air became colder. He worried the Plague-bringer might have mind-linked to Kane and already knew Crukuas' reason for coming to Bone Hollow Cemetery. "You know me?"

"What occurs above the graves is known to us who dwell below, Crukas," Kane said, moving closer.

Crukas stiffened. He wanted to turn and place additional distance between Kane and he, but Sparrow was pressed against the back of his legs. Retreating wasn't possible without tripping over her. Besides, if he wanted the lantern, fleeing wasn't an option. Yet, he wondered, as did Sparrow, if a spirit could inflict damage. The Ghost-flame lantern's magic could revive Kane in his physical form. Kane looked capable of using physical objects to kill or maim intruders.

"I'm a thief," Crukas said. "I never assumed I'd be of importance to those dead and gone."

Kane laughed. His grizzled, gapped beard clung to what little flesh remained on his cheekbones. His rotted teeth were visible through his jaw. The decayed stench of his breath puffed in a small yellow cloud through his jaw and mouth. The clouds resembled the bursting puffs of poisonous spores released from various mushrooms. Even the faint foulness of his inner rot caused Crukas to gag. If he smelled the decay, Kane wasn't a ghost.

Kane narrowed his gaze. His voice held an eerie, mocking tone. "A thief roaming a cemetery can be up to no good. Of course, a notable thief like yourself would be known."

"I never rob graves," Crukas said.

"And yet, you're here," Kane said through a rotted grin.

Crukas nodded. "For other reasons."

Kane snorted his disdain. His eyes narrowed. "You, like the many others before you, have come for the Ghost-flame lantern?"

The deteriorated chimp was almost a full skeletal. Little flesh remained on its chest, back, and legs. Except around its eyes, the face gleamed white bone. Kane's accusation caused the chimp to glare and shriek at Crukas. A rusted rapier was sheathed on its belt and like Kane, the chimp wore pirate garb and a bandana. Crukas held its gaze, which was apparently perceived as a challenge. Chimz released a series of angry sounds and then bore yellowish-black teeth. It held the banana in its left hand and placed its right on the rapier.

"I'm not here to steal your lantern," Crukas said.

The chimp jumped up and down several times with madness in its eyes and shrieked even louder.

"Sir Chimz thinks otherwise," Kane said.

"Sir Chimz?" Sparrow dared to peek around Crukas.

Kane glared at her. "And you are?"

"Sparrow," she said. "Former thief and bounty hunter."

Kane shook his head and sneered. "Never heard of you."

350

"Hmmph." Offended, Sparrow stepped beside of Crukas and crossed her arms. The glow of her eyes brightened, reminding Crukas of a cat. "You know Crukas but haven't heard of me?"

"Aye," Kane said. "*He* has a noteworthy reputation. You? We've heard nothing about you, so you're not considered a threat."

Sparrow scoffed while Crukas fought his spreading smile.

Adgus, Ebden, and Bramnir chuckled.

Sparrow's hands tightened. Her voice deepened. "So this was your pet chimp?"

Chimz hissed and bore his teeth. He leaned forward on his arms and lunged at her. Sparrow squealed and pivoted behind Crukas again.

"You've offended him," Kane said.

With innocence in her eyes, Sparrow faced Crukas. "Does no one have pets any more? Everyone gets offended by the word."

"Though he doesn't speak actual words, Sir Chimz understands seven languages," Kane said. "He's never been a *pet*. He was once a decorated mate alongside me before the rest of our crew mutinied and hung our captain. We fled the ship at the first port we docked; before we, too, became casualties because we had remained loyal to our captain." Kane placed his hand on the chimp's shoulder in the manner a father might his son. "Chimz became my first mate, though we owned no ship. We later joined a pirate crew and sailed the seas until we met our fate in this desolate cove."

Holding his hands slightly above his head to keep balance, Chimz made his way closer to Crukas and peered angrily around Crukas' legs to see Sparrow.

"My apologies, Sir Chimz," Sparrow said. "I meant no disrespect."

Chimz chattered and nodded his head.

Sparrow glanced at Kane. "What's he saying?"

Chimz snarled and hissed.

"He accepted your apology," Kane said.

"He still looks mad."

Kane chuckled. "He understands what you're saying, but he gets frustrated because he can't speak other languages and," he whispered, "he *thinks* he is. So when others ask me to interpret, his frustration sours him. He feels insulted."

Crukas studied the banana Chimz held. "That banana isn't real?"

Chimz sloshed his way back to Kane.

"No," Kane said. "It's carved from wood. He's had it for years. It pacifies him, reminding him of better times. My time to roam tonight is limited, so, *why* are you here?"

"The Ghost-flame lantern."

Kane's eyes blazed redder and his voice snapped. "You said you weren't here to steal it."

"I'm not," Crukas replied. "But if I could persuade you to trade it to me or loan it—"

Kane placed a hand on his hip and reared back his head, cackling like a madman. Chimz howled, jumped up and down, and released a series of short breaths through his broad grin.

"Dat's a *no.*" Adgus shook his head. "I'm a wagering."

Sparrow shook her head. "I agree. Even the chimp laughed at you."

Kane regained his composure. "What kind of thief offers to buy something everyone else would steal at the first given opportunity?"

"A noble one," Crukas said.

Kane humphed. "No such thing as a noble thief."

"I'll vouch for him," Adgus said.

Ebden and Bramnir nodded. "Aye. Us, too."

Kane frowned. "The lantern's how Chimz and I can return to this world so we can reminisce. Without the lantern, we cease to exist. Nothing you offer could ever compensate for its value to us."

"What about peace?" Sparrow asked.

"Peace?" Kane scoffed. "No peace exists for us. Not here. Not in an afterlife, and not even before our untimely demise."

"There's no afterlife?" Sparrow asked.

"*We've* never found it," Kane said.

"But if you could have peace?" Crukas asked.

Kane cocked a weakened brow, his jaw trembled, and he looked as though he was about to cry, if he were able. "If such existed, yes. But such doesn't exist."

"Have you heard of Irmine?" Crukas asked.

"The priestess in Ravensdorf?"

"The same."

"Of course."

Crukas smiled. "She sent me for the lantern."

"Why?" Kane asked.

"I don't know. She's near death. Before she defeated Scorpius, she requested a favor. The favor was to get the Ghost-flame lantern."

"*She* defeated him?"

"Aye," the three dwarves said in unison. "With a bit of distraction."

Kane frowned. "Odd. Truly odd."

"What?" Crukas asked.

"A strange disturbance happened before the lantern summoned us," Kane said. "The whole ground shook. I was awakened *before* the lantern's call."

"Most likely dat was when Scorpius flung all his magic against Irmine's," Adgus said. "We were fortunate he didn't collapse the Dark Ayr Tower down on our heads."

Kane nodded, but he seemed unsettled.

"Perhaps," Sparrow said, "the lantern tethers you and Sir Chimz to this place? If you gave it up, you might find the peace you seek."

Kane's face contorted as he considered her suggestion. "Intriguing to consider, but there are no guarantees."

"Nothing's ever guaranteed," Crukas said.

"That be true," Kane said.

"Since you state that what occurs on the surface is known to you and those underground," Crukas said. "You should know about the Plague-bringer."

"He's no stranger to us," Kane replied. "The thunder of his minions' footsteps quake the ground, similar to the drumbeats before an oncoming war."

"Then he's headed this direction?" Crukas asked.

Kane shrugged. "Hard to predict as the sound grows louder some days and much fainter on others. But the size of his army increases daily."

"Should he succeed in his mission," Crukas said, "he'll no doubt take control of you and add you and Chimz to his undead army. You won't have what you currently do. You and Chimz will be at *his* mercy, of which he has none."

"Chimz and I won't yield to the Plague-bringer," Kane said. "We're protected by the Ghost-flame lantern. He has no power over us."

Crukas said, "Perhaps he doesn't when the lantern has summoned you, but what about during the dormant times when you and Chimz are underground? You would be susceptible to his call as any other corpse. Would you not?"

Kane mulled over Crukas' explanation for several long seconds. "We spent the majority of our living years ensuring we never found ourselves subjected to the harsh rule of another."

"But you weren't ever a captain, were you?" Sparrow asked.

"No," Kane replied sharply. "But a crew is a single body with a captain as its head. The captain acts as an extension of the body and makes the decisions that best suit the crew."

Crukas nodded. "Are you willing to gamble your destiny that he won't venture here? Should he take the two of you under his control, what you have will be gone forever."

Kane gave Chimz a solemn gaze and groaned with slight remorse. "I dislike the thought of that happening to either of us, but what of the afterlife?"

Crukas sighed, wondering how to explain something he didn't fully believe. "If there's nothing after this, what's left to fear? A void? Isn't that peace?"

"I never considered it that way," Kane replied softly. "Pure nothingness would be peace."

"Den you'll part with the lantern?" Adgus asked.

"I don't have the lantern with me," Kane said. "This is a reflection of it."

"See?" Ebden pointed a stern finger at Crukas. "I told ya!"

"It's rumored you hid it between two planes," Crukas said.

"No," Kane shook his head. "That's what I told the pirates who killed me to get it."

Sparrow frowned. "They should've known by killing you that they had no chance of ever finding it."

"They lacked the sense of a jellyfish," Kane said. "But I've hidden it in a safe place. I can't venture there, not in this form. Well, not in *any* form."

"So you're willing to part with it?" Crukas asked.

"Bitterly, but yes," Kane said. "Your reasoning is quite persuasive. Besides, I seem more decayed each time the moonlight summons me. And, poor Chimz, I hardly recognize him anymore. I fear he might one day emerge without his limbs or his head. I couldn't bear to see him in worse shape than he currently is. It's bad enough now."

"Where'd you hide the actual lantern?" Crukas asked.

Kane grinned. "Practically under their noses. Well, that is, when they were still alive."

Adgus looked around. "Where?"

"Not *here*," Kane said in a mocking tone. "In Moonharvest Tavern."

Crukas' stomach churned and Sparrow gasped barely above a whisper.

The three dwarves grumbled.

Crukas shook his head. "It's *inside* the tavern?"

"Not exactly *inside*," Kane said. "More like, *far* beneath it."

"Beneath it?" Adgus said.

"Where the beach meets the cliff wall at the bottom of the bluff away from the piers, there's a small cave," Kane said. "But one can only access it during the lowest tide. The only one of you who could fit is the halfling."

Sparrow's eyes widened.

"See?" Crukas whispered. "You were needed after all."

She frowned. "I'm not fond of the sea or tight places. I dislike the idea of drowning even more."

"Did you forget about the pirates?" Adgus asked. "Ya might not make it to the cave."

"Okay," Crukas said. "We find the cave and send her through? Any traps or locks?"

Kane smiled. "No traps, but you must first obtain the key."

"Key for what?" Adgus asked.

"The chest that holds the lantern. You don't think I'd leave it unprotected, do you?"

Crukas frowned. "I've a feeling that getting the key is going to be difficult."

Kane laughed softly. "You might say it's a challenge."

"Why?"

"The key's inside Chimz's wooden banana."

Chimz held the wooden banana tightly and squealed. He bore his teeth and grunted in a daring challenge.

Sparrow shook her head. "There's no way he'll give us the banana."

"Don't be daft, lass," Adgus said. "*Dat's* not the banana we need to take. It's the reflection of it."

Crukas closed his eyes and sighed. "Where's the real banana?"

"*It's* inside the tavern behind the bar," Kane said. "The dwarves have a better chance of getting into the small cave than the lot of you have in taking the banana."

Kane's decaying jaw widened and he cackled like the crazed being he was.

Crukas turned on his heel and sloshed his way through the cemetery to the dwarves. Sparrow followed.

"Let's go," Crukas said. "We've wasted enough time."

CHAPTER 67

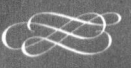

*C*rukas mumbled as they walked to the wagon.

Adgus stomped through the last few steps of the ceme-
tery. "And here I held the relief in thinking we didn't *need* to go to
Moonharvest Tavern. In fact, I hoped we wouldn't have to."

"We're not going to the tavern," Crukas said.

"But ya heard Kane," Bramnir said. "The key's in the tavern."

Crukas sighed. "Provided he's telling the truth. He doesn't want to
part with the lantern. This is a deranged game. One that places all of
our lives into peril. Most likely, we'll all be killed should we follow his
clues. And if that happens, our bodies or what's left of them, will be
stuck in Bone Hollow Cemetery where Kane can mock us."

"So you don't believe he wants peace for Chimz and himself?"
Sparrow asked.

"No," Crukas said. "He wants what he never had when he was
alive."

"What's dat?" Adgus asked.

"Complete control," Crukas replied. "He's taunting us and knows
there's nothing we can do to punish him since he's a ghost."

Ebden said, "The best punishment is to get the lantern. Send him

357

to the grave forever, into the afterlife if one exists. To get the key lies on your shoulders. You're a master thief, after all."

Crukas was surprised by Ebden's sudden courage, being as he was the most timid and quietest of the three brothers. But the curse had awakened Ebden's boldness because, like Crukas, he wanted to live.

"The odds are far too great for us to succeed," Crukas replied.

"Says the master thief," Adgus said with a wink.

"Any theft I've ever done, I've always evaluated the odds, weighed the options, and considered the likelihood of success verses failure," Crukas said. "One thing is certain. Never go in blind."

"Really?" Bramnir laughed. "Do ya think us daft? Ya had no knowledge of Scorpius' tower, and we stormed it all the same. Thanks to Irmine, we succeeded. Surely, dat's not escaped your mind so quickly."

Crukas acquiesced a slight nod and sighed. "True. Other than the tower and not having a map or some blueprint for its layout, I've always been prepared. This time could end far worse."

"Ya *said* time's not on our side," Sparrow said.

"It isn't," Crukas replied.

"Then why make excuses?" Adgus said.

"I'm not. I've risked your lives too many times over something I'm not certain will make a difference," Crukas said. "If Kane's actually telling the truth, we don't have Irmine to rescue us if the situation turns dire."

"We'll worry about ourselves," Bramnir said gruffly.

"What if my assumptions are incorrect?"

Sparrow said, "At least we gave our best efforts. We're this close, so let's see if the key's there. It's better to have tried and failed than to watch Aetheaon crumble beneath the Plague-bringer's control. We've no idea if Kane's setting a trap for us. Overall, it's worth the risk."

Ebden stepped toe-to-toe with him and looked in his eyes. "What's your gut tell you, thief? You and I are tied to dat book, regardless of whether we succeed or not. Search your thoughts. You've brought us 'ere because dat lantern's essential. Irmine needs it."

"I know, but Kane's deceptive."

"So?"

"He's baiting us."

"You've evaluated all of this about the lantern based on *what?*" Sparrow said with disappointment in her voice. "What Kane told us?"

"No. What he intentionally *hasn't*," Crukas said.

"Well, now isn't the time to quit," she said. "We should see if the key's inside the tavern."

He wondered if his lack of boldness to obtain the key and get the lantern had let Sparrow down. Or, perhaps, diminished how she pictured his legendary reputation. Heroes met were often disappointing and dissolved the fantasy image one's mind believed.

Adgus frowned. "Ya can't make such assessments when you've not taken a closer look at Moonharvest Tavern or the cove."

Bramnir nodded. "I agree. Shouldn't we at least travel closer to see what we're up against?"

"I thought you were in agreement that we shouldn't encounter the pirates at all," Crukas said. "You were adamant in not going to the tavern, either."

"I've reconsidered. Call it a change of heart," Bramnir said.

"Really?" Crukas said.

"With all the ruckus and drinking they're doing," Adgus said, "I've gotten more curiosity. I'd like to investigate anyhow."

"You sure it's not the ale that's calling you?" Crukas asked.

Adgus shrugged and rubbed his throat. "Me palate's a bit dry, so no harm in seeing, eh? Besides, we made an oath to Irmine. We should see dat through."

"*We* didn't," Crukas said. "I did."

Adgus grinned. "We're a party. Perhaps *we* didn't swear an oath to her, but we did with *you*."

"Very well. What are your feelings, Sparrow?" Crukas asked.

"You find a way to steal the key," Sparrow said. "The worst part is me crawling through the small cave to retrieve the lantern since I'm the smallest. But you get the key and I'll go inside the cave and find the lantern."

"I'm not sure which is worse," Crukas said. "Finding and stealing the key without being caught seems a greater obstacle."

Sparrow shook her head. "I might fit in small places, but I'm fearful of getting stuck and dying. How about you demonstrate the thieving skills everyone boasts about you?"

"You're in no position to challenge my abilities," Crukas said.

"Nor do you have the right to analyze my fears," she said.

Crukas nodded. "Fair enough."

"Besides," Sparrow said. "You and Ebden are cursed. Fasha predicted my death for pursuing you. Why don't we simply face Death head on?"

"A bold statement for a halfling," Adgus said.

Sparrow shrugged. "Maybe, but running from the problem only delays the inevitable. I'm tired of being scared. If I fail, it won't be because I didn't give my best effort."

"So be it," Crukas said. "You won't be alone."

CHAPTER 68

"**O**ur sorrow calls, through the vacant hall," Strella sang with tears meandering down her cheeks. Orgem's head rested on her upper thigh, and she caressed the side of his bearded face. His eye stared vacantly at the rocky ceiling and an odd smile curled his lips.

Strella was thankful Sparrow's potion had awakened him. After two days, Sparrow had not returned. Strella feared the worst and wondered what fate she'd suffered. She hoped Sparrow was alive and on her way to rescue them, but such hope was dwindling, Strella kept reciting the lines to a ballad in progress to dedicate her blessings for Sparrow. "Straighter than an arrow, on the path bless our sweet Sparrow."

Gynx gnashed his yellow teeth and snarled. "I swear if you sing that line one more time—"

Strella's heart ached. "I know it needs work—"

"Work?" Gynx said. "The words and rhyme *aren't* the problem. Nothing hurts a kobold's ears more than a piercing high tone. You've sung the same line at least a hundred times! Off key, by my ears' evaluation."

"Let her angelic voice ring," Orgem said weakly. "It's the only peace I have to dismiss this horrid headache."

"I can make your headache go away permanently." Gynx hissed and placed his hand on the hilt of his dagger.

Triggor held the prisoner bars with a tight grip. For several hours, he'd pulled, pried, and tugged at the bars, hoping to widen them to no avail. He had given up. The metal hadn't bent in the slightest. "Simmer down, Gynx. We've enough stress 'ere."

"We shouldn't have allowed Sparrow to leave." Gynx paced farther from them.

"Have some faith," Triggor said.

"Yes, please," Strella said. She closed her eyes and sighed. Distressed by the long wait and Gynx's constant provocations, Strella's distress edged closer and closer to hopelessness.

"Faith? In a thief?" Gynx growled. "She stole my crossbow *with* your permission. That was my best weapon for defense should those ghouls—"

Triggor laughed. "What'cha going shoot them with, eh? Invisible bolts?"

Gynx scrunched his face in a soured expression. "That's beside the point. She stole it and Strella's singing for her to be *blessed*. Sickening. Why trust a thief? You can't trust she'll return to free us."

"She's a bounty hunter like us," Strella said.

Gynx shrugged and swung his arm in a violent arc to dismiss her comment. "So she *said*. In my eyes, she's still a thief. *Always* a thief. I've proof and you're all witnesses."

"But, aren't you a thief, too?" Strella asked. "After all, you wish to rob Crukas of the items he's stolen."

"Good to know whose side you're on," Gynx said.

"Sparrow could've shot you, Gynx. You know dat, right?" Triggor said. "Problem solved. No theft of your crossbow then."

"Lost opportunity, for all of you," Gynx said. "However, had she tried, it could've been one of *you* that took the bolt instead. She's never used a crossbow. Of course, that could've been a ruse. But the rest of you are *hoping* she'll come back to rescue us. Preposterous."

"I understand your doubt," Triggor said. "But you forget she's a halfling."

"So?" Gynx turned, crossed his arms, and gritted his teeth.

"Halflings would never allow others to intentionally starve to death," Triggor said. "They'd give up their last morsel if someone else needed it more."

"She's been gone two days. Two days!" Gynx said. His stomach growled. "You hear that?"

"Yah! And dat's why you're at all of our throats," Triggor said. "You're hungry. We are all."

"Starving's more like it," Gynx said. "But Orgem looks like he's near death. We could sacrifice him. With his plumpness, he'd feed us for what? Several days, at least."

"Hey!" Orgem grumbled and tried to hoist himself into a seated position and immediately regretted it. He placed a hand to his head and eased down on Strella's thigh. She rubbed his temples.

"Do you know how disgusting your suggestion is?" Strella asked.

"Of course," Gynx said. "That's why I said it. But, don't criticize until after you've tried it."

Strella placed a hand over her mouth and her cheeks puffed, even though she couldn't vomit if she wanted. She'd already emptied her stomach's contents after wading through the worm dung two days earlier. Covered in the dried filth, her appetite never returned, and after Gynx's sickening suggestion, she didn't think she'd ever eat again. "You're saying you've eaten a dwarf before?"

"No. I *said* I had."

"Dat's a fact?" Triggor cocked a brow. He released the cell bars and turned to face Gynx with a scowl.

Possibly realizing how much he'd offended Triggor, Gynx was silent for several seconds, seemingly choosing his next words or whether he should reply or not. But Gynx didn't seem capable of deescalating any situation and tended to make it worse.

"Well, not the *entire* dwarf," Gynx said with a sly grin. "There were a half dozen of us kobolds, so I only ate a portion—"

Triggor pulled the revolver and cocked the trigger.

Gynx raised his hands slightly. For once, slight fear widened his eyes. "You *did* ask."

"You make the slightest hungered stare at any of us, and I'll put the bullet between your ugly eyes," Triggor said.

Gynx laughed and shrugged. "Sure. Fine. Afterwards, divide me up equally amongst yourselves."

Strella's stomach turned. "Oh, Goddesses help us."

"Don't worry. We won't eat ya." Triggor eyes narrowed and his finger tightened on the trigger. "Probably be too stringy."

"Yeah, well, dwarves have an *earthy* taste. Like thick bog mud that gets stuck to the bottom of your boots. The taste's almost intolerable, but once you get past the gag reflex … You'll eat anything when you're starving."

Triggor's upper lip curled.

"Oh, please stop this conversation," Strella said.

"If you'll quit singing!" Gynx said.

"Agreed! I promise." She waved her hands in surrender. "I'd rather never sing again than listen to your sickening, horrible evildoings."

"Severe hunger does strange things to the mind," Gynx said.

Triggor pointed a stern finger at him. "None of us are dat hungry. So, as you agreed, enough talk about it."

Gynx shrugged.

Fluttering wings buzzed outside the prison bars. Several pixies hovered.

"What's that noise?" Orgem slightly lifted his head.

"Faeries?" Strella said. "Or pixies, perhaps?"

"The latter's correct," the pixie said. "I'm Tamana."

"Why are you in Dark Ayr Tower?" Triggor asked. "Are you Scorpius' patrols?"

"No," she replied with a snorting laugh. "A mutual friend sent us to free you."

"Friend?" Strella rose slightly. "Do you mean Sparrow?"

"Sparrow and Crukas," Tamana said.

Strella wanted to burst into song, but she caught Gynx's soured expression. She blushed and grinned. "She's alive?"

Tamana nodded.

"Neither I consider friends," Gynx said.

Strella glared at him. "You have no friends."

Gynx shrugged and stared at Triggor with spite and anger. "See? I told you Sparrow was in cahoots with him."

Triggor looked disappointed considering Gynx's accusation but said nothing.

Tamana smiled. "Okay, let's say mutual acquaintance?"

"More likely, she's nothing other than a backstabbing thief," Gynx said. "She couldn't return as promised to free us? That tells you all you need to know, Triggor."

"No," Triggor said. "She sent help."

"Yet, she kept my crossbow."

"What's dat matter, you fool?" Triggor said. "As many times as you threatened to kill her, I don't blame her for not returning. Even less likely that she'd willingly hand you a weapon so you could shoot her."

"I don't blame her, either," Strella said. "You were nothing but unkind to her."

"Ladies," Tamana said to the other pixies. "Search the crevices around these prison bars to see if we can find any weakness or a hidden magical lock so we can free them."

Strella straightened, careful not to allow Orgem's head to smack the rock floor. "When did Sparrow alert you to our despair?"

"Two days ago," Tamana said, rising to the ceiling where the metal bar entered the rock.

"Two days ago?" Strella gasped. Sorrow filled her. "That's when she squeezed through the cell bars."

"Yes."

Gynx made fists and glared at Strella. "*Now* you're surprised?"

Strella looked away. Her heart sunk.

Gynx turned his focus to the small swarm of pixies. "You waited two days to set us free?"

"They asked for a delay in releasing you," she replied.

"Why?" Triggor asked.

"Naturally, to place distance between them and you," Tamana said.

Gynx narrowed his eyes at Triggor. "Cahoots, I say."

Strella shook her head slightly and silently berated herself for setting aside her gut feeling when she'd confronted Sparrow in the Mute Changeling.

"I wouldn't say that," Tamana said. "Rather, they thought a head start benefited their safety more so."

"I told ya so," Triggor said. "Had you not treated Sparrow with such malice—"

"She left *with* Crukas," Gynx said. "Either he has no fear of her turning him in for the reward, or she's been in league with him the whole time. She's kept an eye on us and reported our affairs and plans to him. Or did you forget the incident in the supply house?"

Triggor frowned and became silent. His lips tightened. The shadow of disappointment tugged at the edges of his eyes. "I hate to admit it, Gynx, but ya got a point there."

"What did they steal from Scorpius?" Gynx asked. "That would tell us much more. Only a fool would enter this—"

Triggor laughed. "Aye. Dat'd be all of us, eh?"

"Only slightly correct." Gynx snarled and bore his teeth. "I allowed my pursuit of Crukas to get the best of me. However, after Scorpius' lightning blast, I never expected we'd have to enter the tower. I thought we'd find his charred corpse outside, which would've saved us a lot of time."

"Instead," Triggor said. "You were as foolish as us. Fools rush—"

"I didn't rush. I sought to find, capture, and collect his bounty," Gynx said. "Nothing more, which is why I'd like to know *what* Crukas stole."

"What he stole has little importance to you," Tamana said. "But Scorpius paid the ultimate price trying to keep the artifact."

Strella's brow rose. "Scorpius is dead?"

Tamana nodded. "Quite."

Gynx pointed a stern finger at Strella. "Don't start singing about it."

Strella placed a limp hand over her chest and shook her head. "How could I? I've no details to write a tale."

"What did Crukas take?" Gynx said. "Did Sparrow help?"

"I can't tell you what he took, but Sparrow caused a distraction," Tamana said.

"How's dat?" Triggor asked.

Tamana grinned. "She shot Scorpius with a bolt."

Gynx growled. "With my crossbow!"

Triggor howled with laughter.

"I don't find it amusing," Gynx said.

"She had one bolt and didn't miss!" Triggor wiped spittle from his mouth with the back of his hand. "Sheer luck or is she dat good?"

Strella said, "Good for her."

"Whose side are you on?" Gynx said.

"I root for the underdog," Strella said. "Imagine the tale this will make. Sparrow helped kill Scorpius."

"Hardly," Tamana said. "She was a distraction. Enough for the high priestess to strike the deathblow."

"This priestess's name?" Strella asked.

Tamana's face showed no expression. Strella could tell the pixie had said too much and didn't wish to reveal any further details.

"I want my crossbow back," Gynx said. "Sparrow's an outright thief. No way she was ever a bounty hunter."

"Give her the benefit of the doubt," Strella said, even though she couldn't make the words sound convincing. She's was a bard, not a stage actor, and even though she wanted to believe the best in Sparrow, she couldn't. She partially found herself in agreement with Gynx but refused to openly admit it. She wouldn't give the kobold the satisfaction. But the details Tamana had parted with indicated Sparrow was working with Crukas.

"We've already done that," Gynx said. "Look where it got us."

Strella frowned. Her fueled frustration toward Gynx exploded into sheer disdain for the kobold. "*She* didn't put us in this cell!"

Tamana nodded. "No, the kobold chased her into the invisible pit trap. We watched."

Triggor said, "The pixie's right, Gynx. Had you not chased her up the stairs, she wouldn't have fallen through."

Tamana giggled and shook her head. "Running or walking didn't matter. The magical trap was well concealed. If anyone took the stairs without some sort of magic detection, he'd have fallen through."

"Really?" Gynx said. "If that's so, why aren't there a lot more dead bodies?"

"Because Scorpius seldom had guests. If he did, he'd have been a poor host," Tamana replied. "Besides, few intruders ever got past the ghasts. This tower is filled with all sorts of traps."

Another pixie zipped through the air and stopped to hover beside Tamana. "This cell has no openings and no hidden doors. No enchanted doors, either."

Tamana sighed and studied the rock ceiling where the bars connected. "I truly expected these bars would've loosened after the entire tower shook."

Triggor yanked the bars hard. "That look loose at all?"

"That's my point," Tamana said.

"We're stuck in here?" Strella asked.

"Not necessarily," Tamana said.

"What caused the quake?" Strella asked.

"When Scorpius realized he was going to die, he attempted to bring the entire tower down," she replied.

Triggor frowned. "So if he couldn't win, he'd kill everyone else?"

"Apparently," Tamana said. "But he failed."

A pixie shrieked.

Gynx held the pixie tightly in his hand. Apparently, she had flown too close to the kobold. Hunger set in his crazed eyes. "A tasty morsel."

"Set her free!" Triggor pulled the revolver from its holster, cocked the gun's hammer, and aimed at Gynx's forehead.

Horrified, the pixie struggled to break free. Her delicate wings crinkled like a wadded piece of rice paper.

"Go ahead. Pull the trigger," Gynx said. "I'll crush her in my hand before the bullet reaches me."

"I don't think you're dat fast."

"Try me," Gynx said with a deranged stare.

The hovering pixies' magical auras glowed.

"I've not eaten in two days," Gynx said. "Either they release us or I swallow her."

"Threats don't benefit you," Tamana said. "We came to help you escape."

"Two days too late!" Drool dripped off his long, extended tongue.

"In your eyes," Tamana said, "but we *didn't* have to come at all. We could've ignored their request to release you altogether. They'd have been none the wiser. You harm Dewen, and I assure you, this won't end well for you or the others locked in the cell with you."

Strella eased Orgem against the rock cell wall and rose to her feet. "Gynx! Unhand her! Jeopardize your own life if you wish, but not ours. Not like this."

Triggor closed one eye and trained the revolver on Gynx's head. "Aye, listen to the bard, Gynx. Tamana, trust me, we don't approve of his actions and wish none of you pixies any harm."

"The decision lies in the kobold's hand," Tamana said. "Should he harm or kill her, your fate remains inside this cell, however it plays out."

Triggor tightened his finger on the revolver. "Unless he releases her, his death comes quickly."

Dewen's eyes glistened with tears while anger reflected in all the other pixies' eyes. They held no fear of her death, but determined vengeance set in their gazes. Their hands glowed as they drew increased magic, ready to strike a gathered attack.

"Think this through, Gynx," Strella said. "Dewen's not large enough to satisfy a fraction of your hunger. You eat her, then what? Triggor kills you, and even if you survived the gunshot, there's nothing else to feed you. Ravensdorf's only a short distance from the Dark Ayr Tower. Once we're free, we can find sustenance in a tavern or an inn there."

Her words didn't penetrate his crazed mind. Hunger controlled his instincts. Regardless of how intelligent and different he was from his primeval relatives, deep down he remained as ruthless and hostile as the worst of his kind. Was there nothing capable of separating his intellectual outlook from his animalistic instincts? The least thing set him off. Music didn't lessen his bloodlust, and her singing *certainly* didn't. Both made him increasingly hostile. In some ways, and she hated to admit it, she regretted not allowing Triggor to kill Gynx earlier. The kobold's death would've protected them from him. She wasn't sure what Triggor's stance would be, but for her and Orgem, they planned to disband from the group should they manage to find a way out of the cell. Sparrow already had. *Good for her.*

"Gynx," Triggor said. "As much as you and I butt heads, I'd hate to finish you. Don't make me shoot ya. I aim only to kill."

Gynx blinked hard, shook his head slightly, and his eyes mellowed. He had broken free of whatever internal trance was controlling him. After glancing at the struggling pixie wrapped inside his fingers, he uncurled his fingers to release her. When he did, Dewen shot his nose with a blast of blue frost. She flitted upward and to the cell bars, but her flight was not quick or graceful. Her bent wings caused her to stagger through the air, and her face creased with agony.

Gynx snarled with rage, charged after her, but before he got revenge, the other pixies joined their strikes in unison until they rendered the kobold unconscious.

Triggor eased his finger off the revolver and uncocked it. He slid the revolver into its holster and turned to Tamana. "Our apologies for his inexcusable behavior. I beg ya not to hold it against the rest of us. Please help us get out of this cell."

Tamana studied the sincerity in Triggor's eyes. "We'll study the cell bars a bit longer, as long as he's incapable of attacking us again. Restrain him. There's no guarantee how long he'll remain unconscious or how long it might take to find a weakness in these bars."

Strella pulled her rope belt from around her waist and offered it to Triggor. "Use this."

"Aye," Triggor said. He took the belt and flipped Gynx onto his stomach. He tied Gynx's hands tightly behind his back. Then, he removed the kobold's rope belt and used it to tie Gynx's ankles together. "There! Dat should buy all of us more time."

Tamana offered a slight nod, but she obviously held no enthusiasm in helping. "Okay, ladies, some of these bars must've weakened."

"Thanks," Strella said, looking at Triggor. Her words were also meant for the pixies, but Triggor smiled and nodded.

CHAPTER 69

y the time Crukas, Sparrow, and the dwarves trekked along the bluff road to the narrow rocky path leading to Moonharvest Tavern, the drunken ruckus on the cove's beach and docks had diminished and became eerily quiet. On occasion, shadows passed over the rocky bluff. Crukas expected a flock of Ravenfolk to descend upon him and his party.

To prevent risking their wagon and mounts from being stolen, the dwarves left them at the clearing near the cemetery.

Although alarmed by the Ravenfolk's shadows, Crukas said, "It's good we didn't encounter any highwaymen along the way."

"What?" Adgus chuckled. "Why would you—a thief—fear a high-wayman? You'd rob *him*."

"Not likely," Crukas replied. "Highwaymen are more violent when-ever their intended victims stand their ground. They've little to lose. Seldom are witnesses around, so the bodies can be dumped without the fear of someone immediately finding them. On this mountain pass, only a pirate trying to gain more coin for drinks might risk approaching us. But, as you probably noticed, this old road is seldom traveled."

"Aye," Bramnir said. His attention turned toward the beach for a moment. "All's grown quiet."

"Don't be fooled by the deceptiveness," Crukas said. "We're being watched, constantly watched, by the Ravenfolk."

"Even here?" Sparrow asked. "We're still a fair distance away."

"Even here," Crukas said with a soft, serious tone. He searched the bluff again but nothing moved, which made him worry. Had they taken flight while he'd looked away? "Their keen sight is greater than a hawk's or an eagle's."

"You sound paranoid," Adgus said.

"Hardly," Crukas said. "After their Elder Mother was killed, the Ravenfolk built hidden posts in more difficult places to reach. Despite their size, they move stealthier than bats. Their talons are short-sword length and sharper. They can puncture an Orc's skull and your armor offers little challenge should they attack you. The Ravenfolk are small in number, but they're as deadly as a small army."

"Do they ever sleep?" Ebden asked.

Crukas shrugged. "Perhaps they take shifts."

Sparrow said, "How do you expect to steal the wooden banana?"

"First," Crukas said, "we must find it so I can evaluate the *how*. Kane said it was out in the open behind the bar."

"What does dat mean?" Ebden asked.

"I'm not sure," Crukas replied. "Sometimes an obvious item is overlooked without being hidden, especially when things most valued are expected to be buried or locked away. For all we know, Kane lied."

"Lying?" Bramnir asked.

Crukas nodded. "Yes. Telling us it's in the tavern run by Skretch is an obvious ploy to frighten us into not going after it. Anyone entering the tavern puts his life at the mercy of the pirates, and the Ravenfolk are even more suspicious of strangers."

"An outsider wouldn't necessarily know that, though," Sparrow said. "The last thing anyone would be looking for is a wooden banana."

"That's true, too," Crukas said.

"So it's possible Kane's *not* lying, right?" Adgus asked.

"Possibly. A lot depends on how desperate we are to find the key, and if Kane sincerely wants peace for Chimz and himself. There's the slightest chance he hopes we find the key and obtain the lantern, so he goes to rest permanently," Crukas said.

Sparrow said, "His sadness over Chimz's obvious decay seemed genuine."

"Aye." Adgus nodded. "It did. And it should, too, for anyone."

Bramnir's face grew grim. "Aye, but some folk, outside of dwarves, cling to the life they knew."

"Kane is overly skeptical of eternal rest," Crukas said.

"If he's lying," Sparrow said, "then what?"

"We move on," Crukas said.

Sparrow sighed. "Shouldn't I search the cave for the lantern anyway?"

"Without the key," Crukas said, "what's the purpose?"

She shrugged. "Maybe I could find another way to unlock it?"

Adgus grinned. "Aye, it'd be worth a shot, eh? After all, two thieves capable of picking locks increases the odds."

Crukas met Sparrow's gaze and she smiled. Crukas nodded. "You have a point there."

CHAPTER 70

After several labored hours of searching, Tamana and the pixies found a false stone where the cell bars deceptively appeared to be driven through it. With the use of a revelation spell, the pseudo-stone faded and revealed a square door. The door was easier to open than Triggor expected. The door's successful security came from the fact no one could see it, which made it impossible to pick or destroy. Once the pixies opened the door, they fled from the small prison before Gynx awakened, even though he was bound and unable to attack them. Triggor assumed the pixies had also grown tired of dealing with the situation altogether and were ready to leave the tower. For whatever reason, the pixies had fulfilled their favor for Crukas or Sparrow, so they had no reason to stay.

Using his foot, Triggor tapped Gynx between the shoulder blades. Gynx didn't respond, not even with the slightest groan. Gynx's chest moved in such shallow breaths, Triggor thought the kobold had died. "Whatever spell they zapped him with was quite powerful. He's still out."

Strella helped Orgem to his feet. "Good. They struck him with several types of spells. Frost, lightning, and fire. Some blasts appeared to be poison. Not that it matters, of course, because we're safer for their actions. I suggest we leave Gynx behind."

Orgem yawned. In a groggy voice, he said, "I agree."

Triggor chuckled softly and shook his head. "While I'd like to do dat, how would you feel if you were the one left behind?"

"It's not the same," Strella said. "I've lived my life to be trustworthy. I'd never hurt someone like Gynx threatened to do. He's the reason Sparrow fled, and he's treated all of us without any kindness and with pure malice. He lacks the ability to befriend anyone. The closest he comes to the word, *friend*, is that he's a *fiend*. His mind shifts too often and he's unpredictable. I don't trust him."

Triggor shrugged. "I don't trust him, either, but what's trust 'ave to do with it?"

Orgem pointed his stubby index finger at Triggor and snarled. Spittle flew from Orgem's mouth. "He wished to kill me and serve me as his main course! Jest or not, it's inexcusable!"

With his eyes narrowed, Triggor said, "I'd never 'ave allowed it, my friend. Trust me on dat."

Orgem swallowed hard and took a deep breath, apparently trying to soften his anger. "I can't prove it, but I've a gut feeling he's the reason I lost me eye. He half insinuated he was responsible, too, as being the kobold who set the blasting stick in the mine dat caved in on me."

"Dat might be true," Triggor said. "I wouldn't put it past him."

Strella squeezed through the small square door and stood outside the bars. "When we reach Ravensdorf, it's time we go our separate ways. I'm no longer interested in pursuing Crukas."

"Nor I," Orgem said. He turned to look at her. "But me lady, I'd enjoy traveling alongside you."

Strella smiled and blushed. "I'd enjoy your company."

Orgem beamed a wider grin, got on his hands and knees, but suffered more difficulty forcing his way through the cell door than she. After he finally fought his way through and stood, he looked at Gynx on the floor. "What's your decision on Gynx?"

Triggor huffed. "We can't leave him in here."

"We *can*," Strella said.

Orgem frowned and crossed his thick arms. "And we *should*."

Triggor looked at Gynx. Releasing Gynx from the cell was perhaps the worst decision he could make after their escape. Since Scorpius was dead, no one would feed Gynx. Triggor couldn't leave Gynx, regardless of their bad blood. He grabbed Gynx's tied hands and hefted the kobold up and half tossed him through the door. Gynx landed on the hard, dusty floor between Strella and Orgem without uttering a sound. Both stepped away from Gynx and disappointment set in their eyes as they looked at Triggor.

"I can't let him starve to death," Triggor said with a shrug. "And if you've the slightest moral conscience, you'd do the same."

To his surprise, Strella said, "I don't know that I would."

"Aye," Orgem said. "Leave him be."

"Really?" Triggor said.

"Yes. He can't be trusted," Strella said.

"So you'd leave me to starve, eh, Sweetie?" Gynx said, half opening his eyes. He coughed and cleared his throat. "So much for your morals. I heard everything you said. Perhaps you're right. I can't blame you. Leaving me behind is the best option for all of you. If I could've fit through the bars as easily as Sparrow, I'd have left you all behind. No doubt about it. And Orgem, yes, *I* blasted the mine where you lost an eye and almost died."

"You're not helping your cause," Triggor said.

"What's that matter?" Gynx said. "I've the intellect that few of my kin have, but like them, I have no conscience. But I'm in agreement, we go our separate ways. The lot of you was useless anyway. Well, except Triggor here. Him … I'd gladly aid in capturing Crukas. At least, he's the fortitude of mind and the heart to pursue the thief."

"I'm bowing out, too," Triggor said.

Gynx's eyes widened in disbelief. For a moment, he appeared hurt. "Seriously?"

"Aye."

"I'll call a blood truce," Gynx said. "I swear no more animosity between us. We keep the bounty hunt professional and split it evenly."

"No," Triggor said. "They've had a two day head start. Without knowing which direction they fled, we'd waste more time than it's worth to catch them, if we ever caught up at all."

"Than it's worth?" Gynx gritted his teeth. "The amount of gold offered for him is beyond our wildest expectations."

"Aye, tis true," Triggor said with a sigh of reluctance. "But, I've already wasted two years of my life looking for Crukas before you and I aligned to find him. The only reason I joined this group is because of how hard Crukas has been to track. And, he outsmarted all of us."

"My guess is they headed to Pirate's Cove," Gynx said. "At least accompany me there. We've only worked together for a few days."

"It's merely a guess, Gynx." Triggor's stomach tensed. His right hand involuntarily rested on the butt of his revolver and a lump hardened in his throat. He was unable to lessen it after several firm swallows. "No. We've no proof he's headed there. And why there? Pirates would recognize him and probably kill him and us should we intervene. Dat's a bigger gamble than we should risk."

"Fine," Gynx said with a huff. "Who bound my arms and legs?"

Triggor slid Gynx's dagger from its sheath. Strella and Orgem looked at Triggor with pleading eyes and slightly shook their heads. They didn't want Gynx freed, and Triggor sympathized with them. But if he didn't release Gynx, Gynx would most likely become even more hostile and once he wrestled free, he'd try to kill all of them.

"I tied your wrists," Triggor said. He cut the belt binding Gynx's legs together. "I had no choice."

"There's always a choice."

"Not if we wanted the pixies to help us escape, which they did," Triggor said. "And, as you see, dat includes you."

Strella held a defiant air. Her voice rose with a haughty tone. "I'm surprised they stuck around, after you threatened to kill Dewen."

Gynx grunted but didn't bother to glance her direction. "Then,

Triggor, you made the right decision. How about freeing my hands now?"

With a firm grip, Triggor grabbed the front of Gynx's tunic and pulled the kobold to his feet. Triggor stared Gynx in the eyes, searching for any sign that the kobold might be scheming a sudden attack once Triggor freed his hands. But he found the kobold's crazed gaze unnerving and unreadable.

"Can we trust ya won't attack any of us?" Strella asked.

Gynx said, "I'll behave, but should I happen upon one of those pixies—"

Triggor shook his head, released his tunic, and slightly pushed him back. "Dat didn't go so well for you last time."

"They caught me off guard," Gynx said.

"You attacked them," Strella said.

"You're fortunate nothing worse was done to you." Triggor placed the dagger to the rope binding Gynx's wrists and with a swift cut, the blade sliced through the rope. "I'll hold ya to your word."

Orgem huffed.

Gynx glared at the one-eyed dwarf.

"I'm serious," Triggor said. "There are three of us. As I warned before, I only draw my revolver when I intend to shoot, and if I shoot, it's to kill. If I miss, I'm sure Orgem's axe won't, and Strella, uh, she'll—"

Gynx winced and placed his hands over his ears. "Sing a lullaby to release my insanity and rage once again."

"Hey!" She balled fists.

Gynx raised his hands in an innocent manner and laughed. "Can't I jest, in spite of it being true?"

The sinister glint in the kobold's eyes prevented anyone from mistaking his true nature. Gynx couldn't fake playfulness.

Triggor glared at Gynx. "We've wasted enough time in this old tower, Gynx. Let's not prolong our stay with petty arguments, eh? I'd like to find a tavern in Ravensdorf and eat a huge bowl of lamb stew and drink a barrel of strong stout."

Gynx didn't reply in words. A long string of sticky drool stretched from his tongue down to the rocky path. He turned on his heel and headed down the pathway, unashamed of his terrible hunger.

"Dat's more like it." Triggor winked at Strella and Orgem. Neither shared approval of Triggor's impulsive amnesty and were wary of what might occur along the way out.

CHAPTER 71

Crukas stood at the door of Moonharvest Tavern, reached for the handle, and paused. The soft glowing oil lanterns—one on each side of the door—illuminated a small radius around the door and down the stoop, which prevented anyone from sneaking into or leaving the tavern unseen.

The door was unguarded. They had passed no pirates—sober or drunken—along the path to the tavern. In spite of this, Crukas's skin prickled as though someone gently ran a feather across his flesh. The sensation was something his intuition had instilled whenever eyes studied him during the times he needed to act covertly. For a thief, such an alert benefited him immensely by giving him notice, in case he needed to change his tactics or retreat.

Although a lot of pirates in the cove were human and dwarves, the Ravenfolk could quickly discern that Crukas and his companions were not pirates. They didn't fit in.

With his ear close to the door, he listened. No howling laughter or heated arguments were taking place inside. The place was quieter than the cemetery. Well, *almost.*

"Shh!" Crukas pressed his index finger to his lips.

Adgus' eyes widened. He whispered, "A problem?

Crukas nodded slightly. "We're being watched."

"From where?" Sparrow said in a quiet breath.

"The cliffs," Crukas said.

"Ravenfolk?" Bramnir said.

"Yes. But, it's to be expected. Keep your wits, stay alert, and don't draw any unnecessary attention to yourselves."

Crukas eased his hand around the door handle and pushed the lever down. He briefly looked over his shoulder at Adgus and Bramnir. They gave him reassuring nods that they were ready. Crukas pushed the door inward. The iron hinges creaked.

The smell of boiled cabbage and potatoes caused Crukas to cover his nose and mouth with his gloved hand. His stomach turned. The dwarves and Sparrow were used to the odor since cabbage was a staple food and part of their diet, so the aroma didn't bother them. For Crukas, however, the smell reminded him of scrounging for food before his thieving skills matured enough to steal better food.

Crude wooden tables, constructed from scrap slat boards, were positioned in two parallel L shapes closest to the door. Several drunken pirates lie slumped over various sections of the tabletops. A small fire blazed inside the hearth at the far wall.

Occupying the center of the room was a large square bar with jugs of wine and rum. Two barrels of ale were set atop the rough, scarred bar. Crukas couldn't suppress his grin when the three dwarves audibly licked their lips.

Huge mounted heads of strange beasts were displayed on the walls. Some Crukas was thankful to have never witnessed in the wild, and he hoped he never did. The Wierwen attack had been severe enough, which was why when he traveled, he tried to stick to the main roadways and marked paths.

On the other side of the bar were several round tables with lit oil lanterns set in their centers. Even with the soft flickering light, the room was dark, and for a thief, far more inviting. The tables were unoccupied, so he felt he was safer.

Considering the rowdiness of pirates and their excess of drink, the tavern was moderately clean. At this hour, only one barmaid stood inside the square bar alongside Skretch.

"Watch yourselves," Crukas said quietly. He stepped through the door and then allowed Sparrow to pass before him.

Skretch's fierce, keen eyes narrowed, as he watched them enter. He craned his head to the side.

Crukas didn't chance a long stare into the barkeep's eyes, as the Ravenfolk's piercing glares were intimidating. Some claimed they could easily hypnotize other races. Crukas gave Skretch a slight nod and headed to an empty round table at the far side of the tavern. He sat with his back to the wall. The only other exit was a tinted window behind another round table.

Sparrow sat to his left and Bramnir sat across from Crukas. Adgus took the seat to his right and Ebden sat between Sparrow and Ebden.

The barmaid, who appeared to be half elf, left the bar and walked to their table. Her voice was grating and almost dismissive, contrary to how most elves spoke, and perhaps this was because she'd waited on pirates for years. "What'll ya 'ave?"

After she took their drink orders, she returned to the bar and gathered several tankards and filled them with sour mead. Skretch kept his gaze on Crukas' table and bent to whisper in the barmaid's ear.

While the harsh aroma of the boiling cabbage made breathing difficult, a different aroma drifted from the bubbling black cauldron on a steel spit in the fireplace nearest their table. The steam drifting off the pot's rich, brownish-red liquid wafted an oddly sickening sweet odor mixed with the musty scent of a wet animal's hide. Chunks of meat clung to roughly chopped bones and floated with the bubbles.

Crukas narrowed his eyes and looked at the dwarves and Sparrow briefly before he whispered, "I'd stick to just drinks while inside."

Adgus' nose crinkled and his nostrils flared. His lips curled with disgust. "What's dat aroma? Dat's not cabbage and potatoes. Is it the food in dat pot?"

Crukas nodded.

The barmaid smiled as she set their tankards on the table. With vigor, she said, "Today's special. Would you fancy a bowl?"

"Special?" Bramnir's face scrunched. "What's in it?"

"As luck would 'ave it," she said, "a docked ship was infested with Ratkin. Pirates and the Ravenfolk quickly dismembered the pirates the Ratkin, so the meat's fresh. To boot, one fisherman's net caught a merman a few days ago. Its fish tail is mixed in with the Ratkin. The Ravenfolk consider the stew a delicacy."

"A merman?" Sparrow's face paled.

The barmaid shrugged. "He was already dead."

The three dwarves winced and declined by firming shaking their heads. Sparrow's eyes widened, and she placed her hand over her mouth. Her cheeks puffed as she fought sudden nausea.

Crukas grinned. "Don't say I didn't warn you."

"Cabbage I can handle," Sparrow said, "but eating vermin of any sort ... No thanks. And the merman—"

Adgus rubbed his eyes. "I 'ave to agree with you on dat."

Sparrow unexpectedly leaned her head on Crukas' elbow. Before he could jerk his arm away, she whispered, "Is that Chimz's wooden banana."

"Where?" Crukas asked.

"Above the bar, beside the walrus tusk sword."

Crukas took a discreet glance at the bar, pretending to look at Skretch. Crukas used his peripheral vision to study the various trophies locked inside dusty glass boxes on the hanging shelves above the square bar.

A lot of the boxes contained mounted fish and infant sea monsters, which had never been seen outside Pirate's Bay. A few short swords and daggers crafted from sharp, elongated spiral seashells, rested inside glass cases. Amongst these boxes set the wooden banana covered by thick layers of dust, which made it appear rotten.

Crukas wasn't certain he'd accidentally given a tell when he noticed the banana, but Skretch's eyes became more piercing, almost hostile. Perhaps Crukas had stared too long, but had he quickly looked away, he'd have drawn far more suspicion.

Even with so few patrons in the tavern, Crukas didn't calculate a way they could get close enough to steal it without notice. He wondered if Skretch even knew the banana held a key inside. Probably not, as he'd have already used it.

Adgus' stomach growled. "I'm starving but not game enough to consider eating any of *dat* stew. The sour mead's not bad though."

"We're all hungry, brother," Ebden said. "Maybe they 'ave something else?"

"Stale bread would be good," Bramnir said. "Could soak it in the mead."

Sparrow glanced at Crukas. "So, any ideas on how to get the key?"

"None," he replied. "If my recollection is right, this tavern never closes."

"There are few others here," she said.

"We are," he said. "And as long as we are, they'll keep the door unlocked."

"Skretch has to sleep sometime," Sparrow said.

"True, but another Ravenfolk would replace him while he slept."

The barmaid asked, "Anything more than mead?"

"Ya 'ave any stale loafs?" Bramnir asked.

She smiled and offered a slight curtesy. "Sure."

Crukas met Skretch's eyes once more. The barkeep didn't appear uneasy by Crukas' presence, but he seemed to recognize the thief. Crukas hadn't consider disguising himself before entering the bar, as he had each time in the past. Now, he wondered if he should have. It was quite possible Skretch recognized him and held deep suspicions for why Crukas was in Pirate's Cove.

No wanted posters were nailed to the support posts because no bulletin boards were allowed in Pirate's Cove. This didn't mean bounty hunters like Triggor never sought criminals in the cove, but after the Elder Mother's misfortunate murder, the warning had gone out that bounty hunters were *not* welcome.

In Crukas' case, since the bounty on the thief's head was far greater than the worst murderer's, bounty hunters on his trail might have shown his wanted poster to half drunk patrons in the past. And though Sparrow professed to be a bounty hunter, it was unlikely she'd be recognized as one, since Kane knew nothing of her reputation. Like Kane, Skretch seemed unconcerned about her.

Skretch's gaze was more intimidating than anyone Crukas knew. The Ravenfolk's towering size fully backed the fierceness of his eyes. Should Skretch unfold his massive wings, they'd stretch well outside the square bar where he stood. Unlike a raven, Ravenfolk's feathers attached to thick, muscular arms. They could flick out long, razored talons from their fingertips in a moment's notice. The last thing Crukas, or anyone would want to do, was to go hand-to-hand with any Ravenfolk. Their agility, speed, and strength were unmatched by humans, dwarves, and elves. Orcs held equalled strength but lacked the necessary speed to dodge a lethal talon swipe. An orc only held an advantage if he grasped both of the Ravenfolk's wrists and followed through with a harsh headbutt, but getting close enough to succeed was practically impossible. An orc could easily lose an eye to the Ravenfolk's sharp beak before headbutting it.

Long range weapons like bows, darts, and throwing knives were best suited for a successful attack, but using them required incredible accuracy and speed because Ravenfolk used their wings as shields if they noticed the attack before it reached them.

This was why Triggor used a revolver to kill the Elder Mother, provided the gun Triggor possessed was the actual revolver used to murder her. Until Sparrow suggested otherwise, Crukas never considered someone other than Triggor might've taken the opportunity during the scuffle to assassinate the Elder Mother. The crowd, including Crukas, fled so quickly that no one ever questioned Triggor wasn't the murderer. But as Crukas considered this, Triggor's goal had been to take Barnacle into custody. He had no ulterior reason to shoot any Ravenfolk.

"Is there a problem?" Skretch craned his neck slightly and stared at Crukas.

"No." Crukas shook his head and diverted his gaze. "No problems."

"Then why are you staring at me?"

The shrill of his voice sent chills down Crukas' back.

"Was I?" Crukas straightened on his chair. "My apologies. I'm tired from having travelled so long. I must've been deep in thought. Again, I didn't mean to be rude."

"From where have you traveled?" Skretch asked. "For here, you've come to a dead end, a hostile territory."

"I'm beginning to realize that," Crukas said.

Bramnir, Adgus, and Ebden kept their heads bowed while dipping stale bread into their sour mead and eating. Sparrow remained quiet and due to her small size, she drew little attention to herself.

"You look familiar," Skretch said. "This isn't your first visit to my tavern, is it?"

Most likely my last. Since Crukas always disguised himself prior to tonight, the only way Skretch recognized him was from a wanted poster. None were posted, so he hoped Skretch would treat the familiarity as a vague memory. "Actually, I've not been here before."

"All the same," Skretch said, "I've seen you before. Ravenfolk, like crows and ravens, have vivid memories and accurate recollection. We *never* forget a face or an enemy. One's eyes are as unique as fingerprints, and once we've looked into someone's eyes, we don't forget the person."

Crukas shrugged. "Maybe I just have one of those kind of faces, erm, set of eyes."

Skretch cawed a piercing laugh. "The longer you stay, the quicker I'll remember where I've seen you before. Pray you are *not* our enemy."

Without awaiting an answer, Skretch discarded their conversation and turned to the barmaid, bent down, and whispered in her ear.

One of the drunk, unconscious pirates moaned and eased his head up from the table. After blinking several times, he sat up and rubbed his eyes. The door opened and in walked two male pirates and a muscled female pirate. Six stood six inches taller than either of her male companions.

The two males were old, scarred, and wore tattered clothes. Their leathery, dark skin was a testament to their years of sailing the high seas under the relentless sun. One wore a patch over his right eye and most of his teeth were missing. His remaining teeth were black and chipped and ready to abandon his gum-line. The other man was no more handsome and seemed days away from joining Kane in the cemetery. A visible, prominent scar ran along his sparse, gray beard of his left jawline. They followed the female, not as a force capable of protecting her, but because they seemed under her order to do so.

The female pirate held an intimidating, shrewd stare, which intensified when she looked at the awakened pirate at the table. He met her gaze and visibly shivered.

Her human ears were outlined with golden ring piercings and a thick platinum ring protruded from her nose. Her arms and face had been tattooed with burnt wooden splints and ash. Her firm jaw matched her strength and indicated she could probably take as much punishment as she expelled.

"Wal!" she snarled.

His eyes widened. "C-captain Mer?"

"Did you not think I'd find you?"

"I hoped you wouldn't … look for me."

"Where are the others?" she asked.

Wal shrugged and averted his eyes like a scolded pup.

Adgus and his brothers gave Crukas a sly grin, as though he should understand their thoughts. At the moment, however, Crukas was oblivious. Even Sparrow looked confused by the dwarves' sudden epiphany.

"Ready yourself, thief," Adgus whispered and winked. "We may 'ave an opportunity 'ere."

Mer placed her hand on the hilt of her cutlass. "Because of you, our ship sank after hitting a reef. We barely made it ashore in the life raft. You shall pay."

"Take it outside!" Skretch expanded his wings and lengthened his talons. "Or I end you all."

"This doesn't concern you," Mer said, not bothering to glance in Skretch's direction, which could prove to be a deadly mistake on her part. "Wal, rise, and let's go!"

Drunk and stubborn, and probably comfortable that Skretch

would intervene, Wal said, "I'd rather not, Cap'n. Me thinks I'll order another tankard. Sit and I'll order you one as well."

"You can't buy your freedom with a drink, you fool!" She her cutlass. The two older pirates drew theirs as well.

Adgus' brow furrowed deeply as he looked at Crukas. "Thief, ya best take advantage of this distraction, 'cause it's liable to be the only one we'll get."

CHAPTER 72

*C*haos ensued.

Crukas pressed his back against the wall. Adgus and his brothers stood, pulled their axes, and flung over the round table next to theirs.

With a stern frown, Crukas whispered, "What are you doing?"

His whisper was quieter than he'd thought. The dwarves didn't hear him, nor did they reply.

Mer turned at the sound of the crashing table. Her eyes widened when she noticed Skretch's outstretched wings and lengthened talons. He was more menacing than a death angel and less likely to fail at taking her life.

"Ya heard Skretch, ya wench!" Adgus said. "Take your affairs outside, or ya'll be facing more trouble than you wish to find."

Skretch looked over his shoulder and glared at Adgus with fierce, narrow eyes. His high-shrieking voice pricked their ears like sharp needles. "I don't need any aid from you."

Crukas and Sparrow shook their heads at the barkeep's tone. Crukas' ears rang and the room swam around him in a drunken swayed motion. Sparrow leaned against the wall and slowly slid to the floor. Whatever had skewed their vertigo didn't affect the dwarves.

Adgus tilted back his head and howled with laughter. "We be happy to 'elp. We've not split any heads in days now, 'ave we Bramnir?"

"Right!" Bramnir balanced his axe in both hands and positioned his feet to charge at Mer.

Sparrow gave Crukas a confused look. Crukas shrugged. He was as clueless as she. The dwarves never displayed such haughtiness in their fights with the Wierwen or Scorpius. He couldn't tell if it was genuine or simply feigned to create the necessary distraction necessary for Crukas to steal Chimz's banana.

While Mer turned slightly to size up Skretch and the dwarves, Wal shoved the table and drew his rusty cutlass. His stupor caused him to stagger and he fell against the table beside his.

The two older pirates rushed Wal, but even in Wal's drunken condition, he parried their slow attacks with ease.

Mer turned toward Skretch with her cutlass and pressed her free hand against her left ear. The shrill of his voice was affecting her like it had him and Sparrow.

"You should've listened," Skretch said. With a swift backhand of his right wing, he struck Mer's cutlass. The impact pushed her weapon upward, and his right talons slashed her cheek.

Mer stumbled and went with the momentum of the strike. Her back landed atop a table. She rolled off and landed on her feet. She wiped the streaming blood on her face. She looked at her blood-coated fingers and grinned with renewed eagerness.

"You're a fool," Skretch said. "No bounties are collected here."

"He has no bounty on him," she replied. "He's part of my crew. He fled his duties and obligations. I came to fetch him."

"The difference?"

"No bounty. He *belongs* to me."

"Settle your matters outside, as I warned."

Blood streamed from Mer's gash, but the injury didn't perturb her. "Until your interruption, and those dwarves, Wal was seconds from leaving."

"Not without force," Skretch said. "Since you know Wal's where-abouts, all you needed was to wait for his exit."

"It's too late for that." She placed two fingers in her mouth and whistled a harsh cry, almost as painful as Skretch's. The tavern door opened and a half dozen weathered pirates rushed inside.

Skretch appeared more agitated than concerned about the incoming pirates. He rolled his eyes.

The pirates, though eager for a fight, were half starved and yet, Mer demanded them to arrest a crew mate who had come to drink and eat? Crukas was surprised any of them held loyalty to her.

Adgus shouted, "Ya be needing us now!"

Skretch didn't bother looking in the dwarves' direction, but nodded.

The six pirates wailed, raised their weapons, and rushed at Adgus, Bramnir, and Ebden.

Adgus used the axe handle to block one pirate's blade. The emaci-ated pirate was wiry. He didn't have the strength to put the slightest scratch on Adgus' steel handle. Adgus didn't apply much pressure to push the cutlass upward, even though the pirate strained against the dwarf. With a slight thrust, Adgus struck the man in the throat with the handle. The pirate's eyes widened. and He gasped, wheezed, and clutched his throat. Adgus grabbed the pirate's shirt, hefted him up, and hurled him high over the bar like a straw scarecrow.

The pirate struck the lower shelf that displayed the glass boxes and the horrendous crash shattered glass across the floor. The pirate didn't move. Shards of glass protruded from his back and arms.

The Elven barmaid pulled a dagger from her apron and stooped over him for a moment. Apparently seeing the old man was uncon-scious or dead, she dashed at an elder pirate.

Adgus motioned Crukas toward the bar with a head nod and winked. This was the distraction Adgus wanted Crukas to act. While the pirates growled and their clashing weapons struck, no one's atten-tion was on the bar. Crukas slinked along the shadowed corner wall and crept in a crouched position past several round tables until he reached the bar. The flip panel door remained upright after Skretch exited to confront Mer. Crukas passed through almost on his knees to maintain his lowered stance.

Crukas avoided the glass shards while he searched for the wooden banana. The pirate's tattered shirt slowly turned crimson from his numerous lacerations. If the impact didn't kill him, the amount of blood loss surely would.

In between a glossy, spiral-shell dagger and the shrunken head of a strange sea creature was Chimz's banana. He was surprised no one had discarded it long ago. It looked rotten. Did Skretch know what the relic was? At Skretch's height, the banana had not gone unnoticed. With the shelves were destroyed and the glass cases shattered, the relics would have to be gathered after the chaos ended.

Crukas grabbed the banana. It weighed little. He shook it but nothing rattled inside, and his heart sank. Had someone already taken the key?

Holding the banana in his hands, he twisted and bent the banana until it snapped in half. The key was set inside the pith of the wood as though the wood had grown *around* the key. He pried the key loose and then bit the bow of the key and pulled it free. Quickly, he tossed the broken banana on the rubble and tucked the key inside a hidden fold of his belt.

The metal swords and axes struck one another. Crukas crept to the bar opening. He peered around and came eye-to-eye with Sparrow.

"Did you find it?" she whispered.

Crukas smiled and nodded.

Adgus, Bramnir, and Ebden sparred three pirates, and though the pirates might have thought they were holding their own, the dwarves toyed with them to buy Crukas time to find and take the key.

Adgus made eye contact with Crukas. Crukas nodded and grinned. Adgus swung his axe, dislodged the pirate's grip on the cutlass, and sent it spinning across the bar.

Crukas whispered to Sparrow. "We need to return to our table before Skretch notices we were behind the bar."

Before they reached the table, Skretch spread his wings and reared back his head. He opened his mouth and bellowed an excruciating shriek even worse than his previous one. Crukas and Sparrow dropped to the floor and covered their ears with their hands. Even the dwarves stopped fighting, winced, and covered their ears.

The worn pirates cried out, dropped their weapons, and fell to the floor. Their bodies jerked with severe spasms. Blood leaked from their ears and noses. Crukas wasn't certain, but Skretch seemed capable of controlling where he directed the harshness of his shrills. The pirates took the worst of the shockwave sound. After Skretch's shrill ended, the tavern door burst open and four Ravenfolk entered.

They looked at Skretch for direction.

"Take all of them out back," Skretch said. "Except the dwarves, the halfling, and the human beside her. Leave them with me."

Crukas uncovered his ears. Satisfied the reverberating, piercing sound was over, he pushed himself up slowly. He stood and offered his hand to Sparrow. She eagerly accepted it, and he helped her up.

The Ravenfolk shackled the limp, unconscious pirates and dragged them across the tavern to a door hidden behind stack barrels of ale and mead.

"What are you going to do with them?" Sparrow asked.

Crukas gave her a stern look and shook his head. "Not our concern."

"Listen to your friend," Skretch said. "The laws we have don't concern outsiders, but whenever violated, by pirates or others, execution is quick."

Adgus stood and shook his head. He stuck a finger in his ear, as if trying to rid himself of the ringing. "They be on the menu tomorrow."

Sparrow winced.

Skretch directed his gaze at Crukas. "Considering the lot of you were willing to step in and aid us, when, as you can see, it wasn't necessary, your tab is on us."

Adgus' brow rose. "But we just got started!"

Crukas never thought he'd see a creature with a beak smile, but there was no other way to describe the odd curl on Skretch's beak. The Ravenfolk released a long twittering whistle.

Skretch turned to the barmaid. "Give them whatever they wish. No charge. Then we clean up this mess."

She nodded.

Crukas said, "Much appreciated."

"Rewards come to those worthy of receiving them," Skretch said. "Even for a thief."

Crukas' chest tightened.

Skretch winked. He identified Crukas. Rather than waiting for Crukas to reply, Skretch grabbed a broom and started sweeping the glass into a pile.

Crukas returned to the table where they'd been seated. The barmaid brought filled tankards, a large block of hard yellow cheese, and more stale bread.

Sparrow took her seat beside him. "He knows who you are?"

"Seems so." Crukas took a piece of bread and cheese. "Eat up. Afterwards, we find the small cave before the pirates along the shoreline awaken. We need to leave quickly."

CHAPTER 73

The sea's rushing waves crashed on the beach. The brewing offshore storm obscured the faint glow of the crimson moon. Orange-red flashes of lightning danced beneath the dark clouds at the end of the horizon. The wind's direction was being pulled out to sea. The storm was the same one that passed over them when they left Salem.

Crukas, Sparrow, and the dwarves stuck close to the cliff wall. Crukas and Sparrow held lit torches. Crukas would've preferred no torches, as the flickering flames marked their movements. But without light, they'd never find the cliffside crevice with the hidden door during the high tide.

Sand, rock fragments, and broken shells sank beneath their feet. They kept their distance from the anchored ships at the docks. Regardless of the dying campfires, each ship held a watchman, possibly several, to prevent enemy pirates from stealing their wares. Due to the Ravenfolk's fierce law enforcement, small raids between ships wasn't likely, even though no Ravenfolk guards were posted on the beach. Yet, every inch of the bay was under the constant scrutiny from the scattered outposts hidden in the high crevices of the bluffs, which meant Crukas and his party were being watched, too, and with great curiosity.

Skretch had identified Crukas as a thief. If Skretch knew what was inside the wooden banana, he never searched Crukas for the key or asked how the relic had gotten snapped in half. Since the thrown pirate crashed into the shelves and everything shattered on the floor, asking would've been foolish, as anyone would lay the blame on the pirate. Even so, the banana couldn't have been broken in such a manner. Anyone examining the wooden banana's pith could see something had been wedged inside and whatever it was, was gone.

All the same, Sparrow needed to find the locked box in the cavern quickly, and retrieve the Ghost-flame lantern before sunrise. It was unlikely a pirate watchman would confront them alone in the darkness, provided they even noticed them from the ships at all. Three dwarves with heavy weapons were an easy match for a few pirates. However, once the sun blazed over the bay, their activity along the bluff would gather interest. Since pirates fared by looting others, dozens of curious pirates might confront Crukas and his party.

Sparrow risking injury or possible death was in vain, should Kane be lying. Something worse could be inside the cave. But Kane had told the truth about where the key was, which gave Crukas some hope.

A hand clasped Crukas' shoulder.

Crukas turned. "Yes?"

Adgus whispered, "How much farther?"

"I've no idea."

"The braziers on the docks are growing dimmer. Have we gone too far?"

Crukas shrugged. "Unlikely. Kane wouldn't have buried the lantern close to the docks where the pirates held a better chance of discovering it."

Bramnir said, "Dat makes sense."

Sparrow stopped walking and raised her torch. "Listen."

As the receding tide pulled water outward, a bubbling sucking sound came from near the cliffside.

"You think that's it?" she asked.

"Maybe," Crukas said. "Let's see."

CHAPTER 74

When they found where the gluggling sound originated, Sparrow held her torch closer to the smooth cliff wall. After illuminating a small pool of water, she glanced and smiled at Crukas.

"That's it!" Sparrow said.

Adgus combed his beard with his fingers and shook his head. "Dat be an awful small opening, even for a halfling."

She handed her torch to Bramnir. "Tide's almost gone out, but I'll fit. I'm certain."

"Maybe." Crukas handed his torch to Ebden. "But can you hold your breath long enough?"

"Ah, a thief worried about a bounty hunter?" She beamed a smile. "Or are you worried I'll fail and your hope to get the lantern dies with me?"

"Neither," Crukas said.

His convincing tone made her wonder if he meant it or could he hide his emotions that well?

Sparrow placed her hands on her hips and sighed.

Crukas said, "One's occupation has nothing to do with reaching the other side of the wall successfully, if the pool allows access at all."

Adgus snorted. "He has a point."

Ebden stepped closer. "I'd go if it were possible."

"No dwarf's going to fit through there," Bramnir said. "If anyone has the slightest chance, it's Sparrow. We'll tether a thin rope to ya. If ya get into trouble, tug it, and we'll pull you out."

Sparrow studied the pool, took a sharp breath, and nodded.

Bramnir tied a rope around her waist. He checked the knot and tugged. "Dat'll work."

Crukas said, "Just know, the opening might not lead to the other side of the wall."

Her throat tightened. In the light of the torch, the narrow pool took a different form. The length and shape of the pool resembled a fresh dug grave filled with water; one that fit her body, or any halfling her size, perfectly. Chills shot down her spine, and she bit her lower lip.

Fasha's prediction about Sparrow's demise lingered fresh in her mind. *If you choose to go after Crukas …*

She stood right beside the thief. Nothing indicated Crukas was in league with Fasha. But Fasha was the link between her and Crukas, which struck her eerily odd.

Even though the tide had receded, the small opening remained full of water. No pirate or Ravenfolk would expect this to be an entrance to a cave. Besides, the shallow pool might be *too* shallow. A passage under the cliff wall might not be large enough for her to fit through. She could get her head stuck underwater. Despite the dwarves using their strength to pull her out, she might drown before they freed her.

Sparrow lowered to her knees and placed her hand in the pool. She stretched the length of her arm toward the bottom and touched coarse, wet sand. If that was the deepest the water went, she'd barely have room to worm her way to the cave.

Crukas placed a hand on her shoulder. "You don't have to do this. But if you choose to, I believe you can succeed."

Sparrow sighed. "If this lantern's necessary for what you and Irmine need, I've no other choice."

"And if it's a trap?" Crukas said.

"I *know* the risks, Crukas," she replied. "I was never a *master* thief, but my life's been in peril a few times to obtain a valuable piece of jewelry. This is different. It's not for me."

"If you die, and we don't obtain the lantern, your death's for nothing."

Sparrow swallowed hard. "Which is a greater loss, huh?"

"Hey, Crukas." Adgus placed a hand on Crukas' shoulder. "Lighten up, eh? Don't upset her. She doesn't need her confidence shaken any more than it already is, or she's bound to make mistakes."

Crukas nodded. "You're right. That wasn't my goal. I just want her to know—"

"Trust me," Sparrow said sternly. "I know. I've thought my every action through ever since I stayed with Fasha in her spell shop."

"I'd rather risk my life than yours," Crukas said.

She smiled. "Not all of us can gain the glory to save the day. That's the real issue, isn't it? Should I succeed in retrieving the Ghost-flame lantern, you don't get the credit."

"No. I'd rather no one know it were me, or that I came here, but if someone dies to obtain it, it shouldn't be you. This was my mission and I had intended to act alone, but … You've all graciously contributed to see this through." Crukas took an uneasy breath and handed her Chimz's key. "You've all shown me what actual friendship means. Not even the fortune I've gathered over the years could put a dent in what I owe you. *All* of you."

Sparrow detected his sincerity was genuine.

"You owe us nothing," Adgus said. "We understand the value of your quest and what it means for Aetheaon."

Crukas placed his hands on Sparrow's shoulders and peered into her eyes. Though dark, other than the two flickering torches, she could see his eyes.

"Keep your wits," he said. "Expect the unexpected."

She nodded.

Adgus lifted the torch. "Lass, we'll pull you out, if ya need us. But after you enter the cave, there's nothing we can do. We've no way to talk to ya. Our axes can't bust through this cliffside."

"I understand," she said. "Thanks."

Sitting on her knees, Sparrow took a deep breath, held it, and slowly lowered her arms and head into the water. Once her head plunged beneath the salty pool, her chest tightened. The hole seemed to shrink and tighten around her. She hated being in water, especially *under* the water. She wanted to push herself out, but she'd rather drown than to cower at this point.

After being fully submerged, she almost panicked. Her lungs burned. She struggled not to inhale the salty water. In her mind, she hummed a melody that comforted her when she was troubled as a child. She hoped the tune reduced her stress like it had in the past. Patting the sand, she reached toward the cliffside. Her fingers gripped rock. She ran one hand around the crude entrance. Finding finger-holds, she pulled herself into the tight opening, which offered more room than she expected. In hindsight, she wished she'd left her cloak with them because the cloth might snag the rocks and trap her.

While holding the rock, she raised a hand. The cold, cave air chilled her wet fingers. She wanted to shout with excitement. She worried she might have to swim a narrow underwater channel before she reached the end of the pool.

Sparrow pushed against the rock opening until she could sit up in the water. She exhaled forcefully and took in a cold breath of air that chilled her lungs until they ached. She opened her eyes to total blackness and a new fear encapsulated her. What else might be inside the cave? How large was it?

The frigid air assaulted her. She shivered, partly from the cold and partly from her growing fear of the unknown. Drips of water beaded down her face and hair. The water sloshed as she stood and stepped onto the compacted cavern floor.

What I wouldn't give for the heat and light of a torch right now.

Sparrow pulled her cloak tighter and hugged herself. Biting her lower lip to stop her teeth from chattering, she contemplated which direction to go or if she should move at all. Other than the rhythm of her heartbeat ringing in her ears, the only sound that echoed in the darkness was the muffled splashing of the sea's rough tide.

Since the tide had receded, she didn't understand how she could hear the crashing waves from the other side of the cliff wall. Under normal circumstances, Sparrow wasn't fearful of the night, not until she had stayed the night at Fasha's. All the supernatural encounters, the magic spells, and the thought of pirates and highwaymen hiding in the dark had kindled fears she didn't know she held.

Only Chimz could've brought the Ghost-flame lantern into the cave from the pool. He was approximately her height. None of the dwarves with her could fit, and neither could Crukas.

The picture she'd painted in her mind about Crukas was almost the complete opposite of his actual nature. He held compassion for others and even her. He wasn't arrogant and self-centered. Rather than side with the dwarves and dismiss immediate trust, he gave her the benefit of the doubt. He mentioned they might need another thief with lock-picking skills, which made her feel important and necessary. Instead, her size benefited more than actual skills. Somehow, she wasn't concerned about losing her life. But, if she'd chosen not to go through the pool, how would Crukas have retrieved the lantern? Irmine? No. She was too fatigued to journey to Pirate's Cove.

Gynx came to mind.

Kobolds? Could they inhabit this cave? Or maybe Ratkin? Or, perhaps luck favored her, and nothing else resided in the cave. Her skin crawled at the possibility of a kobold colony inside the mountain. The likelihood was probably nil since the Ravenfolk would slaughter and feast on them. The mountain belonged to the Ravenfolk, after all.

How long ago had Chimz hidden the lantern? Why wasn't the lantern visible? When she found the lantern, how would she get it through the pool without dousing the flame? She never considered such outcomes. Did the echoing tide indicate another entrance to this cave that Kane refused to disclose?

The cold metal key Crukas had given her pressed against her wet skin. She slid the key from her pocket and wondered what kind of chest or box it opened. She smacked her head. No wonder she couldn't see the lantern's glow.

Which direction do I go?

The only logical direction was toward the faint, crashing waves to her right. She untied the rope from her waist, as the rope wasn't much longer than the pool's length. Discerning the depth of the dark cave was impossible without light and proper direction. She closed her eyes, since she couldn't see anything at all.

She held her arms ahead of her and walked. After several steps, her hand brushed against the cold, wet wall.

A cool breeze tugged the still, stagnant air away from where she'd emerged. Any draft indicated a possible exit or a way to enter a different chamber. She hoped for a light source, so she didn't need to aimlessly wander like a blind person. Without light, she'd never find the box or trunk. And without the Ghost-flame lantern, she'd never find her way back to the pool.

Sparrow grew desperate and hopeless. For all she knew, she might die wandering through the cave.

CHAPTER 75

long one of Ravensdorf's crude streets, Triggor stomped
ahead of Orgem, Strella, and Gynx as they walked. Frustrated with Gynx's rabid unpredictability, he chose not to look at the
kobold. The least irritant might reignite Triggor's rage. While inside
the small prison cell, Triggor's opportunity to kill Gynx had been
wasted. He didn't like the idea of ending the life of another bounty
hunter, but if he had killed Gynx, Triggor wouldn't have held any
regret for having done so. The kobold's mental state was too unpredictable, and he could turn on innocent folks as easily as he could
criminals. Though Gynx was intelligent, he was an untamable beast
and one *not* to trust.

"I'm in need of drink and food," Triggor said.

"Aye," Orgem said. "All of us be."

Strella tried to straighten the frayed strands of her outfit. She
nodded with tears in her eyes. "Agreed. Then, we go our separate
ways. I need to replace my ruined clothes."

"Aye," Triggor said.

Gynx grumbled under his breath. "You sure you won't accompany
me to Pirate's Cove, Triggor?"

"Quite," Triggor replied. "I think I'll head to Frosthammer instead."

"Frosthammer? Not much to gain from such a frigid trip," Gynx said.

"All the same," Triggor said, "it be better than risking me neck in a bay filled with pirates."

"Wonder which house the priestess lives in?" Gynx asked.

Strella's brow furrowed. "You're itching to die, aren't you?"

Gynx laughed. "At the hands of a priestess?"

"The magic she consults through her hands. After all, she killed Scorpius," Strella said. "With holy magic, too. As vile as you are, she'd destroy you much quicker."

Gynx turned in a flash with his wicked dagger drawn. She recoiled in terror. Before Gynx reached her, Orgem pulled his axe and pressed the blade against the kobold's throat while Triggor cocked his revolver and pressed the barrel against Gynx's temple.

Gynx's eyes bulged with genuine surprise. His dagger dropped to the street with a slight clink.

Partially relieved, Strella grinned and tried to hand-iron the frayed edges of her tunic. "Seems the ideal time for a song, don't you think?"

Gynx cringed. "You wouldn't dare."

"Oh, but wouldn't I?"

"We could end ya right 'ere," Triggor said, "and the townsfolk wouldn't bat an eyelash. Dat be worthy of a bard's hymn, eh?"

With a stiff voice and spittle on the edges of his mouth, Gynx said, "Then do so, please, before she sings."

"I'd rather not have to clean up the mess," Triggor said. "Or, deal with the magistrate when he questions my reason for killing another bounty hunter. Dat is, *if* you're actually registered with one of the Royal Bounty Hunter Guilds."

An evil grin spread across Gynx's serpent-like lips. His eyes regained their normal contempt. He frowned. "You know I am. My reputation is known as well as yours."

Triggor eased the hammer off, sighed, and lowered the revolver. "Then be on ya way."

"Not until I've eaten," Gynx said.

"Fine."

Strella placed a nervous hand to her throat. "You're not … just going to let him go?"

"Aye," Triggor said. "Without a proper accusation filed with a magistrate, it'd be my neck on a guillotine. He'd be dead, and in return, so would I."

Eagerness beamed in Gynx's eyes, much like a child who'd stolen and eaten gooey honeycomb, got caught, but no punishment was administered. Gynx reached for his dagger but Triggor placed his foot atop the hilt.

Gynx snarled. "It's mine! You've already lost my crossbow, now you want my dagger?"

Triggor shook his head. "Nah. You accompany us to The Changeling, fill you gut, and I'll give you the dagger when we're ready to part ways."

Strella swallowed hard. "I'd rather not be seated at the same table."

"Nor I," Orgem said.

"That's fine." Triggor gave Gynx a shrewd glare. "He'll sit with me. But afterwards, Gynx, you take the north road to Pirate's Cove. If ever we cross paths, I'll show no mercy. I'll end you."

Gynx's eyes narrowed. "Not if I see you first."

Triggor pushed Gynx and nodded for the kobold to start walking. After Gynx walked several steps down the street, Triggor picked up the dagger and tucked it behind his belt.

Triggor followed Gynx and Orgem walked alongside Strella without sheathing his axe. As far as Triggor knew, Gynx had no other weapons, but devious folk always found ways to hide extra weapons. The thought of searching Gynx for other weapons disgusted Triggor, and he didn't like the idea of making either of them suffer through such a situation.

CHAPTER 76

$\mathcal{U}$sing the slick, wet wall as her guide, Sparrow bumbled along a winding path in the dark. Occasionally, her foot scuffed a protruding rock on the cave floor, which caused her to trip forward but she managed to retain her balance. She kept going because the crashing waves became louder the farther she walked away from the small pool. She must've chosen the correct direction.

The path seemed endless but in the darkness with her eyes closed, she couldn't properly measure distance. Noises other than the sea waves caused her to stand still and hold her breath.

Several loud shrieks echoed and a breeze rushed overhead.

Bats!

Sparrow didn't fear a flying bat swarm, and their sounds almost made her giddy. The bat colony swooping past her meant there *was* another entrance into the cave, and with them returning to their roosts, daylight must be soon. No bat could enter through the pool, but she couldn't surrender to her excitement quite yet. Their entrance might be too small for a halfling to squeeze through. Bats didn't need a large hole to come and go. But, she hoped their entrance was at least large enough for her.

After the last flittering, chirping bat disappeared, she continued onward.

A chorus of cooing arose. Feathers ruffled. Carrier pigeons? She'd often heard such sounds in the cities, but inside a cave? She opened her eyes and gasped.

Sparrow stood inside a large domed room backlit by glowing, fluorescent blue and green mushrooms. Across the room, near the top of the dome, were pigeons, gulls, and other roosting sea birds. The shadowy crack in the wall behind them was how they'd gotten inside the small cavern.

The lofty dome was large enough to house a monstrous dragon, and to her delight, no dragon was present. No accumulated treasure—at least *not* readily attainable treasure—so this wasn't a lair. The crate or chest with the Ghost-flame lantern wasn't readily visible. If it were stashed in this room, she might spend days searching.

Sparrow sighed her disappointment, almost yielding to the burning tears cresting in her eyes. She'd come this far, put her life at risk, and still she remained empty-handed, failing to find the relic Crukas and Irmine needed.

Her attention turned to the wet, glistening metallic reflections in the luminous glowing mushrooms. Throughout the base of the room were spired rich veins of various ores. They rose from the floor like massive stalagmites. Except these rock formations contained gold, silver, copper, and other ores only an experienced miner could identify. None of their value mattered to her since she didn't have the strength to swing a pickax, but the shimmering, wet ores captivated her. Their vibrance lured her. She wanted to touch the colors, and as she walked between the different formations, she noticed an odd object wedged against an iridescent ruby the size of her fist.

A wooden trunk.

The sides of the trunk had suffered deep scratches and dents where others must've tried to bust it open. One indentation was the length of a sharp axe, but even the weapon had been unable to split the side of the trunk open.

Is this it?

Sparrow slipped the key from her pocket and stuck it inside the lock. It fit. With a slight twist, the lock clicked. She grinned and tucked the key in her pocket. Flipping the latch up, she pried open the trunk. The lantern's bright light emitted a fierce blinding light.

"Ahh!" Sparrow slammed the trunk closed.

The lantern had only been exposed for a few seconds and its beacon left her blinded. The searing light left her dizzy, and she suffered an immediate headache. She patted the trunk until she found the handle on the side. She gripped it, pressed her back against an ore vein, and sat on the cave floor. Numbness spread throughout her body.

She hoped the blinding effect was only temporary. If not, she was doomed to die and rot in this domed room.

CHAPTER 77

riggor held open the door of The Changeling. Strella and
Orgem entered. Gynx stood at the threshold with a
disgruntled look on his face. The kobold's eyes indicated he might
run, not from fear, but because Gynx hated being told what to do.

"Go on," Triggor said with a firm gaze.

Gynx grumbled. "I'd like a few words with the barkeep. He lied to
us. I knew it then and you can't deny it now."

Triggor shrugged and waited for Gynx to go through. The kobold
gave a wary stare at the threshold and after a moment, he stepped
boldly into the tavern.

"Which table are you taking, Triggor?" Strella asked.

Triggor pointed to a round table near the fireplace.

She smiled. "Then Orgem and I will take the one over there."

"Suit yourselves," Triggor said.

Gynx gave a soured expression but offered no insults. He looked at
the bar. "Where's the barkeep?"

Triggor shook his head and shrugged. "Why you asking me? I got
'ere the same time as you."

Triggor sat at the table where they'd met and discussed their plans
to find and capture Crukas. Since those plans had unraveled without

any success, and only Gynx wished to continue the pursuit, Triggor was ready to give the kobold his dagger and part ways. Pirate's Cove was the last place he ever desired to visit again. The only thing he'd be gifted by returning was the rough, scratchy end of a hangman's noose or worse: He'd be butchered and flayed by a Ravenfolk's sharp talons.

The barmaid brought Triggor a tankard of sour mead. He nodded his appreciation and tossed a silver coin on the table.

When she set a tankard in front of Gynx, he said, "Where's the barkeep?"

She shrugged and smiled. "He's not here today."

"Where is he?" he asked with a fierce stare. His jagged teeth formed a grim smile.

The barmaid took a cautious step back. "Sorry. I don't know."

Gynx grumbled and fixated on his tankard with his thoughts having turned inward. He whispered, "Pirate's Cove."

Triggor placed his hand against the side of the holstered revolver and sighed. *Pirate's Cove, indeed.*

Moonharvest Tavern had a good number of rambunctious patrons the night Triggor set foot inside for the first and only time he'd visited the cove. With the hope of capturing a wanted scallawag known to visit the pirate's port often, Triggor expected the tavern to be the best place to wait until Barnacle Reed graced the place. Barnacle's armor made him easy to identify immediately.

Tales were told that Merfolk crafted Barnacle's armor by smelting Mer copper and coating sharpened barnacles into thick layers for his chestpiece and leggings. The barnacles never lost their sharpness. His bracers were fashioned in the same manner. His armor was what earned him the nickname, Barnacle.

The sharp protective armor was why no one could directly place their hands on him and take him into custody. The unusual armor further allowed him to continue his nefarious ways.

Barnacle was a notorious ruffian known to stowaway in small

merchant ships and wait until the ships were far from port. Then, he emerged from hiding. The few who survived his attacks said Barnacle moved silently, much like a shadow. One by one, he attacked and killed the deckhands, tossed their bodies overboard, and waited until the captain left his quarters. Once he took the captain into custody, Barnacle declared the ship as his own.

Somewhere on the high seas was an island reported to be where Barnacle stored his loot. Later, he allowed the winds to catch the plundered ships' sails, which rendered the unmanned ships to go adrift until other pirates found and claimed them. In some cases, the windblown ships hit jagged reefs and ripped the emptied hulls open. The ships sank to the bottom with the other ghost ships in their watery cemetery.

The price on Barnacle's head was nearly one hundred thousand gold pieces and remarkably the reward was far less than the bounty set on Crukas' head.

Triggor often wondered how Barnacle and Crukas matched up, if ever they crossed one another's path. With Crukas' nonviolent reputation, the thief would probably vanish into the shadows without any confrontation at all. As for Barnacle, it seemed unlikely he'd tried to capture or kill Crukas because there'd be no way he could claim the reward without jeopardizing his life.

But the night Barnacle entered Moonharvest Tavern, Triggor's patient wait had almost paid off. Knowing Barnacle's armor protected him from being grabbed directly, and swords and daggers were chipped and dulled by the coated barnacles, Triggor traded for his revolver. He intended to use it on Barnacle.

Arrows flicked off Barnacle's armor, and Triggor wasn't an archer, so he never considered learning to use a bow. The revolver, however, was a weapon he liked. After the pirate taught him how to load, aim, and fire, Triggor never considered using an axe or hammer again. The revolver was lighter, less cumbersome, and better hidden.

Like an arrow, provided Triggor practiced enough, a shot accurately aimed could strike Barnacle's forehead and kill him. Triggor spent hours familiarizing himself with the weapon and practiced shooting the revolver in a thicket far enough from Pirate's Cove where no one could hear the shots. And that night, he was ready. Or, so he had thought.

Moonharvest Tavern was filled with numerous pirates from every shore in Aetheaon. Hostility rose like static and Triggor sensed something was amiss. So many bandits and pirates drank and mocked one another, making challenges and threats, that Triggor wished he'd not entered alone. Though none knew him to be a bounty hunter, he stood out nonetheless. He lacked the scars, tattoos, and missing limbs and eyes the others in the tavern sported. Pirates boasted their toughness based on injuries, and Triggor had none. He was an obvious outsider, not a pirate or a thief, and in hindsight, he was surprised no one called him out openly.

From Triggor's information about Barnacle, the pirate usually worked alone. He wasn't part of a crew and he didn't seek the aid of others, which confused Triggor when Barnacle entered with two other pirates. The trio regarded one another in a protective manner, watching one another's back, and sticking close together.

Triggor eyed them shrewdly, and Barnacle immediately noticed. Triggor should've kept a less obvious stare since he was alone. Not that it mattered. Taking Barnacle into custody was a bigger obstacle since the pirate had companions. Where did their loyalty lie? The temptation to turn on Barnacle for the reward seemed a great enough incentive for other pirates to collect such a rich bounty.

Triggor considered a different approach. The tavern wasn't the proper place to attempt taking Barnacle dead or alive. He held no doubt that numerous pirates in the tavern had bounties on their heads, too.

Barnacle met Triggor's even gaze and since Triggor didn't look away, Barnacle worked his way through the tavern toward Triggor's table. Triggor placed his hand on the revolver, half expecting to need use of it, but instead, three pirates stood at a nearby table with their weapons drawn. They informed Barnacle they were there to take him in for the reward.

Distracted by their threat, Barnacle turned with anger in his eyes.

His two companions rushed the pirates and the clashing cutlasses sent small sparks into the air. Barnacle pulled his short sword and as he did, total chaos erupted. Tables overturned and chairs were thrown.

Skretch shrieked and tried to call order to the disruption.

The piercing, high-pitched shrill Skretch released dropped the pirates closest to him to their knees. Blood leaked from their ears. Perhaps more pirates would've succumbed to the nerve-racking caw but a deaf pirate attacked Skretch, which caused the barkeep to defend himself.

Two more Ravenfolk joined the fight using their talons to impale pirates, slit throats, and gouge out eyes. The Ravenfolk butchered their way through the tavern, trying to reach a female Ravenfolk dressed in an ornamental robe, which Triggor later learned was their Elder Mother. Their goal had been to protect her.

Barnacle turned his back to Triggor and parried a swift blade-thrust aimed at another pirate's throat. Triggor had the perfect opportunity to shoot Barnacle but shooting him from behind wasn't honorary, even for a bounty hunter capturing a known murderer. Had Triggor killed Barnacle in such a manner, he'd never get out of the tavern alive, especially with the dead pirate's body. Too many cutthroats would readily kill him and other pirates would claim Barnacles's corpse and collect the reward. With the Ravenfolk slaughtering pirates to the left and right, the number of casualties meant nothing at this point. No one would be called into account.

Triggor rose from his seat with his revolver drawn and kept it slightly hidden at his side. With the crazed swarm of melee and swordplay around him, the gun held little benefit. Five shots against so many left him vulnerable. The first shot probably would've silenced the fighting for several seconds, striking the pirates with brief confusion. But unless the shot killed his target, the others might turn their vengeance on him. Instead of firing, he pushed through the crowd until he wound his way around to face Barnacle directly, eye-to-eye.

When Triggor prepared to pull the trigger, Barnacle made a desperate attempt to take the gun from Triggor. Everything from that moment forward seemed a blur. Triggor wrestled control of the revolver from Barnacle, and he jerked slightly when gunfire blasted. Barnacle didn't fall. Instead, the Elder Mother cawed in a high shrill of pain and dropped to the floor. All the scuffling died in sudden silence. About half of the surviving pirates scrambled toward the door.

Confused, Triggor checked his revolver. No smoke came from its cold barrel. His finger had never tightened on the trigger.

Fingers pointed and accusations were hurled at him.

"I never fired a shot!" Triggor said.

Barnacle laughed, hurried away from Triggor, and blended into the hysterical crowd. Triggor watched the panic in Skretch's eyes shift to fiery rage. The gunfire was not the reason for the pirates' fear. They feared what was coming, and at that moment, so did Triggor.

Skretch and two Ravenfolk knelt over the Elder Mother's lifeless body. Frantic, they attempted to revive her. Anger rose in their voices and revenge set in their eyes. Apparently the surviving pirates, including Barnacle, understood the fury the Ravenfolk were about to unleash. They rushed over their dead comrades and headed to the door. Triggor holstered his weapon and rushed into the crowd and exited, thankful for the dark of night.

Outside, he searched for Barnacle but in the absence of light, he couldn't find him. Knowing the Ravenfolk possessed night vision, he needed to leave Pirate's Cove altogether.

He ran to the stables, grabbed his mount, and rode south along the bluff road. Although he never fired his revolver and killed the Elder Mother, his guilt overshadowed him. Someone else had taken advantage of Triggor drawing his weapon and acted upon it to frame him.

Triggor wanted to return and explain his innocence, but he doubted they'd listen. His running indicated guilt. No explanation undid his actions. Others had seen the revolver—a rare weapon—in his hand. Who else could they blame? No one.

And worse than falsely accusing Triggor, Barnacle had escaped. Pirate's Cove was the only place Triggor knew the pirate could be found since he didn't possess a revolver. The way Barnacle had laughed when the Elder Mother was killed made Triggor believe the pirate was somehow responsible for her murder. But how? Had one of the two pirates with him carried the same weapon and set him up? Had they staged the distraction so they could kill her?

The day after he'd fled Pirate's Cove, Triggor checked his revolver. The shot was still inside the gun's barrel. He never fired. So who had?

He searched his memories, but the chaos of that night remained a blur. Had it been a planned attack to the Elder Mother? Pirate's Cove's history was no secret. The pirates loathed the Ravenfolk for hostilely reclaiming the ownership of their mountainside.

Killing the Elder Mother didn't benefit the pirates in any way. It made their coexistence less tolerable, and the Ravenfolk would, no doubt, double-down on thinning the pirates' numbers by taking any opportunity or excuse to kill them.

TRIGGOR SIGHED. "Gynx, I'll be going with ya to Pirate's Cove."

Gynx shook from his deep sullen thoughts and his eyes beamed with renewed interest. "Oh? Why the change of heart?"

Triggor grunted and shook his head. "It's not me heart dat's changed. But, more of a mind change."

Gynx rubbed his hands together briskly. "Whatever's changed is of no importance, as long as we find and capture Crukas."

"Aye." Triggor downed his tankard and setting it abruptly on the table with a thud. "Understand, Crukas might not even be there."

"True," Gynx said with a sly grin. "But if not, there's always others with substantial bounties we could capture and return to the closest magistrate."

Triggor gave an even smile and motioned the barmaid for another tankard. She nodded and did a slight curtesy. Triggor met Gynx's excited gaze. He slid the kobold his dagger across the table. Gynx's brow rose in question. Triggor nodded.

"Thanks." Gynx took the dagger and tucked it into its sheath. "Despite our differences, Triggor, you've my word that I've your back."

A tight grin formed on Triggor's lips. He couldn't help but to think the dagger might be what Gynx shoved into his back. The best way to prevent that was to never turn his back to Gynx. "Aye. I appreciate dat. And for what it's worth, I've got yours."

A change settled in Gynx's eyes, unlike anything Triggor had noticed before. Triggor didn't have the heart to tell Gynx that Pirate's Cove had laws against bounty hunters capturing criminals for bounty. Triggor's reason for returning to the cove had nothing to do with finding Crukas. He wanted to plead his case before the Ravenfolk council. It was a bold risk, and one worth taking, provided the council considered and believed his side of how the events had unfolded that night. If not … that was something he'd have to deal with after all was said and done. While the Ravenfolk might believe him, he feared what troubles Gynx might cause beforehand that could ruin his chances to be taken seriously by the council. This meant Triggor would have to keep a cautious eye on Gynx and prevent the kobold from acting irrationally before he scheduled time to be heard. That might prove more difficult than facing the council.

CHAPTER 78

Sparrow blinked hard. Faint images slowly materialized behind the shadowy blotches the fierce light had etched across her vision. Her head throbbed. As her sight began to clear, the feeling in her limbs returned to normal. She never imagined an intense light could render her so vulnerable two different times within such a short amount of time. The lantern seemed much harsher than the lightning, but she was closer to its source.

How much time had passed after she opened the trunk?

The Ghost-flame lantern glowed, even after all these years, albeit *much* brighter than she expected. How had Kane used it without blinding himself? Perhaps he locked it inside the trunk to prevent blinding Chimz. She'd hoped to use the lantern to return to the pool and exit the cave.

Sparrow whispered, "Maybe I can partially open the trunk?"

She stood with her back against a jagged vein of ore. Turning the front of the trunk away from her direct sight, she opened the lid a sliver. The bluish tint of light emitted a weaker beam, so she widened the opening a bit more.

Odd.

The light was not as bright as when she first opened the trunk. The lantern was lit by magic. Had its magic waned? If the light completely extinguished before she reached the pool, she was trapped. She'd die in utter darkness, and most likely her body would never be found.

She set the trunk on a rock, shielded her eyes, and fully opened its lid all the way. The glow was enough to find her way to the pool. She hoped it didn't flare to its full power until after she reached the beach.

Although the trunk wasn't big or cumbersome, she took the lantern and left the trunk behind. By hugging the lantern against her chest and ducking underwater, she could push her way through the small hole to the other side. But would the water damage the lantern and extinguish its glow?

With nimble steps, Sparrow held the lantern. Its blue light illuminated the cave floor up to the high ceiling where the bats nested. The light quashed her fear of what might've been hidden in the dark crevices.

At the pool, she retied the rope around her waist, stepped into the cold water, and slowly submerged. She thought the glow would give her more confidence, and for the most part, it did. But, as she attempted to squeeze through the hole to get outside, the lantern took buoyancy and wedged her abdomen against the upper rock opening. She couldn't push free from the rock without letting go of the lantern. But the lantern tried to tug free of her grip to surface outside without her.

Sparrow held tightly but the lantern pulled harder. To prevent letting go, she outstretched her arms. The rough rock dug into her abdomen. Holding her breath became intolerable. With all her remaining strength she held fast, but it wasn't enough. The lantern slipped free and rushed to the surface. By instinct, she shouted, "No!"

All the air expelled from her lungs. She panicked, clung to the rock, pushing herself downward. Then, she remembered the rope tied around her waist. She tugged it twice, while fighting not to suck water into her lungs. Aching to breathe, and with dizziness overcoming her, death seemed inevitable. Before she lost consciousness, she was grateful knowing she'd served some purpose to aid Crukas. Perhaps she'd redeemed herself of the wrong paths she'd taken after leaving Willows Bend, but she was also a bit sour that Fasha's prophesy had been fulfilled.

CHAPTER 79

The sunrise crept over the sea's horizon. Crukas stood beside the shallow pool, waiting for Sparrow to emerge. He sighed and shook his head. "I should've retrieved the lantern."

"Bah!" Adgus said. "You'd never fit through there."

"I realize that," Crukas said. "At least I'd know what's happening where's she at."

Bramnir offered a teasing smile. "You're worried about her?"

Crukas shrugged. "A bit."

"Ya know, I had me doubts about her," Adgus said. "Dat she'd turn on ya at the first opportunity. Why'd ya trust her?"

"Trust? It's something earned. Without seeing her interactions in person, her words meant nothing," Crukas replied. "She's seems indecisive about which direction she plans to take. Thief, bounty hunter, neither, or perhaps a little of both."

"She put her life on the line by going through the pool," Ebden said. "Doesn't dat count for something?"

"Of course. That's why I'm worried."

Adgus frowned "What? Ya think Sparrow is still thieving even after she became a bounty hunter?"

"Retired bounty hunter," Bramnir said.

Adgus pointed a finger. "Ah, don't be so certain."

Crukas sighed. "I believe she's sincere in giving up both professions. Besides, she won't survive if she continues acting like a bounty hunter."

"How's dat?" Ebden asked.

"Thieving guilds are actively hunting her," Crukas replied.

Adgus' brow rose and his eyes widened. "Dat's the truth?"

Crukas nodded. "She used her knowledge of her thieving guild's members and turned some of them over to magistrates to collect their rewards."

Bramnir whistled. "Dat's cold."

"Yes," Crukas said. "That's why they set a bounty on her head."

"Wait, what?" Adgus said. "Thieves are putting bounties on bounty hunters' heads? Dat's an odd turn, eh?"

"Yes. She betrayed them," Crukas replied. "Not that thieves ever fully trust one another."

Adgus laughed. "Dat was my first thought when we bartered with you. Never in my long life have I ever thought I could ever trust a thief. But ... *you* seem the exception to all de others."

Crukas grinned slightly and his face reddened. He was glad the dim daylight prevented the dwarves from noticing. "I'm at a loss, really."

Bramnir said, "Why?"

"I trust few people. I've always been that way. But I'm changing. The barrels of ale I gave you in return for the ride to Ravensdorf can, in no way, never repay you for your continual help."

Adgus chuckled. "It more than paid for the wagon ride. Us, being here with you, is because we 'ave a duty to defend Aetheaon from the Plague-bringer. There's *no* amount of gold to pay the ransom. Should the necromancer succeed, we all suffer until we crumble to dust."

The four continued watching the small water pool, unaware others were quietly sneaking upon them.

A grim voice caused chills to shoot down Crukas' back, but he didn't jerk in surprise. "What'cha staring at the pool for? Ya 'ave better luck fishing in the sea."

Adgus and Bramnir both turned with their hands on the handles of their axes.

"No." A pirate readied his cutlass and he stood ready to advance fiercely. Three others had their cutlasses drawn. In the dim light, only their dark silhouettes were visible.

Adgus glanced at Crukas. Crukas offered a slight shake of his head. The pirates held the advantage. They could cut through Crukas and attack the dwarves far faster than the three dwarves could draw their axes.

Crukas said, "We're not fishing."

"Well," the closest pirate said. "None of ya can fit in it to take a bath, either."

Crukas laughed heartily, partially rearing back his head, at the pirate's ignorant remark. The pirates' feet shifted in the sand, as Crukas' strange laughter made them uneasy. Adgus, Bramnir, and Ebden gave Crukas unsettled looks, and their eyes indicated they'd thought Crukas had gone mad.

"Bathe?" Crukas said. "By no means. We'd have a difficult time trying to wash our faces. Maybe all the time you spent under the sun on the high seas has fried your brains?"

The dwarves suppressed their laughter, which sounded more like grunts, but their grins were evident.

The pirate took immediate offense at Crukas' taunting. "Careful. Never mock a man who decides whether you live or die."

Crukas frowned and gave a slight shrug. "Are you saying that's *you?*"

The pirate hesitated. He turned to look at his companions. He spoke with a deeper tone. "The four of us."

"Humph," Crukas said. "You'd kill us for *what* exactly? Not for bathing or fishing in his tiny pool, or is it because I pointed out how ludicrous either would be? I'm certain neither are your true concern, correct?"

The pirates murmured amongst themselves. While they did, Crukas watched the water in the pool turn bright blue. Sparrow had found the lantern and was coming through the pool.

Crukas didn't have much time. "Your questions were meant to distract. Your true motive is to rob us, but rob us of what? You see we have no pouches filled with gold or coin. I doubt quite seriously that any of you puny pirates have the strength to tote one of my comrades' broadaxes."

The confused pirates lowered their cutlasses and exchanged whispers. Then, "Why are you looking at the pool?"

Crukas sighed and crossed his arms. "Do you really want to know?"

They all nodded.

Knowing the majority of pirates held an inept fear of the unknown and believed superstitions, Crukas said, "You know of Kane Greaves?"

"Aye. Of course. The mad wandering ghost in the swamp cemetery above the ridge? Some say he was crazy before he died. Others claim his spirit is even crazier. That *is* the Kane you speak of?"

"The same."

Though the pirate tried to sound bold, his voice quivered. "Why should we concern ourselves with him when he's far from the cove? He never ventures from the cemetery."

"Today, he does," Crukas said evenly.

The sunlight was bright enough that the confusion and uncertainty on their faces was unmistakeable.

"Why w-would Kane come 'ere?" the pirate asked.

Crukas narrowed his gaze and in a somber tone, he said, "Revenge."

One pirate said, "We had nothin' to do with his death."

"Does that matter to a mad ghost?" Crukas asked. "He'd still find pleasure in punishing anyone."

"Bah!" another pirate said. "He's a spirit. He can do us no harm."

"His ghostly apparition roams the cemetery, but this morning his resurrection allows him to become fleshly again."

"Impossible," the one who stood as their leader said.

Crukas pointed at the pool. "Do you not see the blue glow of his Ghost-flame lantern in the water pool? We've come to ask his favor, and since you threatened to do us harm, we'll ask him to eliminate you first."

The blue glow of the lantern intensified. Sparrow was close to emerging. Crukas hoped his story played on the pirates' superstitions, and they'd flee. However, should Sparrow emerge with the lantern, his bluff was over.

"You want to wait and see?" Crukas asked.

The pirates took several steps back.

"Or do ya want to test the sharpness of our axes?" Adgus gripped his axe in both hands and growled harshly.

While Crukas' tale distracted them, the dwarves had pulled their axes.

The four pirates offered no reply. They turned and fled.

Adgus, Ebden, and Bramnir howled their laughter. Their jovial moment faded in seconds when the Ghost-flame lantern bobbed on the water's surface but Sparrow did not follow.

Bramnir knelt at the pool. "She's in trouble. She tugged the rope twice *after* the lantern appeared."

CHAPTER 80

*C*rukas grabbed the floating lantern and set it on the sand beside the pool. "Pull her up."

Bramnir stood and pulled the rope. The veins in his forearms swelled as he leaned back and tried to break her free. He shook his head. "Sparrow's stuck. There's no give."

"Surely, the three of you together could?" Crukas' voice was filled with desperation.

"No, Crukas," Bramnir said. "You realize dat as tiny as she is, we'd yank her in half, don't ya? She'd be dead, either way."

Crukas shook his head. "No. She can't die like this."

Adgus placed a gentle hand on Crukas' shoulder. "None of us can reach her. We won't fit. She knew the risks beforehand."

"I can't accept this," Crukas said.

"Death 'appens," Adgus said. "She proved her valor."

"Death can't be her reward," Crukas whispered.

Bramnir tugged the rope again. He hung his head. "Still no give."

Crukas knelt beside the pool and leaned close to the water.

"You won't fit, Crukas," Ebden said. "Face it. She's gone."

"No." Crukas plunged his face into the water. He attempted to go deeper but strong hands pulled him out.

Adgus and Bramnir lifted Crukas to his feet and pressed his back against the cliff wall.

"I know ya want to save her," Adgus said with a grim, fierce stare. He patted Crukas' chest. "But ya ain't able. None of us are."

Crukas sighed. Even if he were strong enough to break free of their hold, Adgus was right, but Crukas didn't want to accept it. He thought of Irmine. Since she was a gnome, she could fit but her poor health prevented it. Even with the fastest horse, they didn't have time to retrieve Irmine and bring her back. Only a portal was the fastest way to transport someone to their location, but none of them had the magical ability to open one.

What about a resurrection potion?

Crukas closed his eyes and cursed under his breath. No. If Sparrow was already dead, bringing her back ... she wouldn't be the same. Such an act was despicable and selfish and put him almost in the same mind frame as the Plague-bringer, who, at the moment was Aetheaon's greatest enemy with his growing undead army. Crukas didn't want Sparrow reanimated under someone else's control.

Adgus looked at Crukas. "Perhaps we should offer some words in ... uh ... remembrance of Sparrow?"

The back of Crukas' throat burned. His heated eyes teared up. Now, he understood even more for why he'd never befriended others. Placing trust and compassion for others made one vulnerable. Loss on a personal level was far greater than any material loss. He detested the building anguish clawing into his soul.

Although he didn't really know Sparrow, he believed she sincerely wanted to abandon the thieving profession. And perhaps the reality of being a bounty hunter weighted a different frustration for her path in life. Both occupations were contrary to the halflings' nature.

Since Irmine had lead him in prayer, Crukas partly understood how to pray. He nodded. "Yes. We should."

The three dwarves bowed their heads and stared at the water pool with somber eyes. Crukas closed his eyes and searched for the proper words. A warmth brushed against his shoulder in passing. The aura was too familiar. He opened his eyes and expected to see Irmine. In a shaky voice, Crukas spoke softly and briefly. When he finished, the three dwarves nodded.

Crukas sighed, picked up the Ghost-flame lantern, and clutched it to his chest.

CHAPTER 81

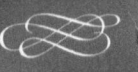

*F*eeling weightless, Sparrow found herself in total darkness. She couldn't move. Even if she could move, she didn't know which direction to take.

Fear crept inside her mind. "Is this what awaits after death?"

Expecting no answer, she was surprised to hear a soft reply. "No."

"Who's here with me?" Sparrow asked.

"That's not important."

"But it is," Sparrow said. "Am I suffering from delusions or am I already dead?"

"Neither, silly halfling. At least, not *yet*," the voice replied. "But if you continue to delay with questions, you'll die. And you'll have wasted more than my time."

"Apologies," Sparrow said.

"Did you find the Ghost-flame lantern?"

"Yes."

"Do you still hold it?"

"No," Sparrow said with disappointment. "It pulled away from my grasp after wedging me under the pool."

"Where's the lantern?"

"It rose to the surface of the pool. I hope Crukas has it."

"If not, my sacrifice is worth nothing."

"Sacrifice? Who are you?"

"Irmine."

"The priestess?" Sparrow asked.

"Do you *know* another Irmine?"

"No. I had lost hope and was certain I was dead. Fasha had predicted I'd die should I pursue Crukas."

"Fasha? The demon witch? Ha! She has no power over me. You're as much a part in defeating the Plague-bringer as Crukas. The two of you aren't alone in this battle. Fate has paired the two of you. *Not* Fasha."

"Why?"

"That I don't know," Irmine said.

"But—"

A beam of bright light broke through the dark nothingness. "There is little time, Sparrow, before your body refuses to allow your soul to return to your body. Follow my light."

Confused, Sparrow said, "I can't move. I have no form."

"You *can* move," Irmine said. "You must will yourself to do so. Should my light vanish, your physical form dies."

"And what of you?" Sparrow asked.

"I'm already dead."

Sparrow gasped, although no physical sound came. "You didn't have to die to rescue me."

"You silly halfling. I didn't come to save you. I came to ensure the the Ghost-flame lantern's safety, but being a priestess, I could not *not* offer aid to you."

"All the same—"

"Defeating Scorpius took a great toll on my weary body."

"I'm sorry."

"Don't be. The cause was worth it. Not only was the mage destroyed, the people of Ravensdorf are liberated from his tyranny. Now, follow."

The light moved away from her, wherever she was, and drifted downward. Sparrow pushed with her mind and somehow kept the glowing orb in sight. Soon, she caught and entered the orb, feeling warmth when she'd felt nothing only moments before.

Ringing surrounded her as she descended like dandelion fluff in the absence of wind. The descent abruptly halted, but only for a moment. Pressure surrounded her and the ringing ceased. Bubbling noises, like a trickling brook, echoed.

The surrounding light brightened for a moment. Sparrow was in the water pool again. Her body was inches away. The hilt of her dagger was wedged in the rocks and had prevented her from swimming to the other side.

"In a moment," Irmine said, "enter your body. Don't inhale, or you'll drown once more. Unwedge your dagger and tug the rope tethered around your waist. After you free yourself, you'll rise to the surface, but they can pull you out."

"Thank you," Sparrow said.

"Hold your thanks. You've not yet reached the surface."

Sparrow felt like crying, but without her body, she had no means to do so. "What should I tell Crukas?"

"You and Crukas must take the Ghost-flame lantern to the battlefront to face the Plague-bringer."

"Why?"

"Further instructions await you there."

"Oh."

"Tell Crukas he must travel to Raven's Point and speak to Garnette."

"Garnette?"

"Yes. In order to defeat the Plague-bringer, we must join with allies who can't succumb to the necromancer's power. Garnette is the matron Living-stone, but she doesn't freely follow or support war. Crukas must convince her kind that they're needed to save Aetheaon as we know it. Persuading their kin isn't an easy feat, but Crukas possesses an uncanny ability to negotiate. He has wit and charm."

"Yes."

"Whether or not Crukas succeeds in gaining Garnette as an ally, there's a portal attuned for all of you to enter. It leads to Zauber, who's gathering leaders for the ultimate confrontation. If Garnette declines, which she may do, hurry to the portal and prepare to go to the battlefront. Tell Crukas I'm sorry I can't offer my aid and protection at a time he needs it most. But he has friends to align with. Now, go!"

Silence followed and the light surrounding Sparrow faded. She entered her lifeless body, reached behind her to find the hilt of her dagger, and pushed it free. After the dagger unwedged, she tugged the tethered rope and hoped Bramnir still held it.

CHAPTER 82

Crukas hugged the lantern to his chest and looked at the pool one last time before he turned to leave. He sighed. "I should've let Sparrow wear the mask."

Ebden shook his head. "No. You'll need it when you face the Plague-bringer."

With a grim expression, Crukas sighed. "She needed it more."

"Confound it!" Bramnir said.

"What is it, brother?" Adgus asked.

"The rope just tugged violently. Help me, brothers. She's alive!"

Hope swelled inside Crukas' chest. Pent-up tears spilled down his cheeks. He never believed in miracles, never expected to receive any, knew he deserved none, but this journey disproved most of his skepticism about friendship, loyalty, and faith.

Bramnir, Ebden, and Adgus pulled the rope with no obvious resistance. Sparrow's face broke through the water's surface. Her weak eyes and bluish complexion revealed how near death she was. Even though she was out of the water, she might not survive.

Adgus and Ebden each grabbed one of her arms. They hefted her up and steadied her on the coarse sand. When they released her, she dropped to her hands and knees, coughed, and sputtered. Water gushed out of her mouth. She coughed again and more water spilled out. After several long seconds, she peered at Crukas and weakly smiled. Her mouth moved, as she tried to speak, but her words could barely be heard. She cleared her throat and spat.

"Much to your dissatisfaction … I survived," Sparrow said.

Crukas set down the lantern and rushed to her. He picked her up and hugged her against his chest like a parent would a child. He offered no words. The tear tracks on his cheeks said more than his words could ever express. His throat tightened so severely, he doubted she'd understand anything he said.

The three dwarves watched with tears in their eyes. Their noses reddened. The happiness and relief they shared ended prematurely.

Four men on black horses cornered them against the cliff wall. Their armor was immediately recognized. They were Dragon Skull Knights from Hoffnung.

A knight drew his sword and pointed it at Crukas. Fresh blood dripped from the tip of the blade. "I hate to interrupt your sentimental moment, but thief, you're being taken into custody for all the crimes you've committed against Aetheaon. You're Crukas, are you not?"

Adgus glared. "If ya 'ave to ask, ya don't know, do you?"

Crukas loosened his embrace around Sparrow and set her down. He stepped between her and the knights. "And if I am?"

"We arrest you in the name of King Erik," the knight said.

"You are?" Crukas asked.

"Captain Noll," the knight replied.

The tears in the dwarves' eyes were replaced by sudden anger. They pulled their axes before the other three knights unsheathed their swords.

"King Erik's dead," Adgus said. "He has been for a long while."

A shrewd grin came to Noll's lips. "In the name of Queen Taube then."

Adgus gave Noll a harsh stare and cocked his head to the side. "Ya be out of your jurisdiction, Dragon Skull Knight or not. Ya won't take Crukas without a fight."

Noll's eyes narrowed. "You three actually think you have a chance against us? Kyrk is a master swordsman. Bennett's fires an arrow quicker than any of you can charge forward. Bigge is a champion when it comes to melee with daggers and short swords. Are you game enough to meet such a challenge?"

"We're willing to find out!" Adgus snarled his upper lip.

Noll nodded. "So be it."

Kyrk and Bigge swung off their horses and Bennett nocked an arrow on his bow. Adgus and his two brothers growled in a low tone with their axes ready.

A heavy thundering of wings descended from the cliff wall. A half dozen Ravenfolk landed and stood behind the knights. Several seconds later, Skretch landed between Crukas and the knights.

Skretch's piercing eyes met Noll's. "*No one* takes another prisoner to collect a bounty in Pirate's Cove. Not even a Dragon Skull Knight. No disrespect to Queen Taube, but you'll respect our laws within our boundaries, or we'll tear you to shreds. As such, you best explain the blood on your sword, knight."

Kyrk and Bigge stepped back and sheathed their weapons. With wide eyes, Bennett eased the bowstring's tension. A Ravenfolk's razor-sharp talon pressed against the bowman's throat.

Noll took a deep breath and sighed heavily. "Self-defense."

"That's yet to be determined," Skretch said.

Noll frowned. "You'd defend the greatest thief in Aetheaon?"

Skretch examined the lantern in Crukas' hand and smiled. "Crukas is under *my* protection. You're forbidden to arrest him, not only in Pirate's Cove, but in any territory outside our domain."

"Is that so?" Bigge asked. He formed fists and set his feet in the sand to get traction. He was a hulk of a man, almost equal in size to a young Orc. "You can't enforce such a law."

"You wish to challenge us?" Skretch cawed three times. The knights looked up. A dozen more Ravenfolk circled the sky above them.

Bigge shrank with slight trepidation. He gave a gruff sigh. "No."

Skretch offered what seemed a satisfied smile. "Come to Moonharvest Tavern. All of you. We've much to discuss." He looked at the Ghost-flame lantern. "*Much* to discuss."

"Oh?" Noll motioned for Bigge and Kyrk to mount up. They did. "Like what?"

Skretch narrowed his eyes. "Crukas is on a mission and the four of you will now escort him to where he needs to travel without causing him any harm. You'll offer your services to protect him."

Noll scoffed while Bigge and Kyrk smirked.

"Why would we do that?" Noll asked.

"If you choose to do otherwise, you're subjected to go to trial over whomever you killed with your blade," Skretch said. "Of which, I'm the judge. Of course, that's *if* you survive to witness your own trials."

For the first time, the knights looked more submissive than defensive and Skretch's threat was clear.

"To ensure you don't harm Crukas or deter his mission, a half dozen of my guardians will escort you. Now, proceed cautiously to the tavern."

CHAPTER 83

On the way to Moonharvest Tavern, Crukas walked beside Sparrow. She was weak. With as much water as poured from her mouth, she shouldn't have survived. Somehow, Irmine must've prevented Sparrow's death.

With the four Dragon Skull Knights riding ahead of them and the Ravenfolk walking behind the knights, Crukas didn't fear a sudden attack from the knights. The Dragon Skull Knights kept their hands in sight and away from their weapons. The knights were wary and fearful of the Ravenfolk.

Crukas whispered, "We thought we had lost you, Sparrow."

"You almost did." Sparrow explained how Irmine had sacrificed herself to save Sparrow and ensure the Ghost-flame lantern was safe.

"Irmine's dead?" Adgus asked.

"Yes," Sparrow said.

"No!" Adgus shook his head. "Dat can't be! Perhaps you were dreaming?"

The knights looked over their shoulders for a moment without saying anything. Crukas placed an index finger to his lips and nodded toward the knights.

Adgus mumbled, "Right."

Crukas remembered something brushing past him when he prepared to speak about Sparrow. The touch was familiar, and now he understood why. Irmine's spirit had passed him. He regretted not acknowledging her presence then.

Crukas closed his eyes and sighed. "No. Sparrow's telling the truth."

"How do you know?" Bramnir asked.

Crukas' jaw tightened. "I—I just know."

They walked in silence for several minutes. Crukas grieved. His favor owed to Irmine had been paid but the met obligation was fruitless and bittersweet. He savored her friendship and missed her companionship more than ever. His chest felt hollow, empty. He'd never see or speak to her again. Without her assistance, he'd have died trying to get the death mask, and Sparrow would've died, even though the Ghost-flame lantern surfaced.

Sparrow whispered, "Irmine said she's sorry she can't aid you ... us."

"*I'm* sorry," Crukas said. "It's because of me that she's dead."

"Ya can't blame yourself." Adgus wiped tears from his eyes. "The only reason I'm alive is because of her. Our fates are not in our own hands."

"She saved me, too," Sparrow said.

Anger stirred inside Crukas. Fate was unfair too often.

Ebden gripped Crukas' forearm. Panic gleamed in his eyes. "What about the curse? How can it be broken now?"

Crukas' jaw tightened. The tome was the reason everything went off course. Had he not stolen it ... "The book! We must retrieve it from her home."

"There's no time," Sparrow said. "You must find Garnette."

Adgus frowned. "Garnette? The Stone Matron?"

"You know of her?" Sparrow asked.

"Every dwarf does." Bramnir rolled his eyes.

"I've never heard of her," Crukas said.

"Well, you're not a dwarf." Adgus chuckled.

Bramnir glanced at Sparrow. "Why does Irmine want Crukas to see her?"

Sparrow sighed. "To plead Aetheaon's need for their aid to fight the Plague-bringer."

"Bah!" Adgus said. "The Living-stone folks don't meddle in the affairs of fleshlings. They never 'ave. They half tolerated dwarves before Dwarven kings expelled 'em."

Sparrow said, "Irmine believes Crukas could persuade them."

"Why me?" Crukas said.

Sparrow shrugged.

Ebden shook his head. "Dat's a waste of time. I agree with Crukas. We need to get the book and find someone who can lift the curse."

"No!" Adgus said. "If Irmine wants us to seek Garnette's council, dat's what we do."

Anger creased Ebden's brow. Desperation rose in his voice. "Dat's easy for you to say, brother. You're *not* the one cursed."

Crukas sighed. "No. Adgus is right. We owe her that at the least."

Adgus nodded. "At the very least."

"What about the curse?" Ebden asked.

"We'll find a way," Crukas said. "There has to be some way."

"There's always death," Ebden said.

"That's true," Crukas replied. He rubbed the protective amulet Irmine had given him. Had her magic delayed the inevitable for him? Unlike Ebden, Crukas no longer feared what hold the curse had or an early death. With the coming battle against the Plague-bringer, he couldn't waste time worrying. Although he sympathized with Ebden, empathy didn't change the situation. Consequences came later.

CHAPTER 84

rukas entered Moonharvest Tavern first. Once inside, Skretch directed Crukas to stand where the square-shaped bar had been. Several barmaids swept the remaining bits of glass shards into small piles. The bar, what remained of it, was in shambles.

Nearly a dozen Ravenfolk rearranged the tables and carried the larger pieces of the destroyed bar. With their wings draped downward, they resembled angelic beings. But their angry, hostile glares when they regarded the dwarves and humans was contrary to anything holy. Vindictive, perhaps, but nowhere similar to protective entities. Yet, they were obedient to Skretch. At least, Crukas hoped they were.

"Here?" Crukas stepped over a splintered board.

"Good enough." Skretch pointed his feathered finger to right side of the room. "Sir Noll, you and your Dragon Skull Knights stand against the side wall."

In a gruff tone, Noll said, "The Dragon Skull Knights are *not* under your command."

"You're not in Hoffnung, Noll, and are subjected to our laws, regardless of the throne you serve or what status you hold. I highly doubt Queen Taube would disagree." Skretch turned his attention to the dwarves and Sparrow. "Join Crukas."

Without a word, they went to Crukas and stood behind him. Crukas shook his head. For the majority of his life, he'd remained solitary and hid in the shadows. He disliked being the center of attention, especially in the company of knights and the Ravenfolk. Life as he remembered would never be the same.

"Look," Noll said. "Allow me to extend my apologies and ask for a truce. We won't harm Crukas or take him into custody. Let us be on our way, and know in good faith that we won't trespass into your cove again. The reputation of the Dragon Skull Knights is known throughout Aetheaon. Our mission's to protect every kingdom in the land. Clearly, our coming to Pirate's Cove and our actions were a mistake on our part."

Skretch shrugged his mighty wings. "Your oversight is excused, but you're not dismissed from your obligation to protect Crukas and his party."

"I mean no disrespect," Noll said. "But, you do *not* hold that authority. Our allegiance—"

"Your allegiance means nothing at this point," Skretch said.

"How do you figure?" Noll cocked a brow.

"Contrary to what you think, you and Crukas are on the same side."

Noll frowned and eyed Crukas. "What? I beg to disagree. No matter the affair, we would *never* side with a thief."

Skretch cawed with obvious amusement. "Then Aetheaon is doomed."

Noll gave his three companions a confused stare. "How's that?"

"Crukas is the only one who's ever gotten Kane to reveal where he hid the Ghost-flame lantern. Kane died to prevent anyone from getting it, and even as a ghost, he's never yielded the information to anyone. Yet, he told Crukas and where the key was hidden." Skretch regarded Crukas for a moment. The look indicated slight admiration, despite the tavern's disarray. "In order to destroy Aetheaon's common enemy who's already attacked Hoffnung, Glacier Ridge, and

Frosthammer, you must ensure Crukas, the lantern, and his party reach their proper destination. These dwarves are worthy warriors, but even they need your help."

"You're referring to the Plague-bringer?" Noll asked.

"Yes."

"He's the reason we came here. Under Caen's orders, we're searching for Dragon Skull Knights at every port and major city. We're currently traveling south to join him at the outskirts of Woodnog."

"Then, after you help Crukas, take him and his party to Woodnog," Skretch said. "He will be needed."

"What's the purpose of the Ghost-flame lantern?" Noll gazed at the bluish glowing lantern.

Skretch shrugged. "I've no idea. Ask Crukas."

Noll met Crukas' eyes. "Well?"

Crukas felt uneasy at Noll's harsh, intimidating stare. "From my understanding, the lantern neutralizes the reach of Mors' power."

"How?"

Crukas sighed. "That we don't yet understand."

Noll glared at Skretch and crossed his arms. "See? This is a waste of our time."

"No, it isn't!" Sparrow stepped beside Crukas. Her face reddened. "Irmine died to protect the lantern because she knew it's essential to defeating the Plague-bringer."

"If it's so important," Noll said, "why didn't *she* disclose the reason for its usefulness?"

Sparrow formed fists and her eyes narrowed like a cat's. "Because she *died*!"

"Yah!" Fury set in Adgus' eyes. He appeared ready to pull his broadaxe and charge Noll. His face flushed crimson and his brow furrowed. "Dat's a good enough reason, eh?"

Noll gritted his teeth. "If it's somehow a weapon, and you don't know how to wield its power, it's as useful as a rock."

Adgus sneered. "Rocks can be mighty weapons, ya know? Especially when they're large."

"What's that supposed to mean?" Noll asked.

Crukas grinned. "Sparrow nearly drowned obtaining the lantern, and while she was close to death, Irmine gave her instructions for us to meet with Garnette."

"I don't know the name," Noll said.

"Of course you don't," Adgus said, mockingly.

"If Irmine's dead, how'd she tell this halfling anything?" Noll asked.

Sparrow explained Irmine's instructions to meet with Garnette and leave through the portal afterwards.

"The Stone Matron?" Skretch asked.

"You know her?" Noll said.

"Of course," Skretch said. "She and her living-stone people protect our western front, ever since the pirates attempted to lay claim to the cove. Few venture into their bluffs and the plateau because of the constant, thunderous vibrations that are felt and heard far before one would reach them."

"I've never ventured there," Noll said. "We've had no need since no cities exist on that plateau."

"Aye. They're the reason for dat," Bramnir said. "The earth quakes beneath their feet when the living-stone people walk, which makes outsiders think the land's unstable. Created by our gods, these living stones were once the protectors of our mines. They guarded us against our enemies until our populations grew and we forged weapons and armor to protect our own armies. They're not known for war. Because of their immense size and chiseled intimidating faces, few enemies 'ave ever challenged them. Most who encounter them, die of fright."

Noll flicked his gaze at Skretch. "You want us to escort them *there*?"

Skretch nodded. "It's essential."

Noll scoffed. "This is based on what a halfling believes a *dead* priestess *told* her?"

Sparrow's face heated with anger. She seethed. "It's the truth."

"I have difficulty finding your story plausible," Noll said. "I'd like more proof than that."

Crukas eyed Noll evenly. "A halfling's nature is to be honest and compassionate."

Adgus suppressed a snicker.

Crukas frowned slightly and gave the dwarf a side-glance before returning his attention to Noll. "I'm certain you've been to Willow's Bend since it's not far from Hoffnung."

"Few halflings ever venture far from the bend," Noll said. "Why would she be here, in a place of thieves and pirates?"

"We needed her help," Crukas said. "None of us could've ever fit through the tight space to reach the Ghost-flame lantern."

Noll looked at Sparrow. "What's Irmine's significance in all this, since she's dead?"

"What more do ya need?" Adgus huffed. "We witnessed Irmine putting her life on the line to kill Scorpius. I'm sure you've 'eard of him, eh?"

"The mage in Ravensdorf? Yeah, we know of him. Is it true, she killed him?" Noll asked.

Crukas nodded. "We were there. Had she not intervened, Scorpius would've killed all of us. Sadly, her victory led to her death. Her unselfish sacrifice should not go unnoticed."

"What proof have you?" Noll asked.

Crukas contemplated showing the death-mask, but the relic wasn't something others needed to know about, especially since he didn't know if Noll and his company could be trusted. Some knights in other kingdoms occasionally went rogue, but none of the Dragon Skull Knights ever had to Crukas' knowledge. However, since King Erik had died, it was possible knights might stray from their allegiances to gain a slight profit.

Before Crukas could answer, Skretch said, "Proof? The partial collapse of the mage's tower was felt here."

Crukas exchanged glances with the three dwarves. Collapse? When they'd left the tower, it was still standing. Perhaps the top of the tower had been blown apart by the mage's magic, but the cylinder walls held. Had it fallen after they left Ravensdorf? What of Triggor, Strella, Orgem, and Gynx's fates? He shook his head.

Skretch continued. "Our sage, Qheith, viewed the aftermath through her crystal orb. There's no way Scorpius survived. Instead of delaying the inevitable with your countless questions, I suggest you prepare your journey while the day's early. Six of my guardians will accompany you."

Noll frowned. "What makes you think Crukas can persuade Garnette to help?"

In a dismissive voice, Skretch said, "He persuaded Kane to give up the lantern, didn't he? Quite a few pirates sought Kane to reveal his secret, unsuccessfully. Crukas might well be the one to convince Garnette that Aetheaon needs their help. Anything else?"

Noll sighed and shook his head. Though he appeared agitated and unenthusiastic by Skretch's demands, he didn't offer further objections. What good would protesting do now?

Skretch sending six guardians on the journey meant he didn't fully trust Noll's intentions. Crukas didn't like the idea of traveling with the Dragon Skull Knights without the protection of the Ravenfolk, either. After all, Crukas had spent most of his youth avoiding these knights from city to city while stealing objects right beneath their noses. The game with the most renowned knights in Aetheaon, on his part, was for sheer amusement. It was no wonder why Noll and the other knights were perturbed because they'd almost captured Crukas. What knight or official would like to be ordered to protect someone they'd hunted for decades instead of rightfully turning Crukas over to a magistrate? None.

Crukas couldn't help but chuckle inside his mind. He could hardly hide the smile begging to spread on his lips. Neither action he allowed to surface because he didn't wish to seem disrespectful to the Dragon Skull Knights or to Skretch. Noll was perturbed enough without further goading.

Crukas found it odd that Skretch was allowing him to leave after stealing the key from inside the wooden banana. But since the Ravenfolk sage had the ability to see Scorpius' demise, he wondered if the sage had foreseen Crukas taking the key and told Skretch before the events unfolded? Skretch recognized Crukas after the skirmish that half destroyed the inside of the tavern but Skretch dismissed Crukas, even though he knew the thief possessed the key.

Was it stealing when Skretch seemingly gave him permission to leave with the key? Irmine had the foresight that Fate and Destiny linked all of them together. Was this why Crukas had gained the same insight as Irmine to get the lantern?

And now, Irmine had spoken to Sparrow for them to find Garnette and request the help of the living-stone people. Strangely, he'd never heard of her or the living stone people. The dwarves knew them and their origin. Crukas hoped they'd help him properly greet her in the appropriate manner.

CHAPTER 85

⁂

Three Ravenfolk led Crukas and the others beneath an overhang in the rocky bluffs that overlooked the vast sea. The smooth rock path was wide enough for two horses to walk side by side. One misstep near the ledge, and the fall was an instant death drop to the jagged rocks protruding through the rough sea waves.

The other three Ravenfolk walked behind the knights to keep Crukas and his party safely separated. Without the Ravenfolk's guidance, none of them would've known this passage existed. From the sea, the lofty height of the mountain was hardly visible, even with a quality spyglass. Due to the shadowed overhang, the path appeared to be a wide crevice etched into the mountainside over time by the wind and sea mist.

The path curved slightly and rose at a slight incline, which led to a vast plateau with tall, luscious grasses, and lavender and pink flowers. An occasional, massive deciduous tree provided shade. The landing was not the highest peak in Aetheaon, but overlooking the sea made the breathtaking view seem so.

For Crukas, this seemed a place dragons would savor. A breeding ground or sanctuary where other races never invaded. However, no dragons could be seen, which gave him a sense of relief. The constant

448

rumbling, shaking ground was the biggest deterrent for anyone exploring the region, especially with superstitious folks.

The three leading Ravenfolk walked to the top of a grassy knoll and slowly disappeared from sight at a sharp descent. The Dragon Skull Knights did the same.

Crukas glanced at Adgus. Adgus kept his attention on the tip of the knoll and never flicked his gaze toward Crukas. The dwarf's attentive stare indicated his anticipation in possibly seeing the stone people he revered.

Crukas whispered, "Be prepared."

Bramnir nodded. "Always."

Adgus chuckled. "Save the words for ya'self. What we might behold is something no one other than a dwarf could prepare for."

Once they ascended the knoll, Crukas frowned. At the bottom of the knoll the land leveled. A sun-bleached, smooth stone about five feet in length, rolled across the tall grasses, temporarily flattening the tender blades. No larger boulders were nearby, Crukas thought it odd for a stone to fall and roll. But then, the stone did something even odder. It rolled back in the direction from which it had come. As the stone rolled and lightly rumbled, a childlike squeal flowed with the gentle breeze.

Crukas said, "Did that stone just laugh?"

The Dragon Skull Knights regarded one another without saying a word, but were clearly confused. Noll glanced over his shoulder at Crukas.

"Aye," Bramnir said.

"I heard it, too," Sparrow said, watching the stone.

"Did the stone make that sound?" Crukas asked.

Adgus laughed. "Of course. Dat's what made the delightful cry."

"The stone?" Crukas said, dumbfounded.

"Aye," Adgus said. "It's a child of the Stone-people. This is a joyous occasion."

"Why?" Noll asked, turning in his saddle.

Adgus laughed. "Because it's the first time I've seen one while I wasn't drunk."

Bramnir and Ebden roared with laughter.

The stone stopped rolling and set itself upright. From this distance, it shouldn't hear them. Little rock arms and legs were suddenly visible.

"And," Adgus said, "it's a child."

"How can you tell?" Noll asked.

"Are ya kidding?" Adgus said. "An adult Stone-person would tower over us."

Bramnir grinned and wiped away a tear. "Truly a momentous occasion."

"Aye," Adgus said. "Can ya imagine what he'd looked like when he was a pebble?"

Bramnir's eyes widened. "I never considered dat."

"A pebble?" Crukas asked.

"Aye," Adgus said. "Ya ever see one of those rock slides but the rocks aren't large. Just hundreds of pebbles skittering down the mountainside with loose soil?"

"Of course," Crukas said.

"Those slides are often started by living pebbles gathering nonliving stones, thinking they are alive, too. Get too many moving around on loose soil ... ya know what happens. They cascade and the increasing weight eventually causes larger rocks to fall as well."

"So they're not isolated to this point?" Sparrow asked.

"Not at all," Bramnir said. "They're elementals."

The Ravenfolk remained silent. Their piercing eyes kept their attention on the rocky ridge. A thunderous stomp echoed. Flocks of birds that had been eating grass seeds and insects burst into flight. The clear sky didn't give the slightest hint of a storm. Another harsh impact rattled the ground, but it wasn't an earthquake.

"Footsteps," Crukas whispered and then pointed.

A rock figure, larger than a small cottage, took another slow step forward. Had the stone person not moved, an unsuspecting explorer might've walked past it or into its path without realizing the rock-being was alive.

Parts of its body were camouflaged by thick moss, small saplings, and clumps of tall grass. Without moving, it appeared nothing more than a huge rock overtaken by nature. Inanimate.

The Dragon Skull Knights, Sparrow, and Crukas held frozen, perplexed expressions. The dwarves grinned and excitement gleamed in their eyes.

"Look, there!" Adgus exclaimed.

A long line of Stone-people marched toward the highest peak.

"Where are they going?" Crukas asked.

Adgus, Ebden, and Bramnir shrugged.

One Ravenfolk, Ashrea, said, "To the throne hall."

Bramnir nodded and pointed a stern finger. "*Dat's* where we need to go."

"You must proceed with caution," Ashrea said. "The last thing you need is for them to mistake you as a threat. I'll speak to them and gain your permission to state your case before them."

With that, the Ravenfolk spread her wings and took to flight.

Noll gave Crukas an uneasy glance and seemingly realized Skretch had told him the truth.

Like Noll, Crukas had never met any Stone-people. They weren't certain how Garnette would react after Ashrea spoke to her. Skretch was the only one Crukas fully trusted because Skretch understood Crukas' reason for taking the key and retrieving the lantern, despite the lantern remaining a mystery to Crukas. Skretch could've easily brought Crukas before the council for theft had he wanted.

Since Skretch had personally chosen the six escort guardians, they should be trustworthy enough to protect Crukas and his party.

Ashrea glided majestically over the plains, past the line of marching Stone-people, and circled briefly before landing before a giant set of mossy, stone columns. Even from the distance, the thrones were identifiable if studied with a critical eye. A simple glance and one might dismiss it as old ruins. Crukas would have.

A half hour passed before Ashrea returned. She landed in front of Crukas and ignored the Dragon Skull Knights. "They've agreed to meet with *only* you, but the knights and your company must remain here."

Crukas gave a slight bow.

"Why must we stay behind?" Noll asked.

"It's what they've requested."

Noll shook his head. "Like I said before, this is a waste of our time."

"You're welcome to address your grievances before their court if you choose," Ashrea said. "To appear before them to air your complaint would be your first and last fatal mistake. Whatever request they initiate is what they expect to receive. What say you?"

Noll gazed at the long line of Stone-people marching toward the throne. The muscles in his throat tightened. In a hoarse voice, he said, "As they wish."

"Very well," Ashrea said. "Crukas, your party should remain here."

"What about all of you?" Sparrow asked.

"Three of us will remain with the knights to ensure they don't shirk their obligation. The other three will lead you."

Crukas gave a slight nod. "Thank you."

CHAPTER 86

*C*rukas never expected two Ravenfolk to grab his shoulders and heft him upward into flight. With their strength, most likely, only one was necessary for the task. He'd stood on high cliffs and atop spiked spires, but during those situations, his feet were *firmly* planted on solid surfaces. Being carried high above the prairie grasses and flowers at a rapid speed made him uneasy, even though a part of him enjoyed the weightlessness, the spectacular view, and gentle breeze. After all, the Ravenfolk might release their hold and drop him to the ground in instant death. Yet, they'd have only done so if Skretch had quietly given them the order to do so.

Skretch didn't act deceptive and approved of Crukas keeping the Ghost-flame lantern safe. Perhaps the Ravenfolk needed Crukas to succeed as did the rest of Aetheaon. Skretch certainly wouldn't have challenged the Dragon Skull Knights in the manner he had, if Crukas' mission wasn't important.

Should Crukas succeed, he wasn't certain what his outcome would be after the battle was settled. Noll and the Dragon Skull Knights longed to take him into custody, more so than they had in the past, which seemed rather odd since the fate of all the living was at stake. Of course, Skretch had berated Noll and his troops and stripped them of any authority, which was a blistering they would never allow to heal. Most likely, they'd seek revenge against Crukas.

Would Skretch continue to protect him?

Considering the ultimate confrontation with Mors, Crukas and Sparrow would be at the center of the battle. Should they defeat the Plague-bringer, Crukas was an easy target to be killed or captured for the reward on his head. He wondered if greed rose supreme once Aetheaon was spared.

Ashrea flew slightly ahead of Crukas. Apparently, she was chosen to be his mediator.

"Any advice?" Crukas asked the Ravenfolk clutching his shoulders. Although their grip was strong, they kept their sharp talons retracted and didn't pierce through his spider-silk armor into his flesh.

Geewk, the Ravenfolk holding his right shoulder, said, "Be gracious and meek. It's highly uncommon for the court at Granite Heights to invite anyone to stand before them, especially humans."

"Rarer than rare," the other, Kooth, said. "They despise any fleshly race and tolerate us because we coexist peacefully and share the mountain with them."

"So," Crukas said, "choose my words carefully?"

Both Ravenfolk shrilled with laughter.

"Yes. State your cause," Geewk said. "Afterwards, if they decline or wish you to leave, do so without argument. We're prepared to fly you back to your party."

"There's never been any animosity between the Ravenfolk and the Stone-people?" Crukas asked.

"No. Both sides favor peace."

"When you reclaimed Pirate's Cove from the pirates, the Stone-people never aided you?"

Kooth said, "We never sought their assistance. Besides, we didn't need their help."

"It's good that you've never had to fight them," Crukas said.

"War's useless against them anyway," Geewk said.

"Why?"

"Few weapons can destroy them. They dull and shatter metal

melee weapons. Arrows flick off them. While cannons might cause damage by gradually chipping away their exterior, getting cannons to the heights of their kingdom is nearly impossible. Dragons' fire wouldn't affect them, either."

Crukas frowned. "So they never die?"

Kooth said, "It'd take several millennia for the weathering elements to wear them down to where they can't function. They prefer the plateau's dry climate. They'd sink in the swamps, but they wouldn't die. The same holds true in the depths of the sea. They'd live, as they don't require air, but they'd probably never resurface."

The two Ravenfolk carried Crukas over the long line of the Stone-people slowly marching to the throne. He counted fourteen and another dozen where the Ravenfolk would set him on the ground. Their harsh vibrating footsteps were felt in the air and the thudding steps forced Crukas to cover his ears.

After they passed over them, Crukas looked to see how far the Ravenfolk had flown. Adgus and the others were specks on the plateau. Too far to aid him should things go awry.

Before he befriended the dwarfs, Crukas never placed his life into anyone else's hands, nor had he ever trusted others. But, in this moment, he felt the painful absence of the dwarves and Sparrow. He missed Irmine even more. He wondered if she were actually dead. Although a priestess, she held mysterious qualities unlike what a spiritual leader should have. Her ties to her deity were strong, perhaps even stronger than she'd known. Her god might've allowed her to travel through the various planes to rescue Sparrow before she'd drown. Was it possible Irmine was still alive?

If any deity read his hopes and unspoken prayers for Irmine's safety, he wished they'd heal her. He needed her alive in this plane, and more than anything, he needed her friendship. He hated the thought of her absence. She'd never given up on him throughout the years, had tried to coax him into abandoning his thieving ways, and perhaps, her prayers were why his outlook on life had changed for the better.

Before the Ravenfolk slowly descended, his thoughts returned to

Jillann and her tragedy when he'd fled and left her for dead in the Gloomy Forest. Rather than holding resentment toward him, Jillann protected him and the dwarves from being killed by other pack members. For that, he was thankful, but he'd have to return to find her in the future, provided he survived his invitation before the Stone-people and whatever Fate offered when he confronted the Plague-bringer. Should he survive the battle and Aetheaon be saved, he'd never be the same person he was before. For a thief to use his skills to prevent Mors from destroying Aetheaon, how could he return to his life as a thief?

The two Ravenfolk stretched their wings and caught the air, which hoisted them upward and prevented Crukas from being driven face-first into the ground. His stomach turned with a slight tickling sensation. They lofted and gently touched down a few feet from where Ashrea stood.

Crukas staggered slightly, after experiencing weightlessness during the short flight and abruptly trying to find his balance. He teetered several seconds with his arms stretched outward to both sides, which reminded him of the times he'd walked a tightrope from one building to another across a city street in the dark. He never expected to feel the same imbalance while standing on the ground. When he looked up, the stone-faced matron's glossy, obsidian eyes studied him. He froze and held his breath, pondering his next step and how to address her.

Her eyes were as large as he was tall and she could smash him with her giant hands with little effort. She sat on her throne, and he couldn't quite imagine how much more intimidating she'd be if she stood. He'd seen Dwarven statues smaller than she. In the throne next to hers sat the king, if his guess were correct.

Garnette's stony mouth opened slightly. "You seek our counsel?"

"Yes."

"Why?"

"The survival of Aetheaon."

Her cold obsidian eyes glistened but hinted no emotion at all. "Survival? To what threat?"

"The Plague-bringer." Crukas explained the Plague-bringer's goal and how the necromancer was sweeping through and claiming the dead as his minions in order to attack larger kingdoms successfully.

The king nodded. "Yes. We've heard of him. He's no threat to us."

"Granitte's right," she said. "No threat at all."

"I gather that, since you're living stone," Crukas said. "Which is why I'm here to plead for your help in this battle."

The king and queen showed no more physical reaction than carved statues. Perhaps they were unable, due to their rigidness.

"If he rids Aetheaon of the pesky races that always try to eradicate one another, what concern is it to us?" Granitte asked. "His task simply would quicken what each culture seems determined to do anyway."

Crukas suppressed his building annoyance and slight anger. "I understand why your kind might dismiss the populations unlike yours. But Aetheaon would lack the proper harmony if our races are destroyed."

"Harmony?" Garnette said. "You came to our plateau with knights. Knights go to war."

Crukas nodded. "They're with us. But not by choice."

"Oh?"

Crukas nodded. "Skretch insisted they accompany us for protection."

"Protection? From whom? Us?" Granitte asked.

"No. The Plague-bringer. They brought me to see if I can persuade you to help us."

"What reason's worthy that we should follow you into battle?" Garnette asked.

"Because our world will be no more," Crukas said.

Granitte grunted. "That's not true. Aetheaon will remain, *absent* the fleshlings. That's what you truly mean, isn't it? Our kind, along with gargoyles and other stone creatures, will carry on."

Crukas nodded. "Your view's more accurate. You'd continue to exist while those of us who are *fleshlings* would not."

"So, this is *your* battle," Garnette said. "Not ours. Why should we meddle in *your* affairs?"

Granitte said, "All fleshlings seek war over peace. There's no end to their skirmishes and claims to land and the treasures buried beneath. We spent enough time as dwarf guardians to realize there's no quenching the thirst for wealth, nor is there ever a true desire for the various races to live peaceably with one another. Even the dwarves fought amongst themselves. Eventually, the Dwarven kingdoms ostracized us, even though we were created to be their protectors. Now, you want us to come to your aid and theirs? Our involvement offers us no benefit, and the loss of all fleshlings might prove tranquil."

The shaking ground increased as the line of Stone-people steadily approached.

Ashrea regarded the coming assembly, but showed no fear.

"You'd prefer a land filled with hordes of undead minions?" Crukas asked.

"They'd be under the control of the necromancer, free from their own lustful thoughts and actions," Garnette said. "They'd be no threat."

"I see," Crukas said. "While I don't understand the full reasons behind the dwarves ostracizing you ... What? Centuries ago? My three dwarf companions revere you. They stood in tears and humbled from seeing one of your youths rolling in a meadow earlier. They were sorely disappointed that you only requested my presence."

"While that may be," Granitte said, "dwarves are more greedy for gold and gems than they are for paying homage to anyone. If my core was filled with precious metals and rare gems, how long before every Dwarven kingdom arrived to destroy us, just to get the treasures inside our bodies?"

Crukas shrugged. "So you won't help us?"

Garnette said, "You never established a valid reason for why we should. As he's indicated, fleshlings are more troublesome than beneficial."

"What if," Crukas said, "your kingdom's threatened *after* the

Plague-bringer takes over Aetheaon? Goblins could view an opportunity to rise from the depths of the mountain caves and capture you to work for them."

Both regarded Crukas before exchanging glances with one another.

"Goblins?" Granitte said.

"Capture us?" Garnette said. "That'd never happen."

"Without humans, dwarves, elves, and orcs, the goblins would never have been driven into the depths of the earth," Crukas said. "They've no fear of the Plague-bringer resurrecting them, as they eat their dead and even the bones of their deceased. And then, once the demons in the depths of Hades discover the goblins have come to the surface, they'll do the same. We *fleshlings* have a purpose, which benefits *you*, despite your evaluation of what you believe us to be. And the Black Chasm ... who knows what monstrosities Tyrann has created inside his poisonous atmosphere? Perhaps, he's waiting for such an opportunity as this to exploit?"

The royal pair sat quietly and unmoving for a while. If they harbored fear, their stolid faces told him nothing.

The queen turned her attention to Ashrea. "Take him to his group."

Before Kooth and Geewk reached for Crukas, he said, "You've not answered my request. Yes or no?"

Geewk shook his head and shushed Crukas with an odd shrill.

Granitte said, "Take him away. The queen and I have much to discuss."

Crukas sighed. The two Ravenfolk grasped his shoulders and took to flight. Crukas worried that he hadn't convinced them of Aetheaon's need for the fleshlings. These would've been the greatest allies to aid them against the Plague-bringer. If anything, the Stone-people's arrival would be a great distraction and enable him to get close enough to the Plague-bringer to destroy the necromancer. Now what?

CHAPTER 87

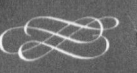

*A*dgus, Bramnir, and Ebden watched the two Ravenfolk snatch Crukas and fly away.

Adgus shook his head and placed his hand on his axe's handle. "There be no way to get to him should things go awry."

Bramnir's eyes narrowed, he grunted, and his jaw tightened.

"I find it difficult to believe," Noll said. "Three dwarves are inclined to follow a thief's orders."

Adgus glared at the Dragon Skull Knight. "We're *not* following his command. We are, however, defending his cause and *dat's* why he needs our protection."

"Exactly what is his cause?" Noll's hand tightened his hand on his saddle's horn.

"Are ya daft?" Bramnir asked. "He and Skretch 'ave already told you."

"We all have," Sparrow said. "Why are you insistent on taking Crukas into custody when greater stakes are at hand?"

A soured expression contorted Noll's face. "Perhaps opportunity graced us during an inopportune time. But Crukas slipped away too many times in the past and since we happened upon him, we sought to take advantage of our fortune."

Sparrow shook her head and grinned. Her catlike eyes narrowed. "You're lying. He took something from *you*, didn't he? A thief bested you. *That's* the real reason you're ignoring Caen's decree to gather the Dragon Skull Knights and instead, you tried to arrest Crukas."

Noll's face reddened. His lips tightened.

"What'd he do?" Mischievousness gleamed in Adgus' eyes, and a sly grin tugged his lips.

"I'd rather not discuss it," Noll replied. "For your information, we never abandoned Caen's decree. We actively search for our brotherhood knights. Yet, you've sidetracked us. For now, we'll do as Skretch requested. We'll safely escort you and the thief to wherever you need to go. Afterwards, Crukas faces me and will answer for his crimes."

"Seems a bit personal," Bramnir said. "Not reward related at all."

Sparrow smiled. "It has to be personal."

Noll said, "It's not your concern."

"Perhaps you should run this past Sir Caen before you proceed?" Sparrow said.

"Lest you forget." Adgus' hand tightened on the handle of his broad axe. "We helped bring down an evil mage. Don't think for a minute we won't protect Crukas."

Noll gave a determined stare. The Ravenfolk escorts moved closer and Noll's expression softened. "So you're essentially thieves, too?"

"Not at all," Adgus said. "But Crukas risked his life to face Scorpius. Dat's a sacrifice worth recognizing and a person worthy of our protection. He didn't do it for himself, but for all of Aetheaon. Dat puts him on the same side as you. Unless I'm missing something, dat's to *your* advantage since you're alive, eh?"

"The priestess died though. Correct?" Noll said.

"Aye." Adgus felt the pang of her loss. He'd not argue the point because she had chosen to sacrifice herself. In a dwarf's eye, anyone who lost his or her life in battle for a greater cause was considered admirable. A hero. No greater cost could be given. Angered, he said, "She gave her life to save us and ensured Crukas got a necessary item."

"That being?" Noll asked with genuine interest.

"Dat's none of *your* concern," Bramnir said.

Adgus said, "If both are willing to die to stop the Plague-bringer, how far will you go? Are you still worthy of the Dragon Skull insignia given to you by King Erik?"

Noll's three accompanying knights held stolid expressions and looked at Noll, seemingly interested in his reply, rather than speaking or allowing themselves to be pulled into the bickering.

Noll's face tightened with sourness. "I'd have died in place of King Erik, if I'd been given the opportunity. Our allegiance to him has never waned. We serve his throne even after his demise, whether Queen Taube reigns or Lady Dawn, we honor our oath."

"Perhaps, after this is all finished," Adgus said, "Queen Taube will grant Crukas a pardon."

Noll took a sharp breath and held it for several long moments. "I wouldn't get your hopes up."

"How will ya feel when a thief becomes a hero?" Adgus asked.

Noll's face reddened even more, but instead of replying, he glanced at the sky beyond where the dwarves stood. Adgus and his brothers turned to see what had captured Noll's attention.

"Your thief's on his way back," Noll said.

Adgus frowned. "Dat's a bit quick."

Sparrow crossed her arms and her voice tinged with disappointment. "Can't be good news."

Noll laughed. "What'd you expect? A thief's job is to steal without anyone seeing him. And you expected him to be a negotiator?"

"Or perhaps," Sparrow said, "he's *that* good."

With scorn, Noll shook his head. "Doubtful."

Bramnir said, "Care to wager on his success?"

"Or," Adgus said. "You'd like to present yourself before the Stone-people's court and convince 'em we need their help. Dat is, if Crukas failed to persuade them? You seem to have better confidence in addressing them."

Noll swallowed hard. "I never implied such."

"Ah, but you did," Adgus said. "By inferring Crukas doesn't possess orator skills because he's a thief, you're implying you could do a better job. The smugness in your tone and your eyes speak volumes."

Before Noll offered a rebuttal, the Ravenfolk gently set Crukas on the ground beside Adgus.

Adgus clasped Crukas' shoulder to help Crukas regain his balance, and then he smiled. "Good you're back. How'd things go?"

Crukas caught his breath and shook his head. Uncertainly reflected in the thief's eyes. "I'm not quite certain what to take away from our conversation."

Sparrow's brow creased. "Meaning?"

Crukas shrugged. "Meaning, they offered neither a yes or a no. They wanted to think about the situation. Nothing more."

"See?" Noll said. "A wasted trip."

"Don't be so certain," Ashrea said. "They're deliberating, which isn't a 'no'. They might still fight with you."

"Now what?" Adgus met Crukas' gaze.

Crukas pulled the two spellbooks from his pouch that Irmine had insisted he take from Scorpius' library. He closed his eyes. "We find the portal at Raven's Point. Irmine said it'll transport us to wherever Zauber is."

Noll's eyes narrowed. "The wizard?"

"Yes," Crukas said. "He's the only one who'll know what to do with these books."

Ebden frowned. "What about the cursed book you left at Irmine's?"

"Yeah," Adgus said. "We need dat one, too."

"I know," Crukas said. "For now, we'll have to wait."

Angered, Ebden said, "If the wizard can use those books in your hands, can't he reverse the curse on you and I. He'd need the book, though."

"Irmine's house is too far out of our way," Crukas said.

Ebden growled and made fists. He gave a frustrated frown at his brothers and walked away.

"Ebden, I understand your frustration," Crukas said. "Besides, anyone else who touches the book will become cursed, too. So Devin can't bring it to us."

"I'll retrieve it," Gishee said.

"You heard what I said," Crukas said. "Anyone who touches the book becomes cursed with the contents inside the book."

The Ravenfolk cocked his head to the side. "Perhaps for humans, but not us."

"You can't be cursed?" Sparrow frowned with curiosity.

"Only if the curse is specified," Gishee replied. "The book you mentioned only seems to affect humans, dwarves, and possibly elves. Not us."

Adgus said, "But you can't know this for certain."

"No. But it's something I should test. Thus far, Crukas and Ebden have handled the book and are still alive. The affects of the curse isn't immediate. If need be, I can take the book to Qheith for her to examine."

Ebden's eyes brightened. "Perhaps *she* can break the curse?"

"It's possible," he replied. "Tell me which house is Irmine's so I can retrieve the book."

Adgus told him the description of Irmine's house and the directions. Not a second later, Gishee took flight and flew toward Ravensdorf.

Adgus exchanged glances with his brothers and Crukas. "Where's dat portal Irmine mentioned?"

"Raven's Point," Sparrow said.

"Then we best be on our way," Adgus said.

CHAPTER 88

Triggor rode his huge razor-snout boar alongside Gynx. The kobold walked while leading his pack-burro with a leather strap. Despite agreeing to accompany Gynx to Pirate's Cove, Triggor wasn't foolish enough to turn his back to the kobold. Too many threats and attacks between them had already occurred. Since Gynx was unpredictable, Triggor wasn't giving him any advantage. In hindsight, Triggor was glad Sparrow had taken the crossbow.

Triggor gave Gynx a side-glance. "What makes you suspect Crukas to go to Pirate's Cove?"

"Seems the least likely place he'd go," Gynx replied.

Triggor cocked a brow. "What's the logic in that?"

"Since we're so close to his proximity, it's likely he'd take a route we wouldn't suspect."

Triggor was impressed. "Aye. Dat's a good point. But I truly don't think he'd venture to the cove."

"No?"

"No."

Gynx frowned. "Then why'd you agree to travel with me?"

Triggor shrugged. "Curiosity mainly. And other personal reasons."

Triggor thought about Barnacle. Would the pirate return to the cove for his next victims? Perhaps the Ravenfolk discovered Barnacle was connected to the Elder Ravenfolk's murder. If so, Barnacle could already be dead. If not, Triggor could be in danger of not only facing Skretch, but being attacked and killed by Barnacle. As on that fateful night long ago, Barnacle didn't enter the tavern alone. Other pirates started the skirmish, which allowed someone to shoot and kill the Elder.

"Personal reasons?" Gynx's brow rose slightly and then creased into a suspicious frown. "Like what?"

Triggor shrugged. "Something dat doesn't concern you and has nothing to do with Crukas."

"Hmm," Gynx said. "Interesting."

"It might turn out to be *more* than interesting," Triggor said.

"In what way?"

Triggor chuckled. "You and I 'aven't quite seen eye to eye and 'ave been at each other's throats since we met. Our trust in one another isn't strong and we're heading into pirate territory. Should things go poorly, we have one another to rely on."

"Enemies often become allies when faced with death from outside forces," Gynx said. "Like I told you at the Mute Changeling, I have your back, despite our earlier differences. Any enemy of yours is my enemy."

The expression on the kobold's face indicated the sincerity of his words. The underlying, sinister attitude he'd exhibited ever since Sparrow joined them was gone. For some strange reason, Gynx despised the halfling. Was it because halflings were the complete opposite of kobolds in nature? Regardless of Sparrow's innocence, Gynx wanted to kill her.

"I 'ave yours as well," Triggor said. And, he meant it.

CHAPTER 89

After waiting a half day longer on the outskirts of the Stone-people's throne hall for an answer, it became obvious Garnette and Granitte held no interest in speaking further.

Crukas looked at the Ravenfolk. "Irmine mentioned a portal at the top of Raven's Point. Do you know the fastest route to reach it?"

They nodded.

Ashrea said, "Yes. We can escort you."

With slight reluctance in his voice, Noll said, "We'll do the same, thief."

"A change of mind or heart?" Adgus said with a slight teasing smile.

"Neither." Noll shifted in his saddle. "But since Crukas risked his life to stand before those living Stone-people, I'll see this to the end. A fool wouldn't have done what Crukas did. Only someone with a genuine purpose would. If Crukas believes he can stop the Plague-bringer, he needs protection. For the Dragon Skull Knights to not do so is treason."

"I appreciate your support," Crukas said.

Noll didn't look him in the eyes and kept his gaze at the ground. As a thief, Crukas understood the dangers when someone refused to

LEONARD D. HILLEY II

look another person in the eyes. This indicated dishonesty or an ulterior motive.

Sparrow said, "Despite your animosity for Crukas, you'll still go with us?"

Noll's face reddened.

Crukas frowned. His gaze flicked between Sparrow, Adgus, and Noll. "Am I missing something?"

The other three Dragon Skull Knights adjusted in their saddles but said nothing.

Sparrow said, "Noll has a grudge against you."

"Oh?" Crukas said. "Grudge for what? Other than being a thief, what trespass have I ever committed against you?"

Noll's lips tightened. "Of course, you'd scheme to deny it."

Crukas shrugged. "Deny what, exactly?"

"Jillann."

Crukas stiffened. He took a sharp breath and failed to hide his confusion. Her name wasn't something he expected Noll to mention. "What of her?"

"At least you don't deny knowing her," Noll said.

"Okay? So I knew her."

Noll's jaw tightened, and his eyes narrowed. He swallowed hard and his nostrils flared. He placed his hand on his short sword. *"Knew?* So, she's dead?"

Crukas shook his head. "Not exactly ... dead."

"You were the last person seen with her." Noll swung his leg over the saddle and slid off the horse. He planted his feet solidly but didn't pull his sword. Two Ravenfolk guardians stepped between Noll and Crukas as a threatening barrier to remind Noll of his place.

Noll said, "No one has seen her since."

Sparrow and the three dwarves exchanged confused expressions. Each shrugged and whispered inaudible questions amongst themselves.

The other three Dragon Skull Knights looked wary and kept their hands on their weapons.

"I imagine that's true," Crukas said. "I'm not sure why this is your concern. What's she to you?"

"She's my sister," he replied.

"Ah." Crukas frowned. "She never mentioned you or that she had any family."

Pain and anger deeply creased the wrinkles around Noll's eyes. His aching loss was obvious. "When I learned she'd fallen in love with someone, my father insisted I find out who she planned to marry. When I discovered *you* were courting her, I aimed to put a stop to it, but then, you and she vanished. Not a word from her or any trace of where she might've gone. Nothing. Word of you stealing in various towns and cities kept my ambition to find and capture you alive. So when I found you earlier, I wasn't going to turn you over to a magistrate for the reward. I wanted to know the truth of what happened to her, even if I needed to beat it out of you."

Crukas shook his head and waved his hands. "No need for physical violence, knight. Until just recently, I thought she was dead."

Noll's eyes moistened slightly. Whether this was from relief in knowing she was still alive or from the growing anger Noll had allowed to fester for so long, Crukas didn't know.

"So she's not dead?" Noll asked.

"No, but she's not the same."

"What's that mean?"

"It's true Jillann and I planned to wed. Had we, I'd have quit being a thief. The thrill of stealing no longer pleases me. Not even then. There's no challenge in it. At the time she and I were together, having a family with her meant everything. It was worth investing in and giving up everything else. But, on the night I planned to ask her hand —" Crukas' voice cracked. He slipped the black gold necklace from beneath his shirt and showed the black engagement ring. "*This* was the ring I planned to place on her finger. But Wierwen attacked us in the forest. One grabbed her, bit her throat, and dragged her into the forest. She never screamed and from the viscousness of the bite, I assumed they'd killed her."

"So, thief, you fled. Like a coward," Noll said.

Crukas sighed. "Honestly, I thought they'd killed her and yes, I fled, but not from cowardice. I'd have given my life to save hers, Noll, just like you said you'd have done for King Erik. I'd have pursued them, but no one should've survived such an attack. The way her throat was mauled, I couldn't stand the thought of seeing her ripped apart and that being my last image of her. Not one day has ever passed that I've not grieved over her."

Sparrow's eyes filled with tears, as did the three dwarves. The other three Dragon Skull Knights bowed and shook their heads in sorrow.

"But she's still alive?" Noll wiped away tears. "How do you know this?"

"On our way to Ravensdorf the other day," Crukas said, "Adgus and his brothers and I were attacked by a pack of Wierwen. Jillann intervened and saved our lives, but she's one of them. Not necessarily their leader, but she apparently holds immense status among them."

Noll closed his eyes. His lips quivered. A tear escaped and meandered down his cheek and soaked into his beard.

"Wait. *She* stopped the charging Wierwen?" Bramnir asked.

"Yes," Crukas said softly.

"So she's a beast now?" Noll said. "Because of you."

"Don't be daft!" Adgus said. "Can't ya see he hurts from his loss?"

Noll stood silent for several seconds while staring into Crukas' eyes. He gave a solemn, slight nod. "When Jillann told father long ago that someone had stolen her heart and she wanted to marry him, I understand why she didn't tell me who she'd fallen in love with."

"What da ya expect?" Bramnir said. "He's a thief, after all."

Sparrow giggled. "The greatest thief known."

Crukas' face heated. "Well, Noll, she never mentioned you. Whatever animosity you hold against me, while understandable, I did nothing to spite you. For her to love me, I was surprised, too. She was far fairer a lady than any heir to a throne."

"That's true." Noll nodded. "Had she mentioned her brother was a Dragon Skull Knight, would it have dissuaded you?"

Crukas grinned. "I'd have been more cautious."

Noll laughed. "Did she know you are a master thief?"

"I'm not certain. I never told her, but with my image on countless wanted posters, surely she knew. How could she not?"

"Our knight brotherhood will seek to protect you in your quest to destroy the Plague-bringer, and afterwards, should we still be alive, I'll appeal to Queen Taube to have you pardoned," Noll said.

Sparrow's eyes widened, and she gasped.

"Dat's quite admirable," Adgus said.

Crukas nodded. "I appreciate that."

"Under one condition, though," Noll said.

"I expected nothing less," Crukas said with a sly grin.

"You and I shall find her," Noll said. "I want her to know I never gave up the search to find her."

Crukas nodded. "I've some explaining to do to her as well."

Noll said, "Then, we're agreed?"

"Yes."

CHAPTER 90

*T*riggor and Gynx arrived at the bluff above Pirate's Cove an hour before sunset. The vista provided a near perfect view of the ships docked in the bay. Several black sails with skulls and crossbones ruffled in the sea breeze. Drunken pirates staggered along the docks. Some shouted slurred insults at one another from opposing ships. Others bellowed loud laughter.

Triggor exchanged glances with Gynx. Both grunted and shook their heads in disdain.

Moonharvest Tavern was on the higher neighboring bluff. Triggor pointed at the narrow, rocky path that led to the tavern. "Dat's where we go."

Gynx huffed and gritted his teeth. "Of course, it'd have to be higher. Good thing the bottom of my feet are calloused like stone."

Triggor chuckled. "Ya should *ride* dat burro instead of leading it."

Gynx grumbled words Triggor couldn't understand. After several moments, Triggor realized Gynx's long, winding tail probably prevented him from riding any mount. He never considered that.

Before heading to the tavern, Triggor considered hiding his revolver in his saddle pouch. Having it holstered on his side would immediately attract the Ravenfolk's attention, but leaving it in the saddle made him defenseless during any conflict. After several moments of reflection, he decided to be bold and accept his fate, whatever it might be. He hoped Skretch allowed him to plead his case and tell his side of what transpired the night the Elder Mother was killed. He feared the Ravenfolk might go into an immediate rage and kill him instead.

Triggor swung off his mount and tethered the boar to a post. He leaned close to the boar's left ear and whispered. The boar chomped its jaws and saliva pooled from its mouth.

Gynx frowned. "Did you just talk to your boar?"

"Aye," Triggor said with a nod and sly grin.

"And he understood you?"

"Of course."

"What'd you tell him?"

Triggor chuckled. "I told 'em to gnash and gut any pirate dat tries to steal him, and to stomp anyone dat tries to take your burro."

"He'll do that?" Gynx asked.

"Aye. Afterwards, he'll eat 'em."

Gynx grinned. "Good to know."

"Keep ya senses, Gynx," Triggor said. "There are eyes everywhere."

Gynx grunted.

They walked toward the tavern. Three pirates entered the tavern ahead of them, but before Triggor and Gynx reached the front door, several Ravenfolk glided downward with loud shrills and landed, surrounding them.

Gynx reached for his jagged dagger, but Triggor placed a hand on Gynx's and shook his head. "They're not 'ere for you."

Gynx frowned and gave Triggor an odd side-glance. "Is this your personal reason for coming to the cove?"

"Aye," Triggor said.

The tavern door swung open. Skretch walked to Triggor, eyed the revolver, and within the next second, he pressed his razor sharp talon to Triggor's throat. Triggor stiffened but refused to close his eyes or blink. Although terrified at having his throat slit open, he kept his gaze locked with Skretch's.

Skretch cocked his head to the side, studying Triggor, and then snatched the revolver from its holster. Skretch whistled softly. "Interesting."

Skretch brought his face closer to Triggor's and for a moment, Triggor expected the Ravenfolk's sharp beak to slice Triggor's nose open. "I wondered when you might return, dwarf."

Triggor cleared his throat. "Do with me what you will. I deservingly face your judgment. All I ask is dat you allow my companion 'ere to leave unharmed."

Skretch's eyes narrowed. "Why should I? You've both a reputation to uphold, do you not?"

Triggor swallowed hard. "I'm not certain what you mean?"

"No bounty hunters are welcome in Pirate's Cover. That's the law," Skretch stepped back from Triggor and looked at Gynx. "You're both bounty hunters. You, dwarf, have earned your name from the weapon you carry. Triggor, eh? Fitting. As for the kobold, he's not free to leave, either, since he's a bounty hunter."

Anger boiled in Gynx's eyes. He gave Triggor a fierce glare. "You set me up!"

Triggor shook his head. "I've done no such thing."

"They *know* who I am," Gynx said.

"Not from me," Triggor said evenly.

Gynx's jaw tightened and he ground his teeth.

"Triggor's not lying to you, Gynx," Skretch said. "We discovered who you are far before you arrived."

"How?"

"That's not important," Skretch said. "All you need to know is, you're not free to go."

Triggor took a deep breath and sighed. "May I speak in my defense?"

Skretch's eyes narrowed. "What do you need to say?"

"I was 'ere the night the Elder Mother was murdered," Triggor said. "But I swear, my revolver wasn't the weapon used."

"Is that so?" Skretch said. "And yet, you fled."

"I know, but at the time, I didn't think you'd believe me. Everyone looked at me. Some even accused me of shooting when I hadn't."

Skretch nodded. "We know you didn't kill her."

"You do?"

"Yes. But fleeing like you did, it certainly questions your innocence."

"Aye," Triggor said. "Dat's understandable. I was foolish to leave as I did."

"But you took the name to boast of your prowess," Skretch said.

"Not by choice," Triggor said. "But if I may ask, who killed the Elder Mother?"

Skretch studied the revolver in his feathered hand for several moments. "One of Barnacle's crew members shot her. During his agonizing interrogation, he confessed that he sold you *this* revolver."

Gynx laughed softly. "He set *you* up."

"Aye." Anger rose inside Triggor because of the setup, but he worried he might not survive the night. "Since you know it wasn't me dat killed her, am I free to leave?"

"Hardly," Skretch said in a low tone.

"What about me?" Gynx asked. "I had *nothing* to do with it."

"No. I require both of your services," Skretch said.

"Eh?" Triggor said with genuine surprise.

"You're bounty hunters and somewhere Barnacle remains unpunished."

Gynx frowned. "You just said bounty hunters can't collect bounties here."

Skretch nodded. "True. But you won't find Barnacle here. He's out on the seas somewhere. We captured and killed most of the pirates he persuaded to kill our Elder Mother. He and a few others somehow escaped through trickery. So, your services to find him won't be in the cove, but on the sea."

"We're not pirates," Triggor said. "I've no idea how to command or operate a ship."

"Nor do I wish to learn." Gynx's eyes widened slightly. "Kobolds *hate* water."

"Perhaps death is a better option?" Skretch asked.

Gynx eyed the two Ravenfolk standing to each side of him. The hunger for blood lingered in their eyes. "I'd prefer not."

"The reward's what bounty hunters seek," Skretch said. "The price on Barnacle's head is only slightly lower than Crukas'. It'd be worth your time to find and kill Barnacle. Bring us his corpse and I'll double the reward. And you're invited to our celebratory feast."

Drool dripped from Gynx's mouth.

Triggor said, "Your offer's more than generous, as I'd like my revenge for how he set me up. But, we don't have a ship."

"I've secured a swift vessel," Skretch said. "Much faster than any Barnacle uses."

Gynx crossed his arms and gave Triggor a stern frown. "Don't expect me to be ya first mate. I refuse to be second to anyone."

With a frustrated glare, Skretch said, "I've handpicked a small crew, too. One with proper knowledge of sailing, capable of following the star charts, and who knows the approximate location of Barnacle's island where stashes his loot. Short of going myself, everything's in order. That should be more than adequate to pay for your services."

Gynx rubbed the stubble on his chin. His greedy eyes gleamed. "Barnacle stores his loot on the island?"

"Yes," Skretch said. "Whatever you find is also yours. Divvy it between yourselves."

"What about the crew's wages?" Triggor asked. "Do they take a cut as well?"

Skretch shook his head. "No. I pay them, separate from your offer."

"Dat's a lot of money just to kill one pirate," Triggor said.

"Even so, it doesn't bring back the Elder Mother," Skretch said. "No amount of gold could ever replace her worth to us. Barnacle's death is as close to redemption we'll ever get."

Triggor frowned. "Wouldn't you rather us capture him alive? So you can take the pleasure in seeing his fear before he dies?"

"I wouldn't risk letting him escape you again," Skretch said.

The remark cut Triggor deeply. He'd had the opportunity to pull the trigger and kill Barnacle in Moonharvest Tavern, but Triggor hesitated. His hesitation set everything else to fall into motion.

Gynx hissed. "See Triggor? I told you a dead body's easier to transport than a living one."

Skretch gave a gentle nod. "Listen to your friend. He's correct."

"We're not friends," they replied in unison.

Skretch sighed. "Perhaps I'm asking the wrong bounty hunters. This venture has no chance of success."

Gynx said, "For the reward you're offering, we'll set our differences aside. We accept the task."

Skretch looked from Gynx to Triggor. Triggor nodded, but only because he feared his refusal might cost him his life. He didn't know whether Gynx could set aside any differences. The kobold seemed more to having his own way other than any compromise.

"So be it," Skretch said.

CHAPTER 91

Dusk was settling when the Ravenfolk reached the peak of Raven's Point with Crukas and the others. The yellow moon glowed between puffy pink and lavender clouds. A stack of roughly hewn rocks formed a large oval outline of a door. It loomed several dozen feet above them at a sharp incline.

"This is the portal?" Crukas frowned.

Sparrow shook her head. "It can't be. It's not activated. It's dead. No magic surrounds it."

Adgus frowned at Sparrow. "You said Irmine told ya to come 'ere."

"She did," Sparrow said. "Of that, I'm certain."

The dwarves searched the surrounding bluff walls.

Adgus' jaw tightened. "This best not be a trap."

Sparrow glanced at Crukas with pleading eyes.

Crukas sighed.

A female Ravenfolk, Qoot, carried a wizard's staff, stepped into the portal opening, and touched the inner stone frame. Her robes indicated she was an apprentice to either a mage or sage. She gently ran the feathery tips of her fingers along the stone. "This structure's new."

"How can you tell?" Crukas asked.

"It wasn't here the last time we patrolled," she replied. "But whatever magic it needs has never been initiated."

Noll straightened in his saddle. His brow furrowed. "Then we've traveled all this way for nothing?"

"We don't know that," Crukas replied.

"For a knight," Qoot said, "you complain far too much."

Bramnir frowned. "Seems suspicious, all the same."

Crukas stepped closer to Sparrow. "Are you certain Irmine spoke to you?"

"Yes."

He bit his lower lip while thinking. He and Ebden had both handled the Cursed Book of the Damned and yet, both were alive. If what Sparrow said was true, and she had actually spoken to Irmine's spirit, she also touched the book. Had she died due to possessing the book rather than suffering severe fatigue after her battle against Scorpius? If so, had she failed to activate the portal before she died? He wished he'd have given her the Death-mask instead.

Crukas walked to where Qoot stood and touched the rocks. The stone was cold. No power radiated from them. If Irmine's magic was attuned to the doorway, he'd have felt and recognized her power. He didn't.

Sparrow sheepishly approached Crukas. "I'm truly at a loss. I know it was her voice. The pitch of her voice is unique. It wasn't Fasha who spoke to me."

"Are you sure Fasha isn't setting us off course?" Crukas asked.

"She tricked me into going through some portal in the tavern beside her spell shop."

"Ah-ha!" Adgus gripped the heel of his axe. "Ya said it right there. A portal. She already sent you through one, so surely this is hers, too?"

"No," Sparrow said. "Fasha predicted I'd *die*. She spoke it as a prophesy, so drowning in the pool would've made her prophesy true. I've no doubt she'd prefer I died so she didn't risk the chance of being wrong. So, she wouldn't have shown me how to free myself. I doubt she has any knowledge of the—"

Crukas shook his head. "Shh."

"Anyway," Sparrow said. "Irmine had already written you her request, Crukas. Something Fasha wouldn't have known."

"That's true," Crukas said. "But it still leaves a problem."

"What's dat?" Adgus asked.

"Without the proper spell, we can't use the portal. Irmine said it'd take us to Zauber, who's currently outside of Woodnog," Crukas said. He looked at Qoot. "Is it possible for you to charge the portal and activate it?"

She shook her head. "No. I haven't any idea where Irmine would've set the opening to appear on the other side. I could activate a destination, but you might end up even farther away."

Noll sighed and then cleared his throat. "Then what's left to do? Head back to Pirate's Cove or south until we make our way to Woodnog where Zauber awaits?"

"Without a portal, that'd take too long," Crukas said.

A ear-piercing screech broke through the air.

The Ravenfolk apprentice said, "Gishee's returned with the cursed tome."

"Dat's pretty damn fast," Adgus said.

When Gishee landed beside the apprentice with the book in his hand, the portal hummed. Crukas, Sparrow, and the apprentice moved away from it.

"Bloody Hell!" Adgus said.

Blue light shimmered and rippled inside the oval doorway. The apprentice marveled. "Why would the book activate the portal?"

"I've no idea," Crukas said.

"Dat's something none of us understand," Bramnir said.

Gishee frowned. "Irmine said she didn't want any others to stray through the portal, so she couldn't leave the portal open. Once I brought the book, the portal would activate but it'll only stay open for a few minutes."

"Irmine's alive?" Adgus asked, before Crukas could ask.

Gishee nodded. "Barely. She could only whisper. Devin said she fades in and out of consciousness."

Crukas swallowed hard. His eyes heated with tears. "Then there's hope she'll recover?"

"He believes so," Gishee replied.

The blue shimmering light made sloshing, watery sounds. Crukas touched the portal. While the icy cold frosted his fingertips, he felt nothing sinister like when he first touched the cursed book. Without looking back, he said, "Are we ready to step through?"

"What?" Noll asked. "You're going to trust a portal that opened the moment the cursed book came close enough to activate it? What if we get trapped on the other side?"

"We accept the consequences, Noll," Crukas said. "We haven't time to debate possible outcomes. We must trust Irmine. We've no other choice."

"There's always other choices," Noll said.

"Yes, but ones dat further delay what's required of us." Adgus frowned firmly.

"Who'll carry the book?" Ebden asked.

Gishee said, "I will."

"And I'll accompany him," Qoot said.

"I'll give Caen your best," Crukas said. "Perhaps he'll understand your lack of fortitude."

"I'm coming," Noll said.

Crukas stepped through the portal. An icy chill shot through his body, and within moments he stood in a forest clearing near Woodnog Swamps. He recognized the trees along the path and after his feet steadied, the eyes of those already gathered stared at him in disbelief.

The wizard, Zauber, offered a slight smile and his brow furrowed with genuine curiosity. "We've been watching this odd empty portal for some time now. It appeared hours ago. Until a few moments ago, it was dead. Thief, did you come alone?"

Crukas shook his head and stepped to the side. Sparrow and the three dwarves stepped out, soon followed by four of the Ravenfolk, and the four Dragon Skull Knights.

Zauber smiled. "What news have you brought us? Are we prepared to battle the Plague-bringer?"

Crukas sighed and revealed the Ghost-fire lantern. "That depends on whether you know how we activate this."

Zauber came closer and examined the lantern. "I've not seen this in ages. It vanished from this plane. How'd you obtain it?"

"Without Sparrow," Crukas said, "we wouldn't have gotten it."

Zauber gave her a slight wink. "With this weapon, we might've found an advantage, but the one carrying the lantern faces the possibility of being killed before getting close enough to the Plague-bringer to use it."

Crukas pulled the mask from his pouch. "Not if I wear this."

Zauber's brow rose. "That looks like Scorpius' Death-mask."

"It is."

"You've been busy, thief," Zauber said. "How'd you manage to steal it?"

"T'wasn't easy," Adgus said.

Crukas explained the battle against Scorpius and how Irmine had nearly sacrificed her own life in order for Crukas to survive and take the mask.

"I see," Zauber said with a smile. "Then, it's time we discuss our plans of attack moving forward."

THE END OF BOOK 5

ACKNOWLEDGMENTS

I extend my heartfelt appreciation to my beta reader, KC Riley-Gyer, whose keen eyes captured errors I missed and graciously highlighted them for me.

I greatly appreciation the fantastic job KC Riley-Gyer did in updating Aetheaon's maps for better clarity.

This book's exceptional cover design by Ellie Douglas brought this story to life. https://www.authorellie.com/covers

ABOUT THE AUTHOR

Leonard D. Hilley II grew up a quiet, shy kid with an inquisitive mind. Learning to read at an early age, he fell in love with books. He read every book he could get his hands on and stacks of dark comics about ghosts, monsters, and creepy things that stalk the night.

Like a lot of boys, he caught beetles, wooly bears, butterflies, and had an ant farm. When he was ten, his interests in science increased even more after seeing a professor's insect collection. Soon he set out on his quest to build his own collection. He learned to rear butterflies and moths to obtain perfect specimens. He learned botany, gardening, and set his goal to become an entomologist.

At eleven, he watched Star Wars on the big screen. His imagination soared. Soon after, he discovered Roger Zelazny's Chronicles of Amber. Six months later, he had written the first draft of a novel. A novel he later discarded, but the characters stuck with him. Years later, these characters came to life in Shawndirea, which Hilley intended to be a background novella for Devils Den. The characters, however, refused to be ignored and took the opportunity to unveil Aetheaon in their first epic fantasy. Lady Squire soon followed.

Shawndirea was Hilley's farewell to butterfly collecting. Those who have read the novel understand why. He has taken Ray Bradbury's advice to heart: "Follow the characters." He does. He follows, listens, and take notes—often never knowing where they're going to take him, but he's never been disappointed in the results.

Hilley earned a B.S. in Biology and an MFA in Creative Writing to combine his love of science and writing.

Sci-fi Titles: Predators of Darkness: Aftermath, Beyond the Darkness, The Game of Pawns, Death's Valley, The Deimos Virus.

Epic Fantasy: Shawndirea (Aetheaon Chronicles: Book One), Lady Squire (Aetheaon Chronicles: Book Two), Frosthammer (Aetheaon Chronicles: Book Three), Shadowfae (Aetheaon Chronicles: Book Four), and Devils Den.

UF/PR: Succubus: Shadows of the Beast (Nocturnal Trinity Series: Book One), Raven (Nocturnal Trinity Series: Book Two), A Touch of the Familiar.

YA UF/Paranormal: Forrest Wollinsky Vampire Hunter; Forrest Wollinsky: Blood Mists of London; Forrest Wollinsky: Predestined Crossroads.

YA Mystery: Dee's Mystery Solvers

www.ingramcontent.com/pod-product-compliance
Lightning Source LLC
Chambersburg PA
CBHW030542020726
47494CB00005B/1453